Into the Vall KT-431-281

A. L. Berridge read English at Oxford and taught for ten years before moving into television, where her production credits range from period drama and thrillers to long-running soaps. Having told stories for other ple all her life, she now writes full-time. She has written two previous els, top ten bestseller *Honour and the Sword* and *In the Name of the King*. L. Berridge lives in St Albans.

Into the Valley of Death

A. L. BERRIDGE

PENGUIN BOOKS

PENGUIN BOOKS

Published by the Penguin Group
Penguin Books Ltd, 80 Strand, London wc2r orl, England
Penguin Group (USA) Inc., 375 Hudson Street, New York, New York 10014, USA
Penguin Group (Canada), 90 Eglinton Avenue East, Suite 700, Toronto, Ontario, Canada m4p 2y3
(a division of Pearson Penguin Canada Inc.)
Penguin Ireland, 25 St Stephen's Green, Dublin 2, Ireland (a division of Penguin Books Ltd)
Penguin Group (Australia), 707 Collins Street, Melbourne, Victoria 3008, Australia
(a division of Pearson Australia Group Pty Ltd)
Penguin Books India Pvt Ltd, 11 Community Centre, Panchsheel Park, New Delhi – 110 017, India
Penguin Group (NZ), 67 Apollo Drive, Rosedale, Auckland 0632, New Zealand
(a division of Pearson New Zealand Ltd)
Penguin Books (South Africa) (Pty) Ltd, Block D, Rosebank Office Park,
181 Jan Smuts Avenue, Parktown North, Gauteng 2193, South Africa

Penguin Books Ltd, Registered Offices: 80 Strand, London wc2r orl, England

www.penguin.com

First published by Michael Joseph 2012
Published in Penguin Books 2013
001

Copyright © A. L. Berridge, 2012
All rights reserved

The moral right of the author has been asserted

Set in 11/13pt Dante MT Std
Typeset by Jouve (UK), Milton Keynes
Printed in Great Britain by Clays Ltd, St Ives plc

isbn: 978-0-241-95410-2

www.greenpenguin.co.uk

Penguin Books is committed to a sustainable
future for our business, our readers and our planet.
This book is made from Forest Stewardship
Council™ certified paper.

ALWAYS LEARNING **PEARSON**

Maps

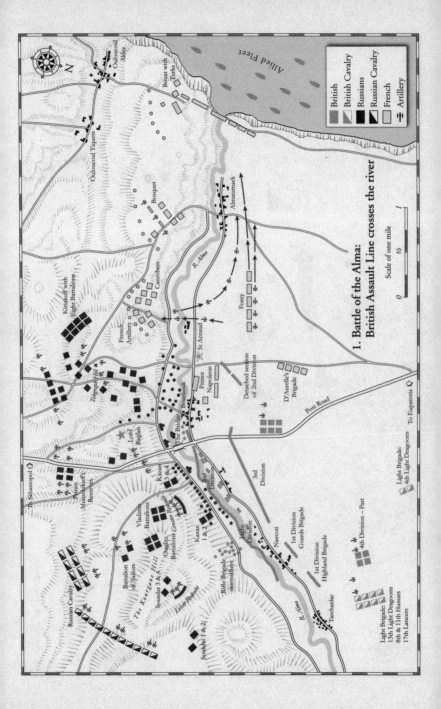

1. Battle of the Alma: British Assault Line crosses the river

Allied Fleet

British · **British Cavalry** · **Russians** · **Russian Cavalry** · **French** · **Artillery**

Scale of one mile

0   ½   1

N

Ouloucod
Ouloucod
Akles
Bouat with Turks

Ouloucoul Tiquets

Bosquet

Almatamack

Canrobert

R. Alma

Forey

Kiriakoff with
Eight Battalions

French
Artillery

St Arnaud

Telegraph Hill

Prince
Napoleon

Bourliouk

Detached section
of 2nd Division

D'Aurelle's
Brigade

The Bridge

Post Road

To Sebastopol

Prince
Mentschikoff's
Reserves

Lord Raglan

Kazan
3 & 4

2nd
Division

3rd
Division

To Eupatoria

Light Brigade:
4th Light Dragoons

Vladimir
Battalions

Kazan
1 & 2

Ouglitz
Battalions

Greater Redoubt

Light
Division

Nacooti

1st Division
Guards Brigade

Battalion
of Sailors

Soushlt 3 & 4

Lesser Redoubt

Rifle Brigade
skirmishers

1st Division
Highland Brigade

Russian Cavalry

The Kourgane Hill

R. Alma

Tarchanlar

4th Division – Part

Soushlt 1 & 2

Light Brigade:
13th Light Dragoons
8th & 11th Hussars
17th Lancers

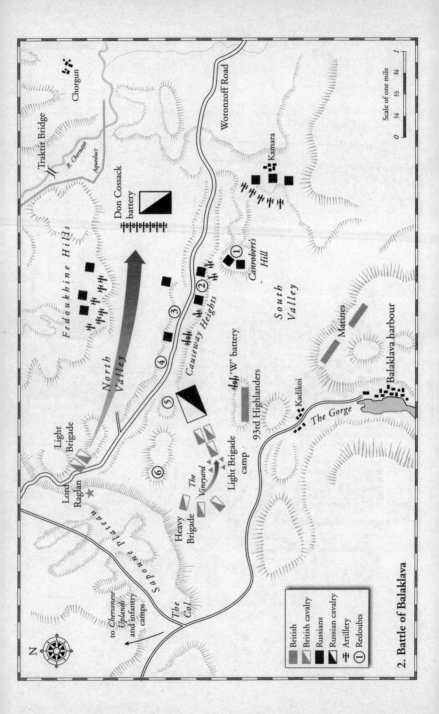

2. Battle of Balaklava

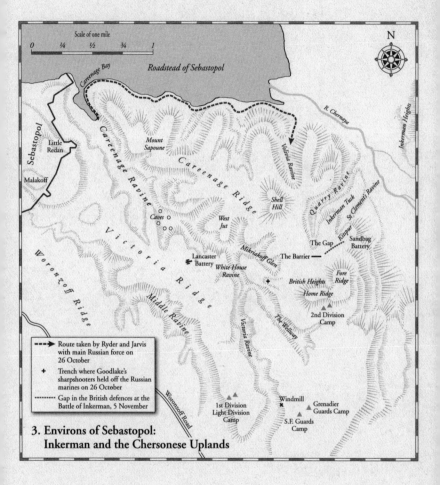

Scale of one mile

0   ¼   ½   ¾   1

N

Roadstead of Sebastopol

Carenage Bay

Carenage Ridge

Sebastopol

Little Redan

Malakoff

Mount Sapoune

Carenage Ridge

Shell Hill

Victoria Ravine

R. Chernaya

Inkerman Heights

Caves

West Jut

Quarry Ravine

Inkerman Tusk

St Clement's Ravine

Kispur

Victoria Ridge

Mikriakoff Glen

The Gap

The Barrier

Sandbag Battery

Lancaster Battery

White House Ravine

British Heights

Fore Ridge

Woronzoff Ridge

Middle Ravine

Home Ridge

2nd Division Camp

Victoria Ravine

The Wellway

➤ Route taken by Ryder and Jarvis
with main Russian force on
26 October

+ Trench where Goodlake's
sharpshooters held off the Russian
marines on 26 October

······ Gap in the British defences at the
Battle of Inkerman, 5 November

Woronzoff Road

1st Division
Light Division
Camp

Windmill

Grenadier
Guards Camp

S.F. Guards
Camp

3. Environs of Sebastopol:
Inkerman and the Chersonese Uplands

Prologue

Meerut – June 1853

Everything looked the same. Heat had dried the nullah to a muddy trickle, but that was usual before the rains came, and Ensign Harry Standish crossed the bridge to the British town with the comforting sense of coming home. Under his breath he was humming 'Widdicombe Fair'.

The Mall was its usual afternoon quiet. The doctor's wife was reading in the shade of her veranda, and when he called 'Hullo, Mrs Carron, I'm home!' her hand flew to her mouth and the book dropped with a smack to the stones. She seemed too startled to return his greeting, and he guessed with amusement she hadn't recognized him. That was fair enough. The boy who left India nine months ago was very different from the eighteen-year-old officer walking home in the triumph of his first-ever battle. He was looking forward to telling his father.

He was still humming as he passed jauntily on to their own bungalow. The white gate looked the same as always, but it bumped open unevenly at his push and he saw with surprise the base was clogged with weeds. There were more growing along the path, and as his footsteps crunched on the gravel the silence blasted back at him like a ricochet from a shot. Where the devil were the servants? Even the path ahead was dirty, its white stones speckled with a spray of earth, but as he neared the house he realized the mud was moving, the random specks resolving themselves into a glinting black trail that reached all the way to the side door of his father's study.

Ants.

His footsteps quickened, slapping urgently up the path. He

dropped his pack, knocked on the door and said, 'Sir?' but the ants were bolder, swarming over his boots in their haste to scurry under the crack of the door. They weren't soldier ants, they wouldn't attack a living man, but he kicked out in revulsion and the door shuddered ajar at the blow. He threw it open wide.

The stench hit him like a wall of heat, sickly, rotten, and tinged with the sourness of whisky. The ant trail trickled past his foot, solidified to an advancing phalanx, and drew his eyes up to the black, heaving mound spread over the floor in the cruciform shape of a man. But the head was monstrous, a gorgon's, surrounded by dark tentacles of ants as they clustered and puddled over what he understood suddenly were sprays of blood or worse. Realization forced his gaze back to the body, following the eloquent curve of the outflung arm to the open hand and the metal object lying silently beside it. There were ants on the gun too.

His throat clenched, and he reeled back through the door, spitting and retching, only vaguely aware of footsteps approaching on the gravel. A voice called 'Master Harry-sahib!' and old Ramesh Kumar came hurrying towards him with a basket, but his smile of welcome congealed into anxiety at the sight of the ants and open door. 'The colonel-sahib . . .'

'In there,' he said, turning away to retch again. 'In there.' He scrubbed his sleeve violently over his mouth and saw with curious detachment the trembling of his arm.

He heard the hoarse cry, then the slow deliberate tread as the *khansamar* backed out of the study to stand beside him. Thank God for Ramesh, he thought dully. The other servants might have disappeared, but the old butler would never desert them. 'For God's sake, Ramesh, what's happened here?'

'My fault, sahib,' said the old man. 'Never does the colonel-sahib send me out of town to market, never in twenty years, I should have known he would do this.' His knees crunched to the ground, and Standish saw with shock that he was weeping. 'Oh, what will we do, sahib, what will we do?'

Ramesh had three times his years and five times his wisdom,

but Standish felt the burden of 'sahib' crash round his shoulders like a yoke. There was no senior officer here, he had no father, there was only himself to be what the old man needed. He swallowed down his own shock and said, 'No one's fault, Ramesh. Now get me water, we're going to clear this before anyone sees.'

'*Han*, sahib,' said the *khansamar* at once, leaping up at the sound of authority. 'Water.' He hurried round the house for the well and Standish forced himself to go back in the room. He wouldn't look at the thing on the floor; that wasn't his father, wasn't the man he'd shaken hands with every night of his childhood, wasn't the respected Colonel Standish who would sometimes forget himself and play bears under the dining table with his boy. He looked at the room instead and only now noticed how much was missing. The bookcase was nearly empty, the candlesticks gone, nothing on the stained tablecloth but a half-empty whisky bottle and a tumbler clouded with finger marks. He lifted them off, and whipped away the cloth as Ramesh staggered back in with a bucket. 'In the middle, Ramesh, clear me a hand-hold in the middle.' His father's waist and strong chest, *the middle*.

Ramesh threw. The water made a red streak in the black, the British army coat of which father and son had been so proud. Standish flung the tablecloth over the terrible head, bent to force his arms under the body, and lifted it with surprising ease. No need to look, no need to flinch, a man couldn't be revolted by the body of his own father. He carried it outside with his head held high in a travesty of pride, and lowered it into the horse trough by the front gate. Little pricks of pain peppered his wrists where the ants bit, but he thrust the corpse under and watched the drowning insects float to the surface in a thick black scum. A paleness glimmered beneath, and just for a second he saw the horror of blood and bone and brain and the eaten-out cavities that had been his father's eyes.

He swung away in shock, furiously brushing the clinging insects from his arms and coat. There were steps at the gate, Dr and Mrs Carron, but Ramesh was running past to meet them, and Standish leaned against the almond tree as he fought to control his nausea. The murmur of voices gave him a moment's space, and he allowed himself to look at the indignity of his father's legs hanging over the edge of the trough. Why had he never seen how thin and frail they were, never until now? A terrible emptiness began to stir in his chest, and with it the first yearning of grief.

He crushed it down ruthlessly to make his mind work. The money was gone, obviously, but it would take more than that to drive a devoted soldier to blow his brains out. What had it done to him, this army he'd given his whole life to? What had it done? He stared at the ground for answers, but saw only faint grey splashes of water already evaporating in the heat.

A woman's voice rose over the others, Mrs Carron saying, 'Oh, Henry, Henry, that poor boy, whatever will he do?' He watched the dark edges of a damp patch magically shrinking, until there was nothing left but a single ant lying crippled and helpless on the burning stones.

PART ONE

The Alma

'Hurrah for the Crimea! We are off tomorrow . . . Take Sebastopol in a week or so, and then into winter quarters.'

Cornet E. R. Fisher, 4th Dragoon Guards, letter of 4 September 1854

I

14 September 1854, 2.00 p.m. to 4.00 p.m.

The bands were playing as they landed in the Crimea. Drums rolled, cymbals crashed, and boats bobbed to the rhythm of *Camptown Races* as they hauled their rafts of soldiers to the shore. The beach was already teeming with them, sunlight blazing in the ranks of scarlet and gold and rifle-green, flashing off brass-fronted shakos and glistening incongruously in the damp black bearskins of the Guards. Private Charlie Oliver of the 13th Light Dragoons watched wistfully from the rail of the steamship *Jason* and wondered why he felt slightly sick.

The other fellows seemed quite happy. The deck buzzed with the speculation of men impatient for their own turn, and Oliver knew he should feel the same. He'd been afraid the Russians would resist the landing, but there'd been no cannon fire, no musketry, no sign of the enemy anywhere, and the British troops panting purposefully up the beach were greeted only by hopeful Crim-Tartar locals, rickety arabas piled high with trade-goods, and strings of depressed-looking mules. British officers were already haggling with the traders just as easily as in the bazaars of Varna, and far across the water Oliver heard the distinctive clonking of camel bells.

'Looks all right to me,' said Fisk, licking up biscuit crumbs from the palm of his hand. 'Don't know why they want to call it Calamity Bay.'

'It's "Kalamita", you ass,' said the knowledgeable voice of 'Telegraph' Jordan. 'Kalamita. It's foreign.'

It didn't really look it now. Specks of red were already appearing above the cliffs as British picquets guarded the road inland,

and those square patches of colour were British regimental flags marking British territory. It didn't sound it either, and Oliver's spirits lifted as another raft landed to the familiar skirling of Highland pipes. The tension of the morning was dissolving into celebration, men shouting and laughing as they waded ashore, and even the dour Highlanders humoured the sailors' mockery of their kilts by prancing up the beach with hands entwined like girls. It was going to be all right. It was going to be all right after all.

Oars splashed below, one of the *Jason*'s own gigs pulling back towards them, and the rail beside him shook with the thump of bodies as men rushed to the side for news. 'Hulloa, Jasons!' called Jordan, clinging on to his shako as the crowd behind shoved him halfway over the rail. 'What's up? Are we off?' Others shouted 'Any sign of the Russkies?', 'Any women?', and Fisk squashed his great bulk next to Oliver to bawl, 'Never mind that, is there any food?'

The coxswain looked at his gig's crew with an air of puzzlement. 'You hear anything, lads? Like it might be the twitter of little birds?'

Hoots of derision exploded round the deck. Jordan cried, 'Have a heart, chum, are we off or not?'

The coxswain grinned up at him. 'Couldn't say, matey. It's coming up for a blow.'

Jordan grinned knowingly. 'What about the Russkies?'

'What Russkies?' said the coxswain, and spat. 'Never a sniff of them; you'll be at Sebastopol in a week.' He rummaged in a sack at his feet then stood precariously and bent back his arm for a throw. 'Here, have a peach.'

The pink fruit came sailing up towards their outstretched hands. Oliver watched it rise, brought his arm smart to the curve and caught it with the familiar smack of a ball in his palm. For a second he was home again, fielding in the deep on a summer cricket field, then Fisk snatched the peach, said, 'Thanks, pal,' and sunk his teeth into the soft flesh.

The group broke up in laughter. The gig was moving on, but no one called after it, no one needed more; a few words and a piece of fruit were enough to make all of it real. Oliver stared at the distant shore, the low-lying cliffs, the green blur of grassy hillocks behind, and knew the intolerable waiting was over at last. The heat and stench and sickness of the camps of Varna were safely behind them, and somewhere in front lay the place they'd set out to conquer all those long months ago.

Sebastopol! The politicians had demanded it, the newspapers screamed for it, even the crowds had shouted it when they embarked at Portsmouth. Sebastopol was the headquarters of the Black Sea Fleet, the prize they must take to avenge the massacred Turkish fleet and show the Russian Bear Britannia still ruled the waves. Britannia wasn't going it alone, of course, there were French ships landing further along the bay and some Turks about somewhere, but Sebastopol could never withstand such a huge and glorious force as this. And Oliver was part of it! He looked down at his own uniform, at the brand-new good-conduct stripe on his dark blue sleeve, and felt the last of his uncertainty swept away on a wave of excitement.

He looked round for someone to share it with, but Ronnie still didn't seem to be about. He hadn't been at parade either, or in the line for their three days' rations, and Oliver began to wonder if he'd been put on some kind of fatigue. It would be beastly to make him miss all the excitement, but he was afraid it was just the sort of thing Troop Sergeant-Major Jarvis would do.

At least the TSM wasn't on deck either, and in his absence the mood was turning almost to carnival. Jordan was conducting a chorus of 'The Girl I Left Behind Me', Fisk gyrating his vast gut in a grotesque belly dance, and Bolton was gazing yearningly at the distant green grass as if at a vision of heaven. Prosser and Moody were actually smiling, and their beautifully polished boots tapped in unison to the music of the band. Even Big Joe Sullivan seemed to have forgotten his own misery for a while, and was scouring the horizon as if eager to find someone to fight. Everyone was excited, and who wouldn't be at a time like this?

Someone wasn't. As Oliver gazed happily round the deck he

saw one man standing apart, a tall, dark and faintly disreputable figure looking down at the sea with a curiously taut expression on his face. He wore a corporal's chevrons on his sleeve, but his hair blew untidily under his shako, his jaw was shadowed by the casual stubble of a man who shaved only when he felt like it, and he was straddling the ship's rail as if he didn't care whether he fell or not. He'd catch it hot if Jarvis saw him, but then he probably wouldn't care about that either. Harry Ryder never seemed to care about anything.

But something was bothering him now, and his tense immobility tweaked Oliver with a sense of unease. Ryder didn't have friends, he was cocky and rude and Jarvis couldn't stand him, but he did tend to know things other people didn't, and no one understood why. Oliver looked furtively over the side to see what was worrying him, but saw only an ordinary empty flatboat tossing and heaving in the swell.

He looked away as Ryder's head turned, but the corporal had seen him and at once relaxed into his usual insolent grin. He swung his leg jauntily back over the rail and said, 'What's the matter, Polly? Don't you want to go to war?'

Oliver flinched at the hateful nickname. 'Of course. It's what we came for, isn't it?'

Ryder had very dark eyes for an Englishman, slanted like an Indian's and gleaming with amusement. 'Is it, Poll? I've often wondered.'

Oliver looked uncertainly at him. It was a moral war, all the fellows said so, they were standing up to Russia to stop them bullying poor little Turkey. He hesitated, but the troop had already spotted Ryder and came flocking round like noisy pigeons, shouting, 'When are we off, Corp?' 'When are we off?'

Ryder shrugged. 'The sea's coming up. With luck it'll be tomorrow.'

'With luck?' said Fisk incredulously. 'The Frogs are nearly all off, there'll be nothing left in the villages once those thieving buggers have been through.'

Ryder smiled faintly. 'There'll be nothing left for anyone once *you've* been through.'

The troop shouted with laughter. Fisk sucked peach from his fingers and grinned.

Moody didn't laugh. 'Don't listen to him, Fisk. The sar'nt-major says we're rostered next, and that's good enough for me.' Prosser immediately said 'That's right' and looked aggressively at Ryder.

Ryder's eyes glinted. 'First rule of toad-eating, Moody. It works better if the man's there to hear you.'

Moody's face turned brick-red, but the laughter was muted and Oliver didn't dare join in. Moody would tell Jarvis.

Prosser certainly would, and his pock-marked face was stiff with truculence. 'Are you saying the sar'nt-major's wrong? Eh? That what you're saying?'

Ryder looked impassively at him. 'The sar'nt-major's right, we're rostered next, but it won't be this afternoon. Only a fool would land cavalry in this swell.'

A bang like a musket shot on the deck behind, then immediately another, the hatches being thrown open to the hold. Their own farrier-sergeant was hurrying up with the vet, and a second later came a screech of tackle as sailors set the hoist to winch the horses from below.

Ryder's face changed. He said something under his breath that sounded dreadfully like 'Christ', then wiped a hand over his mouth and strode across to the farrier-sergeant. 'Hullo, Sam, what the devil are we playing at?'

Oliver licked his lips. The blasphemy was bad, the Christian name almost worse, and he guessed Ryder really hadn't been joking.

'Is he saying it's dangerous?' said Bolton anxiously. 'For the horses? Bobbin's weak enough already, a whole week in a stall not big enough to lie down.'

'Oh, stow it, Tommy,' said Fisk irritably. 'There's no danger, we wouldn't be going otherwise.'

Bolton creased his brow. 'But Ryder says . . .'

'What does Ryder know?' said Fisk, and snorted. 'Giving himself airs like a bloody general. He's a nobody, same as us.'

Oliver glanced across to the hatch. The farrier-sergeant was red faced and waving his arms in exaggerated helplessness, but Ryder stood silent with his arms folded and his head down, giving only an occasional expressive nod.

'Cardigan,' said Jordan, nodding his head wisely. 'Bet you a tanner. This'll be Cardigan wanting to get the Light Brigade off before Lucan's even thought of it. Colley says he'll do anything to show up Lucan in front of Lord Raglan.'

Oliver looked away. Colley was Lord Lucan's servant, and the main source of Jordan's information, but it couldn't be more than silly gossip. All the fellows joked about their commanders, but he knew they wouldn't really order a disembarkation if it wasn't safe.

'First section "G" Troop!' called a squeaky voice by the hatch, and Cornet Hoare came bustling importantly up to the rail. 'Saddles and packs, back here in ten minutes. All aboard for the Crimea!'

Hoare's voice had hardly broken yet, but he represented authority and at once the men dashed whooping for the hold. Oliver glanced doubtfully back at Ryder, but the corporal only gestured with ironic courtesy and said, 'Well, get a move on, Polly. You wouldn't want to lose that nice new stripe.' He was utterly insufferable.

But he was also right, and Oliver pulled himself together to join the race down the ladder. The hold seemed more oppressive than ever after the sunlight on deck, warm and fetid with the stench of sweat and diarrhoea. It was dark, too, illuminated only by the swaying lamps that creaked on ropes overhead, but he picked his way through it with the familiarity of a long voyage and found the unwanted spot in the middle that had been his own bed. His blanket was rolled and ready, his haversack needed only to be slung on his back, but it was the valise that mattered, and he knelt on the damp boards to pack it with care.

These were his personal things. The groundsheet Colonel Lygon had given every man in the regiment when they left for the Crimea. The letters from his sister, precious, marked 'Vicky', and numbered in order. The Adams revolver in its case, good as any officer's, given to him by the squire in his father's old parish. The Christ's Hospital Bible, inscribed with the charge never to forget the benefits he had received from the charity school that had taken in the orphaned boy and given him the education of a gentleman. Oliver stroked the cheap leather with love and stowed the book with reverence. He had never forgotten, and one day he was going to make the School proud.

'Oliver!' called a woman's voice. He spun round in shock, but an oil lamp by the bulkhead showed him only the fair hair of young Mrs Jarvis kneeling by a blanketed figure on the boards. It would take more than regulations to keep out Sally Jarvis when one of her troop needed nursing.

'Oliver!' she said again, waving impatiently. 'Come over, he wants to see you.'

He knew then, knew it before he saw the tortured face of the man in the blanket. Ronnie Stokes. His only real friend in this army, the one man who understood things and would pray with him in the evenings when everything looked dark. They'd prayed yesterday, just last night. Had he been suffering all the time and never said?

'Dysentery,' he told himself, as he clambered over the legs of reclining 'B' Troop to reach the bulkhead. It didn't have to be – the other thing, the disease they'd left behind in the cavalry camp at Devno. He reached the dark wooden wall, but Ronnie's hand came up and his voice said 'Not too close, old man. Not . . . too close.'

Oliver looked down at the boards at his feet. The lamp made a yellow puddle of the floor, and in it he saw the spreading stain of fluid seeping from under Ronnie's body. It was almost colourless, the cracks of the planks clearly visible through it, and the faintly fishy odour told him the rest. Cholera.

He looked up in horror and met the sad eyes of Mrs Jarvis. She said, 'There are orderlies coming, but he wanted to see you before he went.'

'Yes,' said Ronnie, snatching at the word. 'Some things I want you to have.' He moved his eyes towards a shadowy cylinder by his blanket. 'By my valise.'

Oliver's heart thumped. 'You'll want them with you.'

'No,' said Ronnie simply, then closed his eyes in the convulsion of another cramp.

It was unbearable. He said, 'You'll get better, old fellow, lots of chaps do,' but the faint blue tinge of the final stages was already in Ronnie's face. By evening he'd be just another canvas-wrapped corpse floating in the fleet's wake.

'There's no one else,' said Ronnie. 'No auction. Just . . .' Again he nodded at the valise.

Oliver understood. Ronnie had no family, no one they'd have to raise money for by selling his possessions. He said, 'Just to look after, then. Till you join us in Sebastopol.'

There were three items laid out for him: a green bottle of French brandy, a wooden box of cheroots, and the familiar pack of playing cards. It was the cards that hurt most, and just the feel of the box in his hand tightened Oliver's throat. Those evenings of two-handed whist were all that had kept him going during those first dreadful months in the army when he'd been so terrified of Jarvis he could hardly even sleep. He was still scared of Jarvis – everyone was, except Ryder – but Ronnie had helped him master the drill, and in the evenings there'd been those games when they could talk and laugh and it was almost like being back at school.

'Lot of sins for you there, Charlie,' said Ronnie, with a twisted little smile. 'If I only had a dirty book you'd have the full set.'

Ronnie with a dirty book! Oliver tried to smile back, but tears were blurring his eyes and his cheekbones hurt. Ronnie was his own age, just seventeen. He'd endured the training, all the horrors of Varna, only to die now when the adventure was just starting and everything about to be worthwhile.

A voice called 'Come on, chum!' and he turned to see Jordan hanging from the ladder to look for him in the gloom. 'Your mare's on the boat and bloody Jarvis is on the prowl.'

Terror shot through him, and his whole body twitched with the urge to leap up and run. He called back 'All right!' and looked doubtfully at Ronnie.

'You go,' said Ronnie, still smiling. 'I'll see you at Sebastopol.'

Mrs Jarvis smiled too. 'You'd better. If "bloody Jarvis" is on the prowl . . .'

He grinned sheepishly, tucked his new possessions under his arm, and gave a last look down at his friend. Mrs Jarvis was brushing the sweaty hair from his eyes and whispering 'There, my love,' in a soft Cornish voice that made him want to cry. He reached out to grasp Ronnie's dry hand in his own, said, 'God bless you, old fellow,' and turned hurriedly away before the tears could fall.

'Good luck, old man,' said Ronnie, and 'Good luck,' called Mrs Jarvis. 'B' Troop said it too as he passed them, 'Good luck, Trooper. Good luck!' He crammed Ronnie's things into his own valise, snatched up his saddle and bolted for the ladder, but the voices calling 'Good luck! Good luck!' followed him all the way into the sunlight of the world above.

The flatboat heaved as the last horse was swung over the side, and Ryder had to stamp hard to keep his footing. If it was like this in the lee of the *Jason*, how the hell would it be in the crowded mass of boats and rafts that passed for the open sea? One slip on this wet deck could break a horse's legs, and they were short of remounts as it was.

The horses they did have weren't in the best of condition. That was Bolton's bloody Bobbin coming down now, a temperamental little mare who'd never been broken properly, but even she lay inert in the sling, legs stuck out stiffly for whatever ground she'd be plonked on next. The sailors patted her soothingly as they removed the harness and led her over to Bolton's eager hands, and Ryder took some comfort in their steady, sure-footed movements. At least they had trained men with them on the trip.

It was more than he could say of their officers. Poor Cornet Hoare was skidding hopelessly over the waterlogged boards and had to grab the coxswain's arm to stop himself falling. 'I *say!*' he said breathlessly. 'It wasn't like this at Varna!' The boy was reliable enough to follow steady orders, but the only other officer boarding with their section was Captain Marsh himself, a man of such opaque simplicity he was generally known as 'Bog'. The farrier-sergeant had already appealed to him about the conditions, but Marsh's answer was that they'd been ordered ashore, they would go ashore, and the men would just have to make certain there were no accidents.

The men. Ryder studied them as they stood at the heads of their frightened beasts, and felt his confidence sink. From a distance they'd look magnificent, the dark blue jackets accentuating their slim figures and double white overall stripe exaggerating their height, but the yellow and scarlet belts were loose on shrunken waists and the faces beneath the oilskin-covered shakos were a dull grey. They were worn down by months of ill treatment, poor rations, and dysentery, and God knew if they could be counted on in an emergency.

Like this one. The right side was the weakness, and he sighed at the sight of that prize prig Polly Oliver right at the front. Blond and beardless, bright-eyed and oozing pride in his new good-conduct stripe, he'd be as much use as a fly-swat. No, what was needed at the end of that line was bulk, something more like the blubber-lipped ox next to him, who still had bits of peach in his beard even on parade. 'Fisk!' he said. 'Change places with Oliver. Now. Second rank too, Prosser outside, Bolton inside.'

The rear rank should have been safe with Sullivan on the end, but that was before the last day in Varna. Big Joe Sullivan, solid as stone, but he'd got drunk over cards with Bloomer of the 7th and been given fifty lashes for supposedly striking that bastard Jarvis. His back would still be in ribbons, but the real damage was inside, visible only in the hunched body and lowered head that refused to look anyone in the face. Ryder stepped close and muttered, 'You're not fit, Joe, get back on board.'

'I'm fit, Corp,' said Sullivan, but without looking up. 'I'm fit.'

Ryder understood. 'At least take the pack off. We can pile it with the valises.'

Sullivan mumbled something incoherent, but he did lower his broad shoulder to slide the heavy haversack to the ground.

But a second thump echoed it, a man descending from the ladder behind. The tension in the ranks told Ryder at once who it was, and even the sailors stopped chattering to look. He listened to the heavy footsteps prowling slowly to the front, and turned with resignation to face Troop Sergeant-Major Jarvis.

Jarvis wasn't tall, but he held himself so rigid that few of his troopers would have believed it. The massive shoulders and thrust-out chest were daunting enough, but even his face seemed swollen by the excess flesh that formed folds in the whiskered jowls and pouches under the hard little eyes. Everyone on the flatboat watched as he rounded the ranks, stuck his crop under his arm, strained higher on his toes, and stopped in front of Ryder.

Ryder said, 'Sar'nt-major,' and stood to attention. The deck was sopping, the whole platform heaving, but Jarvis would put him on a charge if he didn't do it perfectly. Jarvis would put him on a charge for breathing if he could.

The sergeant-major's eyes crawled over him, searching for that elusive excuse to make him jump. His gaze lingered on the dark shadow of the jaw, visibly burning with resentment at the new regulations that allowed such a sight on his parade, then slid away to the ranks of the men behind. At once he stiffened, and pointed his crop at Fisk. 'These men are out of order! Put them back at once.'

Ryder was careful to keep his voice low, nothing to make the NCO feel threatened in front of the troop. 'Yes, Sar'nt-major, I thought it better to strengthen the outside.'

Jarvis must have heard him, but he wasn't passing up a chance to make the corporal he'd never wanted look a fool. 'Speak up, Ryder, don't be shy. Tell us your opinion.'

Prosser and Moody were already grinning. Ryder lifted his chin and said it again, louder. 'I thought it better to strengthen the outside.'

Jarvis smiled broadly. 'You're a corporal, you're not required to think!' Moody sniggered obediently and Prosser added an extra-loud guffaw.

Ryder ignored them. 'Look at the swell, Sar'nt-major; no one else is landing cavalry. The farrier-sergeant's worried, and we need to take precautions.'

The laughter faded and died. In the sudden quiet the midshipman could be heard addressing the sailors. 'And watch that baggage! It's going to be rough, see, it needs to be dead centre to trim the boat.'

Every head turned to Jarvis. The sergeant-major reddened dangerously and swung round on Ryder. 'You think you know better than our officers, do you? Well, do you?'

A three-year-old knew better than their officers. 'No, Sar'nt-major.'

'No,' said Jarvis, nodding emphatically. 'I gave you an order, Corporal. Now execute it. *At the double!*'

At the double. The boat was swaying beneath them, but men and horses scrambled frantically to get back in their original places. The movement immediately exposed the rank behind, and this time Jarvis didn't bother with words. He pointed the crop at Sullivan's pack, looked on impassively as the man stoically reworked it onto his mutilated back, then strutted complacently on down the line. Ryder watched him with loathing, but could only lead his own horse to the right flank and stand in silence like the rest.

It was too late for anything else. The midshipman was clearly anxious to get under way before the conditions worsened, and waited only for Captain Marsh to take his place before giving the signal to cast off. The tow-boats hauled, the platform heaved, men staggered and righted themselves, and horses whinnied in alarm. Even Marsh said 'By Jove, bit frisky, ain't it?' but they were already committed, every stroke pulling them further and further from the *Jason*'s side. The walls of the anchored fleet receded around them as if they were emerging from a town into open country, and under his feet Ryder felt the full roll of the sea.

He called down the line, 'Arms through bridoon reins, boys, keep those horses steady,' but the boys were even shakier, the neat lines rocking and buckling with every heave of the swell. Even the sailors grimaced as they looked over their shoulders at the water-traffic, and he knew that sailors, like soldiers, had rarely learned to swim.

'Bit crowded, ain't it?' said Marsh, as they skirted a raft of Guards only to find a huge artillery flatboat heaving up beside them. 'Here, Middy, why are we packed so close?'

The midshipman kept his eyes on the artillery raft. 'Not us, sir, it's the Frogs. We had a landing plan and a buoy to mark it, but the French have sneaked out and moved the buoy.'

'By Jove,' said Marsh, struggling to digest this treachery on the part of their allies. 'Given themselves more room, eh?'

The midshipman shrugged. 'So they say. God knows where the Turks will land, they'll be lucky if we've left them a puddle.'

'Never mind the Johnnies,' called the irrepressible Jordan. 'Where's Russ? Looks like we called a war and nobody came.'

Laughter rippled round the boat, but Ryder was watching the approaching shore and didn't feel inclined to join in.

'Nobody?' he said. 'Look again, Jordan. Look at the top of the hill.'

Everyone turned, and the raft was suddenly silent but for the gentle washing of surf. The beach ahead was teeming with red uniforms, but there it was again, a little white flash on the slopes above, a grey blur, then another flash. There were a handful of riders on the horizon, men waiting placidly on horseback, but above their seated figures protruded long-hafted lances with blades that glinted in the sun. They weren't in the uniform of an official Host, they wore grey fur hats rather than shakos, but there was no mistaking them all the same. Cossacks. Not pictures in *The Times* or *Punch*, the real thing, just sitting there watching them. Russian Cossacks.

A low murmur began to buzz about the boat. 'Not many, are there?' said Hoare cheerfully. 'They must be awfully windy to see what's below.'

They didn't look it. Five men in rifle range of thousands, but they trotted along as calmly as gentlemen on Rotten Row, and Ryder saw uneasily that one in a green frock-coat was stopping to write in what looked like a book. What made them so damned confident? Was there a whole army of them just behind those green, inviting hills?

A shout wrenched him back to the flatboat. The coxswain was yelling and waving as the artillery float lurched towards them, a gun rolling loose in its moorings. The raft heaved as the boats tried to turn, horses neighed, men stumbled and cursed, then a violent jolt, a sudden drop, the smashing of wood, and the howitzer came crunching through their side.

The coxswain hauled on a tow-rope, sailors wrestled with the great 24-pounder that was worth all their lives put together, but the platform was tilting like a see-saw, men and horses tumbling towards the rising waves. The troop's right flank was breaking, Sullivan gone and his horse with him, both hurled outboard without a cry. Oliver screamed, 'Take her, take her!' and threw his mare's reins at Fisk even as he slid over the wood towards the foaming sea. Ryder grabbed for him, but the wet sleeve scorched through his hand, Oliver gone, then a blow smashed him sideways as the mare fell after. Fisk had missed her, but at least he understood at last; he was turning with bent knees to hold back the rest.

Ryder swung left. Jordan and Moody had control, that end steady, but Bolton's mare was screaming and rearing on the right, scattering men in fear of her hooves. Jarvis bawled 'Stand steady there!' but the mare was already through them and crashing over the flatboat's shattered side. Hoare's horse was next, and the cornet following, sixteen years old and trying to halt a stallion of seventy stones weight. Ryder flung him backwards, and slid his own haversack to the deck. His shako, sword-belt and cap-box were already off, but there was no time for the boots. Men and horses were struggling and splashing in the water, trapped between two boats pinned together by the anchor of a howitzer barrel. Ryder thrust Wanderer's reins into Fisk's hands, made for the broken side, and plunged into the sea.

A wave broke at once over his head, stinging his eyes and washing wood-splinters into his gasping mouth. He fought the weight of sodden clothing to dodge clear of Bolton's thrashing mare, seized the side to grab a quick gulp of air, and looked round for the men. One was floundering and shouting ahead of the flatboat, but sailors in the gig were already stretching out a boat-hook to bring him in. Oliver was all right too, his damp blond head moving cleanly through the water as he swam back to the raft. Sullivan was the priority, splashing and gurgling with every stroke, weighed down by the bloody haversack there hadn't been time to remove.

Ryder struck out towards him. The trooper was struggling and panicking, but Ryder hauled his arms over a bit of floating wreckage and kept him pinned there until his breathing steadied. He looked back to the flatboat, but horses were still struggling in the gap between the tangled vessels, and would have to be cleared before he could bring Sullivan through. 'Stay there,' he yelled in the man's ear. 'I'll come back for you – stay there, that's an order.'

Sullivan nodded and spat water, and Ryder turned again for the channel. Oliver's horse had fought clear and was ploughing purposefully for shore, but another was already rolling away, a spiral of blood staining the sea about its broken head. Bolton's mare was still thrashing, eyes rolling white, lips retreating from dark gums to show big square teeth, and Oliver was trapped behind her, unable to reach the broken flatboat side. Bolton was crying 'Bobbin, Bobbin!' in an agony of distress and trying to pull her back on board, but the animal couldn't climb in water, she was kicking against the artillery float and would break her back legs. The fourth horse had already done it, and was screaming and writhing as it spun away. Two, maybe three lost, and Ryder knew they had to save the mare.

The flatboat platform was weighed down in the water and the mare had both front hooves on it; she could make it if she had purchase from behind. He put his shoulder to one side of the chestnut rump, and yelled to Oliver on the other side, 'Push her! We've got to push!' For a second it was a toss-up, the fear of an NCO and the fear of the hooves, then Oliver put his shoulder to the mark, and Ryder felt the horse boosted upwards. The water took half the weight, its front legs skittered on the platform, and Ryder kicked down to give himself more thrust. Something solid under his foot gave a moment of purchase, he stamped down and hurtled back up, sending the horse flying upwards to Bolton pulling her bridle from the deck. He grabbed at the boat side, wincing at the splash as a second figure crashed through the surface and whooshed upright beside him. 'Oliver,' he thought, and turned.

A blur of grey, torn canvas, and a face that screamed. The mouth was a cave of teeth in blue distended cheeks, and the eyes black holes in which things squirmed. There were no hands or arms visible, nothing of the man left but a parcelled mummy that bobbed like a giant cork, and a nightmare face so close to Ryder's own its stench seemed almost a parody of breath. His hands spasmed in shock and released their hold on the wood, ducking him once again below the water.

'Cholera,' his mind said. 'Cholera, don't drink it, don't swallow.' He surfaced and spat, aware suddenly of sky above him, the oaths of the sailor pushing at the corpse with a boat-hook, and the terrified wail of Oliver as he batted the thing away from him in childlike panic. It was just a corpse, a cholera victim dropped with insufficient weights from a ship ahead of their own, but for a moment memory had stripped away common sense and showed him the waterlogged and eyeless body of his own father.

He closed his eyes against it, the sound of Oliver's helpless retching blending with an old boyhood tune in his head, *Tom Pearce, Tom Pearce, lend me your grey mare* . . . He wondered if Oliver's grey mare would make it to shore, then became aware of his body rising in the water as the flatboat sprang back to the level. The howitzer must be back on its own float, they were seaworthy again, and a voice was already yelling 'Out of the water! Back on board right now!' Bloody Jarvis. Let him wait.

But Sullivan didn't dare, and Ryder turned to see him abandoning the driftwood and trying to swim. His face was in the water, the soaking haversack weighing him down, he was swimming blind and the freed artillery float driving right at him. Ryder flung forward, but heard the thud ahead of him, a chorus of voices, and saw Sullivan reeling back from the float to vanish beneath the waves.

Ryder struggled past the dead horse, glimpsed the sinking white stripe of a dragoon's overalls, ducked for it and heaved the man up into the air. The sodden haversack pulled against him, Sullivan's big body rolled across his own, then he was back under the water, it was in his mouth and nose, the burn scorching down into his lungs. Unbelievable, ridiculous to drown within feet of a boat, he puffed out his cheeks and kicked down. The haversack banged across his face, his flailing hands struck only Sullivan, and panic swelled in his head, driving out thought and sense, telling him only to breathe, breathe, and breathe air. Again the pain in his chest and throat, his eyes opening with shock and seeing only greyness of water, his ears strangely silent as they closed against the sound of his own drowning. Another desperate heave, but Sullivan's weight was suddenly off him and he shot straight to the surface, blinking and spluttering, feet treading furiously as he coughed his lungs clear. Sullivan was up too, his chin supported

23

by the dark blue arm of another man who looked anxiously at Ryder and said, 'Are you all right?'

Oliver. The frightened prig he'd never thought much of had ignored Jarvis's order and come to help. Ryder spat a last mouthful in reply, and reached out to get a hand in Sullivan's belt. 'Bloody fine, Poll, I'm only doing this for fun. Come on, back to the boat.'

The kid had saved him. Ludicrous, of course, and Ryder struck out even harder against the thought, but Sullivan was coming round and the fact was it took both of them to wrestle him back to the reaching arms of the sailors at the flatboat side. Ryder's pride made him boost Oliver before hauling himself up after them, but it wasn't enough, there was a debt there now, and the man Ryder used to be knew it had to be paid.

But something else had to be paid first, and as he shook the water from his ears he became aware that someone was shouting again and the voice was far too aristocratic to be Jarvis's. He shoved sopping hair out of his eyes and turned.

Another raft had stopped in front of theirs, occupied by a single officer with a crowd of deferential servants. The officer wore the pink pants and blue dolman of the 11th Hussars, but the fur-lined cloak and mane of auburn hair under the busby established his identity beyond all doubt. It was James Brudenell, Earl of Cardigan, commander of the entire Light Brigade, a man with the head of a lion and the brain of a brick.

'A disgrace, sir,' he roared at poor old Bog. 'I won't have one of my regiments paddling about like sailors in front of the entire fleet! What if my Lord Raglan had seen you, hey? A fine thing, 'pon my word, shaming the Brigade before the Commander-in-Chief!'

Ryder stood dripping on the deck, listening to the arrogant aristocratic voice and looking down at Sullivan curled and vomiting at his feet. A man had nearly died. Only a trooper, only a reprobate who'd already had to be whipped like a dog, but a man had nearly died and Ryder's anger seared his throat as if he were back in the water and drowning.

Cardigan ranted on. 'When you order the men to return, it's to happen immediately, sir, *immediately*! You let your own men make a fool of you!'

Marsh's voice sounded half strangled. 'I'm most sorry, my lord. The men will of course be disciplined.'

'See they are,' said Cardigan, waving loftily for his oarsmen to resume. 'Disgrace to the Brigade. You damn well *see they are*.'

Punishment, of course, the commanders' solution for everything that went wrong, and Ryder was under no illusions as to whose it would be. Cardigan was on his way, but the damage was done, he could see it in Marsh's face: the tense, thin-lipped look of an officer who'd been upbraided in front of his men and was determined to pass on the favour as soon as he could. He shouted to the midshipman, 'Get under way, damn you,' then turned ominously to Jarvis. 'Sar'nt-major! I told you to get those men out of the water.'

'And I ordered it, sir,' said Jarvis, turning towards Ryder with a look of pleasurable anticipation. 'They deliberately disobeyed.'

Ryder didn't need to hear Oliver's terrified gasp beside him to understand. It had taken a rough sea and a drowning man to do it, but Troop Sergeant-Major Jarvis had found his chance at last.

The rest of the journey had the blur of nightmare for Oliver. The flatboat was moving and sailors bailing out from the broken side, but part of him didn't care if they sunk or not. His life was ruined and over, and the terror was a clawed hand round his throat.

Why had he done it, why? He'd heard Jarvis's order, what had possessed him to ignore it? He'd never been in trouble before, never even been reprimanded, he'd never been able to bear it and couldn't now. Even a disapproving look from one of the ushers at school had been a torment until he could wipe out the stain with a 'Well done, Oliver,' and a smile. And this would be more than a look. He watched Captain Marsh in conference with Jarvis, he waited for the summons and wanted only to be dead before it came.

'Step forward, Ryder!' called Jarvis. 'Oliver!'

They were on a broken raft that bucked beneath them like an untrained horse, it wasn't like parade and he didn't know the rules. 'Come on, Polly,' said Ryder beside him, and his voice was deep and calming. 'Let's go and have a little chat with the officer.'

He understood that, he could do it, and he followed Ryder across the slopping boards with desperate trust. Captain Marsh didn't seem comfortable either, and that too was cause for hope. He was an officer, he'd always been fair, he must see that no Christian could have let Sullivan and Ryder drown, he must see it, he must.

'Bad business, men,' said Marsh, shaking his head sadly. 'Those Guards spotted us, you know, and his lordship saw it. Disobeying an order and at a time of war.'

The words hit him like stones. The Articles of War, the drum roll before a flogging . . .

'Yes, sir,' said Ryder. 'But not Oliver. He was acting under my orders.'

His head swam with disbelief. *Had* Ryder ordered him? Had he missed it in the noise of the sea? Then he remembered what he'd seen as he'd started up the flatboat side, Ryder going under, Ryder drowning, Ryder in no position to give an order to anyone, and stared at the corporal in something close to awe.

'*Your* orders,' said Jarvis contemptuously. 'You don't give orders, Corporal, your job is to execute mine.'

Marsh cleared his throat. 'Yes, well, that absolves the trooper, Ryder, but I'm afraid it makes matters worse for you. A District Court-Martial . . .'

Could flog him. Oliver's thoughts rushed from side to side, banging against walls of impossibility. Own up, say he'd acted of his own accord – and tell them Ryder was lying. Say nothing, let the corporal take the blame for both of them – and see him flogged. Do the right thing, play the game, but his tongue felt swollen in his mouth and his mind was numb.

'I must speak for Ryder, sir,' said Cornet Hoare. His legs were splayed awkwardly against the rocking of the boat, but Oliver thought he'd never seen an officer look so heroic. 'They were trying to obey the order when the accident happened. Ryder had to go back, sir, he saved Sullivan's life. He saved me too when I nearly went overboard.'

Marsh's face looked quite blank for a moment, and Oliver remembered he liked things kept simple. 'There's Lord Cardigan, you know, Cornet; he'll want an explanation.'

Hoare wobbled as the boat lurched. 'I'll speak to Colonel Doherty, sir. I'll explain. I'm sure he'll be able to satisfy his lordship.'

Marsh's face cleared. 'All right, yes, let's leave it to the colonel. Right, back to your places, men; the sooner we're off this blasted tub, the better.'

A quick movement beside him, Jarvis stepping forward with a reddened face. 'Sir, I protest. My authority. Corporal Ryder defied me in front of the troop.'

Marsh looked irritated again. 'Yes, yes, TSM, quite right, and we'll attend to it at defaulters in the usual way. No need to bother the colonel for that, is there?' He turned on his heel and splashed hurriedly back to the servant holding his horse.

Jarvis seemed to have frozen to the deck. Oliver watched him fearfully, waiting to be ordered back to his place, but the sergeant-major stood quite still and stared only at Ryder as if nobody else existed. The look on his face made Oliver afraid to breathe.

Ryder met the look steadily. After a moment he even smiled.

Jarvis's voice came out so low it was almost a growl. 'I suppose you think you've got away with it.'

Ryder's mouth twitched. 'No, Sar'nt-major.'

'No,' said Jarvis. Oliver became aware of a faint wheezing noise, and realized with shock it was the sergeant-major's breathing. 'No. You're going to wish you'd had that court-martial, I can promise you that.'

'*Damn* it, Jarvis!' yelled Marsh. 'Move, will you? They want to trim the boat!'

Jarvis's colour deepened, but he blinked furiously and shouted, 'Back in line!' in quite his normal bellow.

Oliver stumbled eagerly back to his place in the ranks, hoping for reassurance in the familiar order. He whispered to Ryder, 'He won't really do anything, will he, Corp?'

'To you, Poll?' Ryder's mouth twisted with amusement, but his eyes remained dark. 'Oh, I think you're safe enough.'

He didn't feel it. There was no Misty beside him, no reins through his arm, and the world had changed since he last stood there. It had all seemed as simple as not stepping on cracks in the pavement, follow the rules and be safe, but if an NCO could ignore an officer to hurt a man if he felt like it, then nothing made sense and nothing was safe at all.

The flatboat was breaking up by the time they reached shore, and Ryder knew they'd be lucky to get it back to the *Jason* in one piece. That was a storm brewing in the sky and there'd be no more horses landed tonight.

He splashed Wanderer through the shallows, stretched with the relief of solid ground beneath his feet, and looked around the beach. There were First Division markers to their left and Guards already forming column for a march inland, but the traders were all thronging down by the Light Division, where the cliffs shrank to knee height and a track led up to the country beyond. Their own stretch was bare, except for the distant figure of a single Highlander standing rigid guard over a pile of packs as if he thought the Cossacks might charge the beach for the express purpose of stealing them.

It didn't matter. The bluejackets were already unloading the baggage, and in moments he'd be back on horseback where he belonged. He started towards the scrimmage already forming in the rush for saddles, but hesitated at the sight of Oliver and Sullivan standing apart, dripping and disconsolate, cavalrymen without horses. They'd have a long wait for remounts, poor buggers, and from the look of the sky a bloody wet one. Oliver would be all right, he was young and strong, and anyway that debt was paid, but Sullivan was a different matter. He'd been weak when they started, he'd had a bang on the head and been half-drowned, he'd never survive a night out in a storm.

Ryder strolled over. 'Come on, Joe. Go back in the gig, the surgeon will want to look at that thick skull of yours.'

Sullivan glared at him out of bloodshot eyes. 'I came here to fight a bloody war. You want to stop me?' His scanty hair was plastered to his head and the gash on his brow already swelling.

Ryder hesitated. He'd seen Sullivan as a weakness, then a bulk that could drown him, but now he looked at the beaten trooper and saw only a man. He grinned and shook his head. 'You're a pig-headed bastard, Joe.'

Sullivan looked suspiciously at him, then the corners of his eyes crinkled in a smile. 'And does it not take one to know one, Harry Ryder?'

Ryder laughed and went for his own saddle, but he'd taken only two paces when Marsh called, 'Ah, Ryder, just a minute,' and he turned to see the captain flanked by Hoare and an ominously smiling Jarvis.

'Sir?'

Marsh coughed politely. 'Just lend your horse to the cornet, will you? I need him with me for the patrol, and the TSM thinks you'll be better for a rest.'

On an empty beach with a storm coming. He handed over the bridle without a word, glad at least it was Hoare. The cornet had been a trump on the boat.

Marsh cleared his throat. 'We'll be back in a couple of days, but you can wait with Oliver and Sullivan for remounts from the *Simla*. They'll be landing shortly with Lieutenant Grainger and the rest of the troop.'

Tomorrow perhaps, or the next day. 'Yes, sir.'

'Jolly good,' said Marsh, and turned rather hastily to his own horse.

Ryder politely saluted his back and turned to see Moody at his elbow holding out a saddle.

'Thought you'd better have it anyway, Corp,' he said with a deference that didn't match the malice in his pond-water eyes. 'You'll need something to sit on while you wait.' Beside him Prosser was openly grinning, and Jarvis paused with his foot in the stirrup to watch.

To hell with them. Ryder held out his arms for the saddle, then looked the trooper bang in the eyes and said, 'Thanks, Moody. I won't forget.'

Moody backed away even more hurriedly than Marsh had done. Jarvis mounted heavily, but made no move to join the patrol and Ryder guessed he was waiting to deliver some suitably unpleasant parting shot. 'Yes, Sar'nt-major?'

Jarvis's saddle creaked as he leaned down. 'Oh, come, Ryder. You're not troubled by the thought of a little rain?'

To hell with him too. 'Not at all, Sar'nt-major. I'm wet already, aren't I?'

It was a weak response and Jarvis knew it. 'Well, it'll do for a start, won't it? For a start.' He reached out with his crop, stroked it very gently down Ryder's jaw, grinned broadly and trotted away.

Fury exploded in Ryder's head. The *bastard*. To punish him was nothing, but to touch him like a dog, a tame animal, a creature that couldn't hit back! His fists clenched the saddle, and through the throb in his fingers he felt the pulse of his own heart.

He'd been a man once. He could have thrown down the saddle, pulled that grinning ape off his horse with his own damned crop and beaten the stuffing out of him right here on the sand. But Ensign Standish was dead, had to be, buried with his father in the dust of Meerut, and there was no one here but a lowly corporal who had only to put one foot out of line to be flogged half to death like Joe Sullivan.

The thought of Sullivan swept him with savage fellow feeling. He looked up to the cliffs and the waiting Cossacks, wishing they'd come down and fight, wishing they'd fetch their whole damned army and be done with it. Sullivan was right. This was all that was left now, all there'd ever been for someone like himself. They were here to fight a bloody war, and for the man that was now Harry Ryder it couldn't come too soon.

2

14 September 1854, 4.00 p.m. to midnight

The cavalry patrol made a grand sight as they trotted away down the beach. They'd had a hard landing, poor laddies, and lucky to be ashore at all, but they rode high and proud in their saddles like conquerors in a foreign land, and the lone Highland sentry watched their passage with grave approval. There were two or three of their number left behind, he noticed, but doubtless they'd be on important duty like himself. Niall Mackenzie of the 93rd Highlanders looked at the packs at his feet and shuffled an inch nearer to leave no doubt in whose charge they lay.

A splashing to his front brought his head round fast, and there was a horse coming towards him, a grey horse walking out of the sea and shaking its head vigorously as if it were a normal thing for a British horse to swim to the Crimea. He watched in wonder as it headed towards him, hooves crunching purposefully on the shingle, then thrust a determined nose into his carefully guarded pile of baggage.

Mackenzie forced his features to become stern. 'Shoo,' he said ineffectively. 'Away with you. There's no biscuit here.'

The horse looked reproachful, and he minded guiltily there was a handful in his own pocket. He glanced furtively up and down the beach, but Mr Macpherson was long gone with the rest of the regiment and no other body would pay heed to the doings of a solitary Highlander on picquet duty. Those last cavalrymen might, it could even be their own horse, but when he looked round he saw they too had disappeared.

He held out his offering, and took pleasure in the soft mumble of the animal's mouth against his palm. There was a country feel in it, taking him back to his days as a stalker on the Strathcarron estate before the fearsome Sergeant Macpherson from Kirkton treated him in a pothouse one evening and said, 'Now then, my laddie, how'd you like to come with me and see the world?' Mackenzie looked placidly up at the Cossacks on the cliff and thought he was seeing it now.

But the Russians were turning away. Maybe they'd spied all they wanted, maybe they'd a report to make, but they were trotting their sturdy little ponies away to the distant slope and vanishing from Mackenzie's wistful view. Maybe it was the coming rain they were avoiding, for that was a storm brewing up above or he had never seen one. The traders were of the same mind, and were already beginning to drive their beasts inland, oxen, mules, camels, and even a homely flock of sheep. Maybe that was where those three cavalrymen had gone, or maybe they were pressed close to the cliffs for shelter.

Mackenzie turned regretfully back to the sea. The First Division was almost all in, but a last raft of Guards was approaching and he gave it his full attention. The waves were awful high just here, but the sailors held the raft steady and the Grenadiers laughed and bantered as they waded the last yards through the surf. But at the back came one who did neither, and Mackenzie's eyebrows rose in astonishment as the Guard marched with chin up and rifle held high above his bearskin to save it from the merest splash of spray. It was foolishness, for the empty raft was now springing high in the water behind him, leaping out of the hands of the sailors to hurl itself full at the shore. The man had hardly time to turn before it was on him, and Mackenzie heard him give a great yelp as the raft swept by and buried itself in the sand. The Guard was left floundering in the water, still holding up the rifle but staggering and tottering like a man drunk, while around him his companions slapped their legs and laughed.

Mackenzie watched sorrowfully as he hobbled onto the shingle, followed by hoots of 'Serve him right' and 'Trust Woodall'. The man was clearly hurt, but he asked help of no one and only sat on a rock to remove his boot. It seemed a sad thing to the Highlander, so he strode across and said, 'Here, Tow-Row, let me look at that.'

The man glared up at him with injured dignity. 'No need, thank you, Sawnie. I'm perfectly fine.'

'Aye,' agreed Mackenzie gravely. 'And that's no a gash in your stocking and your life's blood pouring out of it. Let's have a look now.' He closed his brown hand round the man's ankle and began very gently to work down the hose.

The Guard made a resigned noise like 'T'uh!' but his bristliness troubled Mackenzie less than smooth politeness would have done. It was of his own world, and put him in mind of a fox he'd found in a gin once, snarling and snapping at him all the while he freed its paw.

'Oh, that's torn it, that has,' said the Guard resentfully as the stocking fell free. 'What am I supposed to do with *that*?' The exposed foot was puffy and oozing blood from under a torn flap of skin.

Mackenzie hesitated, but a harassed-looking officer was already bustling up, saying, 'Oh, for heaven's sake, what have you gone and done to yourself now?' The Highlander observed the black-looped cocked hat of a medical man, and stood back respectfully to let the surgeon do his work.

But the doctor took just the one look and sighed. 'Woodall, you really are a prize nuisance. You can't possibly march with that, you'll have to rest here till the swelling goes down.' He handed over a dressing, then stopped at the sight of the Guard's pack resting on the sand. 'And that's got to go, you heard the order. Greatcoat and blanket roll with essentials only. Leave it for the next boat back to the *Simoom*.' He hurried away without another word.

The Guard was still a moment, and his hand strayed down to rest possessively on his pack. Then he gave a determined snort, fumbled open the straps, and began to stuff the contents into his already bulging blanket.

Mackenzie watched him curiously. He was a fine-built soldier, this Woodall, and maybe three, four years older than his own twenty-two. He was clean and shaved, everything a sergeant-major would approve, yet there was something faintly pitiable about him for all that.

He said, 'I'll bide with you, you'll no be alone. Some of our regiment did the same as you; I've to guard these packs whiles they send back a boat.'

Woodall made no answer. The man was a squirrel, taking out little packages from his pack and hiding them all over his person: a cake of soap in his pocket, a tin of boot-polish in his coat, another of tooth-powder in his belt. Next came one of those new daguerreotypes, and Mackenzie stared in fascination of the technology. This one was of a woman holding a bunch of roses to her face, but there was something fixed about the smile of her, and the eyes were white and glassy. 'Why,' he said in wonder. 'She looks dead.'

Woodall slammed the picture inside his coat and swivelled round to face him. 'Look, Sawnie, thanks for your help, but would you mind shoving off?'

Mackenzie sighed, and strolled back to his picquet post. The grey horse had gone, but he could hear a sheep bleating above him, the plaintive voice of a late-summer lamb. He turned to look on the grassy rise above the beach, and instantly forgot the sheep. The Cossacks were back, or three of them were, and this time on foot. They weren't for bothering anyone, just standing up against the crest watching what was below, but it seemed to Mackenzie they were looking at one thing in particular, and that was the two British officers perched on the next rise along, studying the land through their glasses. They were senior ones too, cocked hats on the both of them, and the one on the left looked like Sir George Brown himself, commander of the whole Light Division.

Mackenzie reached for his rifle. It wasn't loaded, the orders had been clear as to that, but there was something not just so open about these Cossacks' movements and he wanted the feel of the Minié in his hand. Someone else felt the same, for a puff of white smoke bloomed above the bank and the crack of gunshots drifted down to the beach. He backed seawards to see further, and glimpsed patches of red in the grass, Light Division infantry firing at mounted Cossacks. There was a string of arabas up there too; the Cossacks were attacking them, and the British driving them away.

Mackenzie stroked his jaw. These Russians were said to be canny fighters, so what for would they attack a bunch of native carts in full sight of their enemy? Then the lamb bleated again, and Mackenzie's gaze dropped to see it turning and scampering back across the hill.

Years of stalking told him what to look for. Something had scared it, something in that grey-green mass of rocky hillside he wasn't seeing for himself. 'Open your eyes,' the head stalker had said when he was first learning. 'Still your breathing, take your time, and watch for what moves.' Mackenzie watched and there it was, grey-green moving against grey-green, those men on foot creeping silently across the hillside. That business with the arabas was no more than a distraction, they were after the two exposed British officers not a hundred yards away.

'Look to your backs up there!' he shouted, reaching furiously for his cartridge pouch. 'Look out behind!'

No one responded. The beach was full of men shouting as boats were hauled ashore, the voice of one lone Highlander only more background noise against the crash of the surf. Mackenzie was in with the powder and turning the cartridge smart for the ball, but even as he rammed he saw the Cossacks already twenty yards nearer and their lances ready couched. He fumbled his return, the rod catching in the loops, then a voice said 'What's up, Redshank?' and there was that Woodall still sitting on his rock but with his rifle in his hands.

Mackenzie fair bawled at him, jabbing a frantic finger in the direction of the Cossacks. 'If you've a charge then fire it, man, there are *Russians on the cliff*!'

The Guard's face changed, then there was only a blur of red as he swung on his rock and fired.

It was a bonny shot for the distance, striking a rock not a yard from the leading Cossack. It did the trick too, for the officers jumped like hares and scuttled away down the path, leaving nothing behind but a cocked hat floating gracefully to ground. Shouts from below showed the Fusiliers had been alerted, and in seconds there were half a dozen of them rushing up the hillside. Mackenzie looked back to where the Russians had been and now saw only the unmoving greyness of rocks.

'Did they run now?' he asked the Grenadier. 'Did you see them run?'

The Guard bit the top off a cartridge and spat it out contemptuously. 'Did they run?' he said, pouring the powder neatly down the barrel. 'Frightened rabbits, the pair of them.'

Mackenzie's hand was arrested on its way to his cap pouch. 'The pair, is it?' he said softly. 'I thought there were three.'

They surveyed the deserted hillside in silence. The red coats of the Royal Welch Fusiliers made bright patches in the green as they moved about the paths above, but there was nothing else to see but a seagull soaring and dipping lazily across the darkening sky. Somewhere in the distance came a deep roll of thunder.

The rain came pelting down. Oliver pressed against the cliff to shelter under its tiny overhang, but the waves were crashing on the shingle and filling the wind with spray and sand-specks that blew in his face and stung his eyes. Gulls screamed and clamoured as they swooped inland, and traders shouted in rough foreign voices as they drove the last of their beasts from the shore. Redcoats still swarmed in the areas of the Second and Light Divisions, but the last of the Guards had already marched away, and their own stretch of beach was completely empty. Beside him was only Sullivan, huddled and shivering with his arms wrapped tightly round his knees. There were no medics, no officers, no authority and no order, and Oliver craved them all.

The flatboat had long gone, and he couldn't even see the fleet any more through the grey mist of rain. Somewhere out there was the *Jason*, a warm smelly hold and the familiarity of the regiment. He thought of poor Ronnie but remembered only Mrs Jarvis stroking his forehead and calling him 'my love'. Mrs J was young and her language could be dreadful, but he felt for a moment it would be almost worth dying to have tenderness about him again, someone caring if he lived or died.

Something moved on the bank above. He listened for footsteps, but heard only a soft thump, a rustling of grass, then another thump nearer the edge. Perhaps someone was trying to climb down. It was a strange place to do it, when the bank at the far end sloped down to almost nothing, but the grassy overhang four feet above his head seemed to be vibrating slightly, then a clod of earth dropped and bounced off his boot.

He called up, 'Careful! There are people down here.'

A quick, abrupt movement overhead, and then the grass rustled again, as if something were moving slowly away. Oliver stepped out into the rain and craned his neck to see, but whatever had made the noises must be keeping low to the ground. Perhaps it was a sheep or a wild dog, but surely a startled animal would have bounded away instead of making this slow, stealthy withdrawal.

He moved hesitantly back into the overhang. There was really no need for uneasiness, not with Light Division picquets all over the ground above, but whoever it was had been very furtive. They'd chosen to avoid the camps of the French and the Light Division, and tried to climb down to an area which from above must have looked quite deserted. Oliver remembered the Cossacks, made up his mind, and ducked out into the rain to find Ryder.

The corporal was stretched comfortably beneath another overhang, with his groundsheet wrapped round his body and his shako over his face. Oliver cleared his throat and said 'Corp?'

Ryder tilted up his shako brim to expose one eye. 'Hullo, Poll. What's up?'

He explained. 'Do you think it might be a spy?'

Ryder looked at him without expression. 'The Russians already know who we are, how many we are, they knew we were coming and when. It's all been in the London *Times*.'

'I bet *The Times* never said how many guns we'd got.'

Ryder sighed. 'Remember the Greeks at Varna? They'll try anything to do down the Turks, and we aren't the only ones who can use the telegraph.' He replaced the shako over his eyes and settled his head back in the sand. 'The Russians don't need spies, Polly. If there's anyone prowling it'll only be one of the Johnnies looking for something to pinch.'

Oliver remembered the cholera graves they'd passed that last day at Varna, corpses strewn about the ground where the Turks had dug them up to steal the shrouding blankets. 'I suppose so. I should have thought of that.'

'Good,' said Ryder, without lifting the shako. 'You wouldn't like to move a bit, would you, you're dripping all over me.'

Oliver looked at him with a growing sense of disillusion. Ryder had been a hero in the water, he'd even done that wonderful thing and lied for him to Jarvis, but now he didn't seem to care about anything. 'Do we just stay on the beach, then? In the rain?'

Ryder didn't answer. Oliver looked through the driving mist towards the distant red coats of the Light Division, and then at the little white blobs of the camp beyond. 'The French have got tents.'

The shako rose and fell as Ryder spoke through it. 'The French are organized. The French have got two-men tents they can carry themselves. We're British. We haven't.'

'But we can't just sit out in this all night!' A great wave crashed on the shingle behind him, and he raised his voice in desperation. 'I don't know what we're supposed to do.'

Ryder swept the shako aside and sat up. 'What the hell do you think we do? We get wet, we get sick, and we die, same as everyone else. We don't matter, get that in your head and nail it there, then you'll know what to bloody do.'

His anger was scorching, and Oliver felt his own rise to meet it. 'That's not fair. Sullivan's hurt, there has to be something . . .'

Ryder leaned back against the cliff, and his face was suddenly bleak. 'Never ask anything of the army, Polly. That way you'll never be disappointed.'

Oliver already felt sick with it. He said, 'I'm not asking the army. I'm asking you.'

They stared at each other. A gull flew screaming overhead, an empty, unhappy sound that was lost almost at once in the thunder of the waves.

'Why?' said Ryder. He wiped his face with his sleeve, looked at the sopping fabric and gave up in disgust. 'I'm just a corporal. Why ask me?'

Because he knew things, like he'd known about the flatboat. Because he'd saved Sullivan and told that lie. He said bitterly, 'I don't know.'

Ryder gave a short laugh. He forked his hands through dripping hair, glanced over at the distant figure of Sullivan, and shoved the groundsheet aside. 'All right, Polly Oliver. Let's get even wetter and see what we can find.'

Oliver followed him in meek astonishment, but after a moment's walk he began to fear he'd dragged the corporal out for nothing. The beach was barren of shelter. The cliffs were little more than a perpendicular bank of earth, with no caves or niches to admit a man. There was no pier, no jetty, and the commissary officers had bought and trundled away every cart the traders could supply. The only wagon left was leaning drunkenly on the spindle of its missing wheel, the tide already washing about its timbers like thin grey spit. His foot struck something in the sand, and hope seized him at the sight of the wheel itself.

'Look, Corp,' he said, stooping to drag it clear of the tide. 'If we put this back it would make a shelter.'

Ryder studied the wagon critically. 'If we can lift it.'

Oliver was certain. He could see it in his head, an upright platform of eight foot length, the three of them sitting snug and dry underneath. 'Of course we can,' he said, thrusting his shoulder to the wood. 'Of course.' He heaved with all his might, but the wood ground agonizingly into his shoulder blade and refused to lift an inch. 'If you help me . . .'

'Two's not enough,' said Ryder. 'Not even with Sullivan. But it's big enough for more.'

He gazed round the deserted sand, then stopped to stare at the cliffs on their far left. Two tall red patches were sheltering under the overhang, each with a black top. From this distance it was hard to tell a bearskin from a feather bonnet, but the dark trousers on the one and the kilt on the other set the matter beyond question. A Guard and a Highlander.

'Muscle,' said Ryder with satisfaction. 'They'll do, come on.'

The soldiers watched their approach with the faint smirk peculiar to infantry spotting cavalry reduced to their own pedestrian level. All the Guards were big strong men, but the Highlander was almost as tall and their headdresses brushed the top of the overhang. Oliver felt a sudden awkwardness, but Ryder only smiled and said, 'Evening, gentlemen. Would you like some shelter?'

The Guard's eyes shifted under the bearskin and noted Ryder's chevrons. 'Funny, aren't you, Corporal?' he said with an emphatic sniff. Oliver remembered the 'one rank up' rule for the Guards and wondered if it applied to private soldiers too.

The Highlander's beard was only a soft curly fuzz on his cheeks and his gaze had a steadiness that robbed it of any offence. 'I've packs to mind. Is there room for them too?'

'There will be,' said Ryder, and explained. 'What do you say?'

The Highlander stepped straight out into the rain, but the Guard hesitated and looked at his foot. Oliver's hope sunk at the glimpse of bandage protruding from his boot, but the Highlander had no such qualms. 'Losh, man,' he said cheerfully, offering the Guard his arm. 'It's not your feet they're wanting but the strong arms and broad back of you. They're but laddies, they'll never do it without you help them.'

The Highlander was scarcely older than themselves but the

appeal to his superior strength did wonders for the Guard. 'Never said I wouldn't, did I?' he said defensively, and stepped out with barely a trace of a limp. 'Come on, then, let's see it.'

They set off back across the sand. Oliver still wasn't sure they'd be enough, but Ryder said, 'Get Sullivan, would you, Poll? We'll need someone to place the wheel.'

Oliver lowered his voice. 'But he's been . . . He's been hurt; he can't lift anything, can he?'

Ryder kept smiling for the sake of the others. 'Just get him, Poll, I think you'll find he can.'

It seemed cruel to make an injured man work, but Sullivan almost sprang out of his miserable huddle in his haste to join them, and when he saw what was needed he just spat on his hands and said, 'You lift it, then, and trust me for the wheel.' There was a strength in his voice Oliver hadn't heard since Varna.

They lifted. A Guard next to a Highlander, shoulder to shoulder with two cavalrymen, they lifted together and the wood rose easily in their hands. Sullivan stepped back, the wagon bounced down, and there it was, a long platform more than three feet off the ground, a solid wooden shelter for as long as they needed it. The ground was already ankle-deep in water, but there were five of them to push, and foot by foot they shoved it over the bumpy shingle onto the harder sand, clear of the water, clear of the tide-line, up to the cliff and home.

Ryder gave a little nod. 'We can do better. Sullivan, your things are soaked anyway, give us your blanket and groundsheet. Polly, I want wood, any wreckage you can find, bring it back and get it under the wagon.'

Oliver hesitated. 'But it's wet.'

'Grab it while you see it,' said Ryder. 'Tomorrow there'll be men crawling all over this stretch moaning they can't find any firewood.'

He was right, of course – Ryder usually was – and as Oliver dutifully trudged seawards he began to wonder why. Ryder just knew things. He knew when a horse was ill, he knew about keeping the tents apart in Varna because of disease, he knew how to mix mud and leaves to make a pack that would cool a man with sunstroke. He stuffed straw in his scabbard to stop the metal blunting the blade, and in two days everyone in 'G' Troop was doing it. Trotter said he must have been on campaign before, but he couldn't have, no one had, it was nearly forty years since Waterloo. He might have been in a regiment in India perhaps, but he couldn't have served his time and come out again, he couldn't be more than nineteen.

It made no sense, but Oliver went on rescuing slimy pieces of flatboat and when he brought back his last load the wagon had been transformed. Two sides were draped with weighted groundsheets, and the Highlander was securing Sullivan's sopping blanket to a third. The only open side was against the cliff, but the Guard was stacking packs and saddles to give them further insulation. Sullivan was pillaging them for mess kit, but he straightened as Oliver appeared, and said 'Come on, Ryder wants the wood.'

It seemed inconceivable in this rain, but Oliver had only followed him a few paces before his nose tingled and he looked up to see a faint grey trail curling under the overhang of the bank. As he rounded a little buttress he saw it in front of him, a dark blue figure kneeling by a hole in the sand that was billowing out smoke.

Ryder looked up. 'Quick, Poll! Little bits, I need chips of it.'

He tore scraps off a splintered spar, watched Ryder drop them into the hole, then edged closer to see. It wasn't such a miracle really, the hole was lined with shingle and dry seaweed, but he still held his breath as the tiny flames caught at the wood. One chip hissed and extinguished its kindling, but Ryder threw in another handful of the frondlike weed, struck a Vesuvius and blew it back into life. The overhang kept off most of the rain, a windbreak of rocks repelled the blowing sand, and in minutes the fire was accepting larger pieces of wood and scorching the damp out of them with the strength of its own heat.

Ryder laid wet sticks in a grid across the hole. 'Did you find my coffee ration, Joe?'

Sullivan threw a handful of green beans in a mess-tin, and Oliver watched as they jumped immediately in the heat. The wet sticks spat and stank, but above them rose the unmistakable smell of roasting coffee.

'The kettle's not taken much rain yet,' said Sullivan. 'Will I fill it from my barrel?'

'Ship-water,' said Ryder, making a face. 'Good enough for coffee, but we'll need fresh for the morning.'

Sullivan nodded and emptied his canteen into the big camp-kettle. 'Give us your barrels, then, I'll seek us a stream.' He held out his hand to Oliver.

It was ridiculous. He'd had a bad knock on the head, his back must be in agony, he ought to be under cover trying to get warm. 'It's all right, I'll do it. Give me yours.'

Sullivan's hand stayed outstretched, but his face grew hard and ugly. 'Jarvis had me flogged, Oliver. He didn't have my balls.'

Oliver's face burned red. 'I just think . . . Don't you think it's better, Corp? If I go?'

Ryder was wetter than any man Oliver had ever seen, the sunset shining off his soaked tunic as if he were wearing silver. 'Fifteen minutes, Joe. If you haven't found by then you're to forget it and come straight back. All right?'

Sullivan looked quite different when he smiled. He said 'Thanks, Ryder', took their canteens, and set off towards the cliff with a strut as good as Jarvis's own.

'Flies, Polly,' said Ryder, his hand reaching out to shut Oliver's jaw. 'Now keep stirring, I need to find more wet sticks. When these catch, just let them drop, they'll add fuel.'

Oliver stirred. Rain flicked on his neck and pattered steadily on his back, but the tin stayed dry in the overhang and the beans began to turn brown. The fire was warming his world again, and he wondered how he'd managed to get in such a panic before. The army expected them to use their initiative, they were doing it, and he doubted the French would have managed half so well.

Then Ryder was back, flipping the smouldering sticks down into the fire and slipping damp ones in their place. He wrapped his hand in his wet sleeve to lift the tin, placed the kettle on the newly formed grid, then shook the beans into a rag for crushing.

Oliver watched him covertly. Ryder looked somehow more approachable with his hair dripping and his cheek smeared with charcoal. He'd been friendly, even kind, and his mockery felt no worse than the banter people like Fisk exchanged every day.

He said hesitantly, 'Corp? Before you joined the 13th, were you . . .?'

Ryder looked up. 'What?' His face and voice were both without expression.

Oliver quickly looked back down at the fire. 'Nothing.'

Above the wind and distant crash of the sea he heard Ryder say, 'That's right, Poll. Nothing.'

Sullivan knew better than to waste time hunting for a stream when the beach was full of soldiers who'd have done it before him.

The Light Division were the ones to try. They'd been first to land, and had had time to collect driftwood and do business with the traders. He approached the forward picquet and was immediately confronted by the hulking shape of Private Alfred Flowers, 'Bloomer' of the 7th, the Royal Fusiliers.

Most people knew Bloomer. An East End bruiser with a past Sullivan could only guess at, he was what the colonels called 'colourful' and the lieutenants called 'trouble'. Sullivan had played cards with him over rum one night at Varna, and his head throbbed at the memory. So did his back.

'What's the game, Joe?' said Bloomer, grinning. 'On the shake lurk?'

You couldn't catch Sullivan with the cant. 'Shipwrecked to be sure, but I'm after begging water. Is there any this way?'

45

Bloomer grimaced, an extraordinary elastic movement that brought his lips right up to his nose. 'Only from the sky. Our boys up top will know, they were on the spy this morning.'

Sullivan looked gloomily at the bank above. The land looked barren and the dark already falling.

'Leave it till morning if I was you,' said Bloomer. 'No gammon, Joe, you look done up.'

Sullivan felt a stab of irritation. 'And I'm not then. I'm going right now.'

He began to turn, but Bloomer's lumpy fist closed round his arm. 'Half a moment, racing-boy, half a mo.' He put a large finger to his lips, stooped to a bundle stuffed under a rock, and came up with an infantry greatcoat. 'Get this on you. You're wet through, you need a proper top-tog.'

Sullivan took the coat hesitantly. 'Whose would it be now?'

Bloomer shrugged. 'He won't miss it. Two cholera, two drowned, one with his skull bashed in from colliding with a gun-boat. He'd be glad of a living body to wear it.'

Sullivan thanked him, and set off for the path. The sky was even darker now, but the coat warmed him and he was not going back empty-handed. He wanted to see Ryder's face when he came back out of a dark stormy night with three barrels full of clean water. He wanted Oliver to look at him without seeing a naked back smashed open with the crack of a whip. No one else would. No woman ever would. He would carry those scars till the day he died.

And for what? He thought back to that night in Varna, coming back from the card game to find Johnny Welch dying of cholera, then the devil Jarvis roaring on them for taking extra firewood to keep him warm. He was angry himself to be sure, there was drink inside him and he'd thrown the log back with temper, but Jarvis should never have moved to stop him when it was already in the air. The log struck his elbow, and that was it, assaulting an NCO, strip that man down like an animal and flay the skin off his back while the whole regiment watches.

Ryder was after ending the same way. There was something strange about the corporal, something that didn't fit, and the man Jarvis had spotted it. Ryder could speak rough, but he'd an educated way with him, he was quick with the irony and made Jarvis look an ignorant pig every time he opened his mouth. He was everything Jarvis hated, and sooner or later the bastard would have him. Jarvis broke everyone in the end.

Sullivan adjusted the weight of the water barrels on his battered shoulder and climbed the last two feet of bank to the plateau. At once he saw the sheen of water to his left, a lake surrounded by tall, rustling reeds. It was most likely salt, but the trampled rushes showed at least one other person had been this way, and it would be mad in him not to check. He followed the path, and knelt to scoop up the water in his hands.

One sip was enough, salt and useless, he spat, wiped his mouth, and stood. The surface of the lake was pock-marked with rain, and he paused a moment to look at the distorted reflection of Big Joe Sullivan, the man he used to be. Here was one Jarvis had broken, and devil a bit of fighting left in him now. Those were the grand days, a drop or two of a Saturday with friends, bare fists in the street, then walking back with arms round each other's shoulders, singing with the joy of it all the way home. Not now. How could you fight a man when you couldn't look him in the face?

A black shadow fleeted over the water. Reeds crackled behind and he spun round, but there was no one to be seen. The nearest picquets were right up on the crest, no one else close, it must have been some kind of animal left behind after the trading. He walked back more warily through the reeds, hoping it was nothing with teeth.

It had hands. They came flying at him, one smacking round his throat to stifle his cry, another clutching at the greatcoat, then he was *bang* on his back and the pain screaming through him as the rough ground tore at his scars. The man was on top of him, the reeds closing over them both, hiding them from the picquets, from the darkness and the world.

Sullivan fought. The man who thought he'd never fight again found his hands forming claws as he scrabbled upwards at the face pressing down on his own. His nails scored feebly at the cold cheek, warm blood under his fingers, then a hand swiped at his own face, once and his head banged the path, twice and he hardly even knew. His throat was squeezing, chest burning, his flailing hands missed the face and fell back on the path, stones and mud under his nails. Still he fought, scratching up the dirt, ripping into it, and his mind never noticed he was fighting only earth, never saw the moment his hands stopped moving no matter what it ordered them, never heard the clear clean snap as his neck broke. His mind was fighting alone in a black hole that got smaller and smaller till it was nothing but a pinhole, and then died.

Ryder looked up at the cry of a seagull, then back to the growing darkness of the beach. He was cold and filthy wet, his ears numb from the wind, but there was still no sign of bloody Sullivan. He said, 'Get the others, Polly. The coffee will stew if we leave it any longer.'

They came quickly enough, the limping Grenadier almost hopping in his eagerness to reach the fire, and Oliver filled their mugs with dense black liquid that breathed a second of steam before the wind caught and blew it away. The warm metal tingled Ryder's fingers as the blood moved again, and the coffee itself seemed to burn as it went down. No one took it back to shelter – they were scalding themselves in their haste to drink before it cooled – and the silence in which they finally lowered their mugs was almost religious.

'There'll be more,' Ryder said, laying the kettle in the open to catch the rain. 'Polly, you can make another pot while I go and find Sullivan.'

'Off the beach?' said the Highlander. He turned to study the plateau above them, black and forbidding in the darkness. 'Then I'll come with you a step. I need to stretch my legs.'

If he stretched them any more he'd be taller than the Guard, but Ryder understood the intention and was grateful for it. 'Thanks, Redshank.'

'Mackenzie,' said the Highlander firmly. 'My name's Mackenzie, but I get Niall from most folk.'

The name lay between them like a card on a table, then Ryder said, 'Well met, Niall. I'm Harry Ryder,' and turned to Oliver. The boy said 'Charlie Oliver', then flushed and added, 'Well – Polly.' The Grenadier looked at him with an air of deep suspicion, and said just 'Woodall'. After a moment, he muttered 'Dennis'.

A great wave crashed behind them, an outbreak of shouting greeted another boat ploughing through the surf, and Ryder became acutely aware of how wet he really was. He thrust his mug at Oliver, said 'Won't be long', and turned to stride down the beach. God help Sullivan if anything had happened and he was trapped out in this.

After a few paces Mackenzie appeared by his side. He didn't speak, he was just being there and comfortable about it, and Ryder found his presence reassuring. They walked together along the empty First Division stretch, but the cliffs were still twelve feet tall and Sullivan could never have climbed up from here. Ryder looked ahead to the flags of the Light Division and began to walk faster.

'What's that?' said the Highlander, and stopped quite still. His voice had the flatness of a statement, and Ryder followed his gaze to the cliff. It was still high, no trace of a path, but Mackenzie was looking at a dark shadow at its base, a lump that was the length of a man.

Ryder's throat dried. He walked closer, and there were the white stripes of a 13th Light Dragoon dazzling down the grey overalls that melted into the dark. He knelt with dread to look at the face. The red veins were blue, the jaw sagged open, the eyes mercifully closed, it was a shell of a thing that had once been Joe Sullivan and a man he knew.

'His neck's broken,' said Mackenzie. 'Look, it's loose.'

Ryder looked away. 'Leave it, don't touch him.'

Mackenzie studied the cliffs. 'It's no so much of a drop, maybe just the ten feet. You'd be sore unlucky to break your neck from such a height.'

Or stiff and in pain, dizzy from a blow to the head and unable to react quickly from a slip on wet grass. 'He wasn't well. He could have.'

Mackenzie scratched his head. 'There were Russians up there. Maybe he found one.'

And maybe he didn't. There wasn't a wound on him, and his sword was safe in the scabbard. There was nothing but mud and grit on his hands where he'd tried to stop himself falling, nothing but grazes on his face and neck where he'd struck the cliff as he fell, nothing but death and the guilt of the man who'd sent him to it. Ryder passed the water barrels to the Highlander, slid his arm under Sullivan's shoulders and began to lift.

'Here,' said Mackenzie, coming round to take the feet. 'I'll help you.'

'I can take him, damn you.' He hefted Sullivan over his shoulder, staggered, then forced himself upright. The sodden clothes added to the weight, the body slipped and lolled on his shoulder, but he moved a step forward, then another and another, plodding laboriously towards the authority of the Light Division ahead.

There was none. A section of artillery were crowding from a boat onto the sand, men fighting the black waves to drag the precious gun ashore. A bedraggled lieutenant was yelling at a medical orderly, but when Mackenzie accosted him he only waved them away. 'We've our own dead to deal with, for God's sake, can't you dig a bloody hole?' His eyes were wild in a wind-whipped face, a boy in a nightmare.

They took a pick and blanket from a mountain of hastily landed stores, and climbed the path to the plateau. The left side was no good, there was a big lake there and the ground would be soft, but the grass to the right was already marked with mounds of earth and Ryder guessed he wasn't the first to be told to dig a hole. He laid Sullivan down on wet turf, his face exposed to the splatters of rain, his battered body without so much as a coat to keep out the cold. Far out in the bay twinkled a mass of little lights like a distant city, the warmth and comfort of the Allied fleet. *Play your bands now, you bastards. Let me hear you play.*

He shoved up his sleeves and said, 'Give me the pick.'

'We'll be needing more than one,' said the Highlander, handing it over.

Ryder smashed the axe into the turf. He was vaguely aware of Mackenzie leaving him, but it didn't matter, he was better doing this alone. 'Jarvis,' he thought as he hacked at the ground. If Jarvis hadn't insisted on that flogging. If he hadn't insisted on Sullivan wearing his haversack. If he'd let Fisk hold the line. Jarvis knew perfectly well what Ryder was trying to do, but none of that had mattered beside losing face to a corporal. The knowledge gave a savagery to his efforts as he dug deeper into the soil. Jarvis thought this was the start, did he? Well, maybe he'd got something coming to him too.

Someone stooped beside him, Woodall with a spade. Across the hole appeared Oliver with another, then Mackenzie with a second enormous pickaxe. 'I borrowed them from the Second,' he said, and swung.

They worked together in a silence that was strangely companionable. The roll of the sea receded until Ryder heard nothing but the rustle of wet clothing, the bite of metal into soil, the determined grunts of Woodall and an occasional gasp from Oliver. They wrapped Sullivan in the blanket and covered him deep in the warmth of the earth, then Mackenzie said the service from memory in a voice that made Ryder think of soft streams and green places in a land thousands of miles behind them. The wind and rain still howled about the plateau, but just for a moment there was peace.

They saw movement in the Second Division when they walked back, men milling about and shouting, but Ryder was too wet and exhausted to care. There were picquets all along the beach now, more along the clifftop, and no way for an enemy to get through. The damned place was safe enough, and all he wanted now was shelter and sleep.

Rain had blown under the groundsheets of their wagon and their clothes were already soaked through, but they were soldiers and they made the best of it. Mackenzie lit a candle in a mess-tin, Woodall made more coffee, Oliver produced brandy to season it, and they huddled together to eat their rations. The ship's pork tasted like stringy glue and Ryder wondered gloomily how long it had been in the cask. In the *Culloden* from Portsmouth there'd been barrels of peas chalked 1828.

He didn't feel like conversation. Oliver was too shy, Woodall too dignified, Mackenzie seemed naturally taciturn, and they ate in a silence punctuated only by the stoic chewing of tough meat. Rain peppered the hanging groundsheets and set them crackling in the wind.

An elbow prodded his wet ribs as Oliver turned to grope in the valises piled behind him. 'I don't suppose anyone wants to play cards?'

Then there they were, bright in the candlelight, the familiar faces of a De La Rue set of playing cards, exactly the same in the Crimea as they'd been in England. The groundsheet rustled as everyone sat up at once, and Woodall dug out a notebook and pencil from his extraordinarily bulging coat. 'I'll score,' he said importantly. 'Whist?'

Mackenzie regarded him sternly. 'Not for money, mind. They're very hard on the gambling in the 93rd.'

'Penny a thousand isn't gambling,' said Woodall. He'd removed his bearskin to sit upright, and his flattened hair and square face gave him the look of a hopeful otter. 'Come on, it's not like it's Sunday.'

Mackenzie's face softened. 'Well, if you're set on it.' He too looked younger without his bonnet, a farm-boy on a day out at the fair. 'I'm a canny player, mind, it's only fair to warn you.'

'You look to yourself, Sawnie,' said Woodall, grinning. He licked his pencil and looked expectantly at Ryder. 'Corporal?'

Ryder picked up the deck. They weren't new, there was none of that alien slipperiness of cards that have never carried a man's future on their fall, but they were clean and unmarked and honest. He smiled and said, 'Let's play.'

Mackenzie placed the candle between their feet so they could see the cards, and they played as faceless black shadows in the gloom. Ryder's stripes were forgotten, so was Oliver's youth, they were just four whist players and the only thing that mattered was the game. Even Woodall started to shed some of his pomposity, and said 'Blast it!' with open bitterness when his hoarded king of clubs was trumped. Oliver seemed more confident too, and his playing was first class. Ryder remembered him defying Jarvis in the water and began to think there was more to green Polly Oliver than met the eye.

'Humph,' said Woodall, subsiding muttering over his notebook. 'Luck, that's all, I never held a card. Come on, Mackenzie, we'll thrash them this time.'

But the new game was only two tricks old when a hand jerked aside their blanket screen and a voice said, 'Hullo, this is cosy!'

Four words, and they knew it was an officer. Woodall's head banged against the wagon as he tried to sit to attention, and Ryder had a terrible foreboding of picquet duty.

He said politely, 'We're stood down, sir.'

'Oh yes, yes,' said the officer vaguely, and actually stooped under the blanket to join them. 'But there's been a little trouble, and we're checking everyone's where they should be.'

'Trouble, sir?' murmured Ryder. The officer seemed in no hurry to leave and Ryder was under no illusions as to why. His greatcoat was filthy and sopping wet, his forage cap dripping, and there are few better social levellers than rain.

'Mmm,' said the officer, turning his head to study their little sanctuary. 'Sir George de Lacy Evans's servant's turned up with a knife in his back and a few of the general's things stolen. Probably a local; they've Greeks hereabouts, same as Varna. I say, is that coffee?'

Scrounging bastard. The pot was still half full, and Ryder dutifully held the candle as Mackenzie divided the contents between the five mugs and handed Sullivan's to the officer. Oliver made no move for the brandy, but to Ryder's astonishment the officer produced a silver flask from his greatcoat and poured them each a tot of his own. 'Keeps out the cold,' he said. 'But come on, don't let me stop your game. Mustn't interrupt a whist hand, you know.'

It had been more than a year since Ryder had met an officer who understood private soldiers had feelings too. They played on self-consciously, but the officer seemed quite content to watch and sip his coffee. He was out of the candle's range, but Ryder caught the glint of eyes under the cap brim and knew he was genuinely interested.

When the hand finished he offered him the pack. 'Would you like to play, sir? I don't mind sitting out.'

The officer took the cards with alacrity. 'We might both sit out, Corporal. I'd like to show you something new.'

For the rest of his life Ryder was to remember the moments that followed, as that educated voice taught them a form of whist that would later take England by storm. He remembered the voice and the cards, and most of all the hands of the men who played, all glowing orange in the candlelight. Woodall's, square with oddly flat fingers. Mackenzie's, long and strong and brown. Oliver's, young and grubby, a fourth former back from playing football. His own, earth compressed under the nails where he'd dug a grave in the dark. And the officer's, elegant and white, moving deftly among the cards as he explained what he was doing and why. Ryder's excitement grew as he realized the possibilities. No random turning over a card for trumps, it had to be chosen by the dealer, or the next if he passed. No unwitting fighting against your own side, the dealer's partner exposed his cards for all to see and then sat out the rest as a dummy player.

He said, 'It takes so much luck out of it. It makes it about skill.'

The officer turned towards him, and a flicker of the candle

gave a glimpse of close-shaved jaw. 'You understand, Corporal. Cards are like life and a man makes his own luck.'

Woodall gave a little sniff. 'Still doesn't help if you haven't got the cards.'

Ryder heard the smile in the officer's voice. 'But at least you know what you have, Private. It prevents me taking my own trick – unless, of course, I want to.' The graceful fingers plucked the queen of diamonds from dummy and placed it over his own knave.

'But that's silly,' said Woodall, evidently forgetting he was speaking to an officer. 'The knave was good, wasn't it?'

'Dispensable,' said the officer. 'I need to win the trick in this hand so I can draw your last trumps.'

Mackenzie sounded dubious. 'It seems a sore waste, sir. If you'd played your wee three you could have had two tricks out of it.'

'He still will,' said Ryder, dazed with the intricacy of it. 'That three's the last diamond. When trumps are drawn it will be a winner.'

The officer laughed. 'Bravo, Corporal. I think you will be good at bridge.'

He had a Scottish way of saying the word as if it had two syllables, and his laugh was much more natural than poor old Bog's careful 'haw-haw-haw'. Ryder wondered if he was new to the army, untainted by its rigid conventions, but there was nothing callow about that assured voice, and only a man supremely confident in his own authority would risk such informality with the ranks. Maybe he was one of those independent, much-travelled officers like the controversial Captain Nolan who'd brought their remounts to Varna.

Wet sand blew suddenly into their haven, the cards fluttered and fell, and another man held back their blanket screen to glare inside. His face was invisible in the dark but the stripes on the greatcoat sleeve and the gruffness of the voice were all any of them needed to know.

'And what the hell's going on in *here*?' the sergeant demanded.

'What d'you think . . .' He stopped as the officer turned, and he saw the gold band on the forage cap. 'I beg your pardon, sir, but . . .'

'It's all right, Sergeant,' said the officer loftily. 'The de Lacy Evans business, I suppose? It's all right, I vouch for these men.'

The sergeant cleared his throat. 'Right you are, sir, just doing my duty.'

'Quite right too,' said the officer, looking back at his cards. 'Jolly good. Put the blanket back when you go.'

Ryder wanted to laugh, but the magic was broken all the same. The sergeant left, the hand played out, then their extraordinary officer crouched back on his heels to leave.

'Thanks for the game, chaps,' he said. 'But I'm afraid duty calls.'

Ryder said tentatively, 'The kettle will be full again by now. We could make more coffee.' He wanted to learn more, every hint and strategy this man could teach them.

'Afraid not,' said the officer. 'Jolly decent of you all the same.' He looked curiously at Ryder, then seemed to make up his mind about something. 'You're 13th Light Dragoons, aren't you? I think I saw you . . . er . . . land. Not too many of you, are there?'

Ryder smiled. 'The rest have been sensible enough to stay on board, sir.'

'Quite,' he said. 'But not a lot of cavalry for an expedition like this, is it?'

'There's still the Heavies,' said Ryder. 'They'll be on their way, won't they?'

The officer nodded slowly. 'Still, quite a responsibility for you chaps. Till the Heavies come you're the army's only eyes.'

'We can do it, sir,' said Oliver. He'd slumped low enough to be full in the candlelight, and the pink flush of his cheek suggested the second brandy might have been unwise. 'We can beat the Russkies all by ourselves.'

'Oh, quite right,' said the officer, eyes twinkling in the gloom. He backed away, said 'Well, tally-ho', and ducked neatly under the blanket screen into the rain outside. Ryder watched him walking away towards the crowds of the Light Division, becoming in a moment just another grey man in a beach of grey men.

He closed the flap, and they looked at each other in astonished silence. Then Woodall stretched his legs into the space left by the officer and said, 'Rum fellow.'

'I'd call him a gentleman,' said Mackenzie. 'Ken you ever the like, an officer to sit so natural, drinking and playing with the common folk?'

Woodall sniffed at the word 'common'. 'We're not just anyone, Mackenzie. It's not like we're line regiments.'

Oliver giggled, and slumped even lower against the pile of baggage. Woodall peered down at him and said, 'Too much brandy. Silly young ass.'

'Silly ass,' agreed Ryder, and was surprised to feel a twinge of affection. He dragged Oliver's blanket from the heap, flung it over his recumbent form, and watched Mackenzie tenderly tucking him in. They were a decent bunch, really. He thought of Mackenzie helping him with Sullivan, of Woodall digging a grave despite his injured foot, he remembered Oliver trying to lift half a ton of wagon all by himself, and smiled. Silly ass indeed.

The thought warmed him as he wrapped his own blanket round the damp of his clothes and settled himself to sleep. He'd never had it before, this being part of a group, and of course as an officer it had been impossible. He wondered if that was what their friend tonight had wanted, maybe even more than the coffee. As he drifted into sleep he found himself picturing it again, that solitary figure walking away from them in the rain, as lonely and anonymous as a ghost in the dark.

3
18 September 1854

Two days later Jarvis came back.

It had been fine until then. The weather brightened, Oliver's mare turned up safe in the Second Division, and as far as Ryder was concerned his punishment turned into a holiday. They had transport to fetch water from the villages, they had shelter and wood for the fire, and Woodall made the salt pork edible by frying it in biscuit crumbs. The rest of the troop landed next afternoon, the beach filled with men he knew, but when evening came he and Oliver slipped away to play a game called 'bridge' under a wagon with a 93rd Highlander and a Grenadier Guard. The next night they did it again.

Then the patrol came back. Hoare had the disobedience charge whittled down to 'fined five shillings and taken down six places on the list of corporals', but the ink on Ryder's name was scarcely dry in the Defaulters' Book when Jarvis packed him off for a night on outlying picquet, and followed it up with a day on camp fatigues. The remounts had arrived, Ryder was free to reconnoitre with the others, but Jarvis kept him in camp collecting firewood and water, digging latrines, and cleaning boots for the captain because his servant wasn't feeling quite the thing. When it was too dark for anything else he put him back on picquet and kept him there all night. And when Ryder finally stood down at dawn he was turned out five minutes later to go foraging with the others.

He was still doing it now. He was dizzy with hunger as well as heat, his head ached from two nights without sleep, but Jarvis was looking for a sign of weakness and Ryder was determined not to show him one. He carried his hay-net out of the scrimmage round the oat stack, replaced it on Wanderer's back, and grasped the bridle to keep himself steady. Across the farmyard Jarvis stood watching him, tapping his whip thoughtfully into the palm of his hand.

Fisk galloped through the gate, yelling, 'Threshed oats, boys, the 11th have found a cellar full!' Ryder turned to mount with the others, but his foot missed the stirrup, he clutched at the saddle for balance and felt his head bang against Wanderer's flank. For seconds he was aware only of the surprising cool of the horse's coat against his forehead, the stitching in the leather under his fingers, and the echo in his head of his own harsh breathing. *Jarvis*, he thought. *Jarvis mustn't see*. He dragged up his head and turned.

Oliver was staring in shocked concern. 'You're ill. We've got to get you to a doctor.' Behind him Prosser was grinning all over his smallpox-ravaged face.

Ryder straightened quickly. 'It's only the bloody heat, Poll. Don't come the mother with me.'

He swung into the saddle and turned for the gate, ignoring the guffaws behind. Oliver should know better anyway. Under the wagon had been different, four men brought together by rain and a death, but that was over now and they were back to the business of war. Woodall and Mackenzie had been fetched to their units last night, and in an army of twenty-six thousand he was unlikely to see either of them ever again. Oliver was just another soldier in his troop, and the sooner he realized it the better.

The next farm was only just up the road. He began to hope for full forage then back to camp and a chance of sleep, but as he turned the corner he saw the calm figure of Lieutenant Grainger directing the regiment to form column on the road. Their colonel was there himself, deep in conversation with an aide-de-camp, and

Ryder sagged in the saddle as he realized what was happening. No camp, no sleep, they were off on a bloody reconnaissance.

But Grainger was calling 'G' Troop to fall in on the right flank as designated skirmishers, and at least there was a possibility of action. The troop obviously hoped so, and Oliver was visibly glowing with excitement as for the first time ever he loaded his carbine in earnest. For a moment Ryder was reminded of another boy as innocent and eager as this one, frightened only of being killed before he could achieve something worthwhile. He bit into his cartridge and the vision disappeared in the familiar taste of powder. He was a different man now.

But maybe not different enough, and when Colonel Doherty took his place at the front Ryder was careful to keep his head well down. Jarvis would probably think he was exhausted, but some things were more important than a bullying sergeant-major, and he didn't look up until he heard the order 'The regiment will advance . . . walk – *march*,' and knew the colonel's back would be safely turned.

But Doherty wasn't alone, the ADC was riding beside him, and it looked as if this might not be an ordinary patrol. Ryder watched the two of them talking together, the ADC gesturing eloquently at the distant slopes, and was haunted by a sense of familiarity, a memory of aristocratic hands fluttering descriptively as an officer explained the intricacies of a new card game. He could see no more of the ADC than his elegantly blue-cloaked back, but the slim build was right, the forage cap had the same gold band, it was at least possible. His saddlecloth was only regulation blue, but the horse was a beautiful grey; he thought he might know it again.

Doherty called the trot. Ryder dragged his mind back to the present and looked at the countryside about him. Some of the earlier patrols had reported groups of Cossacks, but there was nothing to see here but empty fields where the wheat had been and stretches of rough grassland dotted with ragged sheep. Two Crim-Tartar labourers mending a fence straightened as they passed, and one waved and called out 'Buono Johnny!' in a deep, guttural voice. 'Buono Johnny!'

Ryder was startled. They must have picked up the phrase from their Turkish allies, but it was extraordinary to hear it out here. *Buono Johnny*, the one greeting the two armies used to each other, the phrase that meant anything from 'My respects' to 'Over here, matey', or even the London prostitute's 'Are you good natured, dear?' The one thing it always meant was friendliness, and that was humbling in these people whose land they were so busy pillaging. The Tartars were of Turkish origin themselves, they were eager to help these foreigners drive out their brutal Russian overlords, but they must surely realize what price they'd pay if the expedition failed. For the first time Ryder felt a determination that it mustn't. As he drew level with the Tartars he called 'Buono Johnny!' back, and was rewarded with a broad brown-toothed grin.

The ADC turned his head towards the voice. Ryder looked at once in hope of recognition, but caught only the blur of a clean-shaven face before the officer again faced front. Maybe he was mistaken. Maybe he wasn't, and here was another man embarrassed by the intimacy of a card game with strangers in the rain. Maybe Harry Ryder was just too bloody tired to think straight and ought to keep his mind on the job.

It looked like taking a long time. They stopped to water at a tiny village and he hoped they'd turn for home, but the ADC was conferring with the colonel and it seemed they had something specific to look for. 'It'll be those Cossacks,' said Jordan knowledgeably. 'Cardigan's sure there's more about, he had us all looking two days ago.' He popped a peppermint in his mouth and sucked complacently.

Whatever it was, it was leading them further and further inland. The farmlands receded behind them, and the grass grew longer, almost feathery, sprinkled with patches of tiny purple flowers that gave off a smell of sage as they passed. A buzzard hovered above them with outstretched wings, eerily silent as it floated down the wind. Ryder listened drowsily to the quiet, familiar sounds around him: the jingling bits, creaking saddles, and thumping of hooves in soft, deep grass.

Someone exclaimed ahead, and the ADC pointed to a distant tumulus. Three riders were watching them from its summit, soldiers in grey-brown coats and high black headgear, and all carrying lances. Not irregulars like the ones on the cliffs, not a wolf-pack, but official uniformed Cossacks, the cavalry even Napoleon had called the best light troops in the world.

'Dons,' said Jordan, slicking the peppermint into his other cheek. 'See the red pom-poms on the shakos? That's the Don Host, ain't it? The beggars the Turks are so scared of?'

Moody sniffed. 'Might not be. The Black Sea Cossacks are red too. So are Siberia. They're bandits, Jordan, you can't rely on anything with scum like that.'

They didn't look like scum to Ryder. Doherty gave the order and the columns turned smoothly towards them, but the Cossacks seemed quite unconcerned. One turned his head to show high cheekbones, dark slants of eyes, and a bearing quite as noble as Lord Lucan's.

Oliver whispered excitedly, 'Do you think they're the ones Cardigan was looking for?' but Fisk's voice answered, 'Don't be such a flat, Polly, there are only bloody three.' So there were. Three men watching more than a hundred riding towards them, and they never moved an inch.

Ryder suddenly felt very awake indeed. He was almost relieved when they closed the distance to a hundred yards and the Cossacks turned casually and trotted away. Doherty was cautious enough to flank the tumulus rather than ride over it, but when they cleared the hump there was nothing in sight but the same three Cossacks, now perched on the crest of a second slope three hundred yards further on.

The patrol continued to advance, and again the Cossacks waited to let them come closer before turning and trotting away. They looked like sentries, a cavalry vedette, but they didn't seem to be signalling, just watching and staying ahead.

'Cat and mouse, by Jove,' said Captain Marsh in front. 'They'll have to bolt in the end.'

But who was the cat and who were the mice? They were being lured inexorably onwards over land none of them knew. When they rode round the hump there were higher slopes ahead, but of the Cossacks there was no sign.

'Gone to ground again,' said Marsh in disgust. 'Not much of a hunt.'

A hesitant voice spoke beside him: Cornet Hoare. 'Could that be them, sir? Over there?'

Every head in 'G' Troop turned. Three horsemen were coming into view on one of the further slopes to their left, their lance-points catching the sun as if they twiddled them in expectation.

'Put on a spurt, by Jove,' said Marsh in admiration. 'They covered that ground damn fast.'

Doherty led them onward, straight for the slope and the horse-men, but his broad back was stiff with tension and the ADC rode down the far flank of the column like a sheepdog looking for trouble. Jarvis was feeling it too, and when Moody said 'We'll catch them this time, won't we, Sar'nt-major?' he only growled 'Quiet in the ranks' and went on staring ahead. Ryder almost felt sorry for him. The men would be looking to Jarvis, but the poor bugger hadn't seen action any more than they had. It was prob-ably new to everyone in the regiment except Doherty, who'd served in India. Just himself and the Old Man.

The colonel's head moved from side to side as he rode, and so did Ryder's own, searching for the danger experience told him must be there. But the sun hurt his eyes, the pain in his head throbbed like blunt knives, his neck ached intolerably, and the effort of looking right, left, right, left was suddenly beyond him. His neck relaxed, his head drooped, his gaze fell on the ground, and then he saw.

Hoof prints. The ground was still soft from the recent rains, and in it were pockets of mud where horses had passed in the last minutes. They weren't from the column, they diverged across the main track and headed with purpose towards a hill on their right flank.

Jarvis was nearest, but there wasn't time to waste on his vindictive games. Ryder called 'Sir! Captain Marsh, sir!'

Marsh turned at once, and his 'Yes, Corporal?' drowned out Jarvis's outraged grunt. Ryder explained, and was rewarded by a sudden exclamation from Hoare. 'He's right, sir, look! Those Cossacks, weren't they much of a size before? Now look, one's half a foot taller than the others. They're not the same.'

'Hmm,' said Marsh, his face even blanker than usual. 'So the first three are hiding about somewhere, eh?'

Ryder looked again at the ground ahead of him. The tracks had multiplied, crossing and blurring with prints so numerous they'd churned up the mud like an insane plough. Hundreds of horses had passed in the last hour, and they too had been heading for that hill.

He said, 'Not just three.'

For a moment no one spoke. As they stared round the horizon even the three decoy Cossacks turned and disappeared down the other side of their mound. The British were alone in the valley, faced with nothing but silence and the watchful hills.

Marsh cantered up to talk to Doherty. The colonel turned his head and Ryder got his own down quick, but the inspection, if there was one, was brief, and less than a minute later Marsh was back.

'Skirmishers to the front! First section "G" Troop to take ground on the right.'

That was more like it. The Russians wanted them to go left, so Doherty was going to damn their eyes and go right. Ryder's tiredness was gone as the files sprung their carbines and spread into skirmish order. The men were the same, he saw it in their faces and felt it in his own, the blood rushing tingling to the skin to tell him to fight or die.

Lieutenant Grainger led them to the foot of the hill, then

divided the line into three. He himself took the right flank where the tracks led, Jarvis took the centre party up the hill, while Ryder led the last six men round to the left. He strained to alertness as they started round, but heard only the soft squelching of their hooves and a faint huffing noise he realized was Fisk, breathing through his nose like a distressed horse.

'Corp,' whispered Oliver. 'Corp!'

Ryder looked round, then saw he was pointing at the ground. Tracks again, two, maybe three horses. Those Cossacks they'd been following hadn't stuck to the route of the main body, they'd gone round the other side of the hill and were –

Right in front of him. A tall ragged shako, a great bearded face with its mouth open, then a blur of metal against the hillside, a lance thrust right at his eyes. His left arm flew up blindly, blocking the haft with a blow that sent pain shrieking up to his elbow, but his right hand was already swivelling the carbine on its chain, up and *bang*, smoke, the acrid powder smell, a spatter of something warm and wet on his neck, and the Cossack falling away backwards with a chest smashed suddenly into scarlet. Behind him were two more.

And in a rush it was back, the old feeling, the need to be alive and to hell with anything that got in the way. His hand let go of the now useless carbine and pulled out his sword, steel flashing as he charged straight at the startled horseman behind the one he'd downed. He forgot who he was, who he was supposed to be leading, nothing mattered but killing the bastard in front of him.

But this was a Cossack, a man trained to the saddle from a child, and he sidestepped so deftly that the ferocity of Ryder's onslaught threw him forward over Wanderer's neck. The lance plunged over him, screeching down his arm and striking the shako with such violence the chinstrap crunched into his nose. Pain, nausea, the old box of tricks, Ryder stayed low and kicked in his spurs. Wanderer plunged forward, crashing broadside into the Cossack's mount and jolting its rider off balance. Ryder threw his body back square in the saddle and plunged forward with the sword, forward and *down* – feel the bite in the shoulder, break the bone then drive fast and savage through the flesh below. The Russian wheeled aside with a yelp, but in a second he righted himself, and it was only when another carbine fired that he turned to trot away. Ryder stared at his retreating back with disbelief. What were these bastards made of?

But there'd been a third, and the soldier part of him was already turning before his mind caught up. Fisk hurtling round the slope, Bolton furiously reloading, then *there* was the Cossack, bloodied in the shoulder but dropping his lance to whirl out his sabre, and there facing up to him with the wobbliest carbine Ryder had ever seen was Charlie 'Polly' Oliver.

'Shoot him, Polly,' Ryder shouted, struggling to turn his horse in a fear he hardly understood. 'For Christ's sake shoot him!'

The bang came almost at once, but the ball went wide, the Cossack only flinched and lunged. Ryder screamed to make him turn, the bastard thinking himself brave to take on a boy barely out of school. His own sword was up again, blood dripping warm on the heel of his hand, but the Cossack reeled abruptly back, turned round and round on his horse then slid slowly down to the muddy ground. Oliver was staring at him in wide-eyed horror, but his sword was bloodied halfway up the blade.

'*Shabash!*' said Ryder before he remembered where he was. 'Bloody well done.'

He looked back for the others. Jordan and Trotter had caught up, Bolton was ramming his carbine, but Fisk sat still in his saddle, looking over Ryder's shoulder with blank eyes and open mouth. Grainger was shouting above them, Ryder heard the word 'behind' and turned.

There was the ambush. There was what they'd have walked into if Doherty hadn't taken them round the other side. Spread over the slopes behind the hill were perhaps four hundred Russian cavalry, some mounted, some climbing into the saddle, and some already moving. Their skirmishers were trotting forward to meet the British, and it wasn't a little party of twenty like Grainger's. There were about a hundred of them coming right this way.

A trumpet behind sounded the recall. *Good plan*, thought Ryder, wheeling Wanderer to execute it. The others were already turning, but Oliver sat motionless, gazing down at the body of the Russian he'd killed himself. The sword in his hand was trembling.

'Come on,' said Ryder. He laid a hand on the boy's arm and sharpened his voice. 'Re-form, Trooper. Back to the regiment.'

Oliver nodded jerkily and began to turn. A musket cracked behind. Ryder yelled again 'Come *on!*' smacked Oliver's horse and spurred his own to the gallop, driving them all back round the cover of the hill. Grainger's team was doing the same, so was Jarvis's, all pelting together after the patrol which was already turning to retreat. The Russians were coming after them, he could see the first skirmishers starting to spill round the hills, but the main body had been much further back, they'd never catch up in time. He slowed to a trot, watched the men re-form into line, took his own place at the end, and drew a long, deep breath of relief.

Jordan was laughing with excitement, Fisk saying 'Bloody hell, bloody *hell*', over and over again, but Oliver seemed shocked and half-dazed, the point missing the scabbard as he tried to sheathe his sword. Ryder hesitated, but then Jordan said, 'Gawd, look at Oliver's sword!' and admiring murmurs rippled down the line at the sight of blood on the blade. Oliver turned pink, but he sat up noticeably straighter and was at least awake enough to wipe the weapon before sliding it home. Ryder smiled to himself, glanced over his shoulder to check the Russians were keeping distance, and felt his own heartbeat return to normal.

Something wet and sticky was crawling up his arm. He looked down to see his sleeve sliced through to expose a long deep gash in his forearm, and felt a sudden stab of pain that seemed to have been only waiting for him to notice it. A vague memory returned of a lance scoring up the flesh, and he realized for the first time how close it had been. One day he wouldn't be sitting here thinking 'Oh look, I'm wounded', one day he'd be the body left face-down in the mud with the others. But not today, maybe not tomorrow, and certainly not now. He clawed in his coat for a handkerchief, and looped his elbow through the reins while he bound up the wound. His tiredness had gone, and the throbbing in his arm was just another pulse like a heartbeat, a proof of his being alive.

The Russians were following. Oliver tried not to keep looking over his shoulder, but it was hard not to snatch glimpses by pretending to adjust the crupper. They weren't chasing or anything, and if they did the colonel would simply order the gallop, but they were following steadily and surely, like a householder making sure the burglar left the premises without stealing the silver. They were just *there*.

And staying there. The patrol was back in the farmlands, but still the Cossacks were behind them, a mass of dark figures following in ominous silence. Oliver glanced down the line, but no one else seemed worried, and Ryder was even humming under his breath as he rode. Colonel Doherty was always calm, of course, and he was still keeping them firmly at the walk. Only the ADC kept looking back at the Russians, but even he looked annoyed rather than concerned.

Chalk track crunched under their hooves as they entered the outskirts of the first village. Doherty halted them as he gave his report to Lord Cardigan, and then Oliver had to look, he had to see if the Cossacks were gaining, but to his enormous relief they were already turning and beginning to trot away.

'Windy buggers,' said Fisk in disgust. 'Don't tell me they're scared of Lord Haw-Haw.'

Jordan laughed. 'Oliver, more likely. He's in a killing mood, ain't you, chum?'

The laughter was kind, even admiring, but Oliver squirmed inside. He'd known he'd have to kill sometime, he was trained and prepared for it, but none of that helped when he came face to face with the Cossack. The man was wounded, Bolton had shot him, but he was still coming, still coming, the sabre slashing straight down, and Oliver forgot he even held a gun in his hand, he was watching something out of a nightmare becoming real. Then Ryder had yelled, Ryder had woken him, and Oliver had done what he'd been trained to do. He'd shot at the man, and when that hadn't worked he'd stabbed him, and then the Cossack was on the ground dead and Oliver had seen he was as young and weak and human as himself.

And Ryder had said 'well done'. He'd killed too, but he'd done it as if it were natural, and didn't seem in the least shaken afterwards. Oliver looked furtively at him, but he seemed quite ordinary, he was leaning forward in the saddle to watch Doherty talking to Cardigan. That was how a soldier was meant to be, so why did it feel so different for himself?

Ryder's face tightened, and Oliver became aware of Cardigan's voice rising angrily. 'And now, sir,' he was saying, 'perhaps you will have the goodness to explain how you encountered the enemy and *failed to engage?*'

Doherty's face went white under the beard, and a low growl murmured through the regiment. Everyone knew it was only the colonel who'd saved them from the ambush, and Cardigan was almost calling him a coward. Ryder muttered '*Bastard*', but then his expression changed and Oliver looked up to see a third horseman slipping out from the column to talk to Cardigan. The ADC was taking a hand.

He spoke very quietly, but Cardigan's face seemed to be growing less mauve. After a moment he cleared his throat and said, 'Oh yes, very well then, perfectly satisfactory. But let me tell you, it would have been a different thing if *I'd* been there, dammit, what?'

The ADC was turning his horse and for the first time his voice was audible. Oliver thought he could even hear a smile in it as he said, 'I'm sure it would, my lord. I shall be sure to say so in my report,' then bowed politely and trotted away.

The voice was familiar, so was that hint of laughter, and Oliver turned quickly to Ryder. Ryder gave a nod of agreement and just for a moment he smiled.

The patrol moved off again, but Oliver was encouraged. It was like an omen, seeing 'their' officer again, and Ryder was already being friendlier, the way he'd been under the wagon. Perhaps he'd only been distant because they were on duty, and this evening he'd keep him company again, let him talk about what had happened with the Cossacks.

He stuck close to Ryder's side as they numbered off back at camp, but they were immediately surrounded by men of other regiments, all desperately jealous the 13th had been first to face the enemy. 'What was it like?' they all wanted to know. 'What was it like?' When they learned Ryder had fought two Russians at once he was practically mobbed. Ryder said only, 'They're damn good, those Cossacks, I'd say they're tougher than we are,' but Prosser and Moody still muttered sulkily together, and Jarvis watched with a lopsided twist to his mouth that Oliver didn't care for at all.

'Just a moment,' said another voice, and he skipped back hastily as Lieutenant Grainger walked through the crowd. Grainger was their best officer, everyone said so, but he was so unobtrusive it was disconcertingly easy to forget he was there.

He didn't miss much either. He stood in front of Ryder, held out his hand, and said, 'Come on, Corporal, let's see that arm.'

Ryder held out his right arm, and now everyone saw the sleeve was flapping open and underneath it was a bloodied dressing that might have been a handkerchief. The crowd murmured, and Cornet Hoare said 'I *say!*' in a tone of unmistakable envy.

Grainger studied the dressing, then looked up. He had a pleasant face, young and friendly, it was only the little crinkles at the corner of his eyes that gave away his age. 'All right, Corporal. Medical orderly – *now*.'

Ryder was never insolent with Grainger. He said 'Yes, sir', saluted as if he meant it, and paused only to check Wanderer's picket pole before walking away.

The crowd hesitated, but someone yelled 'Butcher's out, lads, fresh meat on the beach,' and at once it broke up in stampede. Oliver followed Ryder, determined to wait until they could go together, but Ryder just chucked him his mess-tin and said, 'Get my ration, will you, Trooper? If Fisk gets there first there'll be nothing left but the eyelashes.'

It was probably true, judging by the way Fisk was elbowing his massive way through the mob, but Oliver still knew he was dismissed. That was fair enough, of course, Ryder was an NCO, but as he walked down to the beach he couldn't help wishing their wagon was still there, that Mackenzie and Woodall hadn't left, that things could be back as they were in the storm.

The orderly peeled off the handkerchief with dirty fingernails and peered with drink-sodden eyes at the ensuing flush of blood. 'It's a cut.'

Ryder resisted the urge to show him exactly what a cut was and how much it hurt. 'Just bloody bind it, will you, Merrick? I don't need a surgeon's opinion.'

'Won't get one,' said Merrick, fishing out a yellow-stained bandage that had probably come off six other men before Ryder even saw it. 'Not for something this trivial.'

'Thanks,' said Ryder, resisting the cringing of his flesh as the dressing clamped stiffly over it. 'Good of you to bother.'

'Nah,' said Merrick, grinning. 'I'm sick of boils and cholera. Nice to see a proper wound for a change.'

He was going to see a lot more of them, if those Cossacks were anything to go by. That was an ambush today, a deliberate, planned ambush, and it wasn't hard to guess its purpose. Their

ADC had spotted it, he'd as good as warned them under the wagon when he said the cavalry were the army's only eyes. The Russians wanted to stop them seeing something, and Ryder was afraid he knew what.

An army. Four hundred cavalry didn't just sit about on their own without infantry support, there was a whole damn army assembling out there, and probably getting bigger every day. Five days the Allies had sat around organizing supplies of things they ought to have brought with them, five days the Russians had used to build an army that was all but on the bloody doorstep. They needed to go now, *now*, before it was too late.

But as he walked down to the beach he began to suspect their commanders were feeling the same urgency. The last baggage wagons had gone, the boats setting out for the fleet were carrying sick men back to the *Kangaroo*, and the RSM was standing at the camp markers intoning 'Epaulettes and valises to the boats, see they're marked with your names.' The march was tomorrow, it must be. They were getting off their arses at last and marching out to war.

He strode more briskly onto the sand, threading his way expertly through the cooking fires, but a new sound caught his attention, a lighter note in the hubbub that brought him to an abrupt halt. Three troopers were chatting round a nearby fire, but that was a woman laughing with them, a fair-haired girl in a blue dress kneeling over a sizzling pan, and his heart gave a little jump as he recognized Sally Jarvis.

He shouldn't be surprised. Landing the wives was only one more sign of imminent departure, and of course Sally'd be here. Of course she'd be laughing and joking on the brink of a battle, she was like that, she was the happiest person he knew. There was no surprise in any of it, but still his footsteps faltered, slowed and stopped, because she was Sally Jarvis and he liked to look at her.

It wasn't easy for a woman to look beautiful when she was on the strength of a regiment, but Sally Jarvis managed it. Lucie

Jordan's rouge had run out, she'd stopped bothering with the curling papers, and her face was leathered by sun and bad temper, but Sally was unchanged. She couldn't be more than twenty but she still kept a matronly neatness, her figure always trim, her dress clean, her fair hair scrupulously bound back, and she was always smiling.

The troopers drifted back to their own fires, still grinning happily. Ryder hesitated, but Sally looked up and smiled and it would have been rude to walk away. He strolled to the fire and said feebly, 'Hullo, Sally.'

She fanned away the smoke to examine him with those wonderful dark-lashed eyes. 'You look half dead, Ryder. Is it your arm?'

He blinked. 'It's just a cut. Did the sar'nt-major . . . ?'

Her smile faded, and she turned back to the pan. 'Oliver. He wanted to ask about Ronnie Stokes, poor boy, but I'm afraid he's dead. So is Jimmy Byrd.'

He noticed with compunction the dark circles under her own eyes. 'Was it bad, Sal?'

She stirred the beef. 'It was quick. Byrd wanted me to write a letter for his people.'

Bitterness swamped him. 'Poor sod. What could you say – died of cholera in a war about nothing?'

Her eyes flashed with anger as she looked up. 'I wrote what he bloody wanted, Ryder, what the hell else should I do?'

She'd inherited her vocabulary from her sailor father, and some of the troop thought it fun to make her use it. Ryder wasn't one of them. 'I'm sorry, I wasn't thinking.'

She shrugged and went back to the beef.

He cast about for something that might lift his status from utter brute. 'How did Oliver take it? About Ronnie Stokes?'

That did it, she looked up again and the smile was back. 'He was fine, truly. He was prepared for it and of course he's a Christian. But he's lonely, Ryder, I wish you'd look out for him. He's a nice lad.'

He suppressed a twinge of guilt. 'Then I won't be much good for him, will I?'

She laughed, and began to pile beef into a mess-tin. 'Oh, I don't know. Everyone's going to need friends now, Ryder, even you. They say on the *Jason* we're off tomorrow.'

We. He looked at her delicate hands on the spoon, the glimpse of bare forearm under the loose blue sleeve, and was struck for the first time by the reality of wives at war. 'Why the hell couldn't you stay on the ship? The fleet's going to follow us round the coast, isn't it? They could easily land you all at Sebastopol.'

'Like the heavy baggage?' she said. 'The siege guns? Why do you think women come on the strength if they don't want to be near their husbands?'

The thought of her being near Jarvis turned his stomach. 'It's a sixty-mile march, Sal.'

She began to clean the pan with sand. 'We'll be all right, we haven't the heavy uniforms. Merrick's taking my baggage in the cart, anyway, I'm going to be a nurse.'

He couldn't think of a more revolting job for a woman. 'What does the sar'nt-major think about that?'

'Sixpence a day,' she said, and smiled. 'There won't be much laundry on the march, but you're going to need nurses.'

For a second she looked at him, and he saw in her eyes the understanding that had been missing in the orderly's. Then her face lightened, he turned and saw the sergeant-major standing watching them.

'Hullo, Jarvis,' she said, smiling with pleasure. 'Look, I've cooked you some beef.'

'I can see it,' said Jarvis, not moving. 'Well, Corporal?'

He wouldn't give the bastard the satisfaction. 'Picquet duty, Sar'nt-major?'

It was worth a week of it just for the spark of frustration in Jarvis's eyes. He muttered 'Picquet duty. Parade in ten minutes,' and sat down to eat his beef.

Ryder managed to walk away with a fair appearance of briskness. No sleep, no supper, but Sally had shown concern and Jarvis had just looked petty, there was comfort in that. He felt a slight qualm at the thought of the offhand way he'd treated Oliver, but the kid would have more respect in the troop after today, he wouldn't need the friendship of that well-known callous bastard Harry Ryder. Ryder didn't need it either, whatever Sally said. He managed perfectly well on his own.

The cooking fires were glowing in the dusk like miniature hearths of home. He walked past the laughter and boisterousness in the messes, the pools of quiet as the younger married men were reunited with their wives, the cackling of the older women as they lashed out with ladles at the horseplay of the troopers, he walked alone through it all and wondered why the tiredness was back and throbbing in his bones like an ache.

Oliver peered at the blood beading on the surface of the steak and wondered if it was done. Woodall would know, but Woodall was at the Grenadiers' camp nearly a mile inshore.

'Why are you cooking Ryder's, anyway?' asked Fisk, eyeing it avariciously. 'He'll eat with the NCOs, won't he?'

Oliver knew that now. The others had gone; Ryder wouldn't bother leaving his own mess just for Private Oliver. 'It'll save him time, won't it? He's been on picquet a lot lately, he must be ravenous.'

'Toady,' said Fisk, and went on watching the pan.

Bolton looked up mournfully. 'I'm sorry about Stokes, Ol-Pol. You'll miss him, won't you?'

He already did. He thought with sadness of the cards he'd been so careful to remove from his valise, and wondered if he shouldn't have let them go back to the ship with the rest. What good were they now? Bolton would never follow the rules and Fisk would probably eat them. Aloud he said, 'He's in a better place, Tommy.'

'Isn't everyone?' said Fisk gloomily. He studied his empty mess-tin.

Bolton stiffened. 'Look, Ol-Pol, there's Ryder. On picquet, look, next to Jordan.'

Oliver gazed out over the darkening beach. The inlying picquet was already telling off from parade, and Bolton was right, the last in the line was Ryder. 'That's ridiculous. He was on last night and the night before.'

'When do you think he'll drop?' said Fisk, licking out his mess-tin. 'Bet you a bob it's tomorrow on the march.'

Oliver looked at him in horror. 'Someone should talk to the captain.'

Fisk's tongue stopped mid-lick. 'Give over, Poll, you'll give me indigestion. You peach on Jarvis he'll have you triced up and flogged in a week.'

Oliver's stomach gave a little heave. Fisk might be joking, but he remembered how Jarvis had looked at Ryder on the boat, and was very afraid he wasn't. 'I suppose it's only inlying picquet. I could bring him his supper anyway.'

'No, you don't,' said Fisk, dropping his mess-tin abruptly. 'What if Jarvis sees you, eh? Or Moody or Prosser, which is the same bloody thing. You stay clear.'

Oliver tightened his jaw. 'There's no regulation against it.'

'Oh, blow the regs,' said Fisk. He heaved himself up straight and jabbed a fat finger at Oliver's face. 'Listen, Polly, you listen to your Uncle Albie. You've been getting altogether too close to Harry Ryder lately, and it's got to stop.'

Oliver had never seen him so serious. 'He's my friend.'

'Then he didn't ought to be,' said Fisk. His face was growing redder and he seemed to have completely forgotten the beef. 'Remember Sullivan, do you? Jarvis didn't like him, thought he was disrespectful, he was engineering that one for weeks. And if Jarvis didn't like Joe I'm telling you he fair hates Harry Ryder. There's going to be one bloody big explosion there and when she blows you don't want to be in the middle.'

The unfairness ached in his head. This was how things had felt on the flatboat, everything turned upside-down and wrong. He yearned for the security of his old world, where people cared how he did, where he worked for fear of punishment and was rewarded with a 'well done'.

Ryder had said it, just this afternoon. Oliver relived the moment in his mind and found another memory coming back to him, Ryder shouting 'Shoot him, Polly!' with a desperation that sounded like fear.

He laid the steak in the mess-tin. 'I understand.'

'Good,' said Fisk. 'Cut it in three, Poll.'

He shut the tin with a click. 'No, I'm taking it to Ryder.' He ignored Fisk's outraged splutter, gathered his things and walked away. Moody and Prosser both looked round as he passed their fire, but it didn't matter, he was within the rules, he was safe.

The picquet was on the edge of the main camp on the plateau above the beach. The horses were pegged, ready saddled and bridled, but the men themselves sat chatting in little groups or laying out blankets to make beds. Oliver searched in the dark until he found Wanderer, and there was Ryder behind him, sprawled out on a pile of oat-straw, and already fast asleep.

Oliver stooped to lay the tin by the straw, but it clinked against a stone and at once Ryder's eyes snapped open. Oliver jumped back in embarrassment and said quickly, 'It's just your rations. I thought . . .'

Ryder sat up and ran his hands through his hair. 'No, that's kind. Thanks, Poll.' He smiled wearily and reached for the tin.

Oliver said tentatively, 'I might have overcooked it.'

Ryder was already cutting into it. 'No, it's fine.' He chewed in silence for a minute, then said indistinctly, 'God, this is good.'

Oliver blinked, but Ryder was happy and the blasphemy some-how didn't feel that important. He stood watching him wolf the steak, and realized in a confused way he was happy himself.

He dropped his haversack and blanket and sat down. There was something calming about the picquet line after dark, sitting safe in the shadow of that long warm wall of horses, looking up at the openness of a clear night sky. He leaned back against the straw pile and listened comfortably to the rhythmic munching in nosebags, the odd little snorts, the scuff of an irritable hoof, and the murmur and rustle of men preparing to sleep.

He said, 'I hesitated today. That Cossack. I hesitated.'

'I know,' said Ryder. His voice was very quiet, and Oliver wondered if he felt it too, the peacefulness all around them. 'It doesn't matter, Polly. You won't next time.'

'How do you know?'

There was a clink as Ryder laid down the tin. 'Because today was your first, and that's always a shock. The next will be easier.'

He *had* served before. Oliver considered asking him about it, but it didn't really matter. What mattered was Ryder not minding he knew. 'I think I was scared.'

Ryder gave a funny little chuckle like a snort. 'Good. Fear makes you fast, helps you fight, it keeps you alive. The time to worry is when you lose it.'

He thought about that. 'What if it's bad, though? If I run away.'

Ryder's laugh was louder this time. 'You won't run. You can't. We were alone today, but next time you'll be in the line, and the man beside you will stop you running.'

He thought he understood that. 'You mean you will.'

Ryder shook his head. 'Doesn't matter who it is. It's the man next to you, the one next to him, the man behind, all of you standing together. Imagine moving out of the line, trotting past that lot to run away. Who's going to do that?'

There were stars in the sky, little ones twinkling. 'No one.'

'No one,' said Ryder. He stretched out his legs and settled back with a sigh of enjoyment. 'Because if they do it's all up. If the man next to you breaks, then it stops mattering, you go straight after him, then the whole bloody lot breaks and runs. One man can save a whole army just by standing still.'

Oliver thought back to the afternoon. If any of the others had bolted he knew he'd have done the same. 'Then we all did. Bolton, Fisk, Jordan. You're saying we're all heroes.'

The straw crackled as Ryder turned his head. 'That's the strength of the line, Poll. You'll see.'

The murmuring was dying away around them. After a moment Ryder gave a little snore.

Oliver smiled, and went on looking at the sky. He didn't need to talk any more, anyway. He knew who'd really saved him today, and he would be there again tomorrow, the man who rode next to him in the line.

4

19 September 1854, 3.00 a.m. to 6.30 p.m.

A distant bang cracked into Ryder's sleep. His eyes opened to darkness, the prickliness of oat-straw under his cheek, then it came again, the dull bark of a carbine.

Someone shouted, 'Turn out the inlying picquet! Inlying picquet to fall in!'

He was already moving, thrusting his mess-tin into the haversack, grappling his straw-covered blanket into a roll, turning for Wanderer's picket pole. Oliver stood beside him, pale-faced and bleary, saying 'Should I come? Is it all of us? Should I come?' He said 'Not yet, Poll, go back to sleep,' and swung himself into the saddle.

A pale flash ripped the darkness to his front, another bang, and the ping of a ball whipping past. A trumpet called and Ryder turned to fall in, steering Wanderer through the confusion of snorting horses and sleepy riders asking 'What is it? What's going on?' The crack and flash of another shot, and a yelp from the camp behind. Someone had been hit.

The line was forming, and he placed himself firmly to Jordan's left. Staccato shots ahead suggested the outlying picquet were engaged, and movement shuffled along the line as men sprung their own carbines. Ryder did the same, wondering how the hell he'd know what to shoot at in this dark.

But the officers seemed doubtful too, and Ryder felt the first suspicion of the truth. Marsh moved them out very slowly, an uncertain progress at the walk, and he could hear hoarse, confused voices shouting at each other in the gloom. The shooting didn't seem right either, isolated cracks and bangs from their own vedettes on the crest, and when another ball whined past his shoulder he was almost sure the flash was in their outlying picquet. 'Friendly fire, damn it,' muttered the voice of Lieutenant Grainger behind. 'What's got the Hussars jumping?'

A voice ahead bellowed 'Cease firing! Cease firing!' A moment later the brigade major galloped past their front, shouting it again: 'Cease firing there!' One by one the picquets and vedettes stopped shooting, and a hundred men sat still in their saddles as they strained to listen. Silence. Three hours' sleep, dragged out in the middle of the night, and it was a bloody false alarm.

They draggled back to camp muttering with discontent. The whole camp was roused now, and Oliver said a servant in the Lancers had actually been hit. There was only one other casualty, an 8th Hussar coming in with a rough dressing wrapped round his leg, and Jordan yelled 'Serve you right, you jumpy beggar, some of us need our sleep!'

The Hussar stopped to glare at him. 'Not our fault. There were Cossacks, there bloody were. I saw their fur hats. They were trotting right in front of us.'

'Picking daisies in the dark?' said Jordan. 'Come on, chum, admit it, you lost your bleeding front.'

Ryder had nearly done it himself in Burma, lost his bearings at night and mistaken movement in his own camp for the enemy. He dismounted wearily and said, 'Leave it, Telegraph, it could happen to anyone.'

'Corp,' whispered Oliver, and his shoulders looked stiff with tension. 'Corp, what's that?' He was looking at the sky.

Ryder saw only clouds at first, but they were rising in thick black columns rather than gentle puff-balls, spreading like a stain over the dark blue of the night. The muttering of the picquet lapsed into hush, and faint in the air he knew he was smelling smoke.

'Told you,' said the Hussar in bitter triumph. 'Cossacks. They've gone and fired the village.'

'But why?' said Oliver. 'Why would they . . . ?'

A second cloud was rising now, a dark, roiling plume to the north, and Ryder remembered the trim white-walled houses of the village they'd foraged at yesterday. 'They're cutting off our supplies. They know we're on the way.'

'How can they?' said Oliver uncertainly. 'We didn't know ourselves till last night.'

'Looks like they know more than we do,' said Jordan, tugging his blanket back down from his horse. 'You reckon they'll try to stop us?'

'Wouldn't you?' Ryder thought of other villages they'd passed, of two Crim-Tartars smiling as they mended a fence; he thought of the Russians on the move through the night and the long, long road ahead of them to Sebastopol. He said, 'Forget about sleep, Billy. If Raglan knows what he's doing he'll get us on the road right now.'

Dennis Woodall squinted at the smoke-filled sky and guessed it must be every bit of nine o'clock. At four they'd paraded, four in the ruddy morning, and here they still were waiting for the cavalry escort. He cursed the army's inefficiency and turned back to his letter.

Of course the Frogs have the best of it as usual. They are marching by the lower road, with the fleet to protect their right and the Gallant British to protect their left, and with sea breezes to cool them all the way. We must march right in the sun, and I tell you, Maise, it is set to be a Scorcher.

Summer in England, taking Maisie to the Great Exhibition on a shilling day, *Mr* Woodall out walking with his pretty little wife. Summer and the band playing, Maisie swinging her parasol like a Guard on parade and saying 'Ain't I a lady now though, Denny? Ain't I a lady now?'

His brow creased a little at the thought of that parasol. It had been very dear, and the income from the dad's savings bonds was only just enough for the rent as it was. But she'd seen it and had to have it, like the adorable child she was, that was Maisie for you, that was just Maise.

A fine scattering of ash landed right on the paper. He blew away the grit and wrote on.

And it will get worse. The Russians are burning the villages near the Post Road to Sebastopol, and our water-party say they have filled the wells with earth. How we are to manage on the march I cannot think. They say it will take four hours for us to reach the River Bulganek.

The trumpet at last, and the sergeant-major bawling 'Back to the ranks, *fall in!*' Woodall thrust the letter into his coatee, brushed himself down, and stalked majestically to his place.

'Bloody stifling out here,' said that uncouth Truman next to him. 'You got any water?'

'No,' said Woodall, clapping a hand on his canteen to stop it swishing. 'Haven't you?'

Truman shook his head. 'Thought we'd get a chance this morning.'

Woodall silently congratulated himself on his prudence in having replenished his own supply last night. Overhead the sun was already beginning to feel uncomfortably warm.

By noon it was blazing. Mackenzie tutted sympathetically at the sight of the Guards marching valiantly in full bearskins. The poor creatures must be fair roasting. His own bonnet was not so bad, and at least his legs were cool.

It had been a grand start from Eupatoria, but the bands were quiet now and the colours hung limp in the still heat. No one seemed much for the talking. There was only the swishing of their legs through the long grass, the humming of flies, and the bitter scent of appleringie crushed by the passing of many boots.

'It's a fierce sun, isn't it, Niall?' Young Murray was beside him. His face was flushed and sweaty, and his eyes looked feverish.

Mackenzie passed him his barrel. 'Here, have some more water.'

Murray nodded his thanks and fumbled the canteen to his lips. The poor laddie had only been a day back to duty since the dysentery, but he'd still refused to go to the ships, and Mackenzie understood. It was always better to stay with your friends. As he took back his canteen he looked with pleasure at the sturdy Highlanders around him, marching in perfect step as it might be one single man.

But the country around was not so good, and he pursed his lips at another cloud of smoke in the sky ahead. He would like to catch up with these Russians, and show them what he thought of men who destroyed people's living just to deny their goods to the enemy. Such brave soldiers they must be to kill an old woman's cow and burn a whole village's grainstore out of fear of the terrible avenging army that marched towards them, British and French and Turkish, maybe sixty thousand strong.

He stumbled against something, and looked down to see a man fallen by the wayside. A Coldstream Guard with his bearskin off, twitching and dribbling on the dry ground. Another with the cholera, poor soul, maybe the third he'd seen this morning. Mackenzie broke ranks to move him safely out of the track, then saw the lowered eyebrows of Sergeant Macpherson and quickly slipped back into place. It was a shame to leave the man, but their officers would have made provision for such things. There would be doctors along by and by, litters and wee carts at the rear, that would be the way of it. He turned to smile at Murray, but the laddie's face had changed, the skin round his eyes stood out in white patches like an owl, and his upper lip was swimming in sweat.

'Andra,' said Mackenzie urgently. 'Andra.'

Murray's head turned jerkily towards him. 'It's a fierce sun, isn't it, Niall?' Then his eyes rolled like a horse's and his head dropped suddenly as his knees crunched down on the track.

Mackenzie stopped as the march went on, men parting and trudging past him as if he were a rock in a stream. Andrew Murray from his own Strathcarron, the wee lad who'd only come to the army to follow himself! He hunkered down, wrapped a brawny arm under the bairn's legs, then hoisted him like a sack over his shoulder.

He straightened painfully and saw another man stopped before him, the terrifying Mr Macpherson himself. Mackenzie kept his arm protectively across Murray's body and did his best to stand to attention, but the sergeant only looked sadly at him and nodded his head twice. 'Aye,' he said heavily. 'Aye.' Then he turned and marched on.

Mackenzie adjusted the weight on his shoulder and started after him, one tentative pace after another, until gradually he regained his rhythm and marched again in perfect step with the others.

Ryder's mouth was dry and it hurt to swallow, but he dug in his heels and rode on.

Water. Men had been falling from their saddles for want of it, and the Bulganek could still be hours away. Their small party had empty barrels for all 'G' Troop slung round their necks, and Ryder had another four he'd found abandoned by men too far gone to see a future when they'd ever be filled. He was beginning to fear they never would.

Six villages they'd tried now, but not a drop of water to be had in any of them. This was their last chance, the little hamlet they'd watered at yesterday. It was far enough from the road for the Russians not to have bothered with it, and the bastards couldn't know they were even aware of its existence. It was still a mile away, but Ryder kept his eyes on the sky and prayed for it to stay untainted by smoke.

It was clear. They rode in warily, but the buildings were intact, the villagers greeted them with friendly recognition, and the well, thank God, was clean. Two stout labourers helped them with the bucket, and as one by one Ryder slung the full canteens round his body he felt the sweat on his forehead start to cool. He hadn't even drunk yet, but already the thirst was receding.

'Come on, come on,' said Cornet Hoare, prowling up and down in his impatience to return to the apron-strings of the column. 'Lieutenant Grainger will be worrying where we've got to.'

He wouldn't give a damn when they came back with water. Ryder slung his last canteen and started to help Fisk with the rest.

'Sir,' called Oliver from his post at the far barn. 'Horsemen coming, maybe half a mile. They're Cossacks.'

Ryder stared. Were the Russians burning everything in the whole Crimea just in case the British might have found it? It seemed ludicrous, but Jarvis was sure, he was already leading out the horses, and Ryder turned quickly to join him.

'Just this last bucket,' said Fisk, still filling. 'We can easily outride them.'

Ryder swung round. 'They mustn't even see us here, for God's sake. What will they do to these people if they know they helped us?'

Hoare glanced up at the puzzled villagers, and Ryder saw his face grow older with understanding. 'He's right, Fisk. Come *now.*'

Now it was, and the five of them rode out at full tilt, gobbling up the grass beneath their hooves in the rush to put ground between themselves and the Cossacks. They hadn't been seen, couldn't have, but when Ryder finally looked back over his shoulder he saw black smoke already rising from the distant barns. The Russians were burning the place anyway.

And for nothing. People were being ruined, their livelihoods destroyed, and the stupidity of it banged in his head all the way back. If they'd left a day ago, just one day, all these villages would have been safe. If Raglan had let the ships carry wagons, ambulances, all the things they'd travelled without in the hope of being able to buy them here, if, if, and *if* the British Army had known what it was doing and got on the road yesterday when the French were ready, none of this need have happened.

And men wouldn't be dying for lack of water. The column had progressed two miles since they left it, but the procession was so spread the stragglers were still visible when they regained the Post Road. For the first time he saw the back of the column, a trail of cattle dung, two arabas laden with sick and dying men, medical orderlies stripped to the waist in the baking heat, their fellows in the 4th Light Dragoons scooping up discarded canteens and turning over the shapeless red bundles that were dead men in the grass. The detritus of a mighty army, and this one had yet to face its enemy.

Hoare was already out of earshot, cantering eagerly back to the front, and Ryder turned in desperation to Jarvis. 'Permission to help these men, Sar'nt-major? They're just being left to –'

'Denied,' said Jarvis. 'We're ordered back, now *move*.' He turned and rode after Hoare, followed by Fisk and a subdued-looking Oliver.

Ryder swore under his breath as he urged Wanderer after them. He tried not to look at the trudging men he was passing, the worn, dusty faces that turned towards the rattling and clanking associated with water but saw only the privileged cavalry and turned hopelessly away. Of course they did, and he deserved it. He'd thought the cavalry were suffering enough in their thick uniforms and heavy shakos, but these poor bastards had to carry their own baggage as well. He scanned the faces of the ADCs as they cantered along the flanks, looking for the one he knew, the one who cared about ordinary soldiers, but in this whole damned self-important army that was the one officer he saw no sign of at all.

His horse veered, and there was a man face-down on the ground, surrounded by a cloud of humming flies. He looked away fast, and saw they'd caught up with the First Division. The three Highland regiments were still marching in good order, but a man in the middle was carrying another, and the eyes that met Ryder's were Niall Mackenzie's.

Madness took him. He swung close to the column, unslung a barrel and reached over men's heads to hand it to Mackenzie. 'There's a river coming up, tell them,' he called. 'Take a drink and pass it on.'

Other men crowded round at once. Discipline held and no one snatched, each man taking only a quick frantic gulp, then passing the canteen to the next. Jarvis yelled, 'Back to your place, Corporal, *that's an order!*' but Ryder was beyond caring. He rode to the break between the Scots Fusiliers and the Coldstream, dismounted, and plunged in with his second spare canteen. It was the same here, the way men seized the barrel with shaking hands, water dribbling down their chins as they struggled to make their parched throats swallow. What kind of army made its men march in gear like this, with no provision for sick or wounded? What kind of *men*?

He blundered back to his horse and rode on to the Grenadiers. Woodall was on the outside, thank God, but when he offered him a canteen the Guard mumbled 'I'm all right' and wouldn't meet his eye. A dozen other hands were stretching towards him, voices crying 'This way, Lily,' and one man reaching out a coin, begging 'A shilling, Corp, shilling for a drink.' He pressed the barrel into a sergeant's hands and said again, 'There's a river ahead, tell them it's not far, have a drink and pass it on.'

He had only one more spare canteen. He stopped by the Royal Fusiliers in the Light Division, again the barrel, again the stretching hands, but one was too far gone, and another man was helping him out of the ranks into the gap between themselves and the seaward column. The canteen would never reach them, but there was still his own, it was his to share if he chose. He slid from Wanderer's back and shoved through the ranks on foot.

The Fusilier on the ground looked up at his approach, a dark, hollow-cheeked face with wrinkles at the corners of bloodshot eyes. Ryder knelt beside him, heard the other say 'Here you go, Morry, a bleeding Good Samaritan all your own', and put the mouthpiece to the cracked lips. The elderly man sucked like a starving baby, and Ryder tilted the barrel to give him more. It was almost a shock when the thin hand came up to push the canteen away, and a hoarse voice said, 'Enough, friend, the Bloomer here will want some.'

Ryder knew that name. The notorious Bloomer of the 7th. He looked doubtfully at the broken-nosed companion, but he only grinned amiably and reached out a misshapen paw for the canteen. 'What's your name, Lily?'

'Ryder,' he said, suddenly reminded of who he was and what he was doing.

'Ryder the rider!' The ogre took a long swig of water, smacked his rubbery lips, and winked at Ryder's lack of response. 'You've heard it before, eh?'

'I've heard it before,' agreed Ryder. 'Sorry, I've got to go.'

'All right, Ryder, I won't forget,' said Bloomer. He held out the canteen like a handshake. 'Run along now, and give my regards to Joe Sullivan.'

There wasn't time to explain. He just nodded in acknowledgement and shoved hastily back to his horse. He must be five minutes behind the others.

He urged Wanderer faster, past the Light Division, past the green-jacketed Riflemen, and felt a surge of relief as sunshine twinkled on a thin brown line ahead. The River Bulganek at last. The cavalry advance guard were already fording it, the 11th Hussars dismounting to water, but as he slowed for the bank he was disconcerted to see Lord Cardigan leading his own regiment straight on. True, it was their turn for scouting duty, but surely they'd stop to water first? Then he saw the smoke billowing from the house by the bridge, the flames just starting to take hold, and knew the Russians were only minutes ahead.

He plunged into the river, but Wanderer immediately jolted to a stop and bent his head to drink. Ryder dug in his heels and yelled 'Come on, damn you!' but the poor beast was desperate, and Ryder could only sit and watch in frustration as his regiment disappeared over a distant slope beyond. On a knoll to his right stood a gaggle of Staff with Lord Raglan, studying the land importantly through their glasses. What could they see? General Airey looked agitated.

Wanderer dipped beneath him, the bloody animal trying to roll, but Ryder pulled back hard on the reins. The Staff group was breaking up, an aide being summoned, something was happening, something was wrong. He tightened his legs, kicked in the spurs and drove the horse forward, through the water and out and up the bank. The enemy was ahead, his regiment going to meet them alone, and Ryder put down his head and galloped.

Cossacks again, whole dark ranks of them waiting on the opposite slope, and there was still no sign of Ryder. Oliver gripped his reins firmly and tried to hold on to the calm he'd felt last night. The Cossacks didn't look as many as yesterday, and at least this time they could face them all together. Lord Cardigan certainly looked supremely unworried, and Oliver saw him slap his thigh as he said something to his aide.

'Here we go, boys,' said Fisk. He yanked his gauntlet higher with his teeth and grinned wolfishly down the line. 'Let's get at them!'

Excitement was building like an orchestra tuning up, men fidgeting with bridles and carbines, leaning forward in the saddle as if that would bring the Cossacks closer. Cardigan kept them at the walk still, but Oliver felt his own thighs tense in expectation of the trot. The Russians were already starting to edge down the slope towards them, but he saw with alarm the numbers on the crest stayed the same, more and more of them coming up from behind.

'Two to one,' said someone, and Oliver heard the rustling as everyone looked up.

'T'ain't enough for Oliver,' said Jordan. His cheek bulged a little as he sucked on a peppermint. 'You like this sort of thing, don't you, chum?'

He didn't think he did. He'd dreamed of it last night, the hesitation when he couldn't make his hand move, and then the killing, the way the Russian had reeled back with his belly cut open, and how just for a moment the face looking back at him had been his own. Ryder had said it would be easier this time, but when he looked again at the Cossacks he saw with a jolt that the ones at the front carried guns. He knew what a single shot could do, he'd seen it yesterday when Ryder blew open a man's chest and someone alive was suddenly dead. Dead. The thump of Misty's hooves seemed very loud in the grass.

'Look,' said Jordan, and his chewing stopped. 'Don't think it's another ambush, do you? Look.'

More Cossacks appearing on the slopes to their left, a whole grey mass of them and the sun glinting off their lances. Oliver looked right and saw a shimmer of light over the slopes there too. More lances – or was it bayonets? Was there infantry there too? It *was* an ambush, bigger even than yesterday's, but still Cardigan was leading them on and on, deeper and deeper down into the valley below.

He jumped at the sound of hooves and turned to see Ryder taking up position on his right. Jarvis looked thunderous, and even Lord Cardigan scowled over his shoulder at the disorder in his line, but Oliver was too relieved to care. Ryder was back, and everything would work like before.

But there were more than before, too many even to sit on the crest. They were spreading, trotting from behind the rise to join up with other ridges, and the darkness of them blotted out all the sky. Oliver stared along the growing ranks with rising queasiness, wondering why they didn't charge, do it now, get it over with, and then a single orange flash cracked from the left of the enemy's line. Opening shot. They were engaged.

Cardigan signalled, the trumpeter called, they were halted before the next shots came. Another, then another, then a whole fusillade as the front line of Cossacks opened fire. Oliver felt himself twitching, waiting to be hit, but their own trumpet called again and he sprung his carbine with fumbling fingers. 'Bob and Joe', he knew the drill, he'd done it yesterday, why was it suddenly so difficult? He swung the barrel blindly in the direction of the Russians and pulled the trigger. He had no idea if he hit anyone, it no longer seemed to matter, one ball against so many hundreds. He groped in his pouch for the next cartridge and tried to think only of the drill.

The quiet after the volley was broken by the businesslike rattling of ramrods as everyone loaded at once. For a fleeting moment he thought of the Adams revolver in his haversack, but knew he must save it for when the Russians charged. There was no urgency yet, the Cossacks were too far away for their inferior guns to do much damage, and when Oliver glanced down their own line he saw not a man out of place. The firing was nothing, a bored exchange of courtesies before the main attack.

And everyone seemed so calm! Ryder had talked of the strength of the line, and now he was seeing it for himself. Moody looked positively supercilious, Fisk was muttering to Bolton – 'Tanner on that Cossack officer, what d'you say?' – and Ryder was gazing at the bare slopes around as if they were more interesting than the ones swarming with the enemy. He thought, 'It's only me. I'm the only one feeling – like this.'

Aloud he said, 'What are they waiting for? Why don't they charge?'

'Keep firing, Trooper,' said Ryder. 'They're not going to charge.'

Oliver turned to him in desperation. 'Why not?'

'It's another trap,' said Ryder, casually ramming his carbine. 'There's infantry behind. I saw them from the crest.'

Hope and panic tightened his throat. 'Then we'll withdraw, won't we? I mean Cardigan won't . . . He won't . . .'

The aristocratic bellow must have reached right to their rear. 'Draw swords!'

No. *No*. But his own hand was following the order, a year of discipline moving it all on its own, one more note in a single *shing* of steel. Swords drawn.

'Skirmishers in!' roared Cardigan. 'Trot – *march*!'

Oliver felt his heels dig in, and his mare carry him obediently forward towards the Russians. More shots banged towards them, and he saw Fisk jerk his head as if he felt a ball go past. They were closing the range.

But above the gunfire came another sound, a voice bawling

'Wait!' Hooves thudded behind them, and – oh thank God – Cardigan hesitated and turned, hand up to arrest the skirmishers in their advance. A frock-coated figure in cocked hat was galloping down their flank, a balding, full-bearded man with a jaw that jutted beyond the hat brim. Lord Lucan was commander of the whole cavalry, he outranked even Cardigan, he'd stop this madness and take them back.

'Face front,' said Ryder roughly. 'Face your bloody front.'

Oliver kept his eyes on the Russians, but all his attention was straining towards the angry voices of the British commanders, waiting for the order to withdraw. He heard more horses trotting up behind, but a glance back showed only the 11th Hussars forming to right of the regiment. No retreat. They were going to be made to stand their ground.

A trumpet, skirmishers recalled, but it was only to re-form with the others. The enemy was re-forming too, shifting and growing, two more columns joining from the sides, and the first ranks beginning to pour down the slopes like custard over a pudding. Beside him Fisk said, 'Dear Christ. Two thousand at least. Dear Christ.'

Dear Christ. Oliver was praying himself as they settled beside the 11th, a little body of cavalry four hundred strong, presenting to the enemy in a line only two ranks deep. Lucan and Cardigan were still arguing, but now he saw movement in the hills to their right, grey men bustling round something green. Misty flinched beneath him at the deep, soft boom, then a white puff of smoke drifted across the valley and Oliver saw it, round-shot, a black ball whizzing towards them, sailing over their heads and burying itself with a *crump* in the grass behind.

'Getting the range,' said Ryder. 'They'll do better next time.'

The second ball was closer, and the next ploughed clear into the ranks to their left, exploding in the flank of a horse three files along. Blood and flesh spat out like sparks from a cracker, and a fragment smacked wetly against Oliver's sleeve, gleaming in the dark cloth like a red jewel. He stared in disbelief at the cavity scooped inside the horse, as empty of organs as if a butcher had been at it. The rider was down and clutching his leg, but it was the horse he couldn't bear. Death that quickly, a living creature to just a mound of skin and skeleton; it mocked everything that kept them upright inside their uniforms. Another ball, this time striking in the Hussars, but Oliver couldn't even look.

'Steady, Trooper,' said Ryder.

Oliver turned violently. 'But why are we just standing here? Why don't we retreat?'

'Because we can't,' said Ryder patiently. 'Not without support. We turn now, and they'll have us. We've got to front or we're done, us and that whole exhausted column of infantry behind. They're not ready, Polly, we've got to buy them time.'

Oliver tried to take comfort in the glory of dying to save the army, but the images were stale and cold, his name being read out at the School and it not mattering because he himself was a heap of stinking blood and guts on a field in the Crimea. Heroes didn't count the cost, but he knew now he wasn't one of them and never would be. The Cossacks ahead were taunting them, voices and gestures saying 'Come on, come on, are you scared?' and Oliver knew his own answer was 'yes'.

'Ah, fuck off, you stupid bastards,' murmured Ryder. 'We're not going to play.' He seemed quite unbothered, but Oliver had never heard him use such a word, and his hand was clenching and loosing against the hilt of his sword. It was as if he too were desperate to get it over, as tense as Oliver himself.

Another ball crashed into their ranks, and now he saw it all around him, the same apparent calm belied by taut faces and nervous gestures. Jordan was still chewing, but his jaw was grinding faster than usual and his face was pale. Bolton was fondling the ears of his beloved Bobbin, but the mare was tossing her head at the unusual agitation of his fingers. Jarvis looked as impassive as ever, but as Oliver watched he saw the tip of a pink tongue creep out to flick over dry lips. They all felt it, all of them, and their officers clearly knew it. They were speaking to the men, calming them like frightened horses, 'Steady, lads,' 'Steady there,' 'Steady.' Even Cornet Hoare sat upright in his saddle and said 'Steady, men' in a voice that hardly trembled, and Captain Marsh turned round to smile at him with kindness in his eyes. Oliver was filled with a kind of wonder. Even their officers were hiding fear like his own, but with the realization came a sudden understanding of what courage really was, and that he himself might have it too.

The knowledge roared up inside him and blasted out the fear in an extraordinary light-headedness. Ryder was right, this was the line, and he was part of it. One of the Hussars yelled an insult at the Cossacks, and suddenly Oliver was shouting too, 'Give it up! Go home, you rotten cowards!' They were all at it now, all yelling, some laughing, and Albie Fisk bared his elbow to make a gesture quite shocking in its crudity. Another ball smashed into their line, and Sergeant Priestley reeled back in the saddle with his leg in bloody ribbons, but somehow he still moved his horse through the ranks to Cardigan and said 'Permission to fall out, sir?' His foot hung from his leg by only a strip of skin, he was mutilated for life, but the 13th laughed and clapped, and Oliver clapped too, crying 'Bravo! Oh, bravo!'

Another boom, closer and off to their left, but the smoke was behind them and the soft *crump* of impact threw up a spray of earth at the feet of the Cossacks themselves. Men turned in a single movement, wild hope on all their faces. 'Our guns!' they were saying. 'Our guns at last!' They were only the little 6-pounders of the Light Brigade's own Horse Artillery, but Captain Maude was with them and the next ball whizzed with an almighty crash into one of the Russians' own cannon. It must have been loaded, and for a glorious second the sky flashed orange as the muzzle exploded. Fisk cried, 'Oh, you give it to them, you lovely buggers, go on and give them *hell!*'

It wasn't only their own guns. Behind them the Light Division artillery were unlimbering, big 9-pounder pieces, and behind them, dear God, infantry. More cavalry too, the Lancers were coming, the 8th Hussars, they had support at last, *support*. It came from the very top, for riding down their left flank was a frock-coated staff officer, General Airey himself, along with an ADC in 15th Hussars uniform with a distinctive tiger-skin saddlecloth. The dashing Captain Nolan, the man who knew so much about cavalry he'd even written a book about it. Ryder leaned forward in his saddle, and Oliver heard him say softly, 'Now then, you bastards, now it's *our* turn.'

Their cannon boomed again, and excitement bloomed in the fire of it. The Cossacks were still shooting, but seemed suddenly as harmless as children throwing stones. Nolan called to a friend in the Lancers, 'They're damn bad shots, ain't they?' as if the whole thing were a wonderful game, and for a moment Oliver felt he agreed. The danger didn't matter any more, not now they had a chance to hit back.

But Airey was speaking clearly and authoritatively to Lucan, he was making sweeping gestures, and Oliver felt disbelief wavering through their ranks as they understood. Their infantry were here, they were ready to fight – and Raglan was ordering them to retreat. The rush of excitement banged in his head with nowhere to go, then settled slowly into a lump of nausea in his stomach. Yet again they were running away.

A moment later and it was done. The trumpets called the withdrawal and round they went, round, turning their backs on the enemy just as they'd done yesterday. Their retreat was dignified, but the Cossacks knew they were running, and the sound of jeering laughter followed them all the way back over the hill. Even their own infantry knew it, and he couldn't miss their broad grins and cheerful insults as they marched by. 'Too hot for you, is it?' called a Connaught Ranger. Another just said 'Useless peacock bastards' and spat.

The shame was unbearable. For cavalry to go to the rear! He hoped they still might get their chance, that the skirmish might develop and the cavalry be called back, but the firing grew more sporadic and after a few minutes it stopped altogether. Messengers reported the Russians were retreating beyond the next river, and the whole thing was over with hardly a casualty. The infantry came marching back, smug with the look of men who'd seen their opponents flee the field, and Oliver couldn't look them in the face.

'There'll be another chance,' said Ryder, slamming his sword viciously back into the scabbard. 'There always is.'

Perhaps there would be, but it didn't change what had happened here. Ryder had been right, nothing could have broken that line until their own commanders had done it for them. Oliver had fought through fear into courage and he'd done it under fire, but the sensation of running from the enemy was the same as it had been yesterday, and he was left with only the fear that he'd never be able to face them again.

As dusk fell they withdrew on the river to bivouac in line of battle, and Ryder's spirits rose. They'd advance in the morning when the army was rested, and this time they'd be ready to fight. The Bulganek had been a washout, but this next river, the one the Russians were waiting at, that would be the real thing. He heard its name bandied round the picket lines as he fed Wanderer from the forage net. 'The Alma,' men said. 'The River Alma.' He pictured it on the maps, a thin blue line running across the road to Sebastopol. The Alma.

'Ryder,' said Jarvis. They'd just sat under cannon fire, but he stood in all the formality of the parade-ground. 'A word, *if* you please.'

Oh God, yes, the business with the water, he'd disobeyed another order. The night before a battle, and Marsh was going to fret about another five-bob fine. He said politely, 'Am I under arrest, Sar'nt-major?'

Jarvis smiled. 'Not yet. Lord Cardigan has complained and Colonel Doherty wants to see you himself.'

Doherty! 'Oh, come on, Sar'nt-major, for giving the men some water?'

Jarvis's smile grew. 'The charge is absent from your post at a time of war.'

Ryder stared. 'I was with the army. I was just behind you, for God's sake . . .'

'Explain to the colonel,' said Jarvis. 'At the double now, move!'

Ryder allowed himself to be marched away in a nightmare daze. He was vaguely aware of Oliver's white, shocked face as they passed, but everything else was dim, a background to frantic thought that finally sank into a sick inevitability in his belly. Maybe darkness and the invisibility of rank would save him, maybe it would be better if it didn't, but either way he knew he was finished.

At least Doherty had a tent, and the interview could be held in private. Jarvis marched him in, snapped a salute that made his body vibrate like a tuning fork, and bellowed, 'Prisoner under charge, Corporal Ryder, *sir*!' Ryder slammed his thumb into alignment with his overall stripe, fixed his eyes on the splodge in the canvas where the flag would have been, and saluted in the general area of the man seated on a camp stool in front of him.

There was a moment's silence. Then, 'Thank you, TSM,' said the clipped, well-remembered voice. 'You may stand down now. I'd like to speak to the prisoner alone, if I may.'

Ryder's last hope died. He heard Jarvis's withdrawal and the rustle of the tent flap as it closed behind him, and only then did he lower his eyes to the man on the stool.

'Hullo, Harry,' said Colonel Doherty. 'I think it's time we had a little chat, don't you?'

5

19 September 1854, 6.30 p.m. to 8.30 p.m.

Ryder stood still and tried to keep a grip on reality. It would have been easier out in the open, but the tent shrieked its familiarity with the old world, the Englishman on campaign, everything he thought he'd left behind for ever. Doherty even had a table in front of him with a battered writing desk, two brass candlesticks, and a little ormolu clock that ticked as bravely as if it were in London or Delhi.

'Sit down, won't you?' said the colonel. 'Can't have a conversation while you're looming over me like the Wellington Arch.'

There was only a plywood box labelled HUNTLEY'S BISCUITS, but it seemed no more dreamlike than everything else. He sat and said, 'I'm not asking for anything, sir.'

Doherty was rummaging in a bag, and came up with a red face and a bottle of amber liquid. 'No, but I am, d'you see? So have a drink and maybe you'll tell me what the dickens you're doing in my regiment masquerading as a corporal.'

The drink smelled of whisky and an afternoon he never wanted to live again, but it was a kindness in the circumstances and he managed a small sip.

Doherty looked doubtfully at his own glass. 'Awful rotgut, isn't it? Don't know what St James is coming to.' He sat back, swilled the whisky as if to clean his glass with it, and said, 'I was sorry to hear about your father. Damn shame.'

Ryder looked directly at him for the first time. The jutting beard was greying now, the hair combed flat into two ragged wings, but it was the same determined jaw and kindly eyes he remembered in the man he'd been brought up to call 'Uncle

Charles'. 'You don't believe he actually did what they say, do you, sir? Can you imagine my father cheating at cards?'

Doherty said gently, 'I couldn't imagine him killing himself either.'

Ryder stared into his glass. 'He didn't do it because he was guilty. He did it because he'd lost his job and the means to pay his debts, and because he'd been abandoned by the army that had been his whole life.'

A trumpet was sounding in the camp outside, calling the picquets to parade. Feet pounded past the tent and distant voices barked familiar orders.

Doherty shifted on his camp stool. 'You weren't there, were you? Burma, I'd heard.'

Ryder nodded. 'We couldn't afford a cavalry commission, I went out as an ensign in the 80th Foot. I got leave after Myat Toon's stockade and went home to India, but my father was dead when I got there. I found him.' The sourness of whisky blended with the stench of memory in his mouth, and he had to put the glass down fast. Grass tickled his fingers, and he rubbed them violently against his coat to drive away the ghost of a sensation he knew would be with him till he died.

Something cracked in the silence, a flicker of light, and Doherty touched a lucifer to the candle in the second stick. 'Servants? Surely someone . . . ?'

The phosphorus smell was overwhelming in the confines of the tent, but Ryder welcomed it for driving out the other. 'Only the butler. He'd let the rest go. I had to sell my commission to pay the creditors, along with the house and furniture and everything else. And there was Ramesh, of course, I had to see him provided for.'

'Of course,' said Doherty drily, and blew out the match. 'But yourself? Why didn't you take a commission with the Indian Army? You don't need money for that.'

He almost smiled. 'I needed a respectable background and a father who hadn't been thrown out of his regiment. I worked my passage to England and enlisted there instead. It's all I know, sir. Horses – and the army.'

Doherty nodded. 'But why the 13th, hey? Even with that ridiculous name I was bound to spot you in the end.'

'It was listed under Colonel Lygon, I didn't know until it was too late. Even then I thought it was safe.' He deliberately kept his voice light. 'Who bothers to look closely at a private soldier?'

'I do if he insists on drawing attention to himself,' said Doherty. 'I spotted you on yesterday's patrol.'

He suppressed the jolt of panic. 'Did you tell anyone, sir?' If Marsh knew it would be round the troop in a week. Fisk, Jordan, Prosser and Moody, they'd all know him for what he was, the gentleman serving in the ranks, the butt for anything they chose to throw at him. And as for Jarvis . . .

'No, I didn't,' said Doherty. 'But you should have foreseen it, Harry. You've not changed that much, and of course you're the image of your father.' He stroked his beard thoughtfully and studied Ryder's face. 'But are you like him in other ways, hey? That's the question.'

Ryder stayed wooden under the examination. 'Sir?'

The colonel leaned back on his stool. 'This disobeying orders, causing trouble, all this would be anathema to your father. He loved the army.'

He couldn't keep the bitterness out of his voice. 'And look what it did to him.'

'What some men did, perhaps,' said Doherty. 'But it's still the same army he loved, and it's still the finest in the world.'

'It could be. If the men were treated properly, if our commanders knew what they . . .' He brought himself up sharp. 'I'm sorry, sir.'

Doherty gave a gentle wave of his hand, dispelling the outside world, keeping him in Meerut yarning over a *chota peg* with Uncle Charles. 'No need. We all know Lord Raglan's an old man. Splendid gentleman, of course, but all he knows is Waterloo and what the Great Duke would have done. He will keep calling the enemy "the French".' He frowned briefly at his whisky glass, then cleared his throat loudly. 'But he's trying, my boy, he knows we need to adapt. He said the men needn't shave, didn't he, hey? Said they needn't wear their stocks.'

He thought of the man named Bloomer. 'The Light Division still wear them.'

Doherty grimaced. 'Sir George Brown goes his own way. So do half the others, and Lord Raglan's far too much the gentleman to damn their eyes and make them do as they're told. But he's not getting the support, d'you see, boy, not from them or Whitehall. Not enough money, not enough anything, and the whole commissariat riddled with incompetence. It's not so very different from India, Harry, you'll see.' His fingers were drumming angrily on the table.

For a moment Ryder glimpsed the Old Man's own frustration, the hand-to-mouth existence of a cavalry regiment on campaign. 'Then why are we here, sir? If Whitehall doesn't care? Don't tell me anyone really gives a hang about the Turks.'

Doherty grunted. 'Oh, I expect the Queen does, women are incurably sentimental. But we can't have the Tsar thinking we're back in the Crusades, can we, hey? Wanting to boot the heathens out of Jerusalem?'

He remembered Varna, the brutal way the Turks had treated the conquered Bulgarians. 'But what's it to do with us? We're not a police force for the world.'

The colonel didn't laugh. 'Someone has to be. But it's part of the Great Game, boy, the same old shadow fight with Russia, and this time we really do have to fight her. Let her get away with this, then next thing it's Afghanistan, and after that India. She has to be stopped.'

Ryder looked at the clock. 'The Great Game', Doherty called it, but in the next few hours men were going to be dying for it. He said dully, 'Well then, I suppose we'll stop her.'

'Oh yes,' said Doherty, brooding over his empty glass. 'If we're in time.'

Doubt. The forbidden thing, the always unspoken thing, the Old Man was saying it openly and Ryder felt jolted inside. 'In time?'

Doherty made an impatient gesture that almost swept his glass from the table. 'What do you think this is all about, hey? That patrol yesterday, burning the villages, that foolishness today at the river? They're trying to delay us, boy. They're not ready. If we let them dig in at the Alma they could hold us for weeks, and by the time we get to Sebastopol it'll be a fortress. We've got to smash through them tomorrow, and not stop for anything until we take that damn port and the job's done.'

Instead of which they'd sat for five days on the beach. 'You're right, sir. What we need is speed.'

'Yes,' said Doherty simply. He rubbed his hands over his face, then sat upright at the table. 'Speed – and the obedience of our soldiers.'

Ryder understood. He picked up his glass, placed it on the table, and moved to stand.

'No, no,' said Doherty, flapping his hand irritably. 'You're still Nick Standish's son and I'll help you if I can. Just tell me exactly what happened.'

The story seemed childish in his own ears now he was forced to put it into words. He heard himself say, 'I would have asked the cornet, but he was too far ahead.' He heard himself say, 'I heard the TSM, but he couldn't have seen what state the men were in.' He was damning himself with each and every word, and was soldier enough to know it.

'All right,' said Doherty when he finished. 'I understand. You thought you knew better than the sergeant-major, so you disobeyed his order. And that's why you're here.'

Ryder was confused. 'I thought Lord Cardigan . . .'

Doherty snorted, a splendidly explosive sound in the small space. 'Leave his lordship to me. I shall explain you were absent on other duties and behaved very properly when you saw our situation. I can help you that much.'

Ryder sat forward. 'Then I'm clear.'

Doherty sighed. 'No. Because of what you did with the water.'

It was unbelievable. 'Men were dying, sir. We were having to leave them behind. How could I –'

Doherty's hand flicked up for silence. 'Yes, yes, it was a damn fine thing you did, and a few of the infantry officers have said the same. The cornet even says he'd have given you permission if you'd asked – but you didn't, d'you see? The sergeant-major did quite right in the circumstances and enforced the cornet's last known order, which was to make all speed to rejoin the regiment. And you disobeyed him, Harry. You disobeyed a direct order.'

Ryder stared hard at his boots. Should men be allowed to drop and die in their ranks because their officers didn't know what they were doing?

'And it's not the first time, is it?' said Doherty. 'The TSM's authority has to be upheld, so I'm going to let him have your stripes.'

His stripes. The one thing the army had given him, the one single thing that separated him from the lowest, newest member of the whole damn army. 'But that's unfair.'

'No, it's not,' said Doherty sadly. 'No man can wear the Queen's stripes if he won't obey her orders. You know that, Harry, or you should do.'

The Old Man's face was implacable, and Ryder forced himself to silence. The ticking of the ormolu clock seemed suddenly unbearably loud, a reminder of a whole world lost.

Doherty gave a tiny grunt. 'Oh, I can see how hard it is, boy, of course I can. You're an officer, born and trained to it, and it's hard to take orders from an NCO. But if you can't do it then there's no place for you here. I'll get you your discharge and a passage home.'

Back to England. A job as a clerk, perhaps, sitting in a dusty room with a quill pen, and taking orders from someone he respected even less than Jarvis. 'No, sir. Thank you, but I'll stay.'

Doherty nodded. 'Then you must do it properly. No more

acting on your own initiative. No more disobedience. Not a foot out of line anywhere, do you understand? Not one.'

Be a good little soldier, say 'yes, sir', 'no, sir' to every single stupid order he was given. He closed his eyes and said, 'Yes, sir.'

'Good,' said Doherty. 'There's no need for a parade, just take the stripes off yourself and I'll call it good enough. But make your peace with the TSM, will you, for all our sakes? He's a good soldier, excellent record, twenty years with the regiment. You'd like him if you were his officer.'

Instead of a nobody under his command. Ryder stood without a word and awaited his dismissal.

Doherty stood too. 'All right, then. I'll write to Cardigan, I'll talk to Marsh and Jarvis, but remember I won't be able to help you a second time.'

Ryder stiffened. 'I wouldn't ask you to.'

Doherty tilted his head to one side and regarded him steadily. Then he said, 'I'll keep your secret, Harry. I'll tell Marsh you're only a slight acquaintance,' and held out his hand.

Ryder stepped back and saluted. 'Dismiss, sir?'

For a moment Doherty looked what he was, a tired old man on the eve of a battle. Then he dropped his hand and said, 'Yes, dismiss. You'll understand one day, and when you do we'll talk again. But for your father's sake I hope it's soon.'

Ryder didn't. For a little while Doherty had taken him back, reminded him of a world he used to be part of, but when he ducked out through the tent flap he was back in the one he had to exist in now. 'Out the way, Corporal,' said a young lieutenant bustling importantly up to the tent. 'Hop it back to your unit.'

Maybe he would if he had one, but he looked out over the whole grand army camped by the Bulganek and knew there wasn't a place in it anywhere a man like himself could belong.

Woodall joined the others jostling at the muddy river. He didn't fancy it in the slightest, but if he didn't pretend to fill his barrel like everyone else he'd never get a drink. His canteen was already full of clean well-water, but how could he touch it in front of the others when he'd already told Truman he had none?

'Bloody typical,' said 'Nasty' Parsons, sluicing water down his face and disgusting neck. 'Cavalry camping right on the river, and the rest of us chucked to the outside to protect them. That's what they get for being Raglan's pets.'

'They're not all bastards, mind,' said Jones, a soft-spoken ass Woodall secretly suspected of being Welsh. 'That Lilywhite today, he gave me a drink of his own barrel. Here, he knew you, Woodall, knew your name. Friend of yours, is it?'

He was going to say 'yes', but the stifled sniggering warned him in time. 'I know him, Jones. What of it?'

'Nothing, your lordship,' said Jones, grinning. 'I thought it wasn't likely.'

More giggling, like a pack of beastly street urchins. Woodall reached the stream, and stooped to skim the barrel delicately across the surface as if to avoid the muck swirling up from the bottom.

'Oh, give it here, for Gawd's sake,' said Truman, grabbing rudely at the barrel. 'Scoop now, filter after, we'll be here all . . .' He stopped, looked at the canteen, and shook it. The tell-tale swishing seemed suddenly louder than the river.

'Give that back,' said Woodall, reaching frantically. 'Get your filthy paws off, that's mine.'

'Have it,' said Truman, turning him a face hardened into brown stone. 'I wouldn't touch it to save my life.' He swung round to the others and waved the canteen aloft. 'Look here, boys, Woodall's been carrying clean water all day. Teddy Lloyd fainted from thirst right beside us, and look here!'

'It's river water,' panted Woodall. 'River, same as yours.'

'Is it?' said Truman, and tilted it so everyone could see the clear water that gushed down into the muddy Bulganek. Men's voices hushed to silence on the bank. Someone whispered 'Gawd'.

Truman nodded grimly and shoved it back at Woodall. 'Here,

take it. Wouldn't want to waste any more, would we? Not when it's *yours.*'

Woodall snatched it to his chest and scrambled back from the bank, stumbling away blindly over the grass. He *would* have given Lloyd water, it was Truman who'd said they'd got none and how could he deny it? It was Truman's fault anyway for trying to scrounge off him in the first place. It wasn't a crime not to spend his evening in stupid vulgar talk, but to walk alone to a village and sensibly get water for the morning. Why *should* he have shared it with Truman?

He was far enough away now. No one could see him as his knees sagged and he knelt helplessly in the muddy grass. He thought of his trousers and how he'd have to clean them before he slept, he thought of how the men would look when he faced them in the morning, and most of all he thought of Maisie and of home. Not that awful barracks, but real home, those two little rooms in Goodge Street, and Maisie seated at the upright, playing 'Woodman, Spare that Tree' with the lamplight on her face.

Another picture flitted over it, a candle flame flickering on brightly coloured cards and on the hands of the men who played them. He thought of the wide eyes of a fair-haired cavalryman who bounced with excitement as he said 'That's game, Woodall, that's game!' He thought of the slow, easy smile of a young High-lander who teased him in a way that seemed to mean something like liking. He thought of a dark-haired light dragoon slewed halfway off his saddle to hold out a canteen, saying 'Take it, take it, man, it's water', smiling and holding out his hand.

He had nothing to reach out with, nothing to give. When he looked up there was nothing to see but his own regiment hurry-ing back to their wretched bivouac with an eagerness that puzzled him until he saw the queues forming for the rum casks. There was no comfort there. No slaughtering tonight, and no new rations while the baggage train stayed in its own encampment. The plain was bare of trees, not even a stick to make a fire.

He looked back at the lines for the rum ration, and in the back of his mind he felt the first glimmering of an idea.

They did a grand job by Andrew Murray, with the minister to read the service and the pipes to play him into the earth. Not that it was much of a drop, scarce three feet, but it was more than was given some other poor souls, left behind to die alone. Andrew didn't die alone. He'd died on his friend's broad shoulder, quietly and no fuss, and it wasn't till Mackenzie laid him down by the river he even knew he was gone.

He knew it now. Andrew was with God and rejoicing, but Mackenzie was left with his feet on the grass of a muddy river in the Crimea and the knowledge the laddie would still be alive if he hadn't followed himself into the army. He'd a mother in Strathcarron, and what Mackenzie was to say to her he could not think. The officers would write her, but she hadn't her letters, she'd have to take what they wrote to the postmaster and have him put on his spectacles to tell her her boy was dead. Mackenzie's heart swelled in his body at the thought.

'Always the way of it,' said Farquhar as they walked from the grave. 'The Lord takes the best, and leaves us miserable sinners to drag on in our suffering.'

If Farquhar was anything to go by, then He certainly left the most miserable. Mackenzie hunched his shoulders and began to edge away from the crowd.

Old Lennox trotted after him. 'Come now, Niall,' he said, patting his elbow. 'Come back with the mess. MacNab has thistles gathered to make a fire; you need a wee dram and a warm.'

He didn't want to be treated like a bairn. He wanted Andrew, the frightened gillie who'd turned to the stalker in his first days to say, 'Help me, Niall, I'm scared Mr MacLaverty will turn me off.' He wanted Andrew Murray, who saw him as a man.

He said, 'Thank you, Mr Lennox, but I'll maybe bide a while till I'm fit company.'

Lennox said, 'When you're ready then, laddie,' and gave his

arm another pat before tiptoeing away with Farquhar and Mac-Nab. Mackenzie felt their pity of him like a wall.

'Mackenzie!' called another voice, brisk with purpose. 'There you are, I've been looking for you all over.'

A Grenadier Guard striding through the camp, and Mackenzie could not but smile at the sight of him. Only Woodall would wear his bearskin after dark. 'Are you well, man? There were a muckle of yours down on the march.'

'I'm fine, thank you,' said Woodall, avoiding the eyes of him as he had that first day. 'But here, look what I've brought us.' He opened his bundle to show staves of a broken rum barrel, and stood back with pride. 'There, look – firewood. No one else will have thought of that.'

The gestures spoke of showmanship, but the Guard's eyes held appeal and Mackenzie's heart was stirred. Old Lennox had a fire and he hadn't wanted it, but Woodall was offering him something else.

He said, 'That's a grand find now. Were you thinking we might . . . ?' He jerked his head back towards the river and the cavalry bivouac beyond.

Woodall shrugged carelessly. 'Well, if you've nothing better to do.'

Mackenzie never glanced back at the pitiful mound of earth behind. 'No,' he said, and smiled at the man. 'I've nothing better to do at all.'

The Bridge House was daunting after dark. Only a few hours ago it had been someone's home, but now it was a heap of charred and ash-strewn timbers with jagged spars sticking out over the blackened stones. No one would camp here, it offered the only privacy in the bivouac, and right now that was what Ryder wanted. He sat down on a flower tub, took off his coat, and dug out his knife.

The yellow chevrons were sewn on tight, but he wriggled the blade under the first stitches and pulled them away clean. What did it matter anyway? The stripes had never given authority to change anything, only the duty to enforce orders that would get men killed, and the responsibility to take the blame when things went wrong. He ripped them both away and turned to the second sleeve.

This one was harder. The first stitch was browned, bloodied where he'd pricked his finger as he sewed it on. He remembered the pride he'd taken in it, a laughable thing in a man who'd once worn an officer's epaulettes on his shoulder. Not now. He tore through the last stitches, ripped away the chevrons, and clenched them in his hand.

Footsteps crunched in the debris. A thick shadow took shape as it passed by the lamp on the bridge, but he'd have known who it was anyway. Wherever he'd hidden, Jarvis would have hunted him down.

'I'll have those,' said the sergeant-major. His palm stretched out whitely in the gloom. 'The quartermaster will want them for the next man.'

They were both off duty, and Ryder handed over the stripes without bothering to stand. 'There, Sar'nt-major. Does that make you happy?'

Jarvis looked down at the crumpled cloth, then closed his hand over it in a fist. 'You should never have had them. Never.' His eyes came up again, and Ryder was surprised at the lack of triumph in them. 'You have to earn things like these, Ryder. You have to give yourself to the army if you want her to give anything back.'

Sod the army, he'd given it enough. 'If you say so, Sar'nt-major.'

Jarvis thrust the chevrons in his pocket. 'You don't care what I say, do you? You think you're above the whole lot of us.'

Ryder leaned back against the blackened wall, and felt the warmth of it through his coat. 'If you say so, Sar'nt-major.'

Jarvis was very still. A haze of smoke floated from the ruins and drifted between them like grey breath. 'I know so. I've known it since you first showed up at the Depot. But it won't do you a bit of good now. You'll do what you're told now. And if you don't I'll have the skin off your back before we throw you out in the gutter. You got that?'

'If you say so, Sar'nt –'

The crop shot out to smack against his jaw. The pain of it throbbed like toothache, but Jarvis kept the whip there to hold his face steady and lowered his own to speak right into it. 'And there'll be no more of that, do you understand?'

Worse than on the beach, harder than on the beach, but the penalty for resistance was still to be stripped and reduced to butcher's meat in front of the whole regiment. He swallowed hard and forced out the words 'Yes, Sar'nt-major.'

The crop stroked gently down the line of his jaw and was lifted away. 'Yes, Sar'nt-major,' said Jarvis, and rocked back on his heels. 'Yes.' He looked down at Ryder with evident satisfaction, hitched his overalls over his paunch, then turned and swaggered away.

Ryder didn't move. It was much easier just to stay where he was, gazing at the ruins and looking out over the patches of fire in the British bivouac. Sally would be there somewhere, making her husband's tea. He listened to the distant army noises on the evening air: faint raucous laughter, the barking of an NCO in a picquet, splashing from the river as the Horse Artillery watered, a woman haranguing someone, and far off in the Second Division the tune of a flute. They never changed, those noises. He'd been hearing them his whole life.

He reached in his haversack and drew out the gun. His father's Navy Colt, the one he'd picked up from the bungalow floor where his father's hand had dropped it. It was a beautiful piece, an officer's gun, almost the only thing he hadn't sold. He half-cocked it to spin the cylinder, five chambers greased, the sixth empty for safety, ready for action, ready. He paused a moment, weighing it in his hand. What had his father been thinking when he last held it? What was the final, final thing, the last unbearable image that made him pull the trigger?

Hooves clattered in the darkness, a horseman turning for the bridge. Ryder stood slowly, then caught a gleam of gold from the forage cap, and thrust the gun behind his back. The officer turned his head at the movement, the lamp glowed between them, and in the face of a stranger Ryder saw the start of recognition.

He knew at once who it had to be. The grey horse and blue saddlecloth of the ADC who'd been with them on patrol, the same clean-shaven face, but the recognition meant he was that other man too, the one who'd sat under a wagon in the rain and taught them the game they called 'bridge'. It had been him then, it was him again now, and as if to prove it he gave Ryder a friendly nod.

An officer, an ADC on the eve of a battle, and he paused to acknowledge a lowly cavalryman standing in his shirtsleeves. Something sparked in Ryder, and before he could stop himself he called 'Good luck tomorrow, sir!'

The horseman checked, and looked over his shoulder. 'And to you, Corporal!' he said, laughing. 'And to you!'

He was off again at once, but left behind the echo of that laughter, the natural exuberance of a man on the brink of a battle. As Ryder watched him ride away he became aware that the village too was alive with anticipation, gallopers pounding towards the bivouacs, staff officers flocking round the Post House where Raglan's entourage had set up base. Another ADC turned left at the bridge and galloped towards the distant white tents of the French. This was it, this was business, two armies readying themselves for battle.

But there was a third, and when he lifted his eyes to the slopes beyond he felt his breathing stop. Against the dark folds of the distant hills bloomed little orange blobs, haloed with light. The Russians on the heights beyond the River Alma, sitting round fires of their own. The Russians, waiting for them.

His hand tightened on the butt of the Colt. There was the real enemy, and he didn't need anything more. Smash through them, Doherty had said, and now the prospect filled him with elation. Those jeering Cossacks, the sneers of their own infantry, all of that would be wiped out tomorrow. Perhaps everything would.

Sullivan was right, and in the end there was only this, the one thing that never left him, the need of and joy in a fight.

He looked curiously at the gun in his hand, then stuck it back in the haversack and slung on his coat. As he set off back for the bivouac he began to whistle.

Oliver stared intently at the kettle, and wished Prosser and Moody would just go away. They'd never liked Ryder, and everything they said was a beastly gloat.

'Should have been a whipping really,' said Moody's voice above him. 'But he's lost his pretty stripes, the sar'nt-major says so.'

Bolton made a tutting noise, but Fisk gave an amused snort. 'Serve him right. Let's see him drill like everyone else, eh? Won't be so many of the funny remarks *then*.'

Would the kettle never boil? He'd had to make the fire out of thistles and dried cow manure and the flame was hardly stronger than a candle.

'What do *you* say, Pretty Polly?' said Prosser, and a boot nudged him in the ribs. 'You think it serves Ryder right?'

A familiar sick feeling began to ache behind his breastbone. They'd had people like Prosser at school too. 'It's not my business, is it?'

'Yes it is,' said Prosser, and the boot was harder this time. 'You took him supper last night, you little toady, we saw you. You think it serves your pal right?'

He wasn't going to lie, not for a thug like Jake Prosser. 'No. Men were dying, Ryder helped them, I wish I'd done the same.'

Prosser's mouth fell open, but Moody's tightened to form a line in his face like a slit. 'Disobeyed orders, Oliver? You don't mean you wish that.'

The danger suddenly hit him, he saw it in Bolton's widened eyes and tiny shake of the head. He said hesitantly, 'I just wish the orders had been different, that's all.'

Moody smiled. 'You think the sar'nt-major gave the wrong order?'

'Ol-Pol,' said Bolton urgently. 'Ol-Pol, look, the kettle's boiling.'

Moody stepped in front of him. 'Well, Polly Oliver?'

Oliver blinked at him, trapped. 'I . . . I don't know. I just wish things had turned out differently.'

There was something almost inhuman about Moody. His hair was slicked back so neatly it might have been painted on, and his eyes had the grey flatness of stagnant water. 'Then you're a fool. Don't you realize there's a corporal's vacancy now? You could be in for it, you've got good-conduct, same as me. Don't tell me you'd throw that away for a cocky jumped-up bastard like Harry Ryder.'

'Who's a friend of mine,' said a tranquil voice. Moody jumped back, and into the firelight stepped red and white stockings, a Black Watch kilt, a red coatee, and above them the curly hair and calm smile of Niall Mackenzie.

For a second Oliver couldn't speak. Even Moody was visibly taken aback, and could only twitch his shoulders and say 'Oh, really?'

'That's right,' said Mackenzie kindly. 'And I don't just like what you were saying.'

Prosser shoved straight through to Moody's side. 'And who do you think *you* are, barging into a private conversation? You can't just –'

'Brigade of Guards,' said another voice, and a Grenadier Guard loomed out of the dark, bearskin-tall and ramrod-straight and quite unmistakably Woodall. 'Her Majesty's Brigade of Guards, so don't be giving us any of your lip.' He dumped a bundle on the ground, sniffed in distaste, and said, 'Here, Polly, why does your fire smell of cow shit?'

Fisk stared, Bolton edged discreetly away on his knees, but Oliver just said 'Hullo, Woodall' and grinned.

'Guards!' said Moody, and gave an unconvincing laugh. 'You're infantry in the cavalry camp, that's what you are, and you'll catch it hot if you throw your weight about here.'

Woodall's face froze in disbelief, but Mackenzie laid a calming hand on his arm. 'Losh, man, we're all of the same side, and a battle coming. Let's save it for the heathens.'

His tone was peaceable, and Prosser clearly sensed weakness. 'I thought you Sawnies were supposed to be good at brawling. Savages, aren't you? Like a fight?'

Mackenzie smiled slowly, and Oliver stopped wondering how someone so soft-hearted could be a soldier. 'Aye, we do. If there's a man worth the fighting.'

Prosser stepped backwards, and that menacingly scarred face was suddenly only the badge of a man who'd suffered smallpox. 'All right. All –'

'No, it's not all right,' said Moody venomously. 'He's insulting us, and I'm not having it.' He looked round the bivouac and called to his own mess. 'Here, look, here's fun! We've got infantry come to take a pop at the regiment!'

He made it sound like a rag, and Jordan whooped as he leaped to his feet. They were all coming, Trotter and Blackwood too, and for the first time Mackenzie looked uncertain. Woodall said nothing, but reached down into his bundle and brought out a stave of wood.

Oliver scrambled quickly to his feet. 'It's nothing, Telegraph. They're just my friends, that's all.'

'They're infantry,' said Moody, swinging round to address the crowd. 'You heard them this afternoon, didn't you? "Useless peacock bastards"? They think we're scared to fight.'

A low noise like a growl rumbled from the troop, then into it strode a tall dark figure with an air of assurance that parted the crowd like smoke. 'Do stop shouting, Moody,' said Ryder. 'You'll wake the bloody Russians.'

Ryder himself, as confident as if none of this had happened and it was all a ghastly mistake. The tension broke at once, and Jordan burst out laughing.

Moody reddened with fury. 'Not me, Ryder, it's these friends of yours trying to stir up trouble.'

Ryder looked at him for perhaps two seconds, then turned to

the crowd. 'Jordan, Trotter, Fisk, Bolton, were my friends causing trouble?'

He spoke with a new authority, he spoke like an officer, but when Oliver glanced at his sleeve he saw only the dark cloth and ragged threads of a man with no rank at all.

'No, chum,' said Jordan hastily. Bolton shook his head violently, and even Prosser mumbled and looked away.

'Thank you,' said Ryder. 'Now crawl back under your flat stone, Moody, I've got friends to see.'

Moody was looking at those sleeves. 'Stow it, Ryder, you're no one now. You're not a corporal, you don't tell anyone what to do.'

Ryder took a step forward, just one, and said softly, 'Come on, Moody. Do you really think I need stripes to deal with *you*?'

Oliver had never seen his eyes so dark. It was almost as if he wanted a fight, really hoped for it; he looked as if he wanted nothing else.

Moody's face was yellow. His eyes flicked to the unmoving crowd, then he swallowed and said, 'No. Look, it was just a rag, that's all.'

Ryder went on staring at him for a moment, then his shoulders relaxed. 'A rag?' he said lightly. 'Well, next time you want one you know where to find me, don't you?' He turned his back and strolled to the fire.

The crowd broke up with a murmur of laughter. Moody stalked away with Prosser, and Oliver saw with relief that they walked past Jarvis's fire without stopping. He realized with surprise that nothing had really happened anyway, it was only people being silly because they all felt tense.

And already everything was back to normal. Woodall looked complacent again, and was actually giving his stave of wood to Bolton, saying 'Here, try this for your fire. You'll find it smells better than cow dung.' Fisk was offering coffee, clearly keen to make amends, but Ryder said, 'It's all right, thanks, Albie, we're too many to barge in on you,' and set off to the bank to set up a base of their own.

Oliver never doubted which one he should go to. Woodall and Mackenzie were back, as he should have known they would be, as if they were meant to be a group and together. He watched Mackenzie blowing ferociously on the kindling to get the wood to light, he watched Woodall swinging a heavy kettle as he sauntered back from the river bank, he watched Ryder sprawl on the ground and say, 'Don't suppose any of you bastards thought to get my rum ration,' and felt a warmth inside that defied the cold of the Crimean night.

He rummaged in his haversack and produced the brandy. 'Would anyone like . . . ?'

'You wonder, Polly!' said Ryder, sitting up fast. 'I thought you'd let that go back in your valise.'

Three mugs together were thrust at him and as he poured a generous tot in each he thought of Ronnie and how happy he'd be to see the pleasure his gift was giving. He said, 'I thought we might want it. With a battle tomorrow . . .'

They were quiet a moment, and all their heads turned to the horizon, the dark forbidding slopes and gleam of the Russian fires as they waited on the heights above the Alma.

Mackenzie said, 'I wonder what they're thinking tonight. Are they doing like us, do you think, sitting by their wee fires and wondering how it will go on the morrow?'

'Well, we're not,' said Ryder. He looked strong and confident and the firelight played orange on his unshaved cheek. 'Build up the fire, Woodall, and let's get that kettle on. Now if only we had the cards . . .'

But they did. Oliver had kept them, and he dug feverishly in his haversack to bring them out in triumph. 'We have, look.'

Ryder gave a sigh of pure satisfaction. 'Brandy, fire, coffee on the way, and a battle in the morning. Cut the cards, Polly. Let's play.'

6

20 September 1854, 3.45 a.m. to 3.30 p.m.

Reveille was silent that morning. Men shook their sleeping neighbours and dragged themselves to horse without the aid of either drum or trumpet. It was black dark and two hours before dawn.

The troop groomed their horses in eerie quiet. Ryder listened to the swish of brushes and jingling of bits and felt the sensuousness of ordinary actions performed perhaps for the last time. It was there in the warm velvet of Wanderer's flank under his hand, the slippery smoothness of a buckle, his own quickened heartbeat and the sense of something coming.

It was in the village too, when they went to complete forage. The wind was up, an empty bucket rolling and clattering over the farmyard cobbles, and a dog in the corner barking at nothing. Lamps were lit in the Post House and staff officers passing in and out with a banging of doors, while from out towards the sea came the distant sound of trumpets. 'Oh damn and blast the French,' said a harassed quartermaster, clutching his hat against the wind. 'Do they want *everyone* to know?' He caught Ryder's eye and scowled.

The sky was lightening behind them as they took their beasts to water. It made dark silhouettes of the long line of motionless horsemen, and spread colour over the muddy Bulganek until the whole river seemed to gleam deep red.

Woodall was determined today would be different. He'd little in common with his own mess, of course, and common was the right word for most of them, but last night had left him with a lingering feeling that a battle might be better if you went into it with the support of the men around you. He got up earlier than anyone, started the only fire in the bivouac, and made coffee for the lot of them.

'No, thanks,' said Truman, walking straight past. 'Don't think so, comrade,' said Parsons. 'Teddy Lloyd died in the night, didn't you know?' Jones said nothing, but he'd been a chum of Lloyd's and his silence was somehow worse. Woodall drank coffee by himself and felt sick.

But he'd tried, and when they ranked for the march he told himself it was for the best. A man needed to be hard in a battle, and all that mattered was that he was surrounded by a wall of Grenadier Guards. Jones was still quiet and Truman gave him his shoulder, but Woodall stared at the dirty neck of Parsons in front, and tried to think only of his duty.

He listened to the tramping of feet as the first section of Rifles led off the column, thin blocks of green before their own triumphant red. It should have been themselves next, same as yesterday, but there were line regiments falling in now, the wretched Light Division taking the place of the Guards.

'Cannon fodder,' said Parsons, spitting tobacco juice on the grass. 'Think they'll let the Guards in first against cannon? Let the light-bobs take it, then the Guards can move in and mop up.'

The trumpet at last. Woodall stiffened his spine, waited for the ranks in front to loosen, then his own left foot came smartly forward and they were off. No bands today, which was a pity, but the dark blue legs marched in perfect step, the bearskins added feet to men's height, and he remembered how the rioting mobs back in London had turned tail and fled at mere sight of them.

But were the Russians rabble? 'Cannon,' Parsons had said, and last night Oliver had talked about 32-pounders in the field against them. He shrugged the thought away, but somehow the rifle on his shoulder felt lighter and frailer than it had, and he couldn't help wishing for Ryder or Mackenzie at his side. He marched as he'd wanted in a column of Guards, but even in the middle of it he felt completely alone.

*

They were awful late starting. Mackenzie was sure there'd be good reason for it, but they found the French sitting in the road waiting for them, drinking their morning coffee to while away the time.

Still there was no hurry, and it was a grand feeling to be marching all together, and the fleet keeping pace with them in the sea beside. The great guns of the ships had a longer range than any they trundled with them, and it was barely gone ten when Mackenzie heard them fire for the first time. He could not see what they fired at, but it would surely mean the Russians held their position all the way west to the sea. There was to be no going round.

They halted a mile and a half short of the river. He couldn't see much of it behind the village of Bourliouk straight ahead, but the dark belt of gardens and vineyards marked its path, and here and there he'd a glimpse of shining water. Not what he'd call a river himself, born and brought up by the Carron, but maybe the hot weather had shrunk it.

'It's a bonny name, mind,' he said. 'The Alma. Do you not think?' He turned for Murray's answer, but there was only gloomy Davey Farquhar in his place.

Farquhar never even looked round. 'Ask me after the battle.'

His words dropped clear and hard as pebbles, and for the first time Mackenzie realized how quiet it was. The whole army was silent, twenty-six thousand British soldiers and as many again of the French, all staring ahead with never a word to say. He looked back to the river, then lifted his gaze to the heights beyond and saw.

The Russians. He had thought them rocks at first, those dark grey patches like crags in the folds of the hills, but they were men, thousands of them, enough to blot out the green of the grass. Some were spread like a fringe across the crests and ridges, others clustered in great squares, some gathered behind what looked like little walls and earthworks, and here and there the patches hardened into rigid shapes like teeth. The single white road of the Causeway ran right through the middle of them, and Mackenzie's eyes followed it down from the heights, across the river, and right up to the feet of their own first column of red.

He rubbed his chin thoughtfully. 'Man, that's a pretty position.'

Farquhar didn't answer. No one did, and when a nearby horse let out an angry neigh thousands of heads turned towards it. Mackenzie gave up the idea of conversation, and studied the ground ahead with a stalker's eyes.

It was not so bad. The Russians had the high ground of them, they had cover in the folds of the hills, but there was not so very much in way of fortification. He let his gaze scan slowly from the road ahead westward to the sea, and noted a hill with a dark seam cut across it, earthworks thrown up in front of it like a redoubt, and maybe another smaller glacis up the slopes behind. Way off to right of it was a high crag with a half-built turret on its crown, maybe meant for a telegraph if the Allies had been slower getting here, but no earthworks, no wall, and not so many Russians on it either. Maybe they thought themselves safe there, with nothing to west of them but tall cliffs and beyond them the sea. Maybe they were afraid of the guns of the fleet. Twice it had fired now, like an honest man showing the enemy he was there. He wondered why it didn't fire again.

A voice called 'Loose cartridges!'

Mackenzie's heart leaped like a deer on a gun. He plunged into his pouch, tore open a packet with his teeth and shook the cartridges loose in the bag. They were all doing it, the rattling so loud it was a wonder the Russians didn't hear them. He grinned at Farquhar and said, 'We're doing it now, aren't we, Davey? This is really it.'

'Aye,' said Farquhar, his face queerly white. 'This is it.'

He wondered what they were waiting for. Maybe the commanders were still ordering the battle, for Lord Raglan himself was meeting with the French commander right in front of their lines. He was a poor, wizened creature, this St-Arnauld, men said he was sick and dying, but he'd the flag of their allies and the men cheered him as he came. It seemed to please the old fellow, for he doffed his own hat and quavered the words 'Hurrah for old England!'

Farquhar snorted. 'England, is it, ye fool? Who d'you think *we* are then – a bunch o' lassies?'

Mackenzie sighed sadly, and watched Lord Raglan adjusting his little telescope to study the heights. 'What will be the plan, do you think, Davey? What will we do?'

Farquhar snorted. 'The French are to the right, they'll go to the right, any fool can see that. We're for the left and centre, my man, we're for the big guns and the redoubts and the whole unholy Russian army.'

'Head on, you think?' Mackenzie looked at the wide slope descending gently ahead of them, open and clear all the way to the vineyards and the village. 'But there's no cover.'

Farquhar's face seemed to have no expression in it at all. 'There is not.'

The hooves of old St-Arnauld's departure seemed suddenly very loud. Mackenzie watched him travelling the full length of their own front line, past the Light Division, past the Second Division, past the first lines of the French, becoming no more than a tiny speck in the distance followed only by a cloud of dust. He took a surreptitious nip from his canteen but a flash of colour moved by the French lines and he paused with the water still in his mouth. Surely there were men marching forward down there, right on the edge of the sea. Were the French to try the cliffs?

He plugged his canteen, smiling at the canniness of the plan. That was why the fleet were silent. The French had seen the emptiness of the Russian left and were sending an attack force to take them by surprise. Maybe the French would take out the guns and there would be no need for themselves to march right in the face of them. Maybe the British were to wait and follow west, and there would be no advance at all over the open ground. Maybe . . .

Captain Cornwall's voice called through the silence. 'The regiment will load. With ball cartridge – *load*.'

Their musket butts struck the ground with a single decisive thump. Mackenzie stretched away the barrel with his left hand while his right dived for the cartridge, numbing his mind in the familiar drill. Other voices shouted ahead, a trumpet calling somewhere, but his business was with the Minié and the loading of it. Only when it was done did he look up to see the leading divisions already marching away towards the river, while the green-jacketed Riflemen spread into skirmish order at the fore. The Light Division, beyond them the Second Division, the whole front line was going in. There was no cover, the Russian guns were right above them, but Farquhar was right and they were still going in.

Into the space in front of them rode a single horseman. One look at the lined forehead, curly brown hair and obstinate jaw, and Mackenzie was at once at quivering attention. Sir Colin Campbell was of a different clan entirely, but he commanded the entire Highland Brigade and today he was Mackenzie's chieftain.

'Now, men, you are going into action. Remember this. Whoever is wounded – I don't care what his rank is – whoever is wounded must lie where he falls till the bandsmen come to attend him.'

Off to the sea came another muffled boom from the fleet, but Sir Colin never turned his head, and neither did Mackenzie.

'Don't be in a hurry about firing,' said Sir Colin, and Mackenzie's hand crept furtively back from his Minié. 'Your officers will tell you when it's time to open fire. Be steady. Keep silence. Fire low. Now, men, the army will watch us. Make me proud of the Highland Brigade!'

A bright calm settled over Mackenzie like a fall of snow. The 42nd started forward, his own 93rd followed as easily as parade, and he knew without looking the 79th would be right behind them. The Guards were advancing beside them, the whole First Division going in, and as their feet tramp-tramped into the grass

Mackenzie's spirit seemed to take off and fly out of the top of his own head, soaring like a lapwing into the clear blue sky.

Woodall knew he was going to die. It was madness, walking downhill towards those great guns without so much as a bush to cover them. He watched his own polished boots marching on in perfect step as if they weren't his own feet any more but some terrible machine impelling him forward to mutilation and death.

It was ahead of him already, the dull bark of muskets and sharp ping of the Minié as the skirmishers engaged in the vineyards. There was more of it in the village too, bangs and whining noises as balls ricocheted off walls. He risked a look up, but something like a black ball crashed into the Light Division ahead, earth flew up, smoke blew over, and when it cleared there was a hole in the line, a great ragged gap where men had been. He could see clear through it to the red debris on the grass.

He tore his gaze away and marched on, but this wasn't a column of Guards he was in any more, it was just a bunch of men. Jones's arm brushed against his as it swung, human and vulnerable as his own. Parsons's neck was sunburned and in the centre was a boil. A strange whizzing sound above the Lights, another loud crump, and . . . *dear God*, that thing flying through the air was a man's arm. Jones said 'Whew, that looks hot,' and his voice was suddenly precious, another man at his side. Woodall whispered, 'I'm sorry about Lloyd, Jones,' then said it louder and didn't care.

Two more strides, another ball smashed into the Lights, but as the boom faded he heard Jones say, 'Ah, it was cholera. Not all the water in the world could have saved him. Cholera, that's all.'

His feet faltered, found their step and marched on. Not his fault, just cholera, not his fault at all. He said 'Thanks, Jones' and meant it, and Jones turned to him and smiled.

The ground shook, the sky cracked like thunder, and the world in front was blotted out in a great whoosh of flame. Woodall's feet stopped, his ears went silent, then popped back into sound as men around him yelled 'The village, they've fired the village'.

Smoke billowed back over them, greying out the Light Division ahead. Musketry banged in the gloom, and then a deeper boom as a shell exploded in the midst of it, hurling out fragments of iron and a spray of crimson that seemed to hang in the air before splattering wetly on the men underneath.

'Canister,' said Corporal Gleeson. 'The nasty bastards, that's canister.'

Their feet were still moving, gleaming black boots striding bravely over the grass. Then trumpets sounded the halt, Woodall's toe knocked into Parsons's heel, and the whole column shuddered to a stop on the very edge of the carnage ahead. Relief trickled through him. The generals had seen this was mad, they were going to find another way round.

Voices ahead yelled in the smoke, 'Lie down, the 7th Royal Fusiliers, lie down!'

Lie down? But they were doing it, the whole Light Division, and off to their right the Second were doing the same. Woodall stared in disbelief as the whole assault line ducked to lie flat under the smoke, a prone and helpless target for the artillery above.

Then it was their turn. The Division was deploying into line, and Woodall moved in mindless obedience as the safety of the column split open and spread over the grass, leaving him at the front of a line only two ranks deep. He looked ahead at smoke and helpless men, he saw fire and blackness burst in the middle of them, and when the Guards too were ordered to lie down he did it almost thankfully, closing his eyes and pressing his forehead against the coolness of the grass. If he stayed very still maybe it would all just happen outside him. Maybe it would all just *stop*.

Oliver stared ahead and thought of the strength of the line. His file was almost on the end, but Bolton was his left-hand, Ryder his right, he was safe in the strength of the line.

Beyond Ryder he didn't dare look. The Light Brigade were only on the edge of fire, drawn up on the far left of the British front, but the infantry lay full out in the open to be pulped by the Russian guns. For over an hour now Oliver had sat useless in the saddle, hearing only the explosion of shell to his right and seeing only glimpses of movement as men jumped from the ranks to drag mutilated comrades to the rear.

He guessed what they were waiting for. Everyone did, and all along their line heads were turned towards the distant artillery thumping away down by the sea. The French advance attack had gone in, they were getting a foothold on the cliffs, but surely then it would be their own turn. Surely they wouldn't just be left here, watching the helpless infantry slaughtered right in front of them.

A boom and crash as another roundshot ploughed right into the support line of First Division. He said wretchedly, 'Woodall's in there. And Mackenzie.'

Ryder's head turned sharply. 'That's a block of our soldiers, that's all. Get any closer and you're done.' He looked away moodily, but after a moment Oliver heard him say, 'Mackenzie's all right, anyway; they're as far out as we are.'

It was true. When the infantry spread from column into line the ranks had bulged outward, shoving men further and further out to the east. The Highlanders were on the very far left of the First Division line, little black-and-red specks on the edge of Oliver's sight, surely out of range of the Russian guns. But the Guards weren't, Woodall wasn't, those were British Grenadiers lying on their stomachs like a carpet of red for the Russians to fire into as they pleased. Perhaps the commanders thought the smoke from the village would cover them, but the red must be showing through anyway, and Oliver bit his lip hard to stop it trembling.

'The Brigade will advance! Trot – *march!*'

At last. He dug in his heels and the line moved forward, advancing along the extreme edge of the field of fire. Some of the Light Division were starting to stand now, but others lay unmoving as the cavalry skirted round them, and one man had no head. Oliver forced himself to look past them to the burning village, at the flashes of gunfire in the vineyards, at the River Alma and the bank beyond, where finally they'd get their chance to fight back.

Bolton's mare reared in panic as the first shell exploded to right of them, and Oliver saw little red streaks raked across her flank from the flying splinters. He thought in sudden terror of his eyes, and tilted his head to the left, humping up his shoulder to protect his face. Roundshot blasted past, and poor Bobbin was in a frenzy, cutting right across him and cannoning into Ryder on the other side. For a second they were tangled, the three of them, Bolton crying 'Bobbin, no!' and Ryder's deeper 'Oh, for God's *sake!*' but something else was screaming, a high-pitched wail that ended in the explosion of a shell.

Misty's flank shook, the smoke turned black and red in front of his eyes, and a wet slurry splattered across his cheek. He kept going, scrubbing his sleeve furiously across his eyes, but when he took it away there was a gap to his side and Ryder was gone.

He slewed in the saddle. A bloodied brown mound lay behind, 8th Hussars cursing and skipping round it, but protruding from beneath were patches of dark blue.

'Keep steady, Oliver,' said Lieutenant Grainger from behind. 'You know the drill.'

But it was Ryder. It was his friend, it was Ryder. 'Sir, he might be alive.'

'Then the bandsmen will pick him up,' said Grainger. 'Front and ride on.'

He made himself do it, starkly aware of the emptiness on his right. Ryder said it didn't matter who was beside him, but he'd never imagined it would be nobody. He groped at the memory of that precious conversation, the gift Ryder had left to him, and realized what in the end it had to mean. *He* must be that man, the one on the outside who steadied the others, the one who saved the army by standing still. He dug in his heels more firmly and looked ahead to the shining brown line of the Alma.

Cardigan called 'Halt!' They were stopping again, hardly started and they'd stopped.

'Is it that we can't ford, do you think, Ol-Pol?' said Bolton. The river was only a sluggish stream, but it lay in a deep ditch with steep banks more than the height of a man.

'Must be a bridge somewhere,' said Jordan. His jaw was moving furtively, and Oliver was sure he could smell liquorice. 'Look, there's one of ours already over.'

The gleam of gold on a red saddlecloth caught Oliver's eye. A single rider on a bay horse was trotting casually up the slopes wearing the cloak and cocked hat of the British Staff.

'Doing the heroic,' said Fisk with a sniff. 'Trying to make it look easy.'

'Doing the stupid,' said Jordan. 'Silly beggar's all on his own. I bet he's got lost.'

Oliver didn't care if he had or not. The fact was he was alone and Lucan and Cardigan were making no attempt to cross after him. They weren't looking for a bridge, they were sitting scowling in their saddles, and it was clear that once again they'd been ordered to sit and do nothing.

The Light Division were going in now, he could see the blur of redcoats dashing past to the river and the battle and glory on the other side. He heard the hammering of musketry and the first splashes as the bodies fell. He sat in his blue coat on his beautiful grey horse and wished the enemy would fire on them, wished they would fire on *him* as he stayed steady in the saddle, ready to guard the nakedness of the line.

The ground was vibrating under his cheek. Ryder peeled open his eyelids against the crusted blood and strained to heave his head a couple of inches from the ground.

The world in front made no sense. Smoke billowed over cratered grass, and curious brown blobs leaped in and out of vision, whirling round and round like dervishes at Meerut. One bounded straight past him, and Ryder recognized the long whorled ears and flash of white tummy as it tore by. Hares, lots of them, blundering over the field in fear of the guns.

Guns. A howitzer shrieked overhead, and the crump shook the turf under his hand. Memory rushed back, and with it the realization he was pinned under a dead horse in the middle of a battlefield. Wanderer's face was untouched by the shell that had exploded in his flank, peaceful and out of it, thank God, but Ryder wasn't, and he thrust aside sentimentality to push at the carcase, wriggling his legs to haul himself free. His feet were tingling, his knees screeched in pain, but both were moving, nothing was broken. Wanderer's front legs had buckled under him when he fell, taking the worst of the weight off his master beneath.

It was still too much. If only he could get his chest free, dig in both elbows and really heave, but his free arm sunk weakly in the mud, his neck and shoulders tore from the strain, and impotence broke out in a sweat on his forehead.

But new sounds were approaching, growing closer, and Ryder twisted his neck to see a mass of dark blue legs and black boots thumping towards him over the grass. The infantry assault line was advancing at last, but the neat ranks were bunched and broken as the overlapped Light and Second Divisions jostled to re-form, and what was tramping towards Ryder was no more than a mob.

He supported his head on his elbow and tried to yell. Maybe someone would take a second in this chaos just to tug him free. He shouted again as the first men reached him, but his voice was lost in the blast of cannon, a careless boot kicked away his elbow, and his head thudded hard to the ground. Dazed and sick, he huddled back into the horse, frantically curling his arm round to shield his head, crying, 'I'm not dead, for God's sake!'

'You look pretty dead to me, pal,' said a voice, and a redcoat stooped in front of him. 'You're wearing half a horse on your phizog.' A lumpy fist reached out to shove his hair back from his eyes, and Ryder was looking into a face he knew.

'Thought so,' said Bloomer, nodding in satisfaction. 'Here,

Morry, give us a hand with friend Ryder. Gone and got himself dressed up like Smithfield Market.'

'Ah, but is he kosher?' said the dark man gravely, kneeling and laying down his rifle. One thin hand circled Ryder's wrist and the other slipped securely under his armpit. 'Kick your legs if you can, friend, I'm not the stripling I was.'

'That's the ticket,' said Bloomer. 'I'll lift the nag, you pull.' More redcoats were jostling and pushing past, but he swept a gigantic muscled arm at them, said 'Out the way, daisies!' then pressed his shoulder to the horse and heaved.

Ryder tensed for the pain, but his right foot kicked easily against the turf as the weight lifted, and he slid out as smoothly as a rod from a muzzle. His left foot throbbed abominably, his knees hurt to bend, and his ribs ached as he breathed, but with Bloomer and his friend supporting him he was able at least to stand. He straightened his crushed haversack and said, 'Thanks. Thank you, I'm all right.'

'Sez you,' said Bloomer, cramming Ryder's fallen shako back on his head. 'Come on, Morry, best foot forward, we're sucking hind tit.'

Ryder staggered between them, and by the time they reached the first house of the village he was able to stand unaided to lean against its wall.

'You'll be all right here, pal,' said Bloomer, watching the last Fusiliers disappear into the vineyards. 'There's muftis inside, journalists and the like, I seen them go in. Now if you'll excuse us hopping off, me and Moses are owed a scrap.'

Ryder tried to thank them, but Bloomer grinned through broken teeth, said 'We're square, that's all,' and loped away purposefully for the vineyard. Ryder saw that great-knuckled fist swinging by his side as he ran, and felt almost sorry for the Russians.

He wished he'd a fight of his own to go to, but there was no sign of the cavalry ahead, even if he could have joined them without a horse. He wiped his face with his sleeve and stumbled forward into the smoke-filled village.

A hard central road ran all through. Buildings still burned to either side, but others were stone-built and seemed only blackened by the smoke. White-plastered house fronts were chipped by balls, and green-jacketed bodies of Riflemen lay dead by the roadside, but the Russian skirmishers had already retreated over the river, destroying the bridge behind them. Across the bank Ryder saw only the blossoming yellow muzzles of Russian guns.

A shell smashed through a roof, and red tiles whizzed through the air to crash and ricochet off neighbouring walls. Something dark lurched screaming at his head, and he stumbled back into a doorway, but the object only brushed his shako and flapped harmlessly away. A bird, one of dozens reeling and swooping in the confusion of smoke. He turned for the open door behind him and staggered inside. Just a moment, that was all he needed, a moment to get his head clear and let the nausea and giddiness subside.

It was dark and gloomy, an abandoned house, the promise of a moment's peace. One dark corner seemed especially shadowy but his foot struck an obstacle before he reached it, a boot like his own, and he looked up into a pair of terrified and defiant eyes.

'Shh,' said the man, and a finger appeared in front of his lips. 'Don't want no one coming in, do we?'

A noise behind made him turn sharply before he recognized it as the shallow panting of a man in distress. He saw him then, the hunched figure with its hands clawing its shins into its body, the corn-yellow hair flopping wretchedly over the wringing, tortured hands. A boy, no more, but with the red sleeves and deeper red cuffs of the 33rd Regiment of Foot.

Ryder imagined what it must have been like, the terror of marching into the fire that burned away comrades either side, the seeming normality of houses, the open door like an invitation, a way back to the world lost. He cleared his throat and said, 'You'll feel better outside.'

'What would you know?' said the man in the corner, stepping aggressively forward. A 7th Fusilier, Bloomer's regiment, but in a different league of men. 'You wounded, are you, horseboy? It doesn't bloody show.'

Shame smacked Ryder in the face. He blundered to the door, and out into the smoke-filled air that seemed suddenly fresh in contrast. Across the road he saw surgeons bandaging men with torn and bleeding limbs, soldiers who'd gone down fighting with real wounds, not a cavalryman with bruises from falling off a horse. He'd done nothing in this war. He'd run from the Russians burning that village, he'd sat uselessly under fire at the Bulganek, and today he'd only watched men die. Bloomer had said he was owed a scrap, but so was Ryder, and by God he was going to have it.

The pain and dizziness clarified into hardness, he threw them aside and ran. The bridge was no good, but on his left loomed the fence of a vineyard, the way Bloomer had gone. He hurtled over it and crashed through the rows of staked vines, downhill towards the river, the rifle shots and splashing, the thump-thump of cannon, officers screaming orders. He snatched a bunch of grapes from a laden vine and bit into them as he ran. Sharp popping of skins under his teeth, then the sweet coolness of the juice down his throat, clean and reviving as fresh, clean water. He spat out the stalks, took another bite and ran on, dodging round the green bundles of dead Riflemen in his path.

Then there was colour ahead, redcoats swarming across the river, the last of the assault line crossing to the south bank. He slithered down the slope, and waded straight in. The bottom was slippery and the water cold in his groin, but he hefted his haversack higher and pushed on among the jostling crowd. Bullets whined and skipped over the surface and men dropped either side, pitching back to splash on their comrades behind. A red-coated body floated face-down in front of him, but he nudged it aside with his hip and waded on.

The south side was teeming with their own men, but the bank was steep and fortified with fallen trees, jagged branches sticking out like spears into the faces of men struggling to climb.

A sergeant of the 23rd Foot was straddling one of the trunks and leaning out a horny hand to help his stray lambs up the side. 'Up you come, my boys, welcome to the devil's playground.' Rifles pinged at them, and as Ryder clawed his way up the bank a load of canister exploded only feet away, ripping a hail of iron fragments back into the faces of men emerging from the water. Ryder didn't look back. He straightened on the bank and looked round for someone to fight.

No one. The sharpshooters were on an overhanging ridge above them, the artillery entrenched on the heights, the battle was still to be joined. There was no sign of the cavalry, but around him were men fixing bayonets with grim glee on their faces and Ryder knew this was going to come to steel. He looked for an officer in the chaos, saw a young lieutenant of the 33rd and said breathlessly, 'Permission to join?'

The lad swung round, pistol in one hand, sword in the other, and a grin on his face like a boy at school. 'Oh, come on anyhow, everyone else is!'

He was right. Ryder wasn't very familiar with the infantry units, but surely the 19th had started with Buller rather than General Codrington, while the 95th weren't even Light Division at all. The 7th Fusiliers were panting off after their mad Colonel Yea, but everyone else was simply crowding behind Codrington, anyone who'd lead them against the bastards who'd blown their comrades to bits. 'That's me,' thought Ryder. *That's me.* His carbine was still under Wanderer, but he reached into his haversack and drew his father's Colt. He was Ensign Standish again and it felt like coming home.

A bugle sounded and they were off up the slopes, greenjackets followed by redcoats and one solitary bluecoat, all heading for the guns behind the earthworks of the biggest redoubt. Codrington led them, a distinctive figure on his Arab grey, gesturing stragglers to join them as he went. Their numbers were swelling, a great unruly mob tearing faster and faster up the hill, and when a thick column of Russians began to move silently down to meet them Ryder heard men around him actually cheer. 'Hurrah, lads, here they come!' cried an ensign. 'Now we'll give it them with sauce!'

Ryder wasn't aware of any orders, only the men forming a rough front in which he was quick to elbow a place. He capped his sixth chamber and fired with the rest. Another deep explosion of sound, but this one was theirs, the smoke came from their own guns and the men who fell were Russian. 'That's for Dick!' yelled a man, and another 'That's for Sandy!' A young private with tears on his face was reloading with fast and furious fingers, muttering 'This is for *you*, you murdering bastards. This is for *you*.' Ryder fired at the nearest mounted officer and thought simply 'And that's for me.'

The grey lines rippled flame as Russian muskets returned fire. Ryder felt a thump on his shoulder as the man behind pitched suddenly forward, but only shrugged him away, scraped back the pistol cock and fired again. Again with the cock, the snug feel of a ratchet clicking home, point the thing and fire. The private next to him was already up again with his Minié, squeeze the trigger and fire. A stranger, a bony-faced lad with freckles and ginger hair, but as he turned for the reload the two of them shared a smile.

And Ryder knew him. He knew all of them. These weren't frightened recruits any more, they were veteran soldiers as much as himself. They'd lain under the Russian artillery and seen their friends die around them, they'd had the fear scorched out of them, and they were going all the way.

The Russians saw it, knew it, and broke. A low moan shimmered through their lines as they split, ran, fell away to either side. Into the gap ran the British infantry, in it and up, and Ryder ran with them, wishing only for flatter ground that would be less strain on his foot and aching knee. He could see the summit now, the huge muzzles poking out of rough embrasures: ten, maybe a dozen great field guns, loaded and looking down on them, waiting only for their own infantry to clear before they flamed into life and fired.

Burning iron carved into them, grapeshot exploded wildly in their ranks, but men who'd lain helpless under it for an hour and a half weren't stopping for it now. Flying shrapnel, men dropping, sprays of blood and bone and brains, these were the old things, nothing to stop for, all the more reason to get up there and take those damn guns. No one paused to fire now, it was in with the bayonet and bloody charge. Ryder drew his sword and ran with them. The grass was slippery with blood, the way blocked by fallen Russians, his foot was throbbing, his knee shooting pain up his thigh, but the men behind were pushing him on in this last desperate race for the top.

Again the guns fired. At this range the balls simply drove into them, slicing bloody lanes through their ranks. Men were falling, arms flailing in front of him, bodies crashing against him, and for a moment there was only suffocating redness and death, but still the men behind pressed forward, surging upward, now, now before the cannon reloaded. Ryder gasped and ran, pitching forward on his hands, shove up against the grass and scramble on, hurtling forward to the guns of the big redoubt.

Nearer and higher, and now familiar noises drifting down, the rattle of wheels and chains as the great muzzles slid backwards out of sight. 'Stole away!' men shouted. 'Gone away! They're taking the guns!' Muskets still banged and cracked at them, but the balls were less than stones as their own lines stormed on. One was already there, a red patch streaking ahead to spring up on the earthworks, an ensign waving the colours of the Royal Welch Fusiliers. A boy, no more, he stabbed the staff into the earth and let the flag fly.

The murmur round Ryder grew to a roar as men hurtled towards it, the Welsh to their colour, the rest to plant their own, all aimed like an arrowhead for that little scarlet square flapping lazily in the sky. The bark of a musket and the ensign fell, the standard fluttering down to cover him like a shroud, but another hand seized and thrust it upward, another voice cried 'Come on the Welsh, come on, you bloody Englishmen, come on, come on, come on!'

They came. It was a bloody flag, that was all, but his breath was sobbing with effort as he ran. Codrington was first, his horse springing over the earthworks with cavalry ease, but Ryder was in the next wave, over and at them, sword screeching into the lunge he'd needed for what felt like years, into the belly, twist in the guts under that grey coat, pull out and let the man fall. Blood ran warm down his arm, the smell of it sang. He looked for the next, saw gunners backing a cannon to limber, and leaped at the closest, hacking out with the edge, slice and back for the other, making the air whine with the swing. The man thrashed out with the heavy carriage chain, but Ryder twisted aside to drive the sword under it and home. His knee buckled under the violence of the movement, pain tore viciously up his leg, but still he pulled out ready for the next, bracing his weight against the parapet behind.

But the last gunner was already backing away as the wave of redcoats hit the redoubt. Ryder heard only a terrifying roar, then they were piling up and over, dark legs thumping past him, jarring his back and shoulder as they hurtled over the earthworks after the fleeing guns. He watched with wonder as a single captain of the Welch Fusiliers forced a gun team to stop at pistol point and leave their cannon for the Allies. He looked back at what he thought of as his own gun, a 24-pounder with a bronze barrel and pea-green carriage, and saw an officer of the 95th furtively scratching his initials on it to claim it for the Second Division. The air was thick with cheering, caps and shakos flying in the air, victory, victory, and two of the guns trophies in their midst. The big redoubt was swarming with red, but so was the grass, so were the earthworks, and when Ryder looked at his own right hand the webbing between thumb and finger was encrusted with scarlet.

He sat down on the parapet, suddenly aware how much his foot was hurting. The bloody thing was swelling inside his boot and the leather felt solid as iron. He bent over to loosen it, but at once a blow on his shako sent it spinning back on the caplines, and he flung himself hastily down on the grass. Musket ball. Driving the Russians out of the redoubt only meant their friends on the other slopes could fire into them as they pleased.

But not for long they couldn't. He replaced his shako and peered over the parapet to see the rest of the battle. There was a lot of gunfire over to the west, cannon as well as muskets, hottest round a hill with a half-built telegraph tower and beyond it towards the sea. The French had made it up the cliffs and were fully engaged with the enemy's left. They were too far away to be of help, but the British had their own supports somewhere, to say nothing of the rest of the assault line and the cavalry.

He looked round for them. The 7th Fusiliers were further round the peak, engaged in a firefight of their own, but that still left the rest of Buller's brigade and almost all the Second Division. The 95th were in the redoubt, but there should be another five regiments somewhere. Ryder let his gaze drift down, down back towards the river, and stop at a mass of red soldiery milling around the broken bridge and vineyards at the bottom. They'd hardly started. They'd hardly bloody started and didn't look like moving even now. He followed the line of the river eastwards and saw only the cavalry halted in neat lines of blue. They hadn't even crossed.

'The Guards,' he thought. The support line of Guards and Highlanders, where were they? But the grass slopes were empty of red, no bearskins, no feathered bonnets, no kilts, no bloody nothing but a gentle wind waving the bloodstained stalks of grass, nothing all the way back down to the Alma.

Maybe they'd gone round. He forced himself to hobble to the far wall, but he already knew what he'd see there. For a few moments he'd been stupid enough to get carried away by a flag and the courage of the men around him, but this was the reality of war in this army. On this side too the slopes were bare.

Except for the Russians. There was a second redoubt above the slopes of their amphitheatre, and guns were already being wrestled round to point at their own position. On their left flank were massed infantry, five, six battalions at least, and a hollow to their front was bristling with rows of bayonets, a glistening forest of perhaps four more. The slopes on the right were patched with grey blocks of infantry units, and beyond them the denser mass of a cavalry maybe three thousand strong, enough to swallow their own seven hundred as easily as a python takes a calf. Not that their own cavalry were there to be swallowed anyway, they were down by the river like everyone else. Apart from the 95th, Codrington's tiny force of four regiments was completely alone.

'Oh dear God,' said a soldier in front of him. 'Oh dear God and the Queen of Sheba, we're dead as bloody mutton.'

Ryder rested his back against the parapet, and began to reload.

7

20 September 1854, 3.30 p.m. to 5.00 p.m.

Time had stopped for Woodall. He seemed to have been forever in that bloody field, first lying, now standing, but still just waiting and watching the roundshot roll towards them. Even the officers had tired of cricket jokes, and were lounging listlessly in their saddles, watching the antics of a Maltese terrier as it chased the intriguing black balls over the grass.

No one was frightened any more; they were all too angry. The light-bobs had gone in, so why were Her Majesty's Guards left hanging around like a bunch of ugly bridesmaids at a wedding? To be kept safe, ah yes, he could understand that, but they weren't ruddy safe, they were being shot at and not allowed to so much as chuck a stone back.

Even the guns had become familiar. They gave them all names now, Big Mary for the great 32-pounder, Phyllis for the deep-voiced cannon on the left flank, Gladys for the little howitzer that whined and fell short. But Mary hadn't reached them in a while, nothing was coming from the bigger of the two redoubts, though he could hear them banging away merrily as ever. They had something else to shoot at now, and in the distance Woodall saw redcoats thrusting up the side of one of the slopes.

'We should be there,' said Truman, his face hard and angry. 'They're on their own, poor beggars. We should be there.'

'Aye,' said Jones expressionlessly. 'I've a brother in the Royal Welch.'

For a moment Woodall saw himself reaching out to lay a hand on Jones's arm, he heard himself say 'Don't worry, Jonesy, we'll be going after them in a minute.' He practised the word 'Jonesy' in his head, and turned to make it real, but Jones was looking away, their own General Bentinck was talking to General Airey, and everybody hushed at once. It wasn't dignified to listen, of course, but it was only natural to look, and if he leaned forward a little Woodall found he could hear as well.

'We *are* supporting,' said their general, very properly. 'Look at us, we're here under fire, only waiting for the word.'

General Airey coughed politely. 'I think perhaps when Lord Raglan said "support" he was intending you should *follow* the Light Division. As a support.'

General Bentinck cleared his throat. 'Yes, well, dashed difficult if we're to keep three hundred yards behind. Are we to be exact, do you think?'

Woodall thought General Airey looked rather tired. He began, 'I don't think you need be too particular . . .' but Woodall quickly sprung back into position as the Duke of Cambridge rode up, commander of the whole First Division and the Queen's own cousin. Now they'd see something done, and Woodall was almost surprised to find how much he wanted it.

And almost at once it came, the order they'd joined the army for, 'Forward the Guards!' There was nothing of the machine in it this time, oh no, they were bustling and eager to be off. Not in a rabble like the Lights and the Second, they were going to show the army how it was done. Left foot, right foot, and off over the blood-spattered grass as if they were in Hyde Park. More round-shot came, they parted round it and marched on. More shells, they closed the gaps, and marched on. A low wall separated them from a vineyard, they stepped over it and marched on. Stakes crushed under their boots, vines fell in a rustle of leaves, but still they came on and all he missed was the band.

'Go on!' cried a hoarse voice, and Woodall saw a linesman propped against the east wall, his rifle still in his hands. Both legs were severed above the knee, and blood pumped out to join the growing pool on the ground. 'Go it, beauty Guards! Go in and win!'

For a tingling second their eyes met. Then the march went on and Woodall was swept along with it, but the tingle remained, rubbed into a spark and became a fire. He didn't need a band any more, he didn't need drums or a trumpet, the dying man had passed him something better than either. *Go it, beauty Guards! Go in and win!* He burst triumphantly through the last two vines onto the greensward to the river.

And into hell. The air smashed into colour and noise as canister howled about them, musket balls crashing into the dry leaves of the vines behind. His bearskin was hit, the chain was under his nose before he grabbed it back, but the familiar touch of it kept him steady. Forward and down the bank, slithering down the mud and into the river, rifle *up* and wade straight in. Water sprayed from the slash of balls and the thrashing of wounded men, earth and bark flew at them from the opposite bank as shells tore ragged furrows through the ground. Woodall blinked away the dust and waded on, stride after stride, then up again, bludgeon the broken trees aside with the rifle, and up onto the ball-pocked turf of the other side. They had crossed the Alma.

Two steps in and he felt the difference. An overhang above was sheltering them from the blizzard of shot and shell, the ground here quiet as the eye of a storm. Other redcoats were already clustering in the same place of safety, the Connaught Rangers, the East Middlesex – why, half the Light Division were clinging by the bank in defensive squares as if they expected cavalry.

He stared in perplexity. 'But if they're here, then who's . . . ?'

'Right,' said Jones grimly. 'Who's fighting the bloody battle?'

The first ball ploughed into the earthworks, skimming soil and pebbles off the top and burying itself harmlessly in the turf beyond. Ryder shook the debris off his shako and replaced it more securely on his head. The next would be closer.

He turned at the smack of a hand on a horse's flank. 'Quick as you like, man,' said Codrington gruffly. 'Quick as . . . you like.' The aide nodded tight-lipped, wheeled his mount and sprung over the parapet. Every head in the redoubt turned to watch him gallop away, back over the corpse-strewn ground, back down to the river and their only hope.

Next was a shell, exploding right in the centre and spewing out metal in a fiery spray. 'Out we get, boyos,' said a grizzled Fusilier, skipping nimbly back over the breastwork to crouch against it on the outside. 'Safer out than in.' Others were doing the same, anything to get away from that open centre now the Russians had its range. Codrington shouted, 'No, no, my boys, we must hold in here,' but the fort that had been so impregnable from below was open as a circus ring from above, and the guns of the surrounding slopes were every one lined on it.

Something clattered beside him, a linesman depositing a collection of rifles in a heap. Ryder watched with amusement as he sat down beside them, checking each was loaded, then propping them against the parapet as if preparing for a siege. The tears on his cheeks had dried, but Ryder recognized the ginger-haired private who'd marched up the hill at his side.

He said, 'Can you spare one of those? I wouldn't mind something with a longer range.'

The lad looked up and grinned. 'Course. They're not mine.'

Ryder knew whose they were, the slopes were littered with their owners. He took one and examined it, wondering how different it was from the carbine.

'Here, I'll show you,' said the lad. 'Bleeding horseboys, you don't know which end's up.' He was maybe sixteen years old.

He knew the Minié, though. Another shell burst shatteringly behind them, but the lad never paused in his loading, saying 'Like so, see?' at every step. Ryder wondered where his friends were, then remembered the bitterness with which he'd fired at the Russians and thought he could guess.

On an impulse he said 'What's your name?'

The lad flashed him another grin. 'Come on, what do you think?'

Ryder grinned back. 'Hullo, Ginger, I'm Harry.'

The boy nodded, then abruptly thrust out his hand. 'Pleased to meet you.'

Ryder shook the hand and didn't laugh. He knew the strength of it, this need not to die among strangers. *Did I do that for him or for me?*

Another shell, and they lowered their heads in unison, presenting their shakos to the spray. Again Ryder looked out over the slopes, but saw only a single horseman galloping towards them from the east, a man in the cocked hat of the Staff. Just what they needed, another bloody officer.

The ones they'd got were all shouting orders, but Sir George Brown was so blind he couldn't even see the enemy, and Codrington wasn't much better. Only a colonel of the 23rd sat still and quiet in the saddle, scanning the ground with a field glass. He stiffened suddenly, and Ryder followed his gaze. Those bayonets in the hollow were starting to move.

'Here they come!' bellowed an NCO. 'Face your fronts!'

Men smacked down either side of them, a complete firing line. The range was too far for the pistol, so Ryder shoved it in his belt, sprawled back his legs, levelled the Minié on the breastworks and looked down. The hill was steep, and he could still see only the advancing bayonets, muskets at the slope, not even lowered to fire. They were coming on very slowly, and in a silence that was curiously unnerving.

Gradually a dark line began to thicken at the rim of the hollow, men beneath the bayonets coming into view. Ginger fingered his beardless chin and said, 'They look grey. Seeing colour means they're at five hundred yards, and you set the range like so, see? No, hang on, I can tell heads from shoulders, call it four hundred.' Ryder slid the bar to the mark.

'Don't shoot!' someone shouted. 'Don't shoot, they're French!'

Ryder twisted round. A mounted staff officer by the far wall was gesturing with a pistol, while panicky NCOs bawled 'Don't shoot! Hold your fire!' A bugler called the 'cease fire!' and even

Sir George Brown was saying 'Can't shoot the French, men!' while peering myopically at the advancing line.

They were coming faster, thick and grey, surely grey, were any of the French units grey?

'No!' roared the colonel of the 23rd. He was nearer the front than any of them, waving his sword at the lines as if gesturing them to fire. 'No –'

A shot from somewhere, instantly another, and both hit the colonel. He pitched forward over his saddle, sentence unfinished, but the babble of confusion rose louder than ever. Ryder ignored it to look back at the advancing infantry, very close now, clearly grey, and with spikes on top of their helmets. He'd seen them at the Bulganek, he'd seen them close enough to be sure.

'Russian!' he yelled, 'they're bloody Russian!' and fired right into the line.

Ragged shots broke out alongside, but too few by far. Most were bewildered, all shocked, and none were ready. Officers were still shouting 'Cease firing!' and in the one, two seconds of silence even the advancing infantry paused. Then clear in the quiet came the note of a bugle, a trumpeter calling the retreat.

'What?' shouted Codrington, wrenching round his horse. 'No!' cried Sir George Brown, but the trumpet was clearer and louder, and men drilled to instant obedience were already falling back from the walls of the redoubt. Ryder stayed, Ginger stayed, a colour-sergeant was physically thrusting men back to the breastworks, but the noise was deafening, the confusion total, and at that moment the Russians charged. Down went their bayonets like a wall of spears, and from their grey ranks burst out a triumphant roar.

Earth flew in Ryder's face, and an elbow bashed into his cheek as men outside the parapet scrambled back in to escape the oncoming bayonets. The retreat was still sounding, men breaking and dashing for the far wall and beyond it the slopes to the river. Ryder rolled aside from the stampede, ripped the pistol out of his belt and turned to face the oncoming Russians, *Bang!* and got one, it was child's play at this range. He pointed the Colt like a finger and fired.

'Come on, will you?' said Ginger, tugging at his arm. 'We've got to, come on!'

It was an order, a bloody order, and he had no choice. It looked as if no one did, and as they crossed the redoubt he saw Sir George Brown yelling at the frightened trumpeter, 'But who gave the order, boy? *Who?*' The lad looked about him, then stiffened and pointed at a horseman riding away down the far side. 'Him, sir. There!'

That staff officer again. He was riding encouragingly along their retreating remnant, guiding them towards an advancing scarlet line. The Guards at last, and already starting up the slope. Why the hell had that officer ordered a retreat if he knew they were so close?

Screams behind and musket shots, the Russians had reached the parapet. Sir George was already turning to gallop away, and there was nothing to do now but run. Ryder's knee had stiffened and his foot was swelling, he was hobbling like a bloody cripple, but Ginger took his arm and hauled him on for the sanctuary of the far wall. Russians were there already, swarming round their precious howitzer, but Ryder fired at the nearest and escaped with no more than a gash in his side from a swinging bayonet. Then they were at the parapet, clambering and rolling over it, scrabbling up to run like the others down the slope to safety.

At once he felt it, the terror of a soldier turning his back on the enemy. Muskets banged behind him, balls screamed above, while ahead of him men who'd charged the hill with suicidal courage were tumbling down it like panicking rabbits. He tried to force his leg faster, stamp the ground and ignore the pain, but something barged against his shoulder, Ginger slumping forward with a cry. Ryder's arm shot out to support him, but the boy's legs were buckling, his weight bearing them both to the ground.

The open slope was no more than a shooting gallery. Bullets ripped past in the endless seconds it took Ryder to steady himself, get an arm round the lad's shoulders, and crawl with him behind a wretched little outcrop of rocks. Still the balls followed them, one snicking into their shelter to ping off a rock, and seconds later another chipping past the toe of Ginger's boot. The coat! Ryder in blue could just be a dark stone, but the linesman was a beacon of red on the hillside.

He wriggled out of shelter to drag in the body of a fallen Russian. It was a dead weight over the grass, but he wrestled it into their sanctuary and was already unbuttoning the coat when the next ball came. He felt it before he heard it, a sharp punch in his thigh, a smell like burning wool, then the pain lancing up to his groin and his own voice cursing. It would be the right leg, of course, the only one that bloody worked.

His hands kept fumbling down the row of buttons, tugging the corpse's arms out of the sleeves, rolling him over to strip off the grey coat. It was good and long, very like their own infantry greatcoats, and when he tucked it over Ginger the red completely disappeared. There was still the corpse, and he turned to wedge it into the gap between the rocks. A part of his mind recoiled at using a human being as no more than a sandbag, but the man was dead and out of it, the husk could save the living.

'Won't be for long, anyway,' said Ginger. His voice was monotonic and a fleck of spittle showed at the corner of his mouth. 'The Guards are coming, hey? The good old Guards.'

Ryder looked back down the slope. So far only the Scots Fusiliers were approaching, but in the distance he saw Grenadiers and Coldstream marching up to join them on either side.

'That's right,' he said. 'We're going to take back the redoubt then push the bastards all the way back to Sebastopol.' He leaned back against a rock and took out his powder flask.

Faint shouts drifted up towards them, shouts and the call of a bugle. *Retreat?* Ryder looked wildly round, and saw another Russian regiment advancing over the creases of the hills. It didn't matter, not if there were ten it didn't matter, the Fusiliers had only to hold long enough for the other Guards to join them, then they could –

The shouts were now so loud as to reach to their position. 'The Scots Fusiliers will retreat! The Fusilier Guards *must* retreat!' Again the bugle called, and Ryder stared at the horseman by the trumpeter. That staff officer again, he could swear it was the same, cocked hat, red and gold saddlecloth, bay horse. He was already turning to gallop towards the rest of the First Division, but the damage was done, bloody done, the Fusiliers were turning just at the moment the Russians began to swarm out of the redoubt. Some stood, he saw a group holding fast round the Queen's colour and backing doggedly onto the line regiments behind, but the rest were running, brave men turning their backs on a hail of fire and charging bayonets, redcoats breaking and scattering in defeat.

And the Russians were coming to finish it. They were pouring down the slopes, a whole column heading straight for their own position. He knocked the shako from Ginger's head, tweaked the greatcoat to cover his bright hair, and hissed 'Lie still!' There was only one hope for himself, and he swallowed his revulsion and took it. He rolled painfully onto his side and buried his head and chest under the dead Russian's legs, two corpses together who'd fallen in mortal combat.

The body muffled sound from outside, and all he could hear was his own shallow breathing. There was a strange smell from the dead man's clothes, smoky, vaguely uplifting, ultimately nauseating, but he dismissed it from his mind and concentrated on now. The Russians must be up to them, passing their clump of rocks, but he felt no movement round his legs and no one shouted. The ranks were parting to run round them, intent on nothing but pursuing the British who fled ahead of them like leaderless sheep.

For long minutes he lay quiet and motionless, feeling his anger grow. If the Grenadiers and Coldstream couldn't somehow turn the day, then this was defeat and maybe even massacre. Alone in his black cocoon he felt only a savage rage against the one man who'd caused it all, the officer whose insane orders had broken the biggest British army fielded since Waterloo.

The Guards hooted as the Scots Fusiliers marched sullenly back through the line. Truman called 'Who's the Queen's favourites now?' but Woodall was too angry to join in the laughter. The army was depending on them, that soldier in the vineyard had as good as said so, the Guards couldn't let them down now.

His own battalion wouldn't. Shell was smashing into them from a gun position on their flank, but still they kept going, the rock behind which the fleeing infantry were re-forming to return to the attack. He imagined how they'd look to the Russians, impregnable red and black, striding over the earth like giants from another world. He wished even more they weren't doing it uphill; his calves were beginning to ache.

They marched over the next rise and saw what the others had been running from. A swelling column of Russian infantry was advancing steadily towards them on the left flank, and from ahead were coming two more. Three thick, deep columns against one red line. The battalion halted, the Russian artillery ceased, and in the moment's silence Woodall heard a faint rush of breeze riffling through the long grass.

'Retire!' came a shout. 'The Grenadiers will retire!'

Woodall craned round. The order came again, a staff officer on a bay horse yelling 'The Grenadiers will retire!' then turning to canter towards the distant Coldstream.

Every head turned to Colonel Percy, and Woodall held his breath. Truman muttered, 'Not on your life, chum, not if the bloody Queen ordered it herself,' and while Woodall's soul cringed at the blasphemy he wanted to cheer at the sentiment.

Colonel Percy laughed. 'No, no,' he called to his subaltern. 'He don't mean "retire", he means "dress back" – look, I'll show you.' Then he was giving orders, honest-to-goodness straightforward orders, he was turning their whole left at an angle to face the column on their flank. It was a beautiful movement, smooth as clockwork, and Woodall half expected the polite clapping of the crowds in Hyde Park. In his head he was already writing a letter, *You should have seen us, Maise, you'd have cheered like billy-oh*, but his body did what it was directed and faced front. The Russians were in musket range, their cannon out of it, and now they would come to it, *now*.

The first Russian column faced them and fired. A whole load of bangs, that was all, nothing to men who'd lain under artillery for hours. 'Nothing,' thought Woodall, firing back on the order and slamming his piece to ground for the reload. 'Now you'll get it, you ruddy foreigners, now you'll see.'

Iron flew, blood and flesh flew with it, and still the Grenadiers fired. Again, reload and again, they were quicker and better, their guns more accurate, these Russians must be mad to think they could even dent them. There was hardly a man of their own falling.

'We can hold here for ever, Jonesy,' said Woodall, the familiarity slipping out without thought. 'We're going to break them all through.'

Jones didn't answer. His face was blank, his mouth bleeding, the white of his eyes blotting red. His body banged against Woodall's shoulder and slithered down his chest before collapsing into the grass.

'There goes Jonesy,' said Corporal Gleeson. 'Close up now, keep firing.'

Woodall stared at the percussion cap in his fingers as if he'd forgotten what it was. Did Jones hear him, did he catch it, that last throw of friendship before he died? A ball cracked past his head, he caught up with himself and snapped the cap down on the nipple. He mustn't think about it now, nothing but the gun in his hand and the Russians waiting to fall.

But they weren't falling, the column was still ruddy well there, and swelling at the back like a bat spreading its wings. They were being reinforced from somewhere, and when he looked beyond he saw two, maybe three more columns heading their way. Colonel Hood was bending the rest of their line to blast them from two angles, and that was better, the beggars didn't like that at all, but it would be a different matter when their pals caught up. Well, they'd got pals of their own, come to that, the Coldstream would engage in a minute.

He reached for another cartridge, but another sound pierced the gunfire, a distant bugle, and a call he knew. Someone on their left was calling a retreat.

'Gawd, no,' said Truman, loading like a lunatic. 'If the Coldstream go . . .'

'The Coldstream know their duty,' said Corporal Gleeson, flicking off his used cap with a tiny ping of metal. 'You just keep firing.'

Woodall risked a quick glance away from the enemy. The Coldstream had stopped in confusion, their officers were arguing, and voices yelling 'No!' One mounted officer was turning back to the river, and Woodall stopped with the cartridge to his lips when he saw the same bay horse, same red and gold saddlecloth, same weaver hat and plume.

'Keep firing, I said,' snapped Gleeson, and Woodall quickly bit and spat. The Coldstream would resist, same as they'd done themselves. They must. As he poured the powder down the barrel he found he was saying it aloud. They *must*.

Mackenzie wrung out his dripping sporran and looked up at the slopes ahead. The Coldstream seemed to have stopped, and drifting down towards the Highlanders came the sound of raised voices.

'Will you listen to that now?' he said in outrage. 'Men arguing with their officers!'

Farquhar sniffed. 'No discipline. That's the English for you.'

Mackenzie had to agree. They'd a whole crowd of Light Division way down to their right, bunched up square to face cavalry when any fool could see there was none for miles. There were some for yelling at the Highlanders, saying, 'You're mad, you can't go up there,' and one called, 'Oh let them, let the Scotch do all the work.' Mackenzie smiled at him nicely and called back, 'Aye, we'll do that.'

Their own stretch of bank was clear, and as the last of their number climbed up dripping to join the line he saw they'd somehow crossed that wee bit to the east of everyone else. It was the line of them that was doing it: spread but the two ranks deep, the whole Allied front must reach two, three miles to the sea. It was quieter down this end of things, fewer of the Russian guns pointed their way, but that would change once they knew the Highlanders were on them.

Sir Colin knew they were ready. There was no grand speech this time, he just looked them all over, lowered his brows at the 93rd, who'd maybe edged themselves that little bit nearer the front, said, 'Forward, 42nd,' and led the way himself. First the Black Watch, then themselves, then the 79th, up they went in echelons of regiments, up the hill and into the sudden hail of fire that greeted them from the slopes above.

It wasn't so very accurate, but there was an awful lot of it. The Grenadiers were having a grand battle to their right by the sounds of things, and the Coldstream finally turning off to join it, but there was a fair amount of grey ahead of themselves and Mackenzie's pace quickened in step with the others. It was steep going, but those weaned in the hills of the North weren't to be fickled by a bit of a bank, and those Russians would have the Guards in the flank if they weren't stopped quick. The pipes began again, 'Scotland The Brave', and Mackenzie strode forward with the joy of it, his wet kilt slapping against his thighs, his Minié the sword of a warrior in his hands.

The shooting was louder in front, the 42nd had come to something, and their own chieftain at their head. A cry went up, 'Sir Colin's horse is down!' and now all the 93rd were leaping faster and faster up the steep slopes, and Mackenzie was within sight of the heels of the 42nd when he heard the yell from above. 'Don't shoot, don't shoot, they're French!'

They didn't look it to Mackenzie, that mass of grey swarming towards the Black Watch like rats in a corn barn, but he could see the officer giving the order, one of those staff ones with a plume, very important and in the counsel of Lord Raglan himself. If he said French, then French they would be.

'No!' bellowed a sergeant on the flank of the 42nd. 'No, there's no mistaking them devils!' He raised his rifle and fired right into the middle of the approaching mass.

An NCO to outright disobey an order! But now they were all doing it, and Sir Colin not seeming to mind a bit, he was accepting a second horse from his aide and calmly climbing back into the saddle. Mackenzie's brain gave up the puzzle and concentrated on climbing faster and harder up the slope. The Black Watch was engaged with any number of columns coming against it, and it was time for the 93rd to join. It was a frustration, needing to keep the legs coming up and forward when all he wanted was to stop and fight, but then Colonel Ainslie gave the order and it was the best in the world, the order to 'Advance firing!'

Up to his shoulder came the Minié, a flick of the sights, a touch of the cock, and the relief of pulling that trigger and seeing a man fall! Still his legs were moving, on and on towards the enemy and their faces white with terror at what they saw. A man dropped beside him, but he was to be left for the bandsmen, Mackenzie simply swerved round and went on, his fingers working easily, naturally, in the drill he could do in the dark. On and fire, on and *fire*, and the column was breaking in panic, balls scoring deep furrows down their length, Russians falling and dying as Mackenzie had seen his own comrades fall and die. They were afraid, these poor creatures, afraid to be out in the open without the protection of their big cannon, afraid of the Highlanders marching towards them, blazing out death as they came.

The Grenadiers held on. They had remnants of the 95th fighting alongside them, but Woodall was sure his rate was twice theirs, and the barrel of his rifle was hot to his hand.

And the Russian column was feeling it, wavering, looking round for reinforcements that seemed to have disappeared. Someone shouted down their own line, Truman picked it up, Gleeson, everyone, he cheered himself, and the sound hit the column like a wind. They were reeling back, their rate of fire slowing, now was the time, now, and at last the order 'The line will advance on the centre! Quick march!'

Never mind the quick march, he was all but running and the others with him. One pause to fire, then to hell with it, it was down with the bayonet and charge. The Russians were making noises, an unearthly deep wail as if they were mourning their own loss and defeat. Well, serve them right, they'd get what was coming to them now.

His line crashed into them, in and through, easy as cleaving a mob in the Mall. One man moved to block him, teeth bared and bayonet ready, but he was smaller and bonier than the newspaper pictures, a face like a sad monkey not a raging bear. For a second Woodall hesitated, one man facing another, then the Russian lunged, Woodall whacked the blow aside, turned inwards and plunged the bayonet in the belly. Kill or be killed, that was all. He twisted the blade and found it came out as easily as the sandbag in training.

On for the next, but this one was swerving, and the bayonet jarred against a rib. No time to pull out and stab again, he grunted in frustration and forced the blade through. It was locked, jammed in the ribcage, and cost him agonized and sweating seconds to wrench free, but no one attacked him, the men around were all Guards, and the grey files already scattering before their charge. He paused a second, panting in relief, then wiped his hand down his coat and rushed after them.

The Russians were parting as they ran, and through the opening loomed another green hill with a fortification at the top. Up they went, his calves straining at every step, and Truman muttering 'Bloody hell, what's wrong with fighting on the flat?' A laugh formed in his chest, but he pressed it sternly down and strode on, more of a man than Truman any day. Besides, there were Scots Fusiliers coming up on the left, 7th Fusiliers racing up on the right and some sneaking Coldstream belting up round the back, the Grenadiers had simply got to get there first.

Shots crackled down from behind that low breastwork, the thing was defended after all. Muzzles and bayonets bristled over the parapet, and an officer was riding up and down waving his sword in encouragement.

'Sixpence for whoever downs him!' called Gleeson. 'Come on, Woodall, you're a tidy shot, ain't you?'

He was when he was loaded. His rifle was empty, they all were, they'd fired before the charge. Another volley crashed down, and Gleeson fell on his side with his throat torn open. Woodall's hands were slippery on the barrel as he groped for the cartridge, load, load, quick before they fire again, they'd never reach them in time with the bayonet. He allowed his eyes one glance up as he rammed the charge, and at once wished he hadn't. Poking over the rampart at them was something bigger than a musket. A howitzer, they'd got a ruddy howitzer, and it was pointed right in the middle of their line.

Ryder heaved himself up on his elbows. His legs weren't moving, but he didn't need them for this. He lifted the Colt and rolled sideways to level the barrel over the body of the dead Russian. He'd still got three in the cylinder and was closer than any of the Guards.

The howitzer had to be first. They should have spiked it, why didn't they spike it instead of pissing about scratching their bloody names on it? But they hadn't and there it was, loaded and ready to fire on the advancing Grenadiers. He picked out the man with the linstock, lined the gun for his belly, and fired – one. Another gunner yelled and ran to pick it up, line up and got him – two. The other gunners were backing off, but an officer was screaming at them, waving his sword and yelling, line up and fire – three. Missed, damn it to hell, he was still up and shouting, then a *bang* right by Ryder's cheek and the officer slid down and off his horse.

'Did I get him?' said Ginger, laying down his rifle.

His face was white as plaster, but the eyes glowed like sunshine on wood. Ryder said, 'You're a better shot than me, you beggar.'

A roar swept over both of them as the Guards charged past. It wasn't just Grenadiers now, he saw Coldstream, re-formed Scots Fusiliers, and even remnants of the incredible 7th, who seemed to have finished their own private duel on the right flank. He wriggled round to watch as they stormed the redoubt, laying about them with the bayonet and cheering for bloody England. He couldn't see beyond the earthworks but when bearskins flew triumphantly in the air he guessed the redoubt was retaken. A moment later and a patch of red fluttered again from the top, the colours of the Grenadier Guards.

A lump rose in Ryder's throat, then he swallowed it away. It was too soon to be celebrating. The Grenadiers might have beaten a couple of columns, but he knew how many others he'd seen on the slopes and that they were really no more than an island in the middle. There was their artillery too, and he was hearing even more of it now, big guns out west towards the sea.

'British, aren't they?' said Ginger. 'British guns?'

Ryder stared at him, then strained his neck to look. There was that rocky hill with the telegraph, clustered over with the sky-blue and scarlet of France, but below it was another knoll thrusting into the enemy's own ranks, and from it came the fire of two field-pieces hammering at the Russian artillery. It was too far to see who was with them, but the little white dots looked like the plumes of British Staff, the entourage of Raglan himself.

'See?' said Ginger. He was dribbling a little and had to stop to wipe his mouth. 'British. We're going to win.'

Ryder grinned dutifully, but began to reload. Two guns weren't much. It was good they were penetrating to the west, good the Guards had smashed through the centre, but there were still those Russian columns he'd seen in the east, and they'd be here any minute. As he greased the third chamber he could already hear the rattle of gunfire in the distance and looked up to see another body of the familiar grey figures starting to form on a far ridge. More of the bastards, and coming this way.

'Listen,' said Ginger, and his face had changed. 'Do you hear it? Listen.'

He heard only gunfire and the shouting of Guards in the redoubt, but little by little the voices hushed as if they too were becoming aware of another sound drifting towards them through the hills. He heard it himself now, high and piercing above the banging of the guns, he heard it and knew what it meant. From the hills in the east came the skirling of pipes.

He looked to follow it, and now he saw men appearing on the crest above the enemy, men in red coats and black headgear who might have been Guards but were not. They were firing steadily down into the grey mass, scattering it, driving it back, then advancing to fire again. They were making the Russians *run*.

The music grew louder, and his eyes prickled as he let his gaze drift away over the field. The sound seemed to wash over all of them, the Second Division fighting their way up either side of the Post Road, the French swarming over the telegraph hill, the British guns firing beneath, the Russians limbering up artillery to withdraw from the Causeway, the tall bearskinned Guards standing motionless on the skyline of the redoubt. The Highlanders were coming. There had been Russian columns on that flank, he'd seen them himself, but now there was only the glory of pipes in the hills as the Highlanders marched to join them at the turning of the tide.

8

20 September 1854, 5.00 p.m. to 10.00 p.m.

The cheering from above sounded like victory, but to Oliver the road looked like defeat. Bodies lay beneath their hooves as they climbed, and men were dragging corpses out of the way to allow the gun carriages to trundle past. There were more on the slopes around, grey and red all piled together, and some still moving and moaning.

The cavalry passed them in a silence too deep for anger. A huge, an epic battle had been fought here, and all they'd done was sit in their saddles and glare at Russian cavalry over the river. Lord Lucan had finally led them across anyway, but the Cossacks had gone, and their only orders were to escort guns up to a battle that seemed already over.

By the time they got there it certainly was. The big redoubt was ringing with cheers, flags were being waved and hats thrown, and a bronze howitzer was being hauled away in triumph. Some of the fellows started hurrahing with the rest, but Lieutenant Grainger snapped, 'What have we got to cheer for? We've done nothing.' His usually good-tempered face was hard and unsmiling, his cheek flushed with shame.

Oliver felt it too. The Bulganek had been awful, but at least no one else had died in their place. Here they were surrounded by dead men they might have saved, by living ones who looked at them like dressed-up children in an army of men. Infantry glanced up as they passed, and turned away with smiles of derision. The useless cavalry who sat on their rumps while soldiers fought and died. Oliver clenched his reins till the leather bit his hands, and swore he'd die before he let this happen to him again.

Even the officers weren't immune to it, and Sir George Brown trotted over to say 'Good view across the river was it, Cardigan?' and grin as broadly as one of his own rankers. Oliver hated Cardigan, everyone did, but just for a moment he longed to smack Sir George Brown clear off his horse.

'Meaning what, my lord?' said Cardigan dangerously, drawing up his scrawny frame in the stirrups.

'Oh, nothing, my lord,' said Sir George, smirking insufferably. 'And at least one of your men did his bit, eh? A Lilywhite wanted a bit of action, so he came along with the Lights.'

Cardigan's eyes bulged, and Oliver suddenly remembered he had a reputation for duelling. Perhaps Sir George remembered too, for he added hastily 'Jolly good show too, or so Codrington tells me. Does you credit, old boy,' then turned and trotted away.

Cardigan was left saying 'What? Hey – what?' and Lord Lucan scowling like a thunderstorm, but Jarvis's brows lowered and Oliver suddenly understood.

He whispered to Bolton, 'Ryder, it must be, no one else was down. He's alive.'

'Was, perhaps,' said Bolton mournfully. 'The Light Division's here, Ol-Pol, do you see a dragoon among them?'

Oliver looked quickly up to the smaller redoubt ahead, hunting desperately in the sea of red for the sight of a blue coat. 'He could be wounded.'

'He could,' said Bolton doubtfully. 'If you think that's a good thing.'

Oliver looked back at the piles of bodies behind them, the two bandsmen loading a man on a stretcher, one man out of a thousand on just this one slope. The arabas could pick up men on the flat, but how many were there? How long would it take to carry each one all the way down to the sea and the ships? Even the heaps he could see were already murmuring, crying, reaching out, and a steady mumble growing into a single word, the feeble plea for 'water'. The sun was still warm, and the flies were moving in.

*

Ryder inserted the bayonet into the rim of his boot. There wasn't a spare in the whole army, but he was going to pass out with pain if he didn't cut it off right now.

'You can get another,' said Ginger. 'Lots of dead men here. They won't need them now.'

'Cheery little sod, aren't you?' said Ryder amicably. He gritted his teeth, sliced up through the leather, and looked in disgust at the foot that flopped free. The thing was the size of a melon.

'You won't walk on that,' said Ginger. His voice was weaker now, and his breathing hoarse. Ryder had dressed his wound with the dead Russian's shirt, but it was already soaked right through.

Ryder hauled himself onto a rock. 'If I put my weight on the other . . .' A spike of pain shot through his right thigh, and he ground his palm into the rock to stop himself passing out.

'Don't bother,' said Ginger. 'It can't do the slightest good.'

He knew it. Even if he crawled the mile back to find help, no one would come for one wounded man in two thousand. He slumped back down and looked about the slope in despair.

The only bandsmen were heading down with full stretchers, but others were picking through the bodies now, soldiers and camp followers looking for friends and husbands. Some were looting, and he grimaced at the sight of a drummer boy tugging epaulettes off the shoulders of a fallen officer, but others offered water to those who asked. Perhaps there was hope there.

Or would be if they were visible. He eased Ginger out of the grey coat and said, 'Can you move if I help you? No one's going to see us in here.'

'Can I move?' said Ginger, with the faint echo of a London sneer. He swivelled on his bottom, easing round the rock to face out and towards whatever help there was. 'Get yourself out here, your blue coat might attract the tourists.'

Ryder crawled to join him, and when Ginger offered his hand he took it. The boy's fingers were clammy in his own, and he squeezed tighter to bring them back to warmth.

'Here comes one,' said Ginger, nodding his chin to his left. 'He's got water, look.'

Ryder turned to see a pair of infantrymen working steadily through the carnage. One stooped to offer his barrel to a moaning Russian officer, but as he turned away the Russian's hand came up with a pistol, and Ryder's shout was lost in the bang as the linesman fell. His companion screamed obscenities, and bayoneted the Russian officer twice, three times, shouting, 'You bloody bastard, he was trying to *help* you!'

Ryder's mind whirled in the maze of his own pain. What kind of fanatic would shoot a man who'd just tried to save him? He remembered the smell of the dead man's clothes, the scent of incense. Was that what they thought? They were Christian saints against a devil's empire? Well, it was too late to ask that one, he was as dead as the redcoat who'd helped him. Beside them the fallen canteen bubbled life-giving water into the grass.

But it was a reminder they were still among the enemy, and he let go Ginger's hand to finish reloading his revolver. The lad watched a moment, then said, 'The shot just now. It sounded different.'

Ryder rammed another ball. 'We've got better guns than they have. That wasn't a revolver, just a single-shot pistol.'

'But . . .' said Ginger. 'But . . .'

Ryder looked sharply at him. His breath was rattling and there was definitely more blue in his face. 'Don't talk. It's better if you –'

Ginger made a chopping motion with his hand. 'Colonel Chester. The officer up there. He was shot twice.'

Ryder remembered it, the man waving his sword and crying 'No!' 'That was a rifle, we weren't in pistol range.'

Ginger coughed. 'But . . .' He sucked up another bubbling breath, and coughed again.

Ryder watched him helplessly, then began to arrange the coat back round his shoulders. 'The red still shows at the front, and you'll need this when it gets dark.'

Ginger turned his head to look at him directly. 'No, I won't.'

Ryder saw how dark his eyes were, how grey the freckled skin, and knew the boy was right. He himself would survive, he was sure of it. The bayonet wound in his side wasn't serious, and if they got the ball out soon enough he'd probably keep his leg. He looked at his younger companion and felt ashamed.

'It's all right,' said Ginger. He needed another breath after just three words. 'I ain't got anyone. At home. Have you?'

Ryder said just 'No.'

'It helps,' said Ginger. 'Death or glory. Doesn't matter which. In the end.'

In the end. Ryder gazed over the crowded bodies, most now mercifully still. Some still moaned feebly, one was crying deep jagged sobs like a child's, and somewhere behind him a faltering voice was murmuring the Lord's Prayer.

'No,' he said. 'Nothing matters in the end.'

Woodall eased the last body off his aching shoulders and let it roll down into the pit. A poor end for a Christian, but a chap couldn't leave fellow Grenadiers lying out in the open like rubbish. Some would have to wait for morning anyway, but at least he'd done his bit and volunteered with the others.

He stepped back from the grave to let Truman take his place, but was jolted to see the body in his arms was Jones. 'Ought we to do that? His brother might want . . .'

'Brother's dead too,' said Truman. 'Parsons spoke to a fellow of the 23rd.' He slid the body to the lip of the hole and Jones moved for the last time, rolling lazily onto his back while his upraised arm flopped down on another man's face. Woodall looked away.

'What's it to you, anyway?' said Truman, wiping his hands down his trousers. 'It's not like he was a chum of yours.'

He could have been. 'Common decency, Truman. What's so odd about that?' Behind him Parsons muttered something, and some-one else laughed.

'Woodall!' called a voice. Two men were walking up from the bank, one a tall Highlander, the other a slim figure in cavalry blue.

His fellow Guards were staring, and the knowledge gave an added heartiness to his greeting. 'Mackenzie!' he said, striding towards them. 'And Oliver.' He gave the lad a kindly nod, man enough not to let the cavalry's absolute disgrace of a battle make a difference.

'Can you spare us some time?' asked the Highlander. 'Are you on duty?'

He was missing the point. 'Just lending a hand, you know. Can I help you with anything?'

'Aye,' said Mackenzie, unmoved. 'Ryder's missing, me and Polly are for finding and bringing him in. There's a sore number of bodies, we could do with a hand.'

Woodall's back ached but his fellows were watching, Mackenzie was asking, and something else was digging at him like a memory of Jones and a chance lost. He raised his voice and said, 'Of course, Mackenzie. Anything for a pal.'

They hadn't much time. The gloaming was well advanced and the bodies on the hillside losing colour, every minute making it harder to tell a blue from a red from a grey. The heat of the sun was already gone, and Mackenzie shivered at the thought of wounded men lying exposed through the chill of the Crimean night.

By the time they neared the hill men were calling the Greater Redoubt it was black they were seeking, black rather than dark mauve. He stopped short at the sight of one leaning against a rock, but when he stooped he saw the soldier was red as the others, only shadowed by a grey mantle round his shoulders. He was glad of it, for the boy was dead as stone.

He started to straighten, but something in the lad's posture struck him as strange. One arm was thrust out to his side, and Mackenzie's gaze stopped with a jerk when he saw the hand joined to another's, a second man curled up in the shadow of the rocks. This one looked black in the dark, but Mackenzie knew the colour as well as he knew the face.

He knelt back on his heels and let out his breath in a long sigh. Harry Ryder looked younger than he remembered, and only the wee beard-growth marked him older than the laddie who'd died with him. The sight of their two hands seemed to pierce him some-how, and he reached out his own to touch them in benediction.

And jumped. The redcoat's hand was cold as the Carron in February, but Ryder's had in it a faint warmth. He'd felt the touch too, for the body stirred, the face turned, then the eyes opened and saw him. For a second they stared at each other, then Ryder's mouth smiled.

'Took your time, didn't you?'

Mackenzie grinned. 'Next time we'll leave you all night.' He called to the others 'I have him!' then watched as Ryder struggled to sit up. 'Where are you hurt?'

Ryder raised his eyebrows and glanced down.

Mackenzie studied him. There was a bloodied piece of linen wrapped round his waist, another round his thigh, and one swol-len foot stuck naked out of his overalls. His face had the pale, stretched look of a man fighting pain, and another hour or two of blood loss would be the death of him, but he was a wonderful tough laddie, and when Oliver panted up he broke into a broad smile. 'Hullo, Polly. You made it all right.'

'Course he did,' said Woodall, strolling up behind. 'He only sat and watched, didn't you, Polly? Me and the Scot have been right in the thick of it.'

Mackenzie suppressed the uncharitable urge to kick the Guard in the groin. 'Aye, and yesterday we did nothing while these lad-dies sat under fire. Now take my piece, will you, whiles I carry him down.'

He clambered into a crouch and reached out his arms, but Ryder hesitated and looked at his dead companion. 'I don't want . . . I can't . . .'

Mackenzie remembered the clasped hands. 'A friend of yours, is it?'

Ryder seemed confused. 'Well . . . in a way. I just . . .'

Mackenzie looked from one to the other, unsure what to do, but a pair of boots stepped between them and Woodall's voice said, 'I'll take him, Ryder. That's what you want, isn't it?'

Ryder looked up, and the smile lit his face. He said simply, 'Thanks, Woody,' and reached out his hands to Mackenzie.

He was no more a weight than poor Andrew Murray had been, and Mackenzie hoisted him easily. Woodall carried the redcoat, Oliver followed with the muskets, and together they retraced their steps down to the river. There was a makeshift hospital in the village, but Ryder didn't fancy the butcher's slab and when Mackenzie saw the pile of amputated limbs in the courtyard he was inclined to agree. The man only needed a ball hoiking out and a few decent dressings; he'd be better off in his own camp.

The cavalry bivouac was only a few fires and a great pile of bodies cleared to the edges, but there was a commissary officer dishing out rations and a medical orderly with a proper tent, so they laid the redcoat with the dead, carried Ryder in to the orderly, and set about making a home. Food was what they needed most, but 'G' Troop's butcher was flaying a bullock, and when Oliver told him the First Division men had brought in one of their wounded he gave them a nice piece off the rump for their own suppers. Firewood was the next thing, with not a twig to be found on the barren hillside, but Mackenzie gathered fallen muskets to get them started, while a suddenly tireless Woodall walked back to the river to hack off branches from the trees used to line the bank.

The night was chilly, but Mackenzie borrowed an axe from a farrier and warmed himself by breaking up the musket stocks. His shoulders were weary when he finally sat down by the fire, but it was the grand sort of tiredness that comes from a day's work well done. For himself, he liked the campaign life. Back in the barracks now they'd be parading before watch-setting and being locked in the dormitories, but here was a whole night ahead of them to be their own selves. He watched Oliver queuing at the wagon for his rations, wondered if there might be a drop of rum in them somewhere, stretched out his legs and sighed with sheer contentment.

A woman's voice said, 'Excuse me, soldier.'

Mackenzie turned so fast he near ricked his neck. A woman, and a bonny one, with fair hair and a fresh face. He forgot his aching limbs and sprang to his feet with enthusiasm. 'And can I help you, lady?'

She'd a lovely smile on her, but it didn't reach her eyes. 'The butcher says you brought in a wounded man. Is it Harry Ryder?'

So that was the way of it. 'Aye, he's with the medical man.'

She said 'Thank you,' but her eyes didn't change, and he knew she'd not planned further than that first question.

He decided to help her. 'It's nothing. A wee ball in one leg, they'll patch him up fine.'

Her eyes met his, then quickly slid away. 'That's lucky,' she said. 'We've enough on our hands without Ryder too.'

He dropped his gaze discreetly to her apron and noted the black stains that in daylight would be red. 'Will you bide a while for him? He'll no be long.'

'Oh, no. No,' she said quickly. 'I've only come for more dressings. But thank you.'

She flashed him that smile again, a better one this time, and walked briskly away towards the village. That was a brave lady, to be nursing in those horrors, and to be doing it all through the night. He wondered whose wife she was.

'Who was that?' said Woodall, dropping an armful of branches with a thump.

Mackenzie turned back to watch her. She'd a tidy little figure, and as she passed the next fire her hair shone gold. He reached for his pipe, stuck a twig in the fire, and said, 'That, my man, is what you call trouble.'

*

Merrick gave him a discarded musket to use as a stick, and Ryder was able to hobble to the fire unaided. It was agony but it was possible, and with luck they'd find him a new horse tomorrow. Oliver had retrieved his saddle and carbine from poor Wanderer, he'd kept his haversack the whole time, he had everything he needed to stay on the march with the others. Thank God he was cavalry. An infantryman whose foot wouldn't even fit in a boot would be shipped straight off to the hospital at Scutari, and no one ever came back from there.

He knew he was lucky. Their own bivouac looked all right, the cavalry clean and untouched, but the field beyond was speckled with distant roving lights, the lamps of men still searching through the murmuring wounded and shapeless dead. The infantry camps were quiet and subdued, and from the nearest he could hear the desperate, hysterical sobbing of women. He wondered how high the 'butcher's bill' would be throughout the army. How many had died lying in the field without even a chance to fight? How many in that insane retreat from the Greater Redoubt that shouldn't have happened at all?

He sat down at the fire with the others and tried to eat beef stew. Woodall and Mackenzie were talking cheerfully in the loud voices of men who'd come through when they expected to die, and only Oliver was quiet, the boy who'd yet to fight in a battle at all.

'What will they say about us back home, do you think?' said Woodall. He'd finished his stew and had his bearskin in his lap like a pet cat. 'About today?'

Mackenzie tilted his mess-tin to drink the last juices. 'Mr Macpherson says we'll be in all the newspapers. Even the London ones, maybe with pictures.'

Woodall snorted. 'More than that, you ass. This is history, like Waterloo. Some of our chaps are making a pact to call their first daughters Alma.'

Mackenzie smiled dreamily and reached for his pipe. 'Aye, I can picture a lassie called Alma.'

Alma was a muddy stretch of water bobbing with red-coated corpses. Ryder's leg began to throb, and he massaged it with fire-warmed hands.

'The Guards will come in for most of it, of course,' said Woodall, stroking his bearskin affectionately. 'And the Highlanders weren't bad, I'd never say they weren't. It's the Fourth Division I feel sorry for, poor beggars, stuck guarding the baggage. They'll be a laughing stock back home.'

His voice faded to silence, and he threw a furtive glance at the bowed head of Polly Oliver. Ryder looked at the hunched way he was sitting, remembered a frightened boy in a house at Bourliouk, and felt a tingle of returning anger.

He said roughly, 'Not your fault, Poll, you've got to do what you're told. Everyone will understand that.'

Oliver didn't look up. 'Will they? Telegraph Jordan says they're already calling Lord Lucan "Lord Look-On".'

Ryder pictured those distant blue lines sitting still and useless beyond the river. 'Well, what does he expect? We had the Russians withdrawing, they were on the bloody run, we should have been chasing, driving them back. We should be doing it right now.'

Oliver's head shot up. 'We did chase when it was over, but Lord Raglan ordered us back. We even took prisoners.' His head drooped again and his voice died to a mumble. 'Only Lucan was in rather a bate about it all, and made us let them go.'

Ryder could see it, that stiff-necked bulldog-jawed bastard throwing a fit of pique at being called back. 'For God's sake, what are they – children? Isn't there even one of our commanders who knows what the hell he's doing?'

Mackenzie's brows lowered. 'I'd say they're no doing so bad, Ryder. They've won a battle for us today, if you mind of it.'

His anger was beginning to throb with the ache in his leg. 'No, *you* won it, coming on like you did, turning the enemy's flank. The Guards won it, coming on through fire and steel and not stopping for anything. The 7th Royal Fusiliers won it, fighting all by themselves against that Kazan regiment to stop them sweeping us from the field. The Second won it, fighting up the Causeway. The French won it, going in first and taking that hill with the telegraph, bringing up their guns through the other village, fighting alone for over an hour before we even moved. What have our commanders to do with any of it?'

Mackenzie lowered his pipe. 'But it was our Lord Raglan turned the battle, everyone says so. It was him brought those guns right into the heart of the enemy position.'

He remembered it, those plumes round the two cannon below the hill with the telegraph. 'You mean Raglan was there himself?'

Woodall gave a snort of laughter. 'Only because he got lost. Our chaps say he wanted a good view, so off he trotted behind the French position with all the Frogs gaping after him. They only brought the guns as an afterthought when he said it might be a nice idea. Silly ass.'

Ryder could hardly believe it. 'Worse than silly. What if he'd been captured?'

'But he wasn't, was he?' said Mackenzie, beaming in triumph. 'The Russians were afraid to go near him. We had a prisoner say no commander would be so far from his army, they were sure there were a thousand more of us just behind. A wonderful brave thing.'

'A wonderful stupid one,' said Ryder. 'What good was he to the rest of us out there? How could he send up-to-date orders? Carrier pigeon?'

'That's right,' said Woodall, nodding sagaciously. 'It wasn't the Guards' fault we were late supporting, it was lack of clear orders.'

Mackenzie's grin disappeared. 'There were orders, man, did you not see them? We'd staff officers all about the field.'

'Staff officers!' It all came roaring back, the anger and helplessness as he lay beneath a corpse and listened to the rout caused by the stupidity of one man. He told them all of it, the fatal order to retreat, the same order to the Scots Fusilier Guards, the red lines breaking in disorder. 'I don't know who the hell that man was, but he's got the blood of hundreds on his hands.'

'Here,' said Woodall, sitting up abruptly. 'Did he have a bay horse? Red saddlecloth with gold bits on it? We'd a man like that try it on with the Grenadiers *and* the Coldstream, but it was just a misunderstanding; he said "withdraw" when he meant "dress back".'

'Misunderstanding?' said Ryder, and resisted an insane urge to laugh. 'How could he mean "dress back" when we were sitting in a bloody redoubt? He meant "retreat", he even told the trumpeter what to play.'

Mackenzie's pipe had gone out, there was no smoke as he sucked. 'Well, and maybe there was reason. With the Russians coming for you and the panic that there was . . .'

'There'd have been no bloody panic if it hadn't been for that man.' He saw it all clearly, Ginger propping those rifles against the earthworks, Ginger smiling at him, Ginger dead with his jaw dropped open as Woodall carried him slung over his back. 'He caused the whole thing, he stopped us shooting, he said the Russians coming were French.'

Mackenzie paused with a match in his hand. 'The same man? A brown horse, red saddlecloth?' He cracked the lucifer and applied it to his pipe, cheeks sucking in as he forced it alight. 'Aye, that's a bad mistake. He made it with the 42nd too, but we'd a sergeant spot it in time. Did you not have an officer who knew better?'

He pictured that too, the colonel shouting 'No!' and then the shots, *Bang!* and then *Bang!*, the man falling forward in his saddle. 'One did, but he was shot. Before he could even finish the sentence.'

The fire crackled, and a yellow spark of powder flew violently into the air. Mackenzie pulled the broken musket barrels further out of reach.

'That's . . . odd, isn't it?' said Oliver. He was sitting upright again, and his face looked flushed from the fire. 'Don't you think it's rather convenient?'

'Not for us, Polly,' he said. He felt sick and tired and didn't want to talk about it any more. 'It cost us the Greater Redoubt.'

'That's what I mean,' said Oliver. 'It's what the Russians would have wanted to happen, isn't it? That officer being shot. As if they knew.'

What the hell did it matter now? 'Luck. They couldn't have targeted him, not from the Lesser Redoubt. They'd never have heard him anyway.'

Oliver frowned. 'But the ones coming at you, they could have. If they knew he was warning you, mightn't they have shot him?'

He thought of that silent, deadly advance, bristling bayonets almost gliding up the slope. 'They weren't firing, Poll. If they had been we'd have known they weren't French.'

'Yes,' said Oliver, but his brow was crinkling. 'Only why weren't they? Don't we usually fire before we charge?'

'That's right,' said Woodall at once. 'You don't waste a loaded gun, you fire and then it's in and at them, isn't it, Mackenzie?'

The Highlander didn't answer. 'What's on your mind, Polly?'

Oliver's flush deepened. 'It's just odd to make the same mistake twice, that's all. That staff officer must have realized he'd got it wrong, so why did he do the same thing with the Highlanders? No one's that stupid.'

'Why not?' said Ryder. 'Some of our commanders are.'

Oliver shook his head. 'But it wasn't the commanders, was it? You said it yourself, Lord Raglan wasn't there. This one officer did all these things himself, and every one of them gave advantage to the enemy. That can't be coincidence, can it?'

The only coincidence Ryder could see was the man's stupidity. 'What are you saying, Poll? That one of our officers is working with the enemy?'

Woodall chuckled. 'Oh, come, Polly . . .'

Oliver turned on him. 'Why not, though? How could the Russians know not to fire unless they knew someone up there was going to make that mistake? And how could they possibly know that?'

'How could anyone know?' said Mackenzie reasonably. 'There was no plan beforehand.'

Oliver was knotting his hands in agitation. 'There might have been. We saw an officer like that, too, a bay horse and red saddlecloth with gold lions on it, he was across the river before anyone else. What if he'd been talking to the Russians? He could have, couldn't he?'

Ryder's leg was still aching and his stomach was beginning to regret the beef. 'Oh, don't be an ass. All the Staff are pals of someone, that's how they got here. They couldn't be traitors, Poll, they haven't enough brain.'

Oliver's lower lip was sticking out and his chin was creased. 'That's what you keep saying. You keep saying they're all stupid, they don't know what they're doing. Is that any better than one of them being a traitor?'

Mackenzie said soothingly, 'They're neither, don't you fret on it. They're new to this same as we are, they've maybe made a few mistakes, but we can trust them.'

'I do,' said Oliver, and for a second his voice was high and unbroken, a child fresh out of school. 'But Ryder's saying we've got one so stupid he could lose us a battle by mistake.'

Ryder thought of all the other stupidities that had led them to this. He thought of Doherty talking about the lack of equipment, the poor communication, the officers who ignored Raglan's orders. He thought of the long wait in Varna while the newspapers told the Russians the expedition was on its way, of the chaos of the landing and the sick men who died without tents on the beach, he thought of the sitting around while the Russians had time to gather an army. He remembered the horrors of the march.

He said, 'Never mind that, Polly. We've got commanders stupid enough to lose us a war.'

He heard Oliver's gasp of shock, but couldn't bring himself to care. Innocence had no place on a battlefield, and they'd all have to face it in the end.

'Here,' said Woodall, jutting his jaw. 'Here, are you saying we're going to lose?' He was stroking his bearskin again, hands moving quicker in agitation.

Mackenzie put down his pipe and sat up straight. 'Now, there's no call to be saying that. There've been mistakes made, but we've won the battle, haven't we? Why, the road's clear right through to Sebastopol.'

Ryder swung round on him. 'So why aren't we on it? We ought to be chasing the Russians now, right now, before they get a chance to regroup behind its walls. Tomorrow might be too late.'

'Oh, we're not going tomorrow,' said Woodall, faintly shocked. 'Our officers say there's far too much to do. There's the Frogs, for a start, they took their packs off for the battle, they've got to march back and fetch them.'

'That's right,' said Mackenzie. 'There are all the sick to go back to the ships, and only a few arabas to carry them. Then there's the burying, and only ourselves to do that, and there's the medical supplies for the doctors, they've all to be landed from the ships. Mr Macpherson reckons we'll need all of two days.'

Two days. Two whole days when Doherty said they needed every minute. The folly of it was shocking, unforgivable, and he could hardly trust himself to speak. He said just, 'There you are, then. There you are,' and stared at the fire in black hopelessness. What could he do? Even if he saw that staff officer again, the bastard who'd caused it all, what could he do but salute and say 'sir'? He was nothing, nobody, the army could be destroyed around him and there wasn't a single bloody thing he could do.

'I'm sorry,' said Oliver's voice. 'I've spoiled things, I'm sorry. I was upset about the battle. I do know it's all right really.'

That poor, stupid kid. He made himself look up and say, 'Yes, all right, Poll. It's all right.'

Oliver smiled tentatively. 'I know people make mistakes, but we've still got lots of good officers, haven't we? Like Colonel Doherty, who saved us at the ambush?'

And Codrington with the Light Division, Percy with the Grenadiers, Sir Colin Campbell with the Highland Brigade. Another, young and friendly, who'd wished him good luck before the battle. 'Yes, Poll. Lots of them.'

'Well then,' said Mackenzie comfortably. 'Now have you the cards, Polly? Ryder's hurt, we're all tired, we'd be the better for a game.'

He couldn't see the point in that either. Bridge was like war, you needed skill as well as luck, and with commanders like theirs they were doomed. Luck had saved Raglan today, luck and the courage of his men, but what in the world could save him tomorrow?

He thought of tomorrow, sitting about while the Russians regrouped. The days after that, ambling along while they turned Sebastopol into a fortress. What about the days after that? If they weren't in the place by the end of October they'd be stuck here in the Crimean winter with nothing more than the clothes they stood up in. And if the commanders couldn't look after them in summer, what the hell would it be like in December?

The game began. The coloured cards glowed brightly in the firelight, but in their place Ryder saw rows of scarlet and black and rifle-green, sunlight gleaming on brass as the bands played. The darkness seemed suddenly thicker outside the brightness of their little fire, and he knew that beyond its warmth lay piles of dead men stiffening in the cold.

PART TWO

Balaklava

'Into the valley of Death
Rode the six hundred.'

Alfred, Lord Tennyson – 'The Charge of the Light Brigade'

9

28 September to 15 October 1854

Sebastopol.

They'd seen only glimpses on the flank march south, and the troop was buzzing at the prospect of their first real sight of it. As Captain Marsh led them up the sprawling slopes of Mount Sapoune Ryder heard the sibilance of the same word whispering through the patrol like a constant 's'. 'Sebastopol,' men said. Sebastopol. The town they'd come to conquer.

Marsh halted to inspect it through his field glass, and the position gave them a perfect view. Below them the River Chernaya wound under the Inkerman Bridge into the deep waters of the Roadstead of Sebastopol, and onwards under the boom into the distant sea. There should have been a fleet there, the Black Sea Fleet they'd come to destroy, but other than a few ships at anchor there was only a dark shadow in the Roadstead mouth, and near the shallows of the northern side the tip of a single, listing mast.

Cornet Hoare's mouth was open. 'It's true, then. They've sunk their own ships.'

Marsh's face screwed up as he squinted through the field glass. 'Dashed unsporting, I call it. They might have given us the fun of doing it for them.'

So they might, if the British hadn't hung around for two days on the banks of the Alma and given the Russians time to prepare. Ryder massaged his wounded thigh and wished he could soothe away the bitterness so easily. If the Roadstead had been open the fleet could have sailed in, they could have turned into the Man-of-War Harbour and been right in the heart of the town.

Now it would have to be an entirely land-based attack, and that looked a tough proposition.

Across the Roadstead, the distant North Side of Sebastopol had been their first choice for assault, but the coastal fort of Constantine protected it from the sea, five batteries enclosed it in a circle of artillery, and the solid block of a star fort kept the road open to Odessa and beyond. Raglan had taken one look, and marched the army on round to the south.

Not that the South Side looked much better. Here was the main town, split in two by the Man-of-War Harbour, but while the surrounding wall didn't look too serious an obstacle, Ryder was less sanguine about the bastions. He could see four from where he sat, but last night's patrol said there were more all round the town, doubtless thrown up in response to the helpful warnings of the London *Times*.

And they were getting bigger as he watched. Earthworks were being heaped high in front of them, a turret going up on the round white tower of the Malakoff, and the sited cannon dwarfed by the hulking 64-pounder naval guns being hauled into place beside them. Tiny figures of men scurried like insects to build up the walls, more of them laboured in the nearby quarry, while the brighter coloured blobs were women, hurrying between the bastions with baskets of earth for the ramparts. Some of the blobs were very small, and Ryder felt his throat constrict as he swallowed.

'Why don't they get the children out, poor things?' said Bolton sorrowfully. 'The road's open to the north.'

'Because they're not scared of us, are they?' said Jordan. 'They've seen how slow we are, they reckon they've got till Christmas.'

A shout, someone calling 'Look out, sir!' as Captain Marsh skipped back from the crest, and down below Ryder heard the boom of cannon. The *crump* of the ball smashing into the hillside followed almost at once, and a slab of grey rock sheered clean away to roll down to the Chernaya. A second bang and the ball whooshed over at them, the lines buckling into each other in their haste to back away. The shot gouged safely through the earth on their right, but a horse crunched against him as the ranks tangled and he yelped at the impact on his wounded thigh.

The line backed hastily down the slope to re-form. At least his new mare stayed steady, untroubled by either cannon or jolt, and he urged her easily back into place. She'd been captured at the Alma and he'd never bothered to name her, but now he patted her neck and said 'Natalia'. She snorted peaceably, and he tweaked her ears and said 'Tally'.

He looked up to find Jarvis watching him. He'd seen the collision, of course, and as usual his gaze slid down to Ryder's still-bandaged leg. Hardly anyone in the troop believed his story of a stray musket ball, but it was clearly tormenting the sergeant-major that he was quite unable to prove it. It was a strange army that would blame a man for choosing to fight the enemy rather than rejoin his own unit, but it was Jarvis's army and Ryder guessed the irregularity was eating at his soul. Yet he thought there was maybe something else in it too, and once or twice he'd seen in those piggy little eyes a glint of something very like jealousy.

He could understand that. The whole Light Brigade were panting for a fight of their own, poor buggers, and no one could blame them. The pressure was greater than ever now the Heavies had landed and the Lights lived in dread of their cavalry rivals seeing action first. It was worst for his own regiment. Three times now they'd faced the enemy, three times they'd fought through fear to the action point, and every time they'd been denied it. Ryder could see it in Oliver all the time now, the jumpiness and febrile brightness of the eyes, the desperate need for a fight, any fight, to kill the doubts for good and all.

But as they descended to the plateau he began to see signs of hope. The Chersonese Uplands were rough terrain, a mass of hills and crags and ridges, some no more than bare rock, some covered with jungles of stunted oaks and thorn bushes, but the infantry were already toiling across it, their red coats brightening the barren country like poppies in a field. Artillery was rumbling along the Woronzoff Road, and a trail of ox-drawn carts plodding up from the Col de Balaklava, the smoother route down to the ships. The defences weren't impenetrable yet, the Allies would be ready in perhaps two days, then they could storm the bloody place and be done.

He said, 'It's coming, Poll. Any day.'

Oliver's eyes were anxious. 'But will it be us? They might not think the ground's good for cavalry.'

It was bloody awful for cavalry, riddled with caves and crevices and gashed across the centre by the broad gorge of the Careenage Ravine. 'It doesn't matter. We won't be going in first anyway, not against artillery. We'll be for the final rush, when we can sweep down from the hills and right in their gates.'

Oliver hesitated, and Ryder noticed how tightly he was holding his reins. 'Unless we get another wrong order. Like that officer at the Alma. If somebody sends us against cannon.'

Ryder felt a jolt in the stomach. So that was what he'd been agonizing over all this time. He glanced behind to check Grainger was out of earshot and said, 'Forget him, Polly. He's probably been sent home in disgrace.'

Oliver looked sideways at him. 'So you've been watching for him too?'

He didn't miss much, damn him. 'Come on, we had Staff trotting past every five minutes on the march. If he'd been there we'd have seen him, wouldn't we?' If there was any justice he'd be somewhere behind them, in a hole in the ground at the Alma.

Oliver studied his mare's neck. 'All right, but just for argument. If someone did order us to take that white tower, what would we do?'

With Lucan and Cardigan in charge it was more than likely. He said, 'I tell you what we do, Poll. We take it, that's all. We charge right up and bloody take it.'

Something sparked in Oliver's face as he looked up. 'That's right,' he said. 'Of course we do. That's right.' He smiled suddenly, and the anxiety faded from his eyes.

Ryder grinned back, warmed by a sense of recognition. Oliver wasn't frightened of the Russians, he was afraid of fear. There was the right fire in him somewhere, it would come when he needed it, and that was all that mattered.

Perhaps it was infectious, but the whole column seemed livelier as they trotted down towards the Col. Even the marching feet and rattling of wheels seemed brisker and more businesslike than they had on the march, as if the whole army were rolling up its sleeves and saying 'Now then!' One of the linesmen called 'Hullo, the "look-ons" have been for a look-out!' but Jordan called back good-humouredly 'Look up your backside, flatfoot!' and the whole troop laughed.

'Look at that,' said a voice to his right, and even that sallow Moody had something approaching animation in his face. 'Wait till the Russkies try their teeth on *that*.'

It was certainly a huge gun coming up the road, a Lancaster 68-pounder that must have been dismounted from the ships. Ryder guessed that was where the Russians' own big guns had come from, stripped from their ships before they sunk them, and smiled at the irony of two fleets fighting it out in a land battle. But it was a strange thing for the British to do, and hardly worth it for a two-day storming when the guns would have to be silenced as the men went in. He was still puzzling over it when they passed the artillery team and saw the ox-cart coming up behind.

'Gawd,' said Fisk. 'Gawd, but that's . . .' Jordan was laughing and saying 'What on earth do we want those for?' but behind him Ryder heard the quiet voice of Grainger saying 'Oh God, no. Oh God, no,' and understood.

The cart was filled with digging equipment. Pick-axes, spades, sacks of entrenching tools, all buttressed against the jolting by coils of wickerwork, the familiar cylindrical shapes of gabions. The cart behind had more of them, empty gabions and bundled piles of sacks, all of which he knew with terrible certainty were designed to be filled with earth.

'The siege train,' said young Hoare in front, the question pitching his voice higher. 'Have we landed the siege train?'

Yes, they bloody had. Luck had dealt them a glorious hand, an enemy still unprepared despite all the warnings. Luck had given them a war for the winning in one swift and decisive battle. Luck was offering them a victory their stupidity had never deserved, and Lord Raglan was throwing it away in one move.

He was going to make them dig in for a bloody siege.

He was right. Ryder was right. Oliver saw it in every cart they passed after that, but what was worse was seeing it in the faces of their officers. It was a mistake, they all thought so, and he knew he was struggling to keep faith. It was one thing to doubt some of their officers, he had no choice after the Alma, but a fellow had to believe the commanders knew what they were doing or everything was for nothing.

They rounded the Col into the South Valley of the Balaklava plain, and his spirits rose at the sight of the British Army. The valley lay like a bowl between the curved Sapoune Ridge on this side and the Causeway Heights on the other, a great empty space boasting only a few ploughed fields and vineyards, but today it was full of redcoats and baggage wagons and hummed with the voices of thousands of men. There were gaps among them, bare patches where regiments had already set out for the Chersonese Uplands, but it was still a jolly impressive sight. Even more important, he could see the Guards parading in the distance, and down towards the village of Kadikoi he heard the strain of Highland pipes. Their friends were still here. Every night of the march they'd talked and played cards together, and perhaps it would be the same at Balaklava.

But they'd hardly sat down at the fire that evening when Woodall said importantly, 'We're off tomorrow. Moving to the Uplands to be nearer the action.'

Oliver felt instantly bleak. 'But that's five miles away. How can we play?'

Woodall put the pan on the fire. 'Oh, we may not be that far. They won't put us right by Sebastopol, will they?'

It could still be more than an hour's walk, and Oliver couldn't see Jarvis letting them take out troop-horses. He said miserably, 'Are you going too, Niall? Is it everyone?'

Mackenzie was crushing the coffee beans with unusual vigour. 'It is not. The 93rd are to stay behind like women to guard the base.' He smashed down hard with the rock and sent a little chip of bean flying in the air.

'Oh, hard luck,' said Woodall kindly. 'But someone has to do it, don't they? Can't leave it to those sailors.'

'Or the cavalry,' said Ryder. He was in one of his dark moods this evening, like he'd been after the Alma. Everything about him looked careless, from the unbuttoned coat to the untidy hair, and he kept nudging the fire irritably with his boot. 'I bet we'll be staying too.'

'You are that,' said Mackenzie, with the gloomy satisfaction of a fellow sufferer. 'It's our Sir Colin and Lord Lucan have the charge of it, keeping the gorge open at Kadikoi.'

Oliver reminded himself it was an important job. The gorge was the only route to the ships in Balaklava Harbour, and if the Russians took it the entire British Army would be cut off. Then he thought of the siege happening, Sebastopol falling, the cavalry going home without having fought a single battle, and it was all just too horrid to bear.

'Chin up, young Polly,' said Woodall, rescuing the battered beans from Mackenzie and stirring them into the pan. 'Think of us roughing it in the Uplands while you're nipping in and out of the fleshpots of Balaklava.'

Mackenzie looked at him out of narrowed eyes. 'Aye, that's true. You'll be awful muddy after days in those trenches and the Russians taking pot-shots at you the while.'

Woodall stopped stirring. 'Don't be ridiculous. The Guards don't *dig*. We're there for the fighting, that's all.'

'If there is any,' said Ryder. 'How can you besiege a town from one side? The North's wide open, they can bring in food and re-inforcements, they can hold out for ever.'

Woodall stirred again. 'Oh, I'm sure we won't wait. The artillery will knock down their defences, then it'll be in with the bayonet, just like the Alma.'

'Aye, that's what our officers say too,' said Mackenzie. 'A big bombardment, then a grand battle after. It'll be a sight to see.'

'Then we'd better get a move on, hadn't we?' said Ryder. 'In two weeks that place will be impregnable.' He sprawled on his back and looked at the sky.

Oliver listened to the familiar scrape of the spoon in the pan, and felt a sense of sadness like a song. They might never do this again. This might be the last time the four of them were ever together. He said, 'Shall I get the cards out?'

Woodall poured the coffee. 'Got to give you a last chance at revenge, haven't I? I'm one and sixpence to the good so far.'

'Not for long,' said Mackenzie darkly, sitting up with a look of purpose.

Oliver dug out the box, but Ryder still hadn't moved. He said, 'Ryder?' Then, more tentatively, 'Harry?'

Ryder sat up and dragged his hands through his hair. 'All right, what else is there to do? Let's play.'

Day after day of watching the carts go by. There was a constant stream of them up both the Woronzoff and the Col, gun teams and limbers, caissons with shells, cartloads of timber from dismantled roofs in Balaklava to make platforms and fascines. The Heavy Brigade shared the patrolling now, and most of the time Ryder just sat in the saddle on vedette duty with nothing to do but watch the carts go by.

It was so bloody slow. The gun teams had horses, but the carts were pulled by underfed oxen who nodded in their traces as they strained to haul their loads six miles up to the lines. There weren't enough of them either, and fresh meat in the rations always meant another had dropped dead from overwork. Only one of the regular carts inspired Ryder with any confidence, a green-banded monster pulled by two fat bullocks whose driver wore a corporal's stripes but looked very like Bloomer of the 7th. If anyone could find forage for cattle when half the army was fighting for it then that would be Bloomer.

But the carts weren't the only things moving. Cossacks were about again, little packs of five or six, and nearly every day Ryder had to walk his horse slowly in a circle to show the camp an enemy force was approaching. Once he actually had to gallop the circle to show a bloody great army was on its way, but it seemed to be only a reconnaissance. Lucan led the cavalry to the entrance to the North Valley at the end of the Causeway Heights, but the two forces only glared at each other before a few shots from the Horse Artillery sent the Russians trotting unhurriedly away. If they'd done it to see what the British would do in response to an attack on the Balaklava base, then they certainly had their answer. Nothing.

Nothing. The tents were landed, the field kitchens started again, washing went up on the lines and the camp began to look as permanent as Varna. Only one thing changed, and that was a contingent of Turks beginning to build redoubts along the Causeway Heights. The Allies were here to attack, they were here to take Sebastopol, so naturally Raglan put all his energies into organizing a defence.

The waiting was unbearable. The French opened trenches on the night of the 9th, the British the night after, but all it meant to Ryder was the boom of distant cannon as the Russian guns targeted the work, and the growing number of carts making the return trip with casualties for Balaklava. There was a race going on out there, a race to win a war, and he was stuck on bloody useless vedettes, wanting more than anything just to *know*.

Then it came again, 'G' Troop's turn to patrol the Uplands, and at last he knew the worst. The spires and domes of Sebastopol were almost hidden behind the growing ramparts, and the white tower of the Malakoff had turned into a two-storeyed fortress. Even the Little Redan round the curve was bristling with guns behind walls that were now stone as well as earth. The British lines faced the big Redan and Flagstaff Bastion, and beyond them lay the Central Bastion, the Land Quarantine Bastion, and God knew how many batteries between. Sebastopol wasn't a town any more, it wasn't even a fort, it was all but a bloody castle.

But there were changes on the plateau too. The land was scarred with deep, reinforced trenches, and men were hurrying to lay down gun platforms and shore up mounds of earth. Timber carts were dotted all along the lines with men almost throwing the wood off them to the constant barking of shouted orders. A Lancaster was being hauled onto a platform, a sergeant screaming 'Hold her, *hold her*!' as men strained and heaved like mules in the chains, and the great muzzle bounced and juddered as if in anticipation of the firing to come.

'Oh, well done, our side!' cried Cornet Hoare. 'We're nearly ready, aren't we? It'll be any day now.'

A burly sergeant rolling a gabion glanced round at the voice, and the look on his face stayed with Ryder as they rode on. Raglan might not realize what they were up against, but by God, the men did. Speed, the need of it, he could see it in their faces and voices, in the blur of hands hurling earth into gabions, the savage hacking of pick-axes, the grey exhaustion of the slumped figures toiling back to camp after days and nights without rest. They knew.

'Look,' said Oliver, and he sounded agitated. 'Look, isn't that . . . ?'

Ryder looked. The road ahead was filled with redcoats as they approached the camps, but one gleam of red was higher and moving faster, the saddlecloth of a man on a bay horse trotting out of the end of the Careenage Ravine. He wore the cocked hat of the Staff.

'It's him,' said Oliver. 'The same saddlecloth, look where the sun's catching it. It had gold lions on, didn't it?'

He hadn't been close enough to see. 'If you say so. What's it matter now?'

Oliver jerked his head. 'Only that it's odd. Where's he been? Why haven't we seen him?'

Ryder looked sharply at him. 'Perhaps he was wounded. Perhaps he was at the rear of the march. Perhaps he's a bloody devil who only materializes at suitably dangerous moments. Come on, Poll, give it up, will you? We've more important things to worry about.'

Oliver went pink. 'I was only wondering why he was in the ravine. Jordan says there are Russian sharpshooters down there. He says the men avoid it.'

'All the more reason the officers shouldn't,' said Ryder. 'That's their job, to work out the situation before they give orders. I'd be doing the same thing myself.' He caught himself up fast, but Oliver was hanging his head in embarrassment and didn't seem to have noticed.

Why should he? Ryder wasn't an officer, he was only a soldier with an opinion, and the frustration of it was harder to bear every day. That Staff bastard could go where he wanted, when he wanted; he could investigate, make decisions, make a difference, but Ryder needed permission to so much as set foot outside the camp. He looked again at the weary infantry, he thought of the long hours shovelling earth, hauling heavy guns, running up and down the zig-zags under fire, he thought of being a foot-slogger in the 28th and all he felt was envy.

Woodall looked at his cracked and blistered hands and could almost have wept. Grenadiers on their hands and knees in the trenches, lugging rocks about like navvies! 'What would the Queen think if she saw us now?' he muttered to Truman as they filled a gabion together. 'What would she say to this?'

Truman shovelled in another pile of earth. 'She'd say "Put your ruddy back into it, Woodall, and give over moaning." Come on, she's done.'

The wicker tore his hands as they wrestled the cylinder into place. It wasn't right, wasn't right. They should be guard party, not toiling like this up to the ankles in wet clay. He'd catch a chill, he shouldn't wonder, he always took poorly with wet feet. Overhead the cannon were firing again, boom, boom, boom, and a scattering of earth showered down on his head.

'It's the Frogs causing it,' said 'Nasty' Parsons, dragging up another wretched gabion. 'Ivan knows they're ready. They must have had four hundred rounds against them this morning.'

'The Frogs!' said Woodall. He knelt carefully on a sack to heap brushwood against the mud walls. 'Slipshod, I call it, working at that speed. Slow and steady wins the race.'

'Slow and steady gets blown to kingdom come,' said Truman, his hands sweeping up, down, up, down, filling the gabion with earth. 'They'll be starting on us next.'

'I've seen bunnies up there,' said Parsons, smacking his lips. 'Skipping about like at the Alma. How about it, comrades, fancy rabbit stew?'

'Not at that price,' said Truman, still filling, filling as if he were racing an invisible clock. 'Only a madman's going to go prancing about on top today.'

'Or an officer,' said Parsons. 'Claret-Top's up, I saw him just a minute ago. Lunatic.'

Another boom from above, a soft crump, then a pair of boots crashed down past Woodall's shoulder, knocking a gabion flying. 'Whew!' gasped the linesman, clutching at his hat. 'Hot up there today!'

Woodall stared in horror at the gabion. The wicker had split, it was a pile of earth again, and the whole rampart creaking ominously where the support had fallen out. 'Quick!' he shouted, pressing himself against the wall. 'Another in here, quick!' He spread his arms to hold back the gabions already leaning outward on either side.

He heard frantic movement behind as Truman and Parsons

dragged up the gabion. 'Sorry,' said the linesman's voice. 'It's hell up there, they're peppering anything that moves.'

'Don't ruddy move, then,' said Woodall. He butted his forehead against the top pile of earth in the effort to keep it back. 'If this lot goes, the next ball's coming right inside.'

'Sorry,' said the linesman again. 'We were chasing a couple of Russkies. They're in and out, them bastards, nicking everything they can find. We've lost hats, flasks, blankets, the lot. Bleeding trophy hunters.'

The gabion was in, but it wasn't enough, the others had already bulged apart and the whole ruddy wall was pressing against his chest. 'We need another. She'll go.'

'Coming up,' said Truman's voice behind. There was a reassuring creak of wicker, and a moment's quiet filled only with the panting of men and soft rattle of earth.

'Not just trophies,' said Parsons. 'You heard about the Frogs yesterday? Bunch of Ivans run up saying "Don't shoot, don't shoot, we're English," so the Frogs say "all righty" and back off, and next thing they know they've half their guns spiked. There's sneaky, if you like.'

Something stirred in Woodall's memory, Ryder talking about the Greater Redoubt at the Alma. But that was different, that was a British officer making a mistake, this was the Russians doing it on purpose. 'Disgraceful,' he said, with his nose grinding against mud. 'Lord Raglan should write a letter.'

Truman appeared at his elbow dragging a half-filled gabion. 'Come on,' he called to the others. 'Fill her here, Woodall can't hold it for ever.'

Suddenly he felt he could. Another cannon fired in the world above, the earth vibrated against his body, but Woodall of the Grenadier Guards held firm. The linesman knelt at his feet, sliding in rocks to wedge the wicker tighter, then Truman shoved the gabion home and it held. He stepped back and massaged his arms in relief.

'Nice job,' said the linesman, patting him on the back. 'You're a big beggar, ain't you?'

'Oh, don't encourage him, for Gawd's sake,' said Truman, seizing the next gabion. 'He'll be wanting his picture in the newspapers. Come on, help us fill.'

Not so much as a thank you. He knelt grudgingly back down and said, 'Could have held longer if we'd had proper fascines.'

The linesman made a face. 'I know, we'd a hell of a fall this morning. But what can we do? Russkies got a direct hit on our timber cart.'

Parsons made a vulgar noise with his lips. 'What a stupid waste of shot.'

'Not stupid at all,' said the linesman. 'Don't you get it, Tow-Row? They're trying to delay us. Hold us up while they build their walls.'

A sharp explosion cracked somewhere to their left, then another, then two together. Men were shouting, another bang, and now it was screams, someone yelling 'Christ, Christ, *Christ!*' over and over again.

Truman's face showed white beneath the mud-streaks. 'Sounds like they're succeeding.'

'Grenades,' said the linesman, standing slowly, as if in a daze. 'In the Left Attack.'

Feet thudded down the zig-zags, an officer yelled 'Stretchers to the Left Attack! Where the *hell* are those bandsmen?' The linesman turned and ran.

'But how could they?' said Parsons. 'They've got guard parties, how . . . ?'

'Keep filling, will you?' said Truman savagely, his hands sweeping up and down again, racing, racing, against a clock that wasn't there. 'Shut your mouth and bloody fill.'

Ryder listened to the distant cannon as he watched the carts trundling towards him down the Woronzoff Road. It was mostly empty ones that came back this way, but they were still something to look at and better than nothing.

Something flickered in the far right of his view, movement in the Fedoukhine Hills opposite. A lance glinted, and then he saw them, a little pack of Cossacks trotting quietly down the slopes towards the road.

He touched Jordan's arm. 'Do you want to do it, Billy? While I watch them?'

Even Jordan wasn't excited by Cossacks any more. He nodded silently, moved to the top of their ridge of the Causeway Heights and began obediently to walk his horse round in a circle. Beyond him Ryder saw Hoare leading the others towards them.

He looked back at the Cossacks. They didn't seem aware of the vedettes above and were moving with clear purpose towards the grey line of the Woronzoff. Ryder peered ahead for the object of their interest and saw a distant shape emerging round the flank of the long Sapoune Ridge. Faint on the air he heard the rattle of wheels.

'Hulloa!' called Hoare cheerfully, trotting up to join him. 'Cossacks, is it? Where?' Behind him came Jarvis, Moody, and Fisk.

Ryder pointed. 'I think they're after that cart.'

Hoare stared. 'It'll be empty, won't it?'

The Cossacks were skirting the folds of the Fedoukhine, drawing nearer the road. 'There'll be men in it, sir.'

Hoare licked his lips. 'Of course.'

Jarvis said quietly, 'Engage, sir?'

Of course engage, there were only bloody five of them, but Hoare hesitated and threw a nervous glance back to the camp. 'We're vedettes . . . I don't think we're meant . . .'

It wasn't the Russians that scared him, it was the lack of authority. Ryder looked in frustration at the road and saw two red figures sitting up in the cart, a driver and a loader. A bigger vehicle was just rounding the bend, and God knew how many in that.

'Very good, sir,' said Jarvis expressionlessly, and sat back in his saddle. He knew it was wrong, he must do, but Hoare was the officer and that was that.

The Cossacks were moving faster, and a faint yell of alarm floated up from the cart. It was intolerable, two men to die because six others were bound by the terror of hierarchy. Ryder said, 'We must, sir. They'll be killed. We *must*.'

It sounded enough like an order to wake Hoare. 'Yes. Draw swords, everyone – charge!'

Ryder's sword slid out, his heels digging in, and the mare responded instantly, speeding down the slope with effortless, regular thrusts of her hooves. The Cossacks were alerted, they were turning with lances couched, and Ryder rose higher in the stirrups and went for them.

A bang behind and the leading Cossack flew backwards out of his saddle. Hoare had stopped to fire his pistol. Another shot cracked from the cart, one of the redcoats firing, and a Cossack yelped and dropped his lance. He wheeled away for the hills, but the last three turned for the cart, and Ryder pounded after them, Jarvis right at his shoulder.

The cart had stopped, and the driver was scrabbling behind him for a gun. The other was reloading, but a shot barked from the second cart, another Russian hit and swerving away. Two left, just two, but one already thrusting in with his lance at the help-less redcoats. Ryder charged, crashing his sword two-handed against the lance like a cricket bat, and saw it leap from the Cossack's hands to clatter on the road below. He leaned across to slash at the man, but he was pulling something grey from his belt, the bastard had a pistol. In a second's heartbeat Ryder saw the flash and everything ending, but the gun turned before the bang, the cart lurched from the front, and the bullock dropped on its knees in the traces. The Cossack smiled, a shrug that said, 'Too bad, I'll have a ball for you next time,' then turned and rode away.

Ryder spun for the other, but he was already wheeling away with Jarvis swiping after him. The rest were out of it and gone.

The driver looked all right, Jarvis must have saved him, but the passenger was saying, 'Easy, mates, they've gone,' and for the first time Ryder saw what else lay in the cart.

Bodies. Living ones with grey faces and white eyes, but everything else was red. Red coats, red puddles on the planks, red-stained blankets, red-soaked bandages round arms and legs, and round stumps where arms and legs had once been. Three mutilated men, but with scarce enough limbs between them for two. The lurch of the cart must have jolted them hideously, and one was whimpering like a child.

He looked away in horror, cursing Hoare for not acting quicker, himself for not having *made* him act quicker. The dead bullock stared accusingly at him from the road, even its corpse worth more to the army than the useless cavalry trooper the Cossack hadn't considered worth a ball. Beside him he heard Jordan say just 'Christ!'

The driver of the second cart was shambling towards them. It was Bloomer, he should have known that from the green-striped vehicle, but his face seemed to have sagged, his eyes looked as dead as the bullock's, and all he said was, 'Bleeding lovely, that is. Got tired of looking on, did you? Bleeding lovely.'

Ryder dismounted at once. 'I'm sorry, we came as fast as we could.'

Jordan wiped his mouth with the back of his hand. 'Wouldn't have come at all if it weren't for you, Harry. *Christ!*'

Bloomer's eyes lifted. 'Like that, was it?' He advanced a hairy paw and nudged his knuckles briefly against Ryder's own. 'One on your tibby, Ryder.'

'Well done, chaps,' said Hoare, arriving breathlessly beside them, flushed with the excitement of a first kill. 'Well done, Sar'nt-major, that jolly well scared them. Come on now, better get back to our posts.'

Bloomer swivelled his neck to stare at him. 'I've men bleeding to death here, *sir*. What you want me to do, lug them to Bally Carver on my back?'

Hoare blinked. 'There's your own cart, man, move them to that.'

'I've another six in there,' said Bloomer. 'You want me to stack them?'

Jarvis stretched himself taller in the saddle. 'Watch your mouth, Corporal, you're speaking to a Queen's officer.' Behind him was Moody, bristling with supportive outrage.

An unholy life flashed back into Bloomer's eyes. '*Very* good, Sar'nt-major, I'll just tell Sir George Brown that, shall I? That the cavalry looked on while we had our transport shot to death under us, then left his men to die on the road? *Very* good.'

Hoare twitched in panic. He said 'No, I . . .' and looked back in terror at the heights they were meant to be guarding. 'No, I'll . . .'

'Horses can pull it, sir,' said Ryder. 'Jordan and I can get it to Balaklava.'

Jarvis snorted at the mere idea of a troop-horse pulling a cart, but Hoare was too grateful to argue. 'Yes. Yes, of course, jolly good plan. You and Jordan, then. Come on, Sar'nt-major. Fisk, Moody, back to our posts.' He turned with indecent haste and was at the gallop before Ryder could count three. Jarvis lingered to look murderously at Bloomer, then turned with dignity to follow the cornet.

Bloomer spat. 'Right, Morry, Pepper-Box, relieve these kind gents of their ginghams and get the nags in harness.' He leaned over the side of the stranded cart and bellowed, 'Hear that, swaddies? Going to hospital in proper style. Good as a Mile End funeral.'

A sour London voice answered from the human wreckage in the cart. 'But without the fucking mute.'

Bloomer smacked the cart and laughed. He swaggered back to his own vehicle and stuck a pipe in his mouth, but Ryder noticed the grey look was back in his face, and the hands that patted at his pockets were fumbling and uncertain.

He watched a moment, then was struck with shame. The Fusilier had been in the thick of it under bombardment while he himself sat on horseback and watched carts. He handed Tally's bridle to Morry, walked over and held out a match.

'Ah,' said Bloomer, drawing out the word into a sigh. 'You're a regular out-and-outer, Ryder.' He struck the lucifer, lit the pipe, and leaned heavily against the cartwheel.

This man had saved him at the Alma. 'You came through all right, then?'

'No,' said Bloomer, and winked a droopy eyelid at him. 'I was blown to bits and this is my ghost.' He sucked heavily on the pipe.

'With stripes on,' said Ryder, nodding at his sleeve.

Bloomer shrugged. 'They're two a penny now. We lost half our officers in the first hour.' He jerked his head at the cart and said, 'I'll probably make sergeant after today.'

Ryder didn't want to look again. 'What happened? Direct hit?'

'Not the kind you mean,' said Bloomer. He puffed again and took a deep breath. 'We were working up at a dog-leg on the Left Attack. Lovely bit of work, brushwood, fascines, lick of a broom and you could have ate your vittles off it. Then up comes this staff officer and orders us out. "Bad fall in the Right Attack, you chaps are wanted to dig out." So off we toddle up and down the zig-zags, we get to the Right Attack, and they say no, that's out of date, they had a fall earlier but it's all dug out again and re-inforced proper. Then comes the bangs behind us and back we go, and there it is.'

He heard Bloomer take another long draw on the pipe, but couldn't look at his face.

'Seems we'd only been gone a minute when the Russkies come. You know what they are for the lurking lay, they come at you from the earth and stones. They were straight in, biff our guard party out the way, then in with their grenades and out. Bang.' He removed the pipe again, jerked it at the two carts, and said, 'That's what's left of the guard party, in there.'

The horses were in harness, Jordan was looking round for him, he had to ask now or never. 'The officer, do you know who he was?'

Bloomer massaged his nose as if it were putty. 'Not from the Pope. We call him Claret-Top, for the flashy red spread on his nag.' He paused to fix Ryder with eyes that were suddenly bright and sharp as a bird's. 'Why?'

'Nothing,' he said quickly. 'Nothing. I suppose they're all as bad as each other.'

'Oh, if we're only supposing,' said Bloomer, heaving himself reluctantly away from the wheel. 'I was thinking you might be nosing something. Something that's got a very long tail.'

'And if I am,' said Ryder, suddenly desperate for meaning. 'If I am, are you?'

Bloomer tapped his nose with heavy significance. 'What's in my noddle's staying there, cock. You'd do well to keep yours the same.' He hitched up his trousers and climbed purposefully into his driver's seat.

Ryder walked back to Jordan with a mind crowding with questions. Was it really possible? Bloomer seemed to suspect it and he knew far less than Ryder. Could poor Polly Oliver be right after all, and one of their officers was deliberately helping the enemy?

'If you're ready,' said their driver politely.

The Woronzoff Road was clay beneath his feet, Tally's bridle was leather in his hand, and she came easily, trustingly, seemingly oblivious of the weight she pulled behind. He looked unseeing at the Balaklava plain ahead, thinking back to the Greater Redoubt and letting the memory of anger recreate what he saw. It was all in the open, nothing clandestine about any of it. The officer *could* have been talking to the Russians, he'd ridden up from the east when Raglan had been to the west, but he'd given the orders in front of everyone and with total confidence. He'd kept his distance, it had never been possible to get a good look at him, but it was his job to stay apart and unengaged, to watch and direct rather than fight. He was prepared to fight too, he had a pistol drawn, he'd been gesturing with it in his hand.

Ryder stopped, saw Jordan stare at him, grinned vaguely and walked on. He was hearing it again, the Cossack's gun as he shot the bullock, the sound echoing in the bang of a Russian pistol that Ginger said was different from the shots that killed the colonel. Ryder had dismissed it, assuming the colonel had fallen to a musket, but Oliver had known better, he'd seen the convenience of those two shots in rapid succession. What were the odds of two different marksmen deciding to hit the same relatively unimportant man at the same moment? Say one marksman then, one man firing two shots straight after the other, but there was only one gun capable of that, and it was the one he carried in his own haversack. A revolver. The kind the staff officer had been holding. The kind the Russians didn't have, but the British officers did.

Ryder thought of some of those officers. He thought of Marsh perplexed by anything more complex than a church parade, of Hoare afraid to give the right order because he didn't have the authority, even of Lord Raglan's courtesy that wouldn't allow him to give anything so rude as a direct order. That was how the British Army muddled on, how it always had and always would. He'd seen it as bungling, inefficient, downright infuriating, but just for a moment he saw what else it was and knew it was precious.

Had something got in? Had something crept in and infected it? He'd been so blinded by the incompetence he'd never considered anything darker, but there could be, there could, and there were two cartloads of mutilated men behind him to prove it.

'Slow down, will you, chum?' said Jordan. 'We're going skew, my horse can't keep up.'

He said, 'Sorry, Billy,' and steadied his pace. The plain was beginning to darken ahead of them, the ground was rough and bumpy underfoot, but he forced himself to walk slowly and evenly, and his resolution hardened with every step.

They had music in the Highlanders' camp that night. There were pipes and drums and some of the men dancing, but Mackenzie sat at a fire on the edge of the field with two young cavalrymen and listened to a story that chilled his soul. He busied himself with making the coffee, but it was hard to keep his fingers steady with the evil of what they were saying.

'It's a very, very terrible thing if it's true,' he said. 'Such a way to fight a war!'

'Oh, come on,' said Ryder. He'd a savage, determined look on him tonight, and his fingers were rapping irritably on his knee. 'Ask the Light Division, they'll tell you what kind of war we're in. They've had thieves, night raids, spies pretending to be reporters, the lot. The bastards want to delay the bombardment and they'll stop at nothing to do it.'

'Ah, but those would be Russians,' he said soothingly, pouring the coffee. 'This is one of ourselves we're talking about, and I canna just see it, a man to go against his own army.'

'I know, it's beastly,' said Oliver, biting his nails like a bairn. 'But people do things for money, don't they? We've had deserters coming out of Sebastopol every day trying to sell information. I suppose this could be the same kind of thing.'

Ryder pulled a face. 'It's a hell of a risk. He could have been shot by the Russians, never mind being caught by us. You don't do that for money, Poll, you do it for an ideal.'

Mackenzie put down the pot. An ideal now, that was something he could understand. Even in the 93rd he'd heard men say such things, that the icons in the popish Russian churches were of

Christ and it was hard to war against them on behalf of heathen Mussulmen. There was still such a thing as loyalty, the salt a man ate and the oaths he took, but Mackenzie's family had lost land to the Clearances, Highland chieftains selling their own folk for money, and if it could happen in the country of worth it could happen anywhere.

He groped for his pipe. 'Aye, I would no say it's impossible.'

'I know it's bloody possible,' said Ryder, and he was at it again, tap-tapping at his knee in an endless tattoo. 'What I want to know is what we bloody *do*.'

Mackenzie's fingers tightened on the pipe. 'We will not be doing anything, Ryder. We've no but suspicion, and bad enough at that.'

Ryder stopped rapping and glared at him. 'That's why we need to work out a plan. Why do you think we're telling you? We didn't just want to share the bloody misery.'

Misery was right. Doubts were a terrible thing, gnawing away at a man's peace. He lit his pipe, but over the bowl he saw the fire of Farquhar and old Lennox, his own mess enjoying a crack as they watched the dancing. It would be dismal enough talk, but it would be clean and wholesome and just for a moment he craved it.

He said heavily, 'It's a notion, no more, and to do with our officers. It's not our business.'

'It's everyone's business!' said Ryder in such frustration even Lennox turned to look. 'The bombardment will start any day, and after it a battle. What's going to happen if . . .' He stopped, looked round, and lowered his voice. 'If there's still a traitor giving false orders in the middle of it? This isn't about catching the man who tried to dish us at the Alma, it's about stopping him before he does it again right here.'

Here. Across the field they were starting the 'Reel of Tulloch', and Mr Macpherson himself pointing a toe in the four, but behind the music of the pipes Mackenzie seemed to hear again the great guns of the Alma.

'I wish I'd never thought of it now,' said Oliver wretchedly. 'I thought if it was true the officers would know, I thought he'd be sent home, but he's still here and they're not doing anything at all.'

'How can they?' said Ryder. 'Mackenzie's and Woodall's commanders know one part, Sir George Brown another, and none of them will put it together. We only suspected because we talked to each other: a Highlander, a Grenadier Guard, and a cavalryman who fought with the Light Division. How often does that happen in this army?'

Mackenzie looked round the camp, but Ryder was right, the only regiment here was his own. 'You're saying it's just us, then. That there's no one else in the army who sees it.'

'Just us,' said Ryder. 'If we don't do anything then no one will.'

The silence was long, and in it Mackenzie listened to his own mind. A battle coming, the men in danger of betrayal, and no one but themselves who knew. He was twenty-two years old, second stalker at Strathcarron, he had no business tampering with the doings of officers, but how could he walk away from it now? If he went to dance, even if he went to chat with Farquhar and Lennox, the doubts would come with him like a chattering devil on his back. It might be false, it might be nothing, but one way or the other he had to know.

He blew smoke gently into the night air. 'Very well, then. What do we do?'

Oliver put down his mug. 'There's only one thing we *can* do. We tell the officers.'

Ryder was rubbing his palm up and down his jaw, rasping the bristles like sandpaper. 'Tell them what, Polly? That we think one of the Staff is so awful he's got to be working for the enemy? That's as much as we can say.'

Mackenzie could just imagine having such a conversation with Mr Macpherson. 'No,' he said firmly. 'We must say nothing to anyone until we have proof.'

'But how do we get it?' said Oliver. 'We don't even know who he is.'

'We know the horse he rides,' said Ryder. 'We know his saddlecloth. That's not regulation, it's a personal thing like Captain Nolan's tiger skin. Someone will recognize it.'

Oliver looked no happier. 'No one in our troop did. We all admired it at the river, but no one knew whose it was.'

Ryder shrugged. 'He's hardly come near us. It's the infantry who'll know him, he's at the lines often enough to have his own nickname. We've got to speak to the infantry.'

'Mm,' said Oliver, still doubtful. 'It would be a lot easier if the officers did it. We can't just wander about asking people things.'

'And no need to,' said Mackenzie. He was picturing another man as he spoke, pompous as a king and prickly as a hedge-pig, but a man he knew and was part of them and who he missed. 'Woodall's up there, is he not? We must talk to Woodall.'

Ryder lifted his head. 'Yes, by God, we can trust him. We'll go and see him tomorrow.'

Oliver hesitated. 'But we're patrolling all morning. By the time we've walked out there we'll have to start back for watch-setting.'

Ryder swatted the air. 'We'll get horses, I'll say we're foraging, just leave it to me. But we can't wait, Poll. He's our only chance.'

'And we may be his,' said Mackenzie, the urgency of it striking him. 'It's no just a battle we need to fear, is it? If you're right, this officer is trying to delay the bombardment, throwing grenades and blowing up our men in the trenches. If you're right, then Dennis Woodall is in the most dangerous place of all.'

Woodall looked at the finished trench in satisfaction. Yesterday's damage was repaired, proper fascines to shore it all up, everything ready for the bombardment. 'Tomorrow,' whispered a linesman as they formed line to march back. 'Tomorrow,' muttered a guard party they passed in the zig-zag. 'Tomorrow, comrades,' said Parsons as they arrived back at camp. 'We're stood down, it's all over, the bombardment's tomorrow.'

And about ruddy time. Pack of scarecrows, that's what they were, faces scratched and muddy, uniforms streaked with clay, and feet swelling in their boots from the damp. Parsons was scratching every five minutes, and Woodall had a nasty suspicion he'd got lice. Well, not for *him*. They'd time to sit back now while the gunners did their bit, and Woodall was going to put himself right.

Other men dutifully piled their arms, but Woodall kept his back for cleaning. Other men queued for the rum ration, but Woodall walked all the way to the stream to get a full camp kettle for washing. Other men devoured their disgusting lumps of salt pork, but Woodall peeled off the clean white lard to moisten his hands and polish his boots. His only disappointment was to find yet again the mail brought nothing from Maisie, and he wondered uneasily if she might be ill. People said the cholera was abating in London, but Maise was delicate like himself; if there was something about she was sure to catch it.

He returned drearily to the mess fire to find Truman had swelled the numbers with his mates from the 88th, all lounging round slurping tea and discussing the bombardment. None of his own so-called friends had come, of course; they hadn't been near him in a fortnight. He suppressed a little prick of unhappiness, gulped grudgingly at the tea Truman offered him, and reached to put his kettle on the fire.

It was empty. He shook it in disbelief, and glared accusingly at the others. 'Where's my washing water?'

'You're drinking it,' said Truman. 'What did you think?'

'What – all of it?' In desperation he turned the kettle upside down, but only a few drops fell out. 'How am I going to shave?'

'What do you want to shave for?' said Truman irritably. 'No one has to, it's in the regs.'

He wanted to be clean, but they wouldn't understand that. He clutched his mug and walked away, ignoring Parsons's 'I'll piss it out in a bit, Woodall, you can shave with it nice and warm.' *Animals*.

There was only one thing to be done. He sat down privately behind the NCOs' tent, dipped his razor in the inch of liquid remaining in his mug, and proceeded to shave with cold tea. The drag on his three-day beard brought water to his eyes, but there was a manly pleasure in it all the same. He dunked the razor again, enjoying the familiar rittle of steel against tin, and swept the blade with enthusiasm down the forest of his sideburns.

'You've tea-leaves on your chin,' observed a voice.

Woodall's hand sprang from his cheek, but his heart seemed to bound as well. 'So you've finally deigned to visit, have you?'

'I have that,' said Mackenzie equably, sitting cross-legged beside him. 'Are the laddies no arrived yet? They were bringing horses, I thought they'd be here by now.'

He went on shaving. 'All of us? We might get a card game.'

'They've more on their minds than that,' said Mackenzie. 'You mind that staff officer we talked about after the Alma? Ryder thinks he's maybe a traitor after all.'

Woodall stopped the razor mid-sweep. 'What – Claret-Top? But we said it was all rot.'

'So it still may be,' said Mackenzie. 'But there's more.'

It wasn't much of a story, but Woodall remembered the sound of men screaming 'Christ!' and felt no inclination to laugh. 'Oh yes, I knew all about that. We were in the Right Attack just near by.'

'Were you now?' said Mackenzie, suitably impressed. 'Did you see him about?'

'He's always about.' His mind was that shaken, his mug was halfway to his lips before he remembered what was in it and put it down. 'It doesn't have to mean anything. He always comes up to the lines mid-afternoon.'

Mackenzie raised his eyebrows. 'Isn't that odd now, to be so regular? I thought they went as they were ordered.'

'Well, maybe he's ordered regular,' said Woodall, feeling irritable. He didn't want to think about bad things, he felt like a bit of company and a game of cards. 'Look, it's all perfectly open, you'll see him yourself in an hour or so. He'll have to pass the camp on his way to the lines.'

Mackenzie looked thoughtfully at the crossroads, the Post Road, the Woronzoff, the turning to the Light Division camp, the entrance to the Victoria Ravine. 'I wonder what he'll do up there today.'

'Nothing,' Woodall said firmly. 'We've picquets and guard parties everywhere, they'll be on all night. Even Raglan couldn't get at those trenches now.'

Mackenzie looked quizzically at him, then reached out to pat him on the shoulder. 'Aye, you've done a grand job up there, everyone says so. Has it been hard?'

The sympathy warmed him like a blanket. 'It's been ruddy awful. Two miles the food has to come, we've been getting it stone cold with fat in a skin on top of it . . .'

Mackenzie wasn't listening. He was looking past Woodall at something else, and his shoulders were slowly rising. 'Quick, man, is that him now?'

He turned reluctantly. It was Claret-Top all right, bay horse, cocked hat, that red and gold cloth, cantering casually up towards the windmill. 'That's odd. He's going to be early.'

Mackenzie was rising slowly to his feet, his knees straightening and lifting him in a single fluid movement. 'Unless he's planning on meeting someone first.'

Woodall looked at him in alarm. 'You're not thinking of . . .'

'I'm wanting to know,' said Mackenzie. He was turning his body to follow the horseman round, and Woodall saw his hands stray to his shoulder as if groping for a rifle that wasn't there. 'Send the others after when they come.'

Woodall stood in consternation. 'You're on foot, you can't . . .'

Mackenzie was already moving, the kick of his shoe spraying back mud as his legs pounded into the churned-up turf.

Damned fool. Woodall watched his red coatee streaking round the curve of their camp, then running straight for the Victoria Ravine. He was ahead of his quarry but his instinct was right. The horseman turned left at the windmill, but a moment later he took the right turn and started up the road that ran alongside the

ravine towards Sebastopol. Woodall looked again where Mackenzie had been, but there was no sign of red in the waving grass.

He chucked his razor back in the mug, slung his rifle over his
shoulder, and headed for the camp perimeter. Fool he may be,
but his friend needed support and it was up to him, Woodall of
the Grenadier Guards, to provide it.

Mackenzie ran on. He was at the chase again, and even the thistles that tore at his kilt and hose were Strathcarron and home.

He was safe enough in the ravine as long as his quarry stayed
on the road above. The red coatee was a risk if the man chanced
to look down, but there were rocks and tangled trees in plenty,
there was cover for a man with his wits in him, and for now the
horseman kept his nose safely in front, riding steady and without
hurry for the town of the Russians.

The Highlander ran on. They covered the Victoria in no time,
but as the Second Division camp came up on his right the horseman still followed the road left, cutting the corner and heading
down into the Careenage Ravine itself. Mackenzie's lungs were
burning and there was no short-cut, it would need a horseman to
keep up. Or a Highlander, he told himself between gritted teeth.
Or a Highlander. His feet skimmed the ground, he was fair flying
over it, up to the high ground of the Careenage Ridge and looking down to see what the man did below.

He was riding deep inside the ravine, as if to keep out of sight
of the Lancaster battery coming up on his left. Proof of ill-intent,
maybe, but Mackenzie was puzzled how to follow him. The man
was far below among rocks and gullies, and he'd heard there
were caves down there too. What if he slipped inside one for a
meeting and the watcher none the wiser? What if he disappeared
altogether? Mackenzie could settle to bide his return, but what
good would it be to watch the man ride out and ride back without so much as a glimpse of his face? No, he'd to get closer and
see what there was to be seen. He'd to go in the ravine himself.

He stripped off his coatee, as red a flag as a man could ask, spread it tidy over a thorn as a sign to his friends, then plunged on in his shirtsleeves, over the lip and down. The grass grew sparser, he was running on little more than crumbling earth, and then on stones, great loose mounds of them spread down the slope like beach shale, shifting and sliding and threatening to turn the ankle of him every step. He twisted sideways for the scree-run, jump and slide, jump and slide, the stones pouring and rattling as they carried him effortlessly down. The sound was enough to wake a deaf man, but the rider would have the clatter of his own hoof-beats in his ears, he was hundreds of yards ahead and unlikely to look back.

Someone else was nearer. Mackenzie sidestepped a thorn bush and was leaping into the next stone-slide when a crack echoed into a boom, and a rock beside him jumped to the smash of a ball. Marksman in the ravine, marksman with his sights on him, and as Mackenzie slid past a rocky outcrop a second ball rico-cheted off a boulder and whined a furrow into the brown earth. More than one of them, and himself as exposed a target as a hart on the skyline.

He leaped for the nearest trees. They were miserable twisted oaks, but he smacked his back against the trunk of the nearest and the third ball sang past way wide. He was safe for the moment, but as he strained to peer round his tree he saw his quarry stopped ahead of him, looking to see what was happen-ing behind. The man sat plain upright in the saddle, yet no one took a shot at him and he made no attempt to go for help. He watched maybe one minute, then turned and trotted away.

It was true, all of it true. No honest officer would abandon one of his own to enemy marksmen, none at all. The man was a black-hearted traitor, and Mackenzie pounded his fist on the trunk with fury. He knew the army was no perfect, he knew there were poor officers as well as good, but it was honest, and that man was an evil, a disease like the cholera. He let the heel of his hand grind firmly into the rough bark, then gently, steadily lifted it away.

He must think. He'd no gun and no hope of fighting his way out. Let the sharpshooters' attention once be off him and he could creep away unseen, but now he could only stand useless as a kilted statue and hope they'd find something else to shoot at.

Then a chill settled on the back of his neck as he thought what that might be. Ryder and Oliver would be coming along that road, and when they saw his coatee they'd be straight down after him, clear into a trap of his own making. He looked round for more cover, enough to help him climb back to the ridge, but the nearest boulders of any size were twenty yards away and above them only pebbles and scarred earth all the way to the top. The road itself was out of sight, but above and in the distance he heard the sound of approaching hooves.

Oliver was glad of the excuse to stop. Woodall had clearly never been on a horse before, and his hands were clutched so tightly round Oliver's middle it was difficult to breathe.

'He's gone into the ravine,' said Ryder, stuffing the coatee into his blanket roll and climbing back into his saddle. 'Too steep for the horses here, we'll have to find a path.' He urged his mare forward, searching the sides of the gully.

'Do you want to get off, Woodall?' whispered Oliver hopefully. It was bad enough Ryder lying to get them troop-horses in the first place, but he was sure there was some regulation against making one carry two men.

Woodall's hands laced firmly together round his host's belt. 'I'm quite all right, thank you, Polly.'

Ryder waved them over to the mouth of a track. It was rough, but Oliver had no qualms about following. Somewhere ahead might be the truth, an end to uncertainty, something that would be proof enough to take to their officers. The ground crunched purposefully under Misty's hooves as they went down, down into the ravine.

Someone shouted. The gully was bare, no one in sight, but a voice was bellowing 'Get back! Marksmen, get back!'

Misty's nose bumped into the back of Ryder's mare as she stopped. Ryder was already leaping from the saddle, dragging the pistol from his belt and yelling 'Get out of it, Polly, get back!' as he turned to run towards the voice.

Oliver's hands tugged at the reins before it hit him, Ryder sending him back, a child dismissed from the battle zone. He dragged Misty round and tried to bring his leg over to dismount, but Woodall was still hugging into his back and holding him in the saddle. He screamed 'Let go' and kicked back to free himself, plunging heavily and off balance onto a pile of loose stones. His knee crunched on rocks, but his hands scrabbled at turf, he ignored the thud of Woodall landing behind him and hurled himself forward onto soft ground. The voice yelled again 'Get back!' but a bang wiped out its echo, something cracked off the stones, then another shot, another gun, oh God, how many? He sat up on his tortured knee, saw no one and nothing and shouted, 'Mackenzie!'

'This way,' said a deep voice, and Woodall's arm was round him again, propelling him forward over naked, powdery earth. 'Come *on*, there's cover.'

He saw it ahead of him, a mound of boulders like the remnants of a landslide, grey and smooth and safe. But Ryder was leaping past it, swinging to point his pistol at something Oliver couldn't see, and from its barrel shot a flash of flame. Bang and another bang, then Oliver was at the boulders, Woodall pressing him down, and Ryder crashed in behind them with another man. Shirtsleeved and muddy, torn hose and dishevelled hair, it was Mackenzie himself and in a towering temper.

'Are you deaf, the lot of you? Go back, I said, not run right into it and get yourselves stuck!'

'Our mistake,' said Ryder politely. 'But if you *will* go running about in front of a nest of Russian sharpshooters, what do you expect your friends to do?'

'I had to warn you, didn't I?' Mackenzie glared at them, then shrugged himself lower into cover. 'And I was right to come. I've found out what we wanted to know.'

For a second no one spoke. A pebble skipped loose under Oliver's boot, and rattled ping and ping and ping to the gully below.

'It's true, then,' said Ryder.

Mackenzie's face looked older. 'They didn't shoot at him, they shot at me. He saw them do it, and he rode away. Aye, it's true.'

Ryder's face didn't change. Woodall said, 'Unbelievable. Unbelievable,' but he did believe it, it showed in the bewilderment in his eyes. Oliver believed it too. It was the certainty he'd wanted, but now he had it he'd have given anything to be wrong.

He said miserably, 'Well, at least we can tell the officers now.'

Ryder gave a little grunt of amusement. 'If we get out alive. How many are there, Niall?'

Mackenzie pursed his lips. 'At least three, I'm thinking more likely four or five.'

The far slope of the ravine bulged with cracks and crevices, and yawned with shadowy cave entrances half overgrown by thorn bushes. There could be a whole army facing them and they wouldn't know.

Woodall rested his rifle over a boulder to point at one of the caves. 'That's where the last shot came from. They're in there.'

'If they're all in the same one,' said Ryder.

There was a little silence. Oliver looked up at a faint rattling sound and saw Woodall loosening a packet of cartridges. 'I've got two dozen shots, easy. Ryder?'

Ryder shook his head. 'Only what's in the chambers. Five. The rest's on the mare.'

The silence this time was longer. The musket needed thirty seconds between shots, the pistol was their only realistic chance of cover.

Mackenzie settled himself more comfortably against a boulder. 'We'll have to bide the gloaming. There's o'er many guns against us to risk in daylight.'

Oliver tried not to picture the look on Jarvis's face if they missed parade and came in after dark. He said hesitantly, 'I've an Adams in my blanket roll. And balls and powder.'

They all looked back at the horses. Natalia had stayed near the top where Ryder left her, but Misty had trotted further down and was cropping the grass about forty yards away.

'Not much good there, is it?' said Woodall sourly. 'Why didn't you keep it in your belt? Worried it's not regulation?'

Oliver felt his face burn. He was off duty, he'd thought they were coming out for a talk, he'd been a fool and let them all down.

Ryder leaned over to study the distance. 'Will she come to you, Polly? If you call?'

They were all looking at him now. 'She might. If she can see me.'

'Try it, then,' said Ryder, lifting his pistol and looking back towards the caves. 'Woodall and I will cover, but jump back if we shout.'

He wriggled obediently to the edge of their enclosure and poked his head out between the boulders. 'Misty!' he hissed, feeling stupidly self-conscious. 'Come on, girl. Misty!'

She lifted her head, twitched her ears, then settled back to her cropping.

He heard a stifled snigger behind. Ryder's voice said, 'He can call her Queen Victoria as long as she bloody comes.'

He took a deep breath and edged forward, crouching full in the open. 'Misty, come on!' He groped in his pocket, found half a biscuit, and held it out invitingly. 'Come on, girl.'

She looked at him again, chewing thoughtfully. Then one hoof moved forward, the back leg followed, she was coming, picking her way towards him over the stones. Oliver held his breath, aware of the sudden hush behind him, then called softly, 'That's right, Misty. Biscuit.'

She broke into a gentle trot. She was halfway, more than half, just a little further, and then shouts behind, the bang of Woodall's rifle, and Oliver jumped back. A ball whined past where his head had been, then another crunched into the ground by Misty's hooves. She whinnied and skipped back, tossing her head and looking for Oliver. He half rose, driven desperate by her nearness, but another shot whistled under her nose, she backed and turned away. A moment later and she was back at the grass, as out of reach as ever.

He called wretchedly after her, 'Misty!'

'Leave it,' said Ryder. 'They know what we're at now. They'd like her alive, but if she comes near us again they'll shoot her.'

Oliver slumped down in defeat. It had been their one chance, and he'd lost it.

'Ryder,' said Mackenzie urgently. 'Movement in that opening – there, again. Are they signalling?'

Oliver could see only stony ground between the boulders, but the others ducked their heads and he guessed someone was emerging from the cave below.

'Talk!' a man shouted. 'Just talk – all right?'

The voice was harsh, the words staccato, but it was English and understandable. Ryder looked over his shoulder with raised eyebrows, but when no one else moved he turned back and raised his head a few inches over the boulder. 'All right! Come out!'

Oliver shifted forward to peer down the ravine. He saw movement on the opposite slope, a lone figure emerging from a jagged cave entrance and pushing aside thorn bushes to stand in the open. He was hard to see even there. The long baggy coat was grey, his hat shapeless and black, and only the black cross-belt and ammunition pouch suggested the military.

'The *plastuny*,' said Woodall knowledgeably. 'They hang about the front lines a lot, sniping and looking for prisoners. They've got the Liège carbine, blast them.'

The man cupped his hands to his mouth. 'Surrender now and no one is killed. Throw down your guns and come out.'

'Cheeky beggar,' said Woodall. He finished reloading and clutched the rifle possessively in his hands.

Ryder yelled back. 'Why should we?'

The man spread his hands, open and enticing. 'You have one musket, one pistol. Two shots. We have many more. You may hurt two when we come, but you will all be killed. Surrender now.'

Ryder looked round again, the question in his face.

'We can't,' said Oliver quickly. 'The horses, the guns, the things we know. We can't.'

Woodall was sliding out his ramrod and passing it to Mackenzie. 'Here, if you hand for me we can cut the load time.'

'We can that,' said Mackenzie. 'Give me the cartridges and cap box.'

Ryder smiled and turned back to the Russian. 'Sorry. Here's another offer – just let us leave and we'll wait ten minutes before telling anyone you're here.'

'Sorry,' said the man, with the exact intonation Ryder had used. He gave a single wave, a salute or a goodbye, then turned and walked back to the cave.

Ryder wiped his sleeve over his mouth, and Oliver heard the click as he cocked the revolver. Beside him Woodall laid the rifle again on the boulder, while Mackenzie took out a cartridge and bit off the top. It was only himself who was useless.

'Watch your horse, Polly,' said Ryder. 'See if you can get her nearer when it starts. At worst she'll draw a ball meant for us, at best she'll be close enough for a dash when they're reloading.'

For a moment it was hope, and then he saw the flaw. 'But we don't know how many they are. We can't know when they're reloading.'

Ryder gave him a rueful smile, a schoolboy caught out in a lie. 'Well, it's not all bad. Remember there's something they don't know too.'

The revolver, thought Ryder. It was all going to come down to that. Two shots, they'd said, never realizing he had an officer's gun that fired six balls to every one of theirs. Only five in his case, but he'd got to make every one count.

Mackenzie made a hissing noise. Ryder followed his pointing finger down to the wall of the ravine, but the cave entrance was as impenetrably black as ever.

'Where's your eyes, man?' said Mackenzie. 'Look to your left, among the thorn.'

Ryder stared hard, and now there were glimpses of grey among the dusty green, men moving slowly against the crags behind. He followed their direction and saw another black crack in the stone, a crevice shaped like a pear with the sharp end up. 'They're dividing forces to a second cave. They're looking to outflank us.'

'Oh, are they, though?' said Woodall. He shifted his rifle and squinted down the barrel.

'Don't,' said Ryder. 'There's no chance in that cover, you'll waste –'

Woodall fired. Ryder averted his face from the smoke, then stared as a grey figure crashed out from the thorn and lay still. He turned in amazement to the Grenadier, but he was already taking the next cartridge from Mackenzie and beginning to reload.

He said, 'Bloody hell, Woodall, they'll be after you to join the sharpshooters.'

Woodall kept reloading. 'No thanks. They want us to creep about in the mud, scrape holes and lie down in them for days on end. I mean really, can you see it?'

He couldn't, but the thought made him smile.

'That's three gone in the second cave,' said Oliver. 'If they can spare four, how many have they got in the first?'

Ryder stopped smiling. But Mackenzie hissed again, and then he heard it himself, distant singing, and the tramp of marching feet. He looked up to the road and yelled, 'Here, down here! Russians in the ravine!'

They all joined him, even Woodall shouted 'Here, this way!' but their voices were lost in the singing of the column as they marched. The strain floated down to them over the slopes, a raucous chorus of 'What Shall We Do with the Drunken Sailor?' Naval Brigade, on their way back from the batteries to the ships.

Ryder glanced at Woodall, who nodded, hefted the rifle and fired into the air. Mackenzie's hand smacked out with the next

cartridge before the echo died, but above it Ryder heard the singing from the road gradually fading into the distance, 'Hoo-ray
and up she rises, Early in the morning!' A stray shot meant
nothing on the Chersonese Uplands.

Except to the Russians. A faint rattle of stones to warn him,
then he was whipping round with the pistol yelling, 'Heads
down, here they come!' Woodall was still loading, the bastards
knew it, they'd only got himself to beat. They weren't dawdling
either, the front two were bloody running up the slopes, weaving
as they came. He pointed the pistol at the leading man, antici-
pated the turn, and fired.

Winged him at least, he was crawling back to cover, but there
were two others behind, and shapes already emerging from the
second cave. Too many, but he'd got to buy Woodall time. Behind
him Oliver was shouting at his wretched Misty, but they wouldn't
waste a ball on a horse while there were men to be shot before
they reloaded. Then he saw it, what they thought and what he'd
got to do.

He stood upright behind the boulders and let his pistol sag.
Mackenzie called, 'Get down, you fool!' but the Russians weren't
firing, they thought his gun was empty, they were running to lay
hands on the lot of them and the range was getting better all the
time. The spokesman in front even smiled sadly as he bounded
forward, and Ryder thought 'Friendly sort of chap' as he brought
up the revolver and fired.

Got him dead centre, he crumpled at the waist while his companions stopped in shock. Ryder didn't, he saw one from the
flank lifting his carbine, swung the pistol even as he cocked it and
snapped off a shot at his chest.

And missed. The bastard had sidestepped, a whole shot wasted,
and the gun was levelled at himself. He stumbled back into Oliver
as the ball chipped the boulder, but a rifle crashed beside him and
there was the other front-runner down – Woodall had fired
straight from the reload.

Ryder had two shots left. He jumped back to the barrier, but the Russians were backing to the cave, leaving two of their number flat on the ground. He swung left, the other cave, a man still out there, then a flash, a bang, and a hoarse cry behind. He spun round to see Woodall collapsing, blood on his face and neck and dripping onto his fallen cap. He'd been shot in the head, and Ryder felt a sudden coldness inside his own.

Oliver dropped silently to the Grenadier's side. Mackenzie reached for the rifle and continued the reload, his face as hard as the rocks behind him. Ryder turned away to scan the ravine, but there was no one in sight, the enemy had gone back to ground.

'They'll no try again,' said Mackenzie, ramming the barrel hard. 'Not now they know you've the revolver. We can bide here safe and slip off in the dark.'

Someone muttered, and Oliver straightened with an exclamation as Woodall's hand moved. 'He's . . . I think he's . . .'

Woodall's eyes opened. They were bleary and bewildered, but gradually focussed into awareness. He spluttered, moved his head a fraction, then said, 'I've been hit.'

Oliver bent to examine his skull. 'There's a hole to one side.'

Woodall gave a tiny grunt. 'Big one?'

'Oh no,' said Oliver, but his eyes met Ryder's and he gave a tiny shake of his head.

Ryder saw the fear in Woodall's face and felt a flat sense of fatality. 'That's it, then. We've got to get you to a surgeon.' He turned to Mackenzie. 'We can't wait for dark. We'll cover you while you carry Woodall up, then you can send help back for us.'

Mackenzie considered the distance. 'You'll need more than three shots to cover me.'

'I know,' said Ryder. 'I'm going to get the Adams.'

Mackenzie's eyelids flickered. 'I'm the faster runner.'

'You're also trained with the rifle.'

Mackenzie looked at Oliver, then back at Ryder and nodded. 'Very well.'

'Good,' said Ryder. 'Is the Adams loaded, Polly? Can I just pull it out and fire?'

Oliver didn't answer, and when Ryder looked round he saw the boy was white-faced and shaking. 'You can't. It's my fault it's out there, you've got to let me get it.'

There wasn't time for tantrums. 'Come on, Poll, I'm more experienced. You can take the Colt and help Mackenzie cover me.'

'I don't know the Colt, I know the Adams,' said Oliver. Angry patches of red were burning in his cheeks and his fists were actually clenched. 'It's my horse, if she sees you running at her she'll bolt. I'm faster than you anyway, your leg's still bad. It's got to be me.'

He was right, and Ryder felt something like a knife twisting in his guts. Poor kid, it was a hell of a way to fight his first proper action, but there was fury in his face as well as fear, and it might be enough to carry him through.

He said, 'All right, Polly. I'll cover you, now go and get your bloody gun.'

Ryder talked him through it and Oliver struggled to concentrate on what he was saying.

'Run like hell, don't forget to zig-zag, and if you've heard three shots from us when you reach that rock then drop behind it, understand? Wait for Mackenzie to shout when he's reloaded, then run the last bit. Grab the gun, bring the horse back with you for extra cover, and for God's sake don't forget the ammunition or it's all for nothing. Got that?'

He nodded numbly. Run and get the gun. Get the gun back to them or die. There was a fluttering feeling in the midst of his fear, an excitement at having come to it at last, the place where there weren't any choices and he didn't even have to be brave to make them. Sudden clarity flooded through his head and he looked at Ryder as if he were seeing him for the last time. He didn't actually look that heroic, his hair was tangled and his cheek grazed, but he was the real thing and what one day Oliver aspired to be himself.

He said, 'I'm ready.'

'Good man,' said Ryder. He squeezed Oliver's arm, then released it and stepped back.

Deep breath. Mackenzie had the rifle levelled at the first cave, Ryder was pointing his pistol at the second, they knew he'd go without being told. Another breath – and go. It was running, that's all, back on the cricket field running for the catch curving slowly overhead. Stones rattled under his boots, sucking forward thrust from his run, but Misty turned her head to look at him, he called 'Misty!' and ran on.

Bang! That would be Mackenzie, the Russians had spotted him. He remembered the word 'zig-zag' and struggled to turn right, away from his mare, losing time, losing speed, then a ball went *crack-ping* where he'd been and his mind stopped thinking altogether. Run, just run, another bang behind him, Ryder with the Colt, oh God, Misty was getting nervous and backing away, he yelled 'Misty!' and threw himself from the stones onto grass.

She stopped and looked at him, *biscuit, girl, biscuit, anything you want if you stay where you are right now*. Another bang, that was three, all his cover, he looked for the rock but he'd passed it, in front of him was only the grey flank of the horse they'd given him all those months ago when he'd joined to be a hero. His feet stopped, his hands were touching her, up and to the blanket roll, *don't look round*, unlatching the Adams case, then the butt was solid and grainy in his hand, and he spun round to face what was coming.

Nothing was, he was too far round to be a good shot for the first cave. Something moved in the second, but he wasn't a target any more, he was a man with a gun. Point it, pull the trigger, no need to cock, just pull the trigger, and a man fell. Just a grey shape, but he was a man and he fell. Ryder yelled, Oliver swung round and saw men emerging from the first cave, coming into the open where they could get him. *Where he could get them.* Point the Adams, gun at a target, point it, squeeze the trigger and then a bang of his own making.

The joy of it. Delirium took him as he swung the gun to the

other cave, but no one was there. He sobered suddenly, remembered he had only three more shots and still hadn't got his ammunition. He wriggled his hand under the blanket, pulled out the gun case, and turned to see a man ahead of him, the rifle already levelled on his shoulder. Too late to move, and he felt the bang even before it came.

But it was the other man who fell. Oliver blinked, turned, and saw a Russian outside the first cave pounding away down the ravine, followed by another with a wounded comrade over his shoulder. He looked back to the boulders, but Mackenzie was on his feet and Ryder crossing the slope to greet a group of redcoats strolling down. On the road above stood two empty carts, and beside them a group of Fusiliers with rifles pointing down the ravine. All those gunshots must have sounded like a battle, and they'd come to the rescue, they'd come.

He stood a moment, his throat constricting at the hammering of his heart, then slowly felt his breathing ease. One of the Fusiliers seemed to know Ryder, he was clapping him on the back and laughing, but Ryder only shook his hand, said something, then came walking on towards Oliver.

It was less than two minutes since they'd spoken, but Oliver felt suddenly awkward. He fumbled the battered biscuit out of his pocket and fed it to Misty.

'So how do you feel?' said Ryder.

Oliver looked up. He'd been slow, if the Fusiliers hadn't come he'd be dead, but Ryder didn't look as if he was thinking about that. 'All right. I think it's . . . all right.'

Ryder smiled and said, 'So do I.'

Woodall was a dead weight as they carried him up the slope, and Ryder had a suspicion he'd given up.

'I've had it, haven't I?' he said, clutching at Ryder's sleeve as they laid him down by the cart. 'Polly's right, there's a ruddy great hole in my head. I'm done for.'

'Not you,' said Bloomer, exploring the Grenadier's skull with surprisingly delicate fingers. 'That's the exit hole, daisy, it's been in and out like a knocking-shop grind.'

Woodall flushed, but Ryder saw the fear leave his eyes. 'I won't die?'

Bloomer straightened. 'Couple of days with the sawbones, you'll be going it like a whatsit gazelle.' He turned to bawl at his Fusiliers. 'Right, all the wood in the front wagon for the Left Attack, then I need a volunteer to help me back with this one to Bally Carver.'

He was a grotesque figure for an NCO. His stock had ripped loose, his sleeves were rolled up, and his belly bulging comfortably over his belt, but the men leaped at his orders as smartly as if he'd been Jarvis himself. Ryder watched him with gratitude and said, 'Thanks, Bloomer. That's twice.'

'Nah, we're square,' said the Fusilier, studying him with one eye shut. 'But what's your game, skipping into Devil's Alley like a bunch of Saturday-night flats? What did you expect to find down there, a bleeding picnic?'

Ryder didn't hesitate. 'A rat. The one we were talking about yesterday. It's true, Bloomer. We've just proved it.'

'Ho,' said Bloomer. His eyes gleamed as they slicked round the three of them, then back down to Woodall. 'You put a name to him yet?'

He could only shrug. 'No one seems to know.'

'Someone always knows,' said Bloomer darkly. 'He's noticeable, is Claret-Top, and he'll have to kip somewhere for a start. I'll give it the pig's whisper and see what turns up.'

'No time,' said Woodall, moving his head from side to side as if to throw off something that wasn't there. 'The bombardment's tomorrow. There'll be a battle. No time.'

Tomorrow! He looked desperately at Bloomer, but the Fusilier only nodded. 'We was cutting the embrasures today, cully. Tomorrow for a guinea.'

And a battle after it. He imagined storming Sebastopol with an officer working for the enemy and saw the Alma all over again, the Chersonese Uplands piled with red-coated dead.

'The officers will deal with it,' said Oliver. His voice was stronger, his chin was up, and he looked like something heroic out of *Alton Locke*. 'We have to tell them right away.'

Bloomer's eyes bulged in his face. '*The officers?* Here, where was you when the brains were given out? You don't go near the nobs with something like this.'

'Why not?' said Oliver. 'We don't know who he is, but surely . . .'

'He's a nob on the cross-bite, and that's enough,' said Bloomer. 'It'll be scandal and protect the pals, and all you'll get out of it is a striped shirt. Nah, this is army business and we deal with it army style.' He glanced behind again, then lowered his voice. 'Get him in your sights in a battle, a ball goes whoops the wrong way, and Bob's your very reverend uncle.'

Mackenzie straightened with a jerk. 'That's murder.'

'Is it, noodle?' said Bloomer, and there was a new edge to his voice. 'It's been done before, take my word.'

Oliver shook his head violently. 'No. No. We have to tell an officer.'

Bloomer looked from him to Mackenzie, and curled his lip. 'Then you do it, my biddies, do it and get yourself flogged. Not my hide, is it?'

Doubt and outrage mingled in Mackenzie's face. 'My sergeant would never . . .'

Bloomer pulled a face like a gargoyle. 'A sergeant! He'd be lashed himself if he tried to pass it up. You need a top-nob, a proper big 'un. Know one you can trust, do you?'

Only the man whose help he'd said he'd never ask. But Oliver looked terrified, Mackenzie was glaring at his feet, and Ryder had no choice. 'I'll do it, Bloomer. I'll keep names out of it, but it's got to be done.'

They all stared. The Fusilier peered at him as if examining

a rare specimen, then flopped his shoulders and gave a brisk little nod, like a salute. 'Your funeral, cock. But you tell this very particular nob of yours he needs to move before half after six tomorrow morning. After that I'm looking to my gun.' He closed a baggy eyelid in a meaningful wink, and sauntered back to the carts.

The bombardment would start at half past six. He yanked out his pocket watch and stared at it for what felt like seconds before the digits registered. Ten to four. Fourteen hours to make a difference.

Beside him Oliver was already mounting. 'Time to go, Harry?'

Mackenzie was nodding, Woodall looking up at him with trusting urgency. He put his boot in the stirrup and said, 'Time to go.'

II

16 October 1854, 5.00 p.m. to 7.00 p.m.

Tomorrow. He'd have guessed it anyway when they got back to camp and found half the regiment pouring out to Balaklava. Bolton called, 'Come on, Ol-Pol! We're told to enjoy ourselves in Piccadilly, come on!' and Ryder knew what that meant. They'd be on stand-to from tomorrow, and the officers were giving them a last chance to relax before the battle. Perhaps their last chance to do anything at all.

He said, 'Go on, Poll. I could be a long time with Doherty.'

Oliver hesitated. 'Are you sure you don't want me with you?'

Even Polly Oliver would suspect something if he heard Doherty call him 'Harry'. 'No need to risk both of us. Just go.'

Oliver nodded gratefully, then turned and ran after the others. Ryder brushed himself down, stuck his pride in his pocket, and marched straight to Doherty's tent.

'Won't see you,' said the aide outside. 'Ask an NCO or something, don't bother the colonel.'

To be expected. He stared at the ground and said, 'If you'll just give my name I'm sure he'll see me.'

'Unlikely,' said the aide, scratching a pimple on his neck. 'He isn't even here. Took sick this afternoon, he's in hospital at Balaklava.'

The Old Man ill! 'Is he all right? It's not cholera?'

The aide looked at him, and became slightly more human. 'You really know him?'

'Since I was about six,' said Ryder, feeling sick. 'Is it cholera?'

'Hard to tell,' said the aide. 'Look, you've known him that long, you'll know his servant. Go to the hospital and ask for Syme.'

Drinking lemonade on the veranda a lifetime ago, and Syme saying, 'But do you drink the flies too, Master Harry? Are they part of it?' He said, 'I remember Joe Syme. I'll ask, and thank you.'

He walked fast for the camp perimeter. Doherty was tough, seasoned in India, he'd pull through, he *must*. But there was more than one man's life at stake tonight, and Ryder simply had to see him. There was no one else, and time was running out.

'You're in a hurry, Ryder.'

Bloody Jarvis, standing right in front of him. 'I'm off to Balaklava, Sar'nt-major. I thought we'd been told to enjoy ourselves.'

Jarvis smiled sarcastically. 'Without your friends?'

There wasn't time for his pettiness. He said, 'That's right,' and tried to step past, but somehow Jarvis was in front of him again, that puffed-out chest like a wall between him and where he needed to go. 'Sar'nt-major?'

'None of your games,' said Jarvis. 'I saw you. Trying to see the colonel behind my back.'

Christ! Did the man spend his whole time watching him? 'Sar'nt-major?'

'Don't give me that,' said Jarvis. He stepped closer, and Ryder could suddenly smell him, the warm sourness of an unwashed body beneath the lovingly sponged coat. 'This is how it works, Trooper. You've got something on your mind, you talk to me. I think it merits it, I talk to Captain Marsh. Now then. What's on your mind?'

Impossible to tell either of them. 'It's on my mind that I want to see Joe Syme, the colonel's servant. Is that allowed, Sar'nt-major?'

'Syme,' Jarvis repeated meaninglessly. He stepped back uncertainly, and Ryder didn't wait for him to think of something else. He said, 'Have a nice evening, Sar'nt-major,' and walked straight past.

He'd have liked to run, but Jarvis would be watching and he could only stride away briskly while cursing the bastard under his breath. What the hell was wrong with him? He'd had Ryder's stripes, what else did he bloody want? He glanced back over his shoulder and saw Jarvis still standing where he'd left him, an oddly forlorn figure against the background of the bustling camp.

But the plain sloped downhill to the gorge at Kadikoi, and as soon as he was out of sight he began to run. The battle mightn't be tomorrow, the bombardment would need time to take effect, but Doherty was going to need every hour Ryder could give him. He might be too sick to talk to anyone, he might have to write letters, and God knew how long it would take Raglan to act on those. Ryder ignored the faint protest from his leg and ran on. On down the road, past low stone walls, farmyards, little white houses poking out of the hillside, on and down to Balaklava Harbour and the sea.

The sun was low in the sky when he got there, bathing the orange rippled roofs with rich, warm light. The hospital was right by the waterfront, a converted warehouse, square and ugly, and a linesman outside was washing bloodstains from a battered cart. Ryder paused at the door to catch his breath, then plunged out of sunlight into darkness.

The shutters were all closed. Candles made white blobs along a row of beds down one wall, while hanging lamps oozed light onto the tables where surgeons operated, shining white in the open eyes of a terrified patient, and illuminating the blood-trail to the limbs tub with the brightness of a stained-glass window. The stench was tangible as a brown fog, blood and rum and faeces, vomit and sweat and filth and fear, a thickness of air that muffled the feeble moans and sobs like a blanket. Above it rasped the grinding of a saw.

'What's your business, Trooper?' said an orderly with a filthy apron. 'We're too busy for visitors.'

He couldn't make his mind work. 'I . . . I just . . .'

'Ryder!' said a woman's voice. Quick, light footsteps, and Sally Jarvis walking towards him out of the murk. A white headscarf covered her hair but even in this horror the smile was hers. 'What is it? Is it your leg?'

He seized the inspiration. 'That's right,' he said to the orderly. 'I need stitches out. Here and here.' He bunched up his coat to show the bandage round his waist.

The orderly sighed heavily. 'Can you stay and do it, Mrs J? We've got a double amputation coming.'

'Of course,' she said, pulling up a stool. 'Come on, Ryder, overalls off.'

At any other time he'd have loved to have Sally's hands on his thigh, but not here and not now. He stripped and sat on the stool, keeping his eyes open for where Doherty might be. The beds were rough pallets, perhaps just for the night's casualties before they were taken to the ships, and there was no sign of Woodall. There had to be more rooms somewhere.

Sally knelt in front of him and produced a pair of scissors. 'These don't look bad. Couldn't Merrick do it?'

He felt clammy with shame. 'I didn't ask him, Sal. Sorry.'

'Doesn't matter.' She brought the scissors to the first stitch and he winced at the coldness of metal against his skin. 'I've got time, my shift's finished.'

The orderly was going through a door at the back, and he caught a glimpse of corridor and more rooms behind. Doherty must be down there somewhere, but the doorway was guarded by a redcoat as well as another orderly.

He said casually, 'Is Joe Syme here? Colonel Doherty's servant?'

She laid her palm on his thigh to pull the skin taut, and in spite of himself he stirred at the touch. 'He's in with the colonel. Why?'

It was a lot harder lying to Sally than it was to her husband. 'I'd like a word with him, that's all.'

She looked wordlessly at him then bent again to her work. 'I see.'

A fat black fly landed lazily on her headscarf. He stared at its aimless crawling, afraid to strike so near her head. 'All right. It's Doherty I need to talk to. Can I see him?'

Her fingers stilled a moment, then he felt her teasing out the last stitch. 'He's in his own room, they'll never let you in.'

'Would you ask for me? You're a nurse, you can get in anywhere.'

She knelt higher to get to his side, and the fly flew away in irritation. 'What are you up to, Ryder?'

Always questions. 'It's important, Sal. Can't you just trust me?'

She peeled off the dressing round his middle. 'You know what Jarvis will do if he finds out. Isn't there enough trouble without you always looking for more?'

He kept his voice light. 'I never look for trouble.'

She glanced up at him, and for a moment he wished he did. 'No?' she said, and began working up the scar in his side. 'Everyone knows you went in at the Alma by yourself.'

'I didn't. It was a stray bullet, the sar'nt-major knows.'

'This is a bayonet wound,' she said, snipping another stitch. 'What did they do, throw it at you?'

He jerked away from the softness of her touch. 'I only want to see the bloody colonel. Please, Sally, what harm can it do?'

'With you, I don't know.' She brushed away stray cotton and sat back on her heels to study him. 'You promise it's nothing against Jarvis?'

'Of course,' he said, stung. 'I don't peach. Why would I when he's bound to find out?'

'I don't peach either.' She thought for a second, then stood and slipped her scissors into her pocket. 'I'll ask for you. It'll probably be no but I'll ask. Get your clothes on and wait here.' She turned and walked away.

He dressed quickly, steeling himself for the 'no' he knew he'd deserved, but he'd only just got his boots on when she was back.

'He'll see you,' she said. 'But he's bad, you'll have to be quick. He needs to sleep.'

He wouldn't sleep after what Ryder had to tell him, but it had to be done. He followed Sally through the guarded portal, down a filthy corridor lined with makeshift beds, and saw Syme standing by a bare wooden door. Time swam for a moment as he looked at that seamed and leathery face that hadn't changed over thirteen years.

Sally murmured 'This is Ryder' but Syme was obviously prepared for the alias. He said, 'So it is, miss,' with a flash of humour in his eyes, then opened the door smartly as if to a court-martial. Ryder thanked him gravely and walked in.

The smell. Familiar at Varna, constant on the *Jason*, there was no mistaking the stench of diarrhoea. Doherty was clearly aware of it too, and fixed his eyes fiercely on Ryder's as if he could stop him even seeing the smell. He looked faintly ridiculous in a voluminous white nightshirt, but held himself upright against the grimy pillow and said, 'Good of you to come, Harry. I was thinking of you.'

Ryder believed it and was ashamed. 'I'm sorry, sir. About last time. I acted like a cad.'

The Old Man smiled. 'Boy in a temper, that's all. I was the same at your age.' His voice was more breath than sound.

Ryder swallowed. 'I said I didn't need your help, sir, but I do. The army does. It's important.'

Doherty focussed his eyes as if he were suddenly resuming his uniform. 'Then sit down and tell me. I've nothing better to do.'

Ryder perched on the edge of the bed and told him. Everything, all of it, as calmly and impersonally as he could. The colonel listened without comment, sipping constantly at a glass of cloudy water, and once batting out a lightning hand to swat away a fly.

Then he said, 'You know it's all supposition, don't you? You know that?'

'What happened in the ravine . . .'

'Proves nothing,' said Doherty. His legs moved restlessly

beneath the sheet, and he was obviously in pain. 'Who's to say the officer saw your man at all? He heard firing, he got out of it, and jolly sensible too.'

'But the grenades in the trenches. He told the men . . .'

'Out-of-date information,' said Doherty. 'Happens all the time, and you know it.'

He must be pretty far gone to admit it. 'I know, sir. I can explain any one of these things – but all of them together? Surely you can see it.'

Doherty made a sideways chopping movement of his hand. 'And what if I can? What are we supposed to do? Tell me that, will you, Harry, for I'm damned if I see it myself.'

Ryder saw how his eyes wandered, how the tip of his tongue kept flicking out to wet his lips, and felt the flatness of failure sinking in his chest. 'We can warn people.'

'Who?' said Doherty, and again his body writhed. 'Tell the men they can't trust their officers? Tell Lord Raglan he can't trust his messengers? Destroy the whole wretched army without need of a traitor at all?' His face spasmed, and he controlled it with an effort.

It was hopeless, the man was in agony. 'I'm sorry, sir, I'll get Syme.'

Doherty's hand flashed out again in the same chopping gesture. 'No. It's important. Have to make you understand.' He eased himself back against the pillow and tried again. 'Look. If you knew who the beggar was, that's one thing, hey? Pack him back to England, proper investigation at the right time. But you don't. We don't know anything.'

'The saddlecloth. Someone will know.'

Doherty closed his eyes. 'Come on, Harry, you used to have a brain in your head. Why do you think those marksmen didn't shoot him today?'

'Because they knew he was a friend. Because . . .' He stopped as he saw it. 'The saddlecloth. It's to mark him out.'

Doherty nodded, still with his eyes shut. 'Have to be something, wouldn't there? That's all the cloth is, just a signal. His own is probably quite different.'

It had been their only clue. 'Then all we know is a staff officer on a bay horse.'

Again the colonel nodded. 'You really want me to go to Raglan with that?'

He was in no state to go anywhere. 'We can't just do nothing.'

'You must,' said Doherty, and his eyes snapped open. 'You must, I want your word.'

He glanced helplessly at the door. 'I can't, sir. I can't let it happen again.'

'Say it does,' said Doherty. He reached for the water, but snatched back his hand as another convulsion gripped him. 'Good officers ignored him at the Alma, they'll do it again now.'

Ryder picked up the glass and put it to the pale lips. 'And if they don't?'

Doherty sipped, grimaced, and gestured the glass away. 'Then a few men die. But if we go into battle with men afraid of their own officers, men refusing the orders that could save them, how many will die then?'

There was no answer. He put down the glass, stared at its smeared surface, and remembered another just like it a long time ago.

'No one will want to hear it, boy,' said Doherty, and his breath came in audible little pants. 'Take this story to anyone else and you're finished.' His face was contorting, his voice little more than a croak. 'I can't save you. Even if I were fit I couldn't. I need your word, Harry. You'll be . . .' He hunched forward suddenly and screwed his eyes shut.

Ryder leaped for the door. Syme took one look at his face and rushed in with Sally straight behind. Ryder hovered helplessly as they eased Doherty back onto the pillows, but Syme threw an agitated look over his shoulder and said, 'Better go, sir. It's not doing him any good. Better go.'

Sally didn't seem to have noticed the 'sir', she was slipping an arm round the shoulders of the colonel of the regiment and feeding him sips of water. Ryder looked at the tortured man whose peace he'd just destroyed, and backed quietly out of the room. He closed the door after him, watching the little vignette of tenderness narrow to a crack then disappear.

The corridor seemed even dirtier and more chaotic than when he walked in. There was no hope here, no solution for him or for anyone, and all he was doing was making things worse. He walked blindly back towards the main hall, not even seeing the patient figures lining the walls until one stirred and said his name. Woodall, of course, how could he have forgotten? Woodall, huddled on the floor under a filthy blanket, even the bandage round his head black with dirty fingermarks. Ryder dropped to his knees beside him. 'How is it?'

Woodall shifted fretfully. 'Awful. Everything's filthy. I could die in this rotten place and no one would care.'

He tried to smile. 'You've only just got here. I expect they've still got casualties from yesterday.'

'Oh, I know,' muttered Woodall. 'The ones Claret-Top did for. It's a proper mess in there, I've seen a linesman who's lost both legs.'

Ryder remembered what he'd seen in the cart. 'That's bloody bad luck.'

A little fierceness crept into Woodall's feeble voice. 'Not luck, it's that ruddy traitor. I hope they hang him.'

They'd never even catch him. Ryder looked at Woodall's haggard face and red-rimmed eyes, and knew the Guard had nearly died for this. So had Oliver, so had Mackenzie, and a ginger-haired private who couldn't have been older than seventeen was already rotting in a hole at the Alma.

'We will get him, won't we?' whispered Woodall, as if in sudden doubt. 'That's what you said.'

Ryder made up his mind. 'Yes, that's what I said.' He struggled to his feet and held out his flask. 'Keep your pecker up, Woody. I'll come back when I can.'

Something startled flitted across the Guard's face, but he took the flask and said 'Thanks' in a ghost of his grand manner. Ryder smiled and walked away. Out down the corridor, out through that hellish main hall, out into the fresh air where he could find some space to think.

He walked to the waterfront. It had been so beautiful when they first arrived here, sky blue and sparkling in the sun. Now the shore was lined with bell-tents and littered with the carcases of broken boats, while baggage mules and oxen nosed at rickety stacks of boxes outside ramshackle huts. The water was brown with animal filth and debris from the distant fleet, the bay crowded with packed vessels and dominated by a frigate in for repair, its empty masts pointing like jagged fingers at the greying sky. Dusk was already falling, and tomorrow the guns would start.

He had to do something. They were all at it, Bloomer, Doherty, even Sally, all telling him to keep his head down, leave it alone, but he hadn't given his word and he had to do something. What, though? Doherty said he'd act if they could identify the man, but the saddlecloth had been their only hope. Bloomer might pick up something, but their best chance had always been the officers, and they were the very people he could never ask. He walked on past the noise and stink of Cattle Wharf, and knew he was praying for a miracle.

Then he saw him, an officer leading a horse from the path round the headland. The forage cap was lined with red and gold, undress uniform for Staff as well as ADCs, but the greatcoat that concealed his rank was the ordinary muddy grey of the infantry, his horse was grey rather than brown, and the saddlecloth was a regulation blue. And Ryder knew the face. He'd seen it last under a lantern at the Bulganek, when everything had looked dark and this man had changed everything by wishing him good luck.

He stepped forward and said, 'Sir.'

The officer stopped. 'Hullo, Trooper, how's the bridge?'

He remembered. He'd seen Ryder's stripes had gone, but it

hadn't changed anything, he'd even bothered to stop. He was the first officer Ryder had met who treated men like people, who was interested in their ideas, the first who thought about being an individual in a world of dull and random luck. Doherty had said to tell no one, but if there was a man in this whole mindless army who could help them it was this one.

'Sir, can I talk to you in confidence about something? It's important.'

The officer tipped his head on one side. 'In confidence, Trooper?' He looked around, then looped his reins over the horse post by the entrance to Cattle Wharf. 'Well then, we can't talk here, can we? Let's find somewhere quieter.'

Privacy was hard to come by on the waterfront, but not if a forage cap had the right gold band on it. The officer led him past a marine sentry to a row of dilapidated storehouses set back from the quay, pulled open a sagging door, and waved him straight in. 'I don't think we'll be disturbed here, do you?'

It was unlikely. The boxes piled on the boards had a dusty, forgotten look, despite the urgency of their labels. In a corner lay a heap of opened packs, linen spilling on the floor along with pipes and soap and tragic little pictures in frames, oddments of comfort for men who lay dead at the Alma or toiled in the trenches with nothing but what they stood up in.

The officer lit a stump of candle in a tin lid, placed it on top of a greenwood box marked PERISHABLE, then pulled the door gently closed.

'Come on then, old man, fire away.'

It was strange being in the candlelit dark again, as if they were back under the wagon, and Ryder found it surprisingly easy to talk. The officer showed no impatience or incredulity, and his only noticeable reaction came at the description of the saddle-cloth, when he gave an admiring little laugh and said, 'Someone's got jolly sharp eyes.' Other than that he was silent.

Ryder finished and said, 'That's it, sir.' He held his breath for the reaction.

'All right,' said the officer at last, and Ryder thought he sounded more tense than angry. 'Tell me – what makes you think this is so urgent now?'

'The bombardment. There'll be a battle after it, won't there? And if it's tomorrow . . .'

'Tomorrow?' said the officer. There was a rustling sound as he shifted his weight against the wall. 'Now how would you know that, I wonder?'

He couldn't betray Woodall. 'I can't say, sir, but I'm sure. That's why I went to see the colonel, but he's too sick to act.'

The officer nodded. 'All right. Who else have you told?'

He had to be careful now. Spreading mutinous talk could get him flogged. 'No one, sir.'

The officer smiled. 'Come now, there must have been someone. A soldier doesn't speak to his colonel without talking to others first.'

'No, sir,' said Ryder. 'But I did.'

The officer laughed and leaned back against the boxes. 'Do you play chess, Trooper? You'd be uncommon good at it.'

Not as good as this man was. He'd seen the weakness in the story at once, and would never believe it unless Ryder explained. 'I'm sorry, sir. It's just that I don't get on well with my officers. It's my fault, I've been in trouble, but I can't expect them to listen to me now.'

There was a brief silence, then the officer straightened against the wall. 'I think you'd better tell me, don't you?'

The man was friendly, he seemed understanding, but it was still a hell of a risk to criticize one officer to another. 'Sir, I don't . . .'

The officer sighed, and offered him his flask. 'See it from my point of view, will you, Ryder? Suppose I stick my neck out over this only to find out you're a known troublemaker whose word isn't worth tuppence? If I'm to trust you I need to know it all.'

No one knew it all. But the drink helped, and he managed at least to talk about Marsh and his own disobedience, about the personal hostility between himself and Jarvis. 'And you, sir? I don't even know your name.'

The officer turned the flask over in his hands. 'Probably better that way, don't you think? I doubt the army would approve. Call me "Angelo", if you like. It seems to have the right conspiratorial ring.'

His smile was infectious, but this wasn't a game. 'You'll have to tell someone though, won't you, sir? If you're to do anything.'

'Oh yes,' said the officer, slipping the flask back in his coat. 'I'll have to tell someone. But you need to stay out of it now. Tell no one else.'

Relief relaxed him even more than the brandy. 'I won't, sir. Only the others.'

The officer looked up. 'The others?'

'You met them. The Guard, the Highlander, my friend in the 13th.'

Angelo nodded slowly, and paced back to the boxes. 'And they're all investigating? Like you?'

Ryder woke to the danger. He'd a right to risk his own neck, but no one else's. 'I doubt it, sir. They're very loyal.'

'So are you,' said Angelo, and Ryder could hear a smile in his voice. 'But you're the leading spirit, I'd guess. Without you they'll let it drop.'

Ryder knew the diplomatic answer. 'I suppose so.'

'I suppose so too,' said Angelo. 'It's just you, really, isn't it?'

'Just me.'

Angelo leaned against the boxes and bowed his head. After a moment he said, 'Will you promise me to do nothing? To sit quiet, say nothing, and leave it to me?'

'No, sir,' said Ryder.

Angelo looked at him, but this time he didn't laugh. 'All right. But you must understand you have more at stake than I do. For an ordinary soldier to involve himself . . .'

He stopped abruptly, and then Ryder heard it himself, foot-steps slapping smartly towards their door. A voice yelled 'Oi, you can't go in there!' but it was tailing away and the footsteps moved past them towards the road. Angry voices were raised in the distance. Angelo moved to the door, listened, then turned to rest his back against it. 'He's gone,' he said, and smiled like a naughty schoolboy.

It was impossible not to like him. 'It could be more dangerous for you, sir. If you're talking to people, and he hears about it . . .'

'Oh, I can look after myself,' said Angelo. He hesitated, then brought something out of his coat, a long, thin object that flashed in the light of the candle. 'They call it a stiletto in Italy. Look, I'll . . .'

He stepped forward, but something banged to the floor and darkness sprang between them as the candle fell. 'Damn,' said his voice. 'Can you . . . ?'

It was right by Ryder's feet. He stooped to retrieve it, but froze with his hand on the tin. The voices were coming nearer again, someone speaking with angry authority.

'Then you *find* them, Captain, I don't care how long it takes. I've the best part of a thousand men sleeping rough in the trenches and I'm not going back without those tents.'

Someone mumbled, then a rattle and creak suggested the opening of a door near by.

Ryder straightened with the dead candle and found Angelo standing right next to him. His figure was rigid with tension, and Ryder understood what was at stake. To be found in a dark room with a private soldier was a crime even more shameful than his father's.

He said quickly, 'It'll look better if we . . .'

The officer hesitated, then seemed to relax. 'Quite right,' he said, and slipped the knife back in his coat. 'Meet back at my horse. Will you . . . ?' He nodded at the door.

Ryder opened it and stepped out into the lamp-lit dusk. Angelo was right behind him, tall and straight of back and already bursting into speech. 'A disgrace!' he declared. 'Utter disgrace, you did quite right to tell me. My Lord Raglan will have something to say . . .' He turned as if only just noticing the commissary officer a few feet away and beyond him a furious colonel of the Light Division. 'You there, you – Captain! What the devil do you mean by it? These stores should have been distributed weeks ago!'

Ryder slipped discreetly past, marvelling at his companion's effrontery. Whatever rank he was hiding under the greatcoat his voice had enough authority to terrify the commissary officer into babbling explanations and the colonel to complacent silence.

He waited outside Cattle Wharf and a minute later Angelo joined him, smiling with suppressed glee. 'Time to go, I think, before they start asking questions. But I'll need you to contact me if you find out any more.'

He was serious about this, he really was. 'Of course, sir. Right away.'

'And no one else,' said Angelo sternly. 'Me first before anyone, do you understand? There's a disused well outside Kadikoi, you can tuck a note under the canopy and I'll check it every couple of days. All right?'

Ryder nodded wordlessly.

'But you're to tell no one else. No one's to know you've spoken to me, not even your friends. That's a condition, Ryder. Do you swear it?'

The man was trusting him, he couldn't be asked to trust other people he didn't know. 'All right, sir. But you won't just ignore it, will you? You will do something?'

'Oh yes,' said Angelo, and smiled at him. 'I think I can promise you that. Now off you go, we can't be seen to leave together.'

He was right, of course, and Ryder's confidence rose as he walked away. Angelo knew what he was doing, he understood the seriousness, he was exactly the ally Ryder had prayed for. He turned at the hospital for the long walk back up the gorge, but the steepness was nothing now, and even his knowledge of the coming bombardment was only a sign that somehow and at last the Allies were fighting back.

*

Angelo watched him go with regret. Harry Ryder seemed a like-able young man, decidedly intelligent for his rank, and it was scarcely surprising his officers resented him. The whole thing was altogether a pity.

Not least for himself. He stood irresolute for a moment, then led his mare back round the bend, up the winding road towards the headland, then off into the yard of the last farm. There was no sign of its Bulgarian owner, but that was of no consequence. It saved him the tedium of explanations.

There was no one in the stable either, but he'd always enjoyed tending his own horses. No servant ever put the same care into it, and the bond between a man and his beast might be the only thing that saved him on a battlefield. He worked without hurry, seeing the mare comfortably settled in her stall before grooming the bay and laying the saddlecloth with some reluctance on his polished back. Blue was such a flat, dull colour, and did nothing to highlight the stallion's magnificent bronze tones. He looked so much better in the red.

Well then, the red it would be. One last time for the joy of the danger in it, then he would put it safely away for the war. It would hardly be wise to leave it here anyway, since Kostoff could never be trusted to burn it. He would promise to do it, he would swear on his mother's grave, then he would sell it to buy the attentions of some poor wretched serving girl too poor to refuse. That was the kind of mistake he himself would never make. He couldn't afford to make any at all.

He paused as he tightened the girth and wondered briefly if he'd made one this evening. He'd hesitated, certainly, and it was a shame he'd been interrupted, but the truth was he'd liked Harry Ryder and couldn't honestly regret not killing him. There were other ways of keeping him quiet, and what, after all, could the man do? A private soldier without the support of his officers, what could he possibly do? Poor Ryder. He wasn't even on the right track.

He swung into the saddle with a sense of elation and rode

straight out for the headland. There was a British battery sited on one of the slopes, but he gave them a friendly wave and rode by. He waved to the Highlanders' picquet too, to the cavalry vedettes at Kamara, to the Turks labouring at the redoubts, he waved to them all and rode by, speeding to the gallop for the North Valley and the race to the Chernaya. It didn't matter who saw him, they'd never recognize him again. None of them would ever know that Mikhail Andreievich Kalmykoff had just given them a wave and passed by.

12

17 October 1854, 5.30 a.m. to 2.00 p.m.

Ryder was dreaming of Sally Jarvis touching his thigh. A faint rumble disturbed him, but Sally's hands were warm, her dress seemed to be falling off, and he didn't want to wake just yet. Then a second deep vibration trembled through the ground and he opened his eyes. Oliver was sitting up one side of him, Bolton opposite, the others responding to the movement with groans and curses.

'The bombardment,' said Oliver. 'Must be.'

'Not yet, Ol-Pol,' said Bolton blearily. 'We'd have been called.'

A third boom, unmistakably cannon, and then a trumpet calling 'Boots and Saddles'.

'Now we bloody are,' said Fisk, bashing his elbow into Ryder's shoulder as he hauled up his braces. 'Trumpet's late, that's all.'

It wasn't. Ryder struck a match when he got outside and his watch gave the time as half after five. The bombardment had started all right, the sky above the Sapoune Ridge was lit in intermittent flashes to the distant boom of artillery, but something had gone wrong.

Everyone knew it. The parade in the dark was a fumbling, awkward business, sergeants' voices rough from abrupt awakening, responses slow from men half-asleep at their horses' heads, and all eyes fixed on those ominous cracks of light that illuminated faces like signals from a shuttered lantern. Horses fidgeted at the sound of the guns.

'Wait a bit,' muttered Jordan. 'The light's wrong, ain't it? Oughtn't it to be away from us, blazing at the Russians?'

Lieutenant Grainger heard him, and Ryder saw that old-young

intelligent face turn to the hills, the orange flicker striking his cheek like a slap. Then he faced front again, and his silence was worse than words.

Another, louder boom, then another even deeper, a whole salvo of artillery from beyond the ridge. The noises were overlapping now, faster and more frequent as cannon answered cannon, a solo bombardment becoming a battle.

'They're firing back,' said Cornet Hoare. 'I bet that woke the beggars!'

No one answered. Distance made the sounds deceptive, the Sapoune blocked anything like a meaningful view, but the bombardment had started early and Ryder felt a deep, sick certainty as to why. The Russians had fired first. They'd shot at men still asleep and unprepared, robbing the Allied attack of surprise and coordination, reducing it to a ragged fire of reprisal as one by one the batteries hurried into readiness. The Russians had known exactly what was planned, and it wasn't hard to guess who'd told them.

Light was coming, a faint yellowing of the gloom, then the self-important clip-clop of hooves as old 'Look-On' arrived for his usual morning visit. Lucan seemed not to notice the flashes and bangs as he trotted with his entourage to inspect the terrain, and when he returned to their lines the order was the same as every day. Stand down.

File away in turn, secure the horses in the lines, shove a handful of forage at the poor beasts who probably wanted water more than anything, then crawl away to be miserable at leisure. Only one thing was different. The RSM stood at the horse-lines telling everyone, 'No leave, no permissions, all confined to camp. We're on stand-by for when the attack goes in.'

It was beginning to feel more like 'if' to Ryder. The bombardment had got off to the worst possible start, and if the Russians had done serious damage before their own guns opened then it was unlikely to get better. The men knew it, they were murmuring in groups, looking ominously towards the Col de Balaklava.

'What about the fleet?' Fisk was saying. 'I thought the ships were going to blast the Russian forts.' 'Oh weren't they, though?' said Jordan, unsmiling. 'I don't hear nothing from the sea, do you?' Ryder heard only the gulls, their calls high and plaintive at the disturbance in the sky.

Hot tin brushed his fingers, Oliver passing him a mug. 'Coffee.'

'Thanks, Poll.' He took a sip, and let the truth of their situation sink in.

Oliver said, 'It's our traitor, isn't it? He met the Russians last night and told them.'

'Yes,' he said. 'It's him.'

Dawn brightened to full morning, and the constant dull rumble began to seem like something that had always been there. Marsh relaxed the orders to send them in threes to water, but otherwise there was nothing to do but sit and speculate. In desperation Ryder dealt a game of two-handed whist, but even that couldn't keep out the sound of guns that hammered relentlessly like punctuation to his thoughts.

Oliver wasn't much better, and Ryder watched with dry amusement as he scooped up a trick he hadn't won. 'It's not our fault, Harry. We did all we could. Even if Colonel Doherty had acted, it would have been too late.'

Perhaps. But the fact remained the bombardment had been crippled, maybe fatally, and there would be no battle today. Again they'd been delayed, again the Russians had bought time, and it was the same bastard responsible for all of it. He'd got to be stopped, got to be, but all Ryder could do was pin his hope on Angelo and play bloody cards.

An even louder thunderclap crashed in the distance, and the ground shook. The sky above the Col shimmered in a brighter flash from below.

'A magazine,' said Oliver, staring at the Sapoune Ridge as if to look right through it. 'That's a magazine, isn't it?'

'Ours or theirs?' said Ryder. 'Lift your hand, Poll, I can see every single card.'

Ten minutes later and there came another, a crash that echoed in the ground beneath them and blew brown dust over their cards. A group from 'B' Troop clapped and cheered, and someone called 'Go it, the gunners!' but Ryder dealt the new hand in silence. The firing continued, but the noise seemed thinner than before, as if he'd lost hearing in one ear. Then heads were turning to the front of their own camp, and Ryder heard it himself, the rattle of wheels rounding the Col.

Carts. Three, four, a little stream of them with infantry escort, casualties being brought down to Balaklava. Men surged towards them, all pretence lost, and even Marsh called, 'Hey, you there, any news?' Ryder and Oliver threw down their cards and ran with the rest.

The first cart didn't stop, but one of the linesmen called over his shoulder 'Mont Rodolphe's gone, the French battery. The Frogs are out of it.' The second cart halted and was immediately surrounded by clamouring dragoons, but Ryder ran past it to the back of the procession. The last cart had stopped by a crowd of 8th Hussars, but its escort were 7th Fusiliers and the one at the back was Bloomer.

He was already talking to the Hussars, but his voice was quieter than usual and Ryder had to strain to hear. 'We was cover-party, bringing up shells to the Left Attack, we saw it all. Bang-smack on the magazine on Monty Rudolph, fifty men dead in a second. Smoke cleared and there they were, black as burned crackling and nothing white but their teeth.'

'Stow it, Flowers,' said a sergeant. 'No need for croaking. The Frogs will have it up again in no time.'

'Not they,' said Bloomer. 'They'd another blow straight after. They've no heart in them, poor beggars, their officers are standing them down.'

'Ah, but we're Englishmen,' said the sergeant, grinning round at the assembled cavalry. 'Trust me, lads, we'll have the Redan down this afternoon, then it's in with the steel. We might even leave something for you "look-ons" to do!'

The sally was greeted by predictable groans and hoots of derision, but Ryder knew it was meaningless. There'd be no attack today, and with the French out there mightn't be one for weeks. He looked at Bloomer and the Fusilier gave him the tiniest nod of his head.

He backed out of the crowd and waited for Bloomer to sidle out to join them. 'You all right?'

'Oh, in prime twig,' said Bloomer. He took off his forage cap and blew out his cheeks. 'The Russkies fired first, you know that?'

'We guessed,' said Ryder.

'Well, I'm guessing too,' said Bloomer. There was a hard red line on his forehead where the cap had bitten into the flesh. 'I'm guessing your man had something to do with it. You know where he went last night? Sebastopolly, that's where. He was twigged crossing Traktir Bridge.'

More proof, useless proof of what they already knew. 'Maybe he'll stay there.'

'And maybe he won't,' said Bloomer. 'How'd the parlay go with your officer pal?'

Ryder looked away from the cynicism in his eyes. 'He's sick.'

'Sick,' said Bloomer expressionlessly. 'I near as a toucher shot the cat when I saw Monty Rudolph. But I can't say I expected no better from an officer. Did you?'

He wasn't going to blame the Old Man. 'He'll act if we get the name.'

'So will I,' said Bloomer. 'And I may just have something handy.' He glanced back to see the sergeant still holding his audience, then lowered his voice to a hoarse whisper. 'You know a village called Kamara?'

'Of course.' It was on the lower slopes of the Causeway Heights, not far from their own camp.

'Good,' said Bloomer. 'Because I'm blowed if I do. But whisper says there's nice pickings there, and a bunch of prigging coves have spotted Mr Claret-Top hopping along regular of a Sunday morning to visit a flash crib down the lane. Something of the fish smell about it, he always slinks round the hedges so no one don't see which house. The lads reckon he's got himself a convenient, but nine's a funny time of day to chase a skirt.'

'Always nine?' said Ryder, ignoring Oliver's mystified face.

'Very particular,' said Bloomer. 'Stays an hour, maybe more, but always there for nine.'

The cart was beginning to move again. 'Thanks, Bloomer. I won't forget.'

'Nah,' said Bloomer, sticking his cap back on. 'Like I said, this is army business. Forget the officers, pal, we'll nail this Joe ourselves.'

The cart bumped away, and Ryder's excitement rose in the rattle of its wheels. A mistake at last, and a big one. It was the first rule of war, never to let the enemy know where you were going before you got there, and this stupid bastard traitor had broken it in trumps.

'We can't really forget the officers though, can we?' said Oliver, as they set off back to the fire. 'You'll have to tell the colonel.'

'He's sick, remember? He wouldn't listen anyway, he told me to leave it alone.'

Oliver stopped in consternation. 'Then we must. That's an order, an order from our commanding officer. We can't just ignore it.'

'Oh, can't we?' Ryder said cheerfully, walking on regardless. 'It's for the good of the army, he'll thank us in the end.'

Oliver hurried after him. 'He won't. You couldn't even tell him, you'd be admitting we disobeyed orders.'

He'd forgotten what an irritating prig Oliver could be. 'He won't argue with success, Polly, the military never does. Look at Nelson.'

'We're not Nelson,' said Oliver passionately. 'We're private soldiers, we can't act like officers. We can't do it, Harry, you must see that.'

They were back at the fire, the cards lying exactly as they'd left them. 'Look, leave Doherty to me, will you? I told you, I know him a little, he'll be only too pleased if we catch this bastard out.'

'How can we?' said Oliver. 'I'll be on vedettes, I start on Friday.'

He was just making difficulties. 'Swap with someone for the day. You're with Grainger, you know he doesn't mind.'

'There's no point,' said Oliver. He sat down like a sulky child and began to collect the scattered cards. 'We can't watch the meeting without an officer.'

He looked at the top of that blond head and wondered at its obstinacy. There'd been a time when Polly Oliver trembled at his sarcasm, but never again, not now. He'd fought a damn good action yesterday, and the frightened boy was gone for good.

He sat back down. 'All right, why can't we?'

'Because it's Sunday,' said Oliver, blowing dust off a card. 'We'll still be at Divine Service.'

He stared in disbelief. 'That's ridiculous. We'll just have to miss it, that's all.'

Oliver looked nervous again. 'It finishes round about nine. You could still be at Kamara for quarter past.'

'And what good's that? We'll never know which house he's in unless we're there to see him arrive. No, we can't let the chance go for something as stupid as a Church Parade.'

Oliver looked up in horror. 'But that's a *blackguardly* thing to say!' His mouth was hanging open, and he looked genuinely distressed. 'Church isn't stupid, you know it's not. All those fellows gone to eternity just this morning!'

Ryder bit his lip. 'All right, look, I know it's important, but we can say our prayers another time. We just have to get out of it now.'

Oliver still looked shaken. 'No one can unless they're on duty. No one gets leave from Divine Service.'

The cannon went on firing beyond the Sapoune, banging and banging as if it would never stop. 'Then we'll go without it.'

Oliver stared at him, clearly too shocked to speak.

Ryder gestured dismissively. 'Come on, people do it all the time. How do you think Bloomer's friends learned about this in the first place?'

Oliver suddenly found his tongue. 'They were looting. They're criminals. We're not, and I'm not going to do it.' He slid the cards back in the box and closed it with a snap.

Ryder knew defeat when he saw it. 'Then I'll do it alone.'

Oliver shook his head violently. 'It's even worse for you. You've been warned already, and you know the sergeant-major would love an excuse.'

He thought of Jarvis watching him yesterday, and shrugged uneasily. 'It's only missing a church service.'

'No, it's not,' said Oliver. 'It's lying to get out of one in order to go and spy on an officer when you've been directly ordered not to. It could hardly be worse.'

He knew it. He knew it was a flogging offence and he'd very little chance of getting away with it. He stared at the fire, and it took him a moment to realize the damn thing had gone out.

Oliver turned for the miserable pile of roots that was their only remaining firewood. 'It could still be all right. Colonel Doherty might be better in a few days. And you wouldn't have to disobey him, you could just ask what he thinks.' He looked up with appealing eyes.

Ryder tried to smile. 'Yes, all right, Poll. Maybe I'll do that.'

He wouldn't, but he couldn't tell Oliver what he was really going to do. He couldn't tell anyone his only hope left was the mysterious officer he knew as Angelo.

Kalmykoff stretched luxuriously in the rose-scented bath water and took another sip of champagne. French, as he liked it, without the added sweetness of their own Ay-Danil variety. Doubtless there would be shortages now the invaders were wrecking the vineyards, but that could soon be rectified once they were driven out. He listened to the pulse of distant artillery, and felt it stir him more than the champagne.

A door opened, and he looked through the painted screens to see his uncle entering the chamber. Lieutenant Colonel Sergei Paulovich Kalmykoff was an imposing figure in eyeglass and full dress uniform, but the wispy grey hair and anxious expression robbed even the medals and scarlet sash of the power to intimidate.

'Here you are, Mikhail,' he called, laying a pile of clothes over a chair. 'Gasha's done her best, but really, dear boy, it looks as if you've been sleeping in them.'

'I have,' said Kalmykoff, and grinned. 'In Kostoff's barn most nights. Tell Gasha it's good for my soul.'

'But not your linen,' said his uncle. He sat down at the table and studied the chessboard. 'What have you done here? You've made two moves!'

'Only one,' said Kalmykoff. 'But I think it was the right one.' He thrust himself upright and reached for a towel. 'How is it going?'

His uncle was still frowning at the chessboard. 'Not so well. The British are pounding the Redan. If they reduce it they could storm us by this evening.'

'They won't,' he said, stepping out of the tub. 'The French have stopped for now, and Raglan would never be so rude as to attack without them. That is how he thinks.'

'Is it?' said Sergei. He began to slide forward a bishop, then changed his mind and put it back. 'You're very certain, Misha. Is every Englishman so easy to read?'

He began to towel vigorously down his body. 'Not all. Ryder puzzles me, he is not the right type for a private soldier. And then there is our Mr Shepherd, who is the right type for nothing, and what goes on behind his face nobody knows. Count Ignatieff says, "You deal with him, Kalmykoff, you're half English, you understand these people," and I consider myself quite insulted.'

Sergei gave a dramatic little shudder. 'I don't blame you. No disrespect to your mother, dear boy, but couldn't you work with civilized people like the French?'

He walked out through the screens, noticing with amusement his uncle's averted face. 'It wouldn't work with the French. An officer gives an order, the men argue, and the majority carries the day. That's the curse of revolution, Uncle – men who think for themselves.'

'Are you being ironic again, Misha?' Sergei moved his knight and set it down with a defiant *click*.

'Possibly.' He looked over his uncle's shoulder, reached for a castle and slid it deftly into place. 'Mate in two, I think.'

Sergei leaned forward to scan the board, and Kalmykoff turned tactfully away to dress. 'Is my horse ready, Uncle?'

'Of course,' said Sergei, sitting back with slumped shoulders. 'But really, must you go back? Count Ignatieff has other . . . helpers. You're not essential.'

'He would have none if it weren't for me.' He slipped on his shirt, cool and smooth against the rawness of his skin. 'Someone has to meet with animals like Kostoff to get the names and contacts Mr Shepherd will need next month and the next.'

The guns boomed again, and Sergei flicked away a tiny flake of plaster from the chessboard. 'It won't last that long.'

'It could last for ever if we go on as we are.' He looked at the board and marvelled at its simplicity, black against white in neat, still squares. 'You know what's wrong with this war, Uncle? That no one wants to fight it. We build our walls of stone, the Allies build theirs of mud, we are all careful and cautious and look only to defence. We need to be bold, to attack, to bring the battle to the enemy and drive him from our land.'

His uncle was silent a moment, then he flipped over his king and looked up. 'We cannot. In numbers we can match them, but they have their ships, they have better guns . . .'

'A fig for their guns!' He tugged out a chair and sat to face Sergei at the chessboard. 'There is no heart in their cause. We have the Church, we have men like Admiral Korniloff who the men will die for, we have . . .' He stopped, disturbed by Sergei's expression. 'What? Uncle, what?'

Sergei reached out to take his hands. 'The Admiral fell at the Malakoff not an hour ago. There has been no official announcement, but he died, Misha, died a Christian, and almost his last words were "Defend Sebastopol".'

Kalmykoff gripped his hands. 'Well, then, that is a proper end for a great man. To die rallying your troops, to die fighting – all the pain in the world would be nothing to that.'

Sergei relaxed his hold. 'He leaves a widow . . .'

'Who will be proud,' he said, and knew it for truth. 'Think if Sebastopol were taken, to be captured, humiliated, helpless. Korniloff's death is the only one for a man, and I pray for as good a one myself.'

Sergei pushed back his chair and stood. 'Do you pray, Misha? Sometimes I wonder.'

He laughed. 'I pray for battle. We have a perfectly good field army at Chorgun, we must go out, attack, draw our cautious enemy into a fight we can win.'

Sergei shook his head. 'If he is cautious he will not be drawn.'

Kalmykoff smiled. 'If we know the right bait he will be. Take the British cavalry. Lord Raglan is proud of them, he wishes them kept safely in their bandbox, so.' He picked up a black knight and moved it behind a defence of pawns. 'But what if we threaten something he values even more?' He slid a white castle alongside the black queen.

Sergei thrust his hands into his pockets. 'What does Lord Raglan value more than his cavalry?'

'His guns. Their Wellington never lost a gun, remember, and Raglan was his secretary. If he thought his guns were under threat . . .' He took the castle with the black knight. 'Now see how his knight is exposed to our queen.'

Sergei wasn't even looking. 'These are men, not chess pieces.'

'Yes!' said Kalmykoff. 'That is why this will work. Raglan who lives in his hero's shadow, Lucan and Cardigan who have been so shamed by doing nothing they would charge a fleet on the water to regain their honour. They are flesh-and-blood men with flesh-and-blood weaknesses, and one wolf among the sheep can destroy them all.'

'You've changed, Misha,' said Sergei, turning away to grope for the bottle. 'We should never have let you train so long with the Cossacks. You don't care for Russia any more, only your own skill.'

'And the other way is better?' He took a long, cool drink of the champagne. 'The old ways died at the Alma. Prince Menschikoff was so certain of them he did nothing to fortify the city, and if it weren't for Todleben, where would we be now? An engineer is saving us, an engineer and the heroism of women and children who work all night to build up our walls.'

'Yes, heroism,' said Sergei, drawing himself up and looking almost impressive. 'Heroism for the greater good, for Russia and the people, not for themselves and their own pride.'

'And what do you call it, our army against their army and the one who kills more wins?' He drained his glass and slammed it back down on the table. 'I am the future, me and people like me. The day will come when you look from your trenches to other men in other trenches and you will ask, "Isn't there a better way?" Well there is, Uncle, and you're looking at it.'

Sergei's kindly mouth had hardened into obstinacy. 'It's against the principles of war.'

'Principles!' he said. 'Look at this game. White is now winning, but suppose I take this bishop and move it sideways, like this?'

Sergei stared. 'But the bishop can only move on the diagonal.'

He smiled. 'The bishop can move any way I want. The rules are in your head, not on the board.'

Sergei shook his head and turned away. 'I could never argue with you, Mikhail Andreievich.' He took out his eyeglass and began to polish it on his handkerchief.

Kalmykoff looked at his hunched shoulders and was sorry. 'No, I'm talking foolishness. I've been alone too long, perhaps. I've missed the company of my own kind.'

Sergei replaced his monocle and blinked experimentally. 'Then don't go back. I beg you, Misha, for your safety as well as your soul. This young cavalryman of yours, if he talks to anyone else . . .'

'Ryder!' He pulled on his frock-coat and grinned at his reflection in the mirror. 'Don't worry, Uncle, I know exactly how to deal with him. He has given me the weapon himself.'

Ryder watched the butcher's cart trundling towards the gorge. The rations cart had already gone, and even Oldham, the senior captain, was relaxing the stand-to by letting 'A' Troop go for forage. Now was his chance.

He still needed an excuse, but there was a perfectly good one in his own overalls. He'd had it seen to yesterday, of course, but the officers didn't know that, and Hoare at least was still pleasingly blind to guile. He checked Oliver was still deep in innocent conversation with Bolton, then scribbled his note and went in search of the cornet.

Hoare was standing alone by the forge cart, chewing his lip and looking despondently towards the Col. Ryder saluted smartly and said, 'Permission to leave camp, sir. Just for an hour or so.'

Hoare hesitated. 'Well, you know, Ryder, we *are* on stand-by.'

The poor idiot probably thought there'd still be an attack today. 'It's my leg, sir. Merrick's in Balaklava, and I need my stitches out.'

Hoare wavered, and Ryder saw uneasily that Jarvis was watching them. 'Well, I don't know. The hospital will be awfully busy with casualties from the bombardment.'

Jarvis was moving nearer. Had he heard? 'I know, sir, but I want to be fit for when we're called to battle.'

Hoare brightened at once. 'Yes, of course, you need your leg right for that. Off you go then, and come straight back.'

Ryder saluted and turned swiftly for the perimeter, but the hated voice called him back. 'Ryder. One moment.'

If Sally had told him, he was finished. 'Yes, Sar'nt-major?'

'Your leg,' said Jarvis. 'Why didn't you have it done yesterday?'

He said, 'I didn't think of it then, Sar'nt-major,' and prayed hard.

Jarvis snorted. 'Didn't want to do it in your own time, you mean. Well, you can pay us back by taking picquet tonight, can't you, Trooper?'

The relief was so great he could only say 'Thank you, Sar'nt-major' and walk hastily away. God bless Sally. She'd said she wasn't a peach, and she wasn't.

He set off across the plain at a brisk trot. He had no need to run this time, he wasn't going as far as Balaklava, but the urgency was still driving at him and his feet started to thump faster and harder on the turf as he pounded down the slope towards Kadikoi.

He knew the place he was after. Three withered juniper trees stood just off the track to the Highlanders' camp, and between them was the disused well, long boarded up with rotting planks. When the white walls and red roofs of the village came up on his left he turned off the road, walked confidently towards the juniper trees, and stopped dead.

Turks. A whole bunch of them had spread away from the Highlanders and set up camp round the trees. Two stretchers stood propped against a tree trunk, three tents were up, and a man in a dirty white apron dropped from a wagon to hurl the contents of a brimming bowl across the track. This was a sick camp, it was here to bloody stay, and the well stuck right in the middle of it. A man was even sitting on the planks while he rolled bandages and hummed tunelessly between fleshy lips. The postbox was blocked.

He considered brazening it out, leaving the note anyway, but abandoned the thought as soon as it came. The Turks might read it, but Angelo never would, he'd never expose himself as publicly as this. This one, stupid well had been their only means of contact, and now it was lost.

He turned away, still furiously hunting for answers, but as he reached the road the air exploded in a tumultuous roar from the sea. His mind shook, and it took him a second to remember the fleet. These weren't single cannon shots, they were full broadsides crashing out from upwards of six hundred guns, and for a moment he could only crouch against the dry-stone wall and cover his head with his hands.

It was impossible to think, and after a moment he stopped even trying. The world was one vast noise, and against it he was as insignificant as an insect, scurrying round trying to change things that had long ago been sealed. Even the disaster of the well had been inevitable, just one more sign of his utter powerlessness. A cart rattled by, packed with wounded and mutilated men from the trenches, and he hardly even blinked at it, seeing only the same old horror that never looked like ending. He felt movement on the grass verge, but just kept his head down, waiting for whoever it was to pass. Then a hand touched his arm, a voice said 'Ryder?' and he jerked round to find himself face to face with Sally Jarvis.

For a moment he thought he was dreaming again, but she was wrapped in a plaid and carrying a basket, and if she was about to stroke his thighs she didn't look it. She said, 'Are you all right?' and shook his shoulder as if to wake him.

He made an effort. 'Come on, Sal, can't a man have a moment to himself?'

She released his shoulder and sat down beside him. 'Not if he looks like he's thinking of shooting himself.'

He thrust away the image. 'It's just the row, that's all. How can you bear it?'

'Oh, I'm used to it,' she said, smoothing her dress over her knees. 'It makes me think of Falmouth and the salutes when a ship came in. I'd always watch in case it was my father.'

He could see it suddenly, little Sally jumping and waving her handkerchief at the sails sweeping into the Carrick Roads. She was still that girl now. She must have been in the thick of it down in the hospital, among the stench and screaming, but her face and hands were scrubbed clean and her hair tied back so tightly it was lifting the delicate skin of her forehead.

He looked away. 'Thanks for not telling Jarvis. About yesterday.'

'Of course I didn't.' She sounded thoroughly indignant. 'I don't interfere in regimental matters, you should know better.'

He did really. Back in barracks a woman had only to stick a foot the wrong side of the blanket screen to bring the wrath of the gods on her neck, and he could only imagine how Jarvis would react if his wife started telling him about men in his troop.

But that was a thought, and with it came a flicker of hope. 'Sally, if I really needed to get out of something, would you tell the officers my leg was bad and I had to go to hospital at once?'

She didn't hesitate. 'Not if it wasn't. The surgeon would have to look at it, and you couldn't fool him.'

'What if I cut it? Gashed it myself?'

Nothing shocked her. 'If you did it thoroughly enough for the surgeon, it would be too bad for you to do anything else. What is it, Ryder? Can't you trust me enough to say?'

Her hand was back on his forearm, not a dreamlike soft white-ness but a work-reddened, warm reality. He said roughly, 'Leave it, will you? You can't help, so that's that.'

She drew back her hand. 'Maybe I could if you actually both-ered to tell me. Have you thought of that?'

He heard the temper in her voice and felt wearier than ever. 'Look, I'm sorry, Sally, but it's private. It's not the kind of thing –'

Her hand smacked down so hard on the turf he realized she'd only just not hit him. 'Oh, go to hell. You think you're the only person who cares about the army?'

He stared at her. Her cheeks were pink, her mouth pale, and her eyes blazed with passion. 'The army's just a job to you, isn't it? But it's my family, don't you understand, the only one I've got. I'll do anything to save it if you'll only bloody let me.' She slumped back against the wall and was silent.

The gunfire seemed a long way away now, something distant in another country. 'You know, don't you? You know what this is about.'

'I know some of it,' she said, and the anger was out of her, she sounded like an unhappy child. 'The colonel's in a fever. He talked a little.'

Someone else he hadn't bothered with. 'Is he bad? Should I . . . ?'

'No, no,' she said gently. 'He'll be all right, I think, it's just that stage. But he talked about it, it was on his mind. Don't worry, you know I won't tell anyone.'

He looked at the grass and realized he did know. He could trust her as much as any of his friends, maybe even more. He said, 'I'm sorry. I'll give you all of it if you want, but you mustn't even tell Jarvis. Nobody at all.'

She said, 'I know what "nobody" means. Tell me.'

He did. Not about Angelo, because he'd given his word, but otherwise he told her everything because none of it mattered any more, and there wasn't even hope. He said, 'I just don't know what to do. This Sunday was our first real chance, and thanks to the bloody army I can't even use it.'

She brushed grass off her skirts. 'I wouldn't say that. You could watch him, see who he's meeting. You might even hear something.'

'How can I?' he said savagely. 'Don't you understand? Some-one's got to be in Kamara to watch this bastard arrive, and no one can do that but an officer.'

'Or a woman,' she said, and smiled.

Kalmykoff watched with satisfaction from the slopes above the gorge. It didn't really matter if Ryder saw him in the cavalry camp, but it was certainly simpler if he wasn't there at all. Those two heads were very close together, and it seemed likely the dragoon wouldn't be moving for quite some time.

It was still strange he should be here when his fellows were all in camp. Was it possible he'd been trying to access their letter box? That he'd actually managed to discover something danger-ous? Kalmykoff considered, then relaxed. No, he would hardly have brought the woman with him for something so secret. Ryder was merely doing what he always did, refusing to stay where he was meant to be and going his own way.

Which, of course, was what Kalmykoff was here to stop. He cantered cheerfully into the Light Brigade camp, an ordinary ADC on a black horse with a green saddlecloth and no bad associations for anyone. The men lay about like ragged street beggars in St Petersburg, but he picked his way through to the 13th Light Dragoons, chose an oafish-looking type who was stirring something unpleasant in a pot, and said, 'I say, can you point me out Troop Sergeant-Major Jarvis?'

The oaf gaped, looked about him, then pointed at a stocky figure by a fire on the edge of the camp. 'There, sir, shall I . . . ?'

'No, no,' he said soothingly. 'You're busy.' He ambled back to the open ground, rode slowly along the camp's perimeter, then reined to a stop in front of the TSM's fire.

'I say there,' he said, leaning confidentially down from the saddle. 'Can you help me a moment?'

The creature gawped and scrambled at once to its feet, panting, 'Yes, sir, of course, sir.'

Kalmykoff concealed his amusement. The man was a troglodyte, little over five feet tall but as broad round the chest as a man could reach. The jowly face was reddened and creased with anxiety as he straightened his coat and said, 'Troop Sergeant-Major Jarvis, sir.'

The tedious insistence on title of the little man. 'Sergeant-Major,' he said gravely, touching his hat for the pleasure of watching the animal salute. No wonder he disliked Ryder, poor creature, they were species and worlds apart. 'I wonder if you could explain to me the markers here and where each of the regiments is camped? They're having a little difficulty with deliveries.'

The NCO drew himself up with pride, adding perhaps two inches to his height. 'Of course, sir. No trouble at all, sir. I'll take you round now, sir.'

'Oh, no need,' he said. 'But perhaps you could draw me a little map?' He drew a paper and pen from his sabretache and offered them with a smile. 'The Heavies too, if you can.'

The sergeant-major took the sabretache with reverence. 'I'll be honoured, sir.'

Kalmykoff watched without interest as he began to pencil clumsy black lines over the paper. It didn't matter in the least what he drew, it was merely an excuse for casual conversation. 'Sorry, I'm terribly bad at all the uniforms. Rather new at all this, actually. You're a 13th Light Dragoon, aren't you?'

'That's right, sir,' said Jarvis, frowning with concentration as he drew. 'Colonel Doherty. Didn't you come out with us one day on patrol?'

God in heaven. Kalmykoff stared at the bent head in consternation, but the man didn't seem to see anything odd in the fact his horse and trappings were now so different. Perhaps he saw all senior officers as godlike beings who could dress and do as they liked.

He pulled himself together. 'That's right. Matter of fact I made a few friends among your chaps that evening. You're a colourful lot, aren't you?'

'Sir?' said Jarvis, pausing to write in a number.

'Well, a lot of characters, shall we say? There's that trooper of yours everyone's talking about – Ryder, is it? We all know about *him*.'

Jarvis's pencil stopped on the paper. 'Ryder?'

'Kind of name you can't forget, isn't it? Particularly the way he's putting himself about with the ladies.' He allowed himself a jocular little chuckle.

'Ladies, sir?'

Time to offer something more specific. 'Well, so they say. Saw him with one just now, as it happens. Pretty little thing, blonde hair and a blue dress. Cannon going off all round us, and there he is canoodling in the gorge!'

Something extraordinary was happening to the sergeant-major. His face was becoming almost purple, and the pencil drooped unregarded in his hand. 'Just now?'

'Oh, I know. Have to say I'd no idea you fellows had so much time off, but he's always about, isn't he? I've seen him myself wandering about Balaklava.'

'Have you?' said Jarvis, and actually forgot the sir.

He couldn't pretend not to notice a growl like that. 'I say, is there a problem? I thought you'd know all about it.'

Jarvis bent back to the map, but his lines were even thicker and blacker than before. 'No, sir. I didn't.'

On the hook, and time to reel him in. 'Oh, no one's complaining, we all find it terribly amusing. We've all been scamps in our time, haven't we?'

He rather doubted the sergeant-major had. He stood to hand back the sabretache, and whatever was gleaming behind those porcine little eyes certainly wasn't humour. 'Here you are, sir, I hope it's all right.'

'Wonderful,' he said, studying the scrawl with admiration. 'And you'll forget about that other business, won't you? I was talking out of turn.'

The Neanderthal brow knitted in confusion. 'But, sir, if he's been camp-breaking . . .'

'Then you'll know how to stop it in future, won't you? Look, I forgot myself, I was talking man-to-man, and we wouldn't want to get anyone into trouble, would we?'

The sergeant-major looked squarely at him, then stepped back and saluted. 'No, sir.'

First lie, and Kalmykoff knew he had him. He looked at the map again, said, 'Here, Sergeant-major, I hope you'll let me . . .' and held out a crown.

Good heavens, the man actually hesitated. 'Just doing my job, sir.'

Kalmykoff pressed the coin into his fleshy palm. 'Oh, no, Sergeant-major,' he said quite truthfully. 'I think you'll find you were doing mine.'

13

22 October 1854

Sally remembered Sunday mornings. Toiling up Church Street, fingers crushed in her mother's tugging hand, the feel of clean linen and the smell of lye. Gentry in carriages, discarded seamen with crutches, worn-down women going to pray the sea would give back their men, all had bustled up the street together to the clamour of bells. Now she was alone, her unwashed hair squashed under a Crim-Tartar headscarf, and she walked through vineyards to Kamara to the sound of guns.

She hardly noticed them now. Six days the bombardment had gone on, every day less effectual than the last. Her patients told her it was pointless, that the Russians simply built up by night whatever the British destroyed by day, and the ships had given up completely. Everyone knew there'd be no attack now, or if there were it would come from the Russians. The men had been on stand-to in the saddles all night because of some rumour of an assault on Balaklava.

It had helped in a way, and Jarvis had been too tired to argue when she told him she had to go to the hospital. The lie still made her uncomfortable. Jarvis had given her the army for a family, he'd saved her when she was destitute and there was no one else. The lie was a poor return for his kindness, but he'd never have let her do anything for Ryder, not even if it meant ending the war tomorrow. And that was sad, because her husband was a good man.

She emerged from the vineyard and looked at the higgledy-piggledy scattering of houses dotted over the slopes above. The grandest were surrounded by tall trees and hedges so she could see only their orange-tiled roofs peeping out, the smallest had rough wooden fences strung with wire, but what connected all of them was the central chalk track that ran up like a spine to the ridge above. That must be the key. There would be little side lanes for people to reach the houses to right and left, but no rider could get to them without climbing that track. She needed only to watch it, note which lane this officer took, then follow him to learn the exact house. She had also to do it without attracting his attention, but she had come prepared.

The clock of a distant church struck the three-quarters as she started up the track. Perhaps that was where most of the inhabitants were, since Kamara seemed deserted apart from herself. High on the ridge was a picquet of pink-trousered 11th Hussars, but they were watching the Causeway Heights, not the village, and she needn't worry about them. A tethered goat bleated, and a gaggle of dirty geese honked from behind a fence, but even they fell quiet when she pulled on her gauntlets, took knife and shears from her basket and set about cutting furze. The stems were too tough now for forage, but it made good kindling and it was common to see peasant women collecting it.

She worked with enthusiasm, and had almost forgotten what she was here for when she heard hooves on the track behind. She stooped to put more gorse in the basket and shot a quick glance sideways as she rose. A black horse, not a bay, but lots of officers had more than one. She saw no weaver hat either, only the blur of a forage cap as she turned back to her cutting, but that again was natural off duty. It could still be him.

He was coming slowly and would turn off soon. She sawed hastily through more stems, piled them loosely in the basket to make it look fuller, then straightened to stretch her back. He was passing now, and out of the corner of her eye she saw the flash of a bright green saddlecloth. A doubt crept in, but she dismissed it at once. Who else would be coming to this deserted place when the British Army were at Divine Service? She dropped shears and gauntlets in the basket, put the knife in the pocket of her apron, and turned round.

Only just in time. He was steering his horse down a path to the left, passing a white house with its own little orchard, and already disappearing out of sight. She hefted the basket on her hip and hurried after him.

The path was narrow and dark with trees. She started cautiously down it, but there were brambles snaking right across the grass, and she had hardly taken six paces when one caught at her skirts, jerking her back in a tremendous rustling of leaves. The horseman looked back at once, but after only a quick glance he turned and rode on. She was an ordinary peasant woman, he'd seen her cutting furze and knew she was harmless.

Relief made her want to laugh. How easy it was really! He had no suspicions, it didn't matter if he saw her. Nor could she lose him. He couldn't ride fast on a path so narrow and winding, and even if he vanished after turning a bend the houses were so far apart she'd still know which he'd gone into. She untangled herself without hurry and walked on.

And there he went, turning off the track just before a bend. Thick trees made a screen between them, but there was obviously a house there, she'd just give it a glance as she walked casually past. She kept going, here was the bend, a quick look left – and her heart jumped. It wasn't a house, just a little fenced paddock, and he was only dismounting to leave his horse. He'd be coming back, she couldn't possibly stand and wait, she had no choice but to walk on by.

She turned the bend, walked to the next, and stopped in frustration. This was hopeless. She could keep going, hope to hear him coming behind, then look round when his steps turned off, but he might take ages in the paddock, he might even come out and go the other way. Ryder would be here in twenty minutes and she'd have nothing to give him. He'd say it wasn't her fault, but they'd still have to wait a whole week to get another chance.

She wasn't having it. She carefully unravelled three of the thickest and thorniest bramble stems, then calmly entangled them in the skirts of her own dress. She'd done it by accident once, so why not twice? Even if he was another five minutes he'd see nothing odd in a woman taking so long to free herself if she didn't want to tear her only frock. She tossed her basket and shears lightly across the path as if she'd dropped them, then stood and waited.

The distant clock struck nine. As the last strike faded she heard footsteps, and to her relief they were heading this way. She turned at once to the brambles, working at them with obviously ineffective bare fingers, and listening to the steps coming closer. She backed respectfully into the hedge to let him pass, but a pair of polished shoes stopped in front of her and a deep voice said something in a tongue she'd heard many times at Varna.

Bulgarian! She looked up and saw not a staff officer, but an elegant figure in a brimless black hat and a green coat fastened at the neck like a cloak. He was a gentleman and presumably offering to help her, but damn and blast him, he'd come at the worst possible time. She smiled and said 'Ne, ne', plucking a fold of cloth away from the thorns to show how easy it would be, but the wretched thing snagged and caught, and now it was the Bulgar who smiled. He stooped to untangle the bramble at her hem, sliding a hand under the skirt to lift it clear. His fingers brushed her leg, and she hesitated, uncertain, but then the hand slid up to her thigh and she was sure. She wrenched backwards into the brambles, clenched her fist and punched him full in the face.

He tottered back across the path, straightened and massaged his jaw, but the look on his face made her suddenly afraid. He was a Bulgarian gentleman, wealthy and in with the Russians, she was a woman and a Crim-Tartar peasant, and ought to be grateful for any sign of his favour. She said 'No, wait,' but he was already coming at her and his palm smashed with full force into the side of her face. Blood filled her mouth, a back tooth gone, he was pressing her back into the brambles, and his hands seized her wrists.

'Kostoff!' cried a voice. 'Kostoff, *nyet*!' and then words that turned blessedly to English. 'For heaven's sake, let her go!' The Bulgar hesitated, his fingers tightening on her wrists, then he flung them away in disgust and stood back.

Her heart was slamming in her chest. She took a deep breath, dragged her sleeve across her mouth, and steadied herself against the brambles. The voice was still talking, and sense returned as she realized who the speaker must be. The language was English, she was looking at a British officer in cloak and forage cap, but he was the traitor and their enemy.

It was almost impossible to believe. The man was no more than thirty, with frank, clear features and a boyish smile, and when he saw her looking he nodded and touched his hat. 'All right, my dear,' he said, in a soothing voice that suggested his tone was all he expected her to understand. 'Cut along now, it's all right.'

She pulled herself free of the last clinging thorns. The officer was placing a firm hand on the Bulgar's back to urge him along, but as she grabbed her basket to follow them she saw with amazement they were walking through a gated entrance right in front of her. They knew she was there and couldn't fail to see them, but clearly considered her no more observant or dangerous than a mule.

She let out her breath in a single, painful laugh. It was done. She had only to wait to point out the house, then she could bask in Ryder's gratitude and leave the rest to him. The thought was warming, and as she walked back out to the central track she saw even the grey sky shimmer with a hint of sun.

The padre closed his book and blinked as the parade dissolved into stampede. Ryder barged his way through the jostling bodies and was clear for the horse-lines where Moody was already waiting, Bolton and Jordan coming up behind. He released Tally and had a foot in the stirrup when a voice behind said, 'And where d'you think *you're* going?'

Ryder brought down his boot with deliberate slowness. 'Forage party, Sar'nt-major. Captain Marsh gave us permission last night.'

'Very good,' said Jarvis, not blinking. 'Give your net to Fisk, I want you here.'

It was unbelievable. 'But Captain Marsh said –'

Jarvis raised his voice. 'And when Captain Marsh wishes to relieve me of my responsibilities he'll tell me to my face. I need you to dig a grave.'

Ryder's temper rose to boiling point. 'Captain Marsh gave me permission, and I'll –'

'You'll stay right here, Private,' said Jarvis. 'You think the captain cares who goes on a forage party as long as it's got?' He tugged the forage net from Ryder's mare and tossed it to Moody. 'You're in charge, Moody, and if you're not back in an hour I'll have the hide off you. There's a war on, even if ex-corporal Ryder hasn't noticed.'

Moody smirked, toady that he was, and began to lead the others away. Ryder looked at Jarvis in helpless hatred, but the man was already turning and waving him to follow.

'Cholera,' he said over his shoulder. 'Captain's servant. Report to me when you're done, I need latrines dug too.'

Ryder took the spade he was offered, but could hardly think for fury. A burial party was never one man, there were plenty who could have helped him, but this was nothing to do with burials or latrines, this was bloody Jarvis's spite. He'd never get to Kamara now, there'd be no hope of seeing what the traitor did or who he met, no chance of getting the evidence they needed. He swung the spade like a pick and hacked it into the earth.

The only comfort was Sally. She'd realize something had kept him and would come straight back. If she'd identified the house they could still salvage something. They could search it, perhaps find out who owned it, and next week they could try again.

Next week. A whole bloody week lost, thanks to bastard Jarvis.

He thrust the spade back in the earth and went on digging his grave.

Sally watched the road in frustration. Where the hell was Ryder? Perhaps there was a stand-to, perhaps he'd had difficulty getting away from the forage party, but somehow or other he'd been delayed and they were running out of time.

She was supposed to go back. She'd promised she would, but this was a better chance than they'd ever imagined. They'd always planned to watch, but the Bulgar spoke English and they might even be able to listen. Ryder would. He wouldn't be afraid, he'd sneak right up to a window or doorway and listen for all he was worth. What if there were a battle before next Sunday, what if this man did it again, ordered innocent, trusting boys to their death, and all because she wouldn't take the opportunity that was here in front of her right now?

The clock struck a quarter to ten, and she made up her mind. She planted her basket conspicuously by the opening, and set off a second time down the dark and brambled path. It seemed even quieter than before, and her footsteps sounded harder and more urgent as she hurried back to the house with the gate. She hesitated, wondering what to use for a marker, then untied the apron and left it at the bottom of the hedge. Silly really, since it was more than likely Ryder wouldn't come at all.

The gate was unlatched, and moved smoothly under the push of her hand. She stepped through and found herself on a gravel path leading through overgrown grass to a big white house with tall windows. They were terrifying, those windows, like eyes all staring at her, but she walked across the grass to avoid the crunch of gravel, and no one came or shouted.

When she reached the walls she ducked low and out of sight. The nearest window was less than three feet from the ground, the shutters were open, but the glass reached to the bottom and it was shut. She crouched in silence for a moment, but it was ridiculous, she couldn't even hear a muffled voice. She peered out along the front of the house, but the line of glass was everywhere unbroken by the bar of a sash. They were all closed.

She thought for a moment. If the men were in this room she'd surely have heard something, however faint. She crouched a little higher, and then slowly, carefully, nudged her head up between the shutters to peer inside.

At first she saw nothing but the daylit garden reflected in the dark glass, but as she pressed her face closer she made out a big square room filled with strange white shapes of furniture covered in dust sheets. The house was unoccupied, its owners had fled the invasion and left their property behind. Most others had taken their furniture with them, but perhaps these were British expatriates who hoped to return, or perhaps there hadn't been time.

What mattered was there was no one there. The sash made no more than a faint, low creak as she slid it upwards, and she needed to open it only halfway before she was able to wriggle through. She sat up on bare polished floorboards, looked round at the elegant legs of a piano beneath its dust sheet, and suddenly felt like a burglar.

But she wasn't, she was a spy for her country and men's voices were talking close by. Afraid to risk footsteps, she crawled quickly over the dusty floor and slipped under the piano. It was a big one, the kind they called a 'grand', and a man would need to bend right down to see her underneath the dust sheet. She wished it were nearer the door, the voices were very muffled and indistinct, but none of the other furniture offered such good shelter. She crouched in her little tent, tore off her headscarf, and strained to listen.

It was hard to make any sense of it. The language was English, but there were three different voices, and only one spoke clearly. One man had a high, querulous voice that distance blurred to a refined whine, the Bulgar was mumbling and his accent thick, but the third man was her gentleman, the chivalrous traitor who had saved her outside. Even he was hard to follow, his voice kept coming and going, and his footsteps creaked as he paced. She heard the word 'Balaklava' clearly enough, and then something about ships. If she could just pick up the thread it would be easier to guess the rest, but the most she had were partial phrases. Then one word stood out, and it was one her father had used when speaking of something all sailors feared. The word was 'fireship'.

Now she knew what to listen for. She heard the words 'cut one out' and then 'powder in the hold' and the last of her doubts disappeared. This was treachery of the worst kind and Ryder had been right all along. 'They'll escape in the dinghies,' said the gentleman's voice, clearer as if he were facing her way. 'Light the fuses, then go.'

A mumble from that Bulgar, damn and blast the man, why couldn't he speak up? But the gentleman seemed to be standing still at last and she heard his reply. 'No, no, we have your information, you need do nothing more. Borisoff will organize the assault, then our seamen will come before dawn. It's only a distraction for the main attack, after all.'

The Bulgar was clearer this time. 'When? Is it still this month?' She held her breath for the answer, praying the gentleman would stay where he was just a moment longer.

'Oh, yes, the 24th. The reinforcements must be here by then.'

She stared blindly at the dust sheet. The 24th was two days away. This was crucial, vital information, and they'd so nearly missed it. Thank God she'd ignored Ryder and risked it, thank God she'd –

Footsteps again, but louder and closer, directly outside her room, but the next sound was the clunk of a bolt being pulled back. The front door! They were leaving, and in a minute she could be out and running home with the kind of information that could win a war.

'You go out the back way, Kostoff,' said the gentleman, his voice shockingly near. 'There'll probably be a set of angry uncles waiting outside the gate after that business with the woman. Really, you should know better.' She heard a rattle and creak as the front door opened.

'Oh, I do, your honour,' said Kostoff, for the first time clearly audible. 'She wasn't local, no one will bother after her. Just an Englishwoman looking for something to steal.'

'English?' said the gentleman. 'You're sure?'

'Of course,' said Kostoff, with a note of injury in his voice. 'She spoke to me, your honour, she said "no, wait". You know my English is as flawless as your own.'

Sally listened harder, but everything had gone very quiet. Then came another creak and a soft bump as the door closed. The bolt clunked home.

'Yes,' said the gentleman, sounding tired. 'Yes, and that blue dress, I've seen it before. If it hadn't been for the apron and head-scarf . . . *Damn* it, I think we're watched.'

Another moment's silence. Sally became aware of a rhythmic thumping in her throat she knew was her own heart.

The other man spoke at last, and the querulousness was no longer a whine but an aristocratic threat. 'You've compromised my house? Do you realize what you're saying, both of you? You've compromised *me*.'

The gentleman sounded deferential. 'I'm sorry, sir, I stopped him at once. But you're right, we'll leave by the back way, and this animal shall wait half an hour before he follows.'

Kostoff sounded belligerent. 'Then how will I . . . ?'

'We don't need any more from you,' said the aristocratic man. 'I'll send a message if something arises, but none of us must come here again. Understood?'

A shuffle of feet, then the aristocrat's voice saying 'Good'. She heard footsteps striding away over polished boards, turning fainter down a corridor, then the soft bang of another door. The Bulgar was silent.

She tried to think. It wasn't a disaster. They'd never expected to catch the traitor today, but she'd seen him, would know him again, and had all the evidence they needed. But how had he known her, what made him think she was dangerous? Perhaps he'd noticed her on the march, and just knowing she was an army wife was enough.

The Bulgar was pacing in the hall. If only he'd go and do it somewhere else! She was getting cramped under the piano and didn't want to wait the full half hour before she could escape. The footsteps stopped, and she pictured him standing in indecision. Then he started again, two quick steps to her door, then a firmer, less hollow sound as he turned to come in.

Fear fluttered in her chest. He couldn't possibly see her, but she saw his polished black shoes and grey trousers, and the nearness tightened her throat. What could he want? There was nothing in this room but shrouded furniture, and he wasn't going to uncover it – was he? A sharp whipping noise, and she saw a white dust sheet billowing to the floor in front of something big and red with clawed wooden feet. An armchair, a velvet-covered armchair, and his legs turned to face her as he sat down with a sigh. The creak of a chair-back, then another rustle, a firm *snip*, the crack of a match and a moment later the smell of a cheroot.

Relief trickled through her. He was only having a smoke. Fool that she'd been to think otherwise, or imagine a brute like that would suddenly decide to play the piano. She almost giggled, but recognized her light-headedness in time and forced herself calm. He was still here and very close, and now she didn't even dare move to relieve her cramped thighs.

A faint sound turned her head, a gentle thump-thump from the window. A gust of wind must have got up and was playing with the shutters. The sound was not repeated and the Bulgar didn't move, but alarm was suddenly shooting up inside her as if to come screaming out of her mouth. The window! She hadn't dared close it for fear of the noise, and if the wind came in he was bound to feel it, to turn and see it, to know she was right here.

She froze in her position while her mind ran. Please God let the wind drop, let him not feel it, let him get up and go somewhere else, *please God make him go*.

Ryder's fear was choking him like the dust of the shovelled earth. Where the hell was Sally? At half past she'd have known he was late, at twenty to she'd have known he wasn't coming, she should have been back by ten at the latest.

He'd looked at his watch at ten, at five past, at the quarter, he wouldn't look again till he'd finished the grave. What was she doing? What else could she do but come back? Then he thought what he'd have done himself, hurled out the last shovelful and stood back. 'Report to me,' Jarvis had said, and so he would – after he'd been to Kamara to fetch Sally.

He picked up the bucket, stuck the spade over his shoulder, and strolled out from the camp perimeter. He was a poor trooper on some obscure work-fatigue, a man no one would look twice at, and not till he was past the first fold in the hills did he throw down bucket and shovel and start to run.

Run. His boots slithered on the smoothness of long grass, he stumbled against concealed rocks, banged into an oak, swung his arm round its trunk and ran on. On past the low slopes of Number 2 redoubt, Turks looking down and waving, 'Yes, yes, Buono Johnny to you too,' then on to Canrobert's Hill, skirt it and up, more Turks looking down from the earthworks, 'Buono Johnny, Buono Johnny, but I've got to bloody *run.*'

Into the vineyards, find the path and crash through. The vines were sad things now, stripped by the scavengers of the army, that same army he was trying to save and that was doing everything in its bloody stupid power to try and stop him. Well *sod* the army, sod everything it stood for, he was here for Sally and the rest could go to hell.

Kamara, the centre track, and no sign of her anywhere. She must be here, she was hiding, they'd said to meet here, but he turned round and round, saw a goat, some screaming geese, nothing and nobody else. There were too many houses, lots of little paths to get to them, dark green entrances all the same – and a basket of gorse laid by one of them with a pair of shears laid neatly on top.

*

The wind banged the shutters harder, and a gust of air flicked up the corner of a dust sheet. Sally stared intently at the Bulgar's legs as they fidgeted, tucked in, then straightened as he stood. He was walking to the window, and a moment later she heard it shut. He was too far away to see now, and she made no attempt to stoop lower for a better view. She didn't want to see or hear anything but the sound of him going away.

Silence. He was just standing there, and she imagined him thinking. She tried to put words into his mind – burglars, just burglars, been in and gone, leave it and go home.

His shoes creaked, then a new noise, a sudden exclamation. What had he seen? She was invisible, screwed up small as a child playing hide-and-seek, her dress tucked tight about her, but still he'd seen something and his feet were turning towards her. She stared at the bottom of the dust sheet and saw his shoes coming purposefully back into view. He was following something, and now she saw it herself, a faint brightness in the dusty floor. Her dress had made a trail as she crawled, and it led right under the piano.

Terror wiped out thought. She backed away an inch or two, but there was nowhere to go, nothing to do but stare at the sheet, waiting to jump as it was ripped away. Fragments of panicked hope flickered and went out. Hit him, buy herself seconds to run – but the window was shut and the door bolted. The knife – it was in her apron outside. Why hadn't she listened to Ryder? Why had she . . . ? She stared at the sheet, and it trembled, lifted, and a face loomed in the opening, upside-down and nightmarish, the thick lips twisting into an ogre's smile.

'Hello, English lady,' said the Bulgar. 'Have you come back for some more?'

The path was dark, he'd got to the last house and seen no sign. She must have left one, and he retraced his steps more slowly, studying the entrance to each house as he went. The Colt was capped and ready in his hand.

The third house had an iron gate, and his attention quickened as he saw it swinging slightly ajar. Had Sally crept in here, perhaps to listen at a window? He stared at the ground around it, saw something pale under the hedge, and drew out a brown Crim-Tartar apron.

Faint but high, a woman's scream. He swivelled round and it came again – Christ Almighty, she was in the house! The gate flew aside as he charged through and down the path, cocking the revolver as he ran. Damn the windows, that was the scream of a woman in fear for her life, and Ryder threw himself full at the door. It held at the top, some kind of bolt, but he gave it his shoulder and crashed the thing through.

An empty hall, but an open door to the right and Sally's voice crying 'Here!' He hurtled through, saw the blue of her dress as she was shoved across the room, but in front of him a big man in green, then a flash of light as a blade slashed within an inch of his face. He stepped back fast, brought up the gun, and yelled, 'Drop it, you bastard, drop it now!'

The man bared his teeth with a sound like a hiss, but the knife was still weaving. The blade was near a foot long, curved viciously to the tip, and the edge already tinged with blood. *Sally.* Fury exploded in his head, his finger tightening to the trigger, but Sally's voice cried 'No!' and brought him sharply to his senses. This man could be vital, they'd got to take him alive. He said again 'Drop it', and motioned downwards with the barrel.

The man hesitated. He probably hadn't understood the words, but seemed to recognize the gesture, and at least lowered the knife to his side.

Ryder stepped cautiously towards him, extending his left hand, but Sally screamed 'Watch out!' and the man moved, one hand streaking for the pistol, the knife snaking up savagely at Ryder's groin.

He leaped sideways and back, the blade slashing harmlessly at his coat, but the man had the pistol barrel and was twisting it in Ryder's hand. It was pointing everywhere, and Sally in the room, he must not, *must not* pull the trigger. The blade whipped at him again, he grabbed in desperation at the knife hand, clamping his fingers tight round the man's wrist. For a second they faced each other, hands to hands in a grotesque dance, then Ryder lowered his head and moved in. Wrestling now, gun and knife, hands sliding on the metal, slippery with sweat. He had to put the knife out of it, free himself to get two hands to the gun. Twisting the wrist, bending it back, clenching his teeth with effort, the intimacy of another man's breath in his face. The fist unclenched, the knife dropped, but the man's other hand slid down the pistol, jolting Ryder's finger on the trigger. Light cracked, a bang and the bitter powder smell, the revolver was loose in Ryder's hand and the man slumped gurgling to the floor. Half his face was shot away, and his heels drummed horribly on the wooden boards.

Ryder looked away. His own fault, he should never have cocked the gun if he didn't mean to use it. 'Is there anyone else, Sally?'

'No. I'm sorry, the officer's gone.'

He allowed himself to look at her, and was shocked at what he saw. Her hair was dishevelled, one cheek stinging red, but almost worse was the way she was huddled against the wall with her arms wrapped tightly across her chest as if she fought not to scream. She was watching the man on the floor, and he saw her wince as he gave a last gurgle and died.

Then he was barging through the shrouded furniture, reaching for her, seizing her hands, but at once he felt their stickiness and stared in horror at the palms. The cuts were superficial, only fine scratches, but they blurred into an image of a curved blade being slashed at the face of a girl who'd tried to fight back with only her bare hands. Anger tore at him, and he could only grapple her into his arms, whispering, 'I'm sorry, oh God, he hurt you, I'm so sorry.'

She lifted her face, and he felt her arms slip round his neck. He pressed his cheek against hers, suddenly dumb in astonishment. The feel of her bare neck under his hand drove him to tenderness, and before he could stop himself he stooped to kiss it. Her face slid round, he was kissing her cheek, her throat, then there were her lips and he kissed them too.

Her face jerked back at once, and he opened his eyes. For a moment they looked at each other, then gently, wordlessly, she took her hands from his neck and stepped back. As his breathing slowed he seemed to feel the beat of his own heart.

He said, 'I'm sorry.'

She shook her head. 'An accident. Silly. We were overwrought.'

He still was. She left a tiny smear of blood on her cheek as she pushed back her hair, and the sight twisted his guts. 'Oh God, I should never have let you come here.'

'But you should,' she said, and managed a little smile. 'I've learned so much. Listen.'

He took out his handkerchief and wiped her cheek while she told him. It was hard to take in at first, hard to think of anything but some Bulgarian bastard hitting her, but the importance of the dates struck home. He said, 'Give me more detail, will you, Sally? I need the exact words.'

She took the handkerchief. 'Why?'

'I have to tell the officers if we're to stop the attack on the fleet. Only it has to come from me, Sally. No one else must know you were ever here.'

She looked away. 'Because of Jarvis.'

'You know how he'd take it, what it would mean.' He hesitated, studying her. The redness of her face was already fading, but the scratches on her hands could be dangerous. 'Will he wonder about those?'

'Not if I cut firewood when I get back,' she said, wiping them absently on the handkerchief. 'All right, I'll tell you again.'

Her calm was astonishing. He looked out of the window as she talked, memorizing the words, shutting his mind to the reality of the danger she'd been in. But she was still in it, and as she finished he saw a flicker of pink moving beyond the gate. The bloody picquet, they'd heard the shot and must be checking all the houses.

He said urgently 'Is there a back way out?'

She was already heading for the door. 'Yes, come on.'

He glanced back at the window – and froze. Men were walking through the gate, three hussars, but the fourth was a short stout light dragoon he'd have known anywhere. Jarvis. Jarvis had known he wanted to go out, he'd known he'd break camp, he'd deliberately watched and followed. He'd lost him in the lanes, but the shot had drawn him, the bloody, bloody shot, and he was right outside with Sally still in the house.

'Ryder?' said Sally.

The woman who'd risked rape and murder to help him, whose life and marriage he was about to destroy. He grabbed her arm and hurried her through the hall. A door, thank God, a back door, and beyond it a garden and a low wall. 'Go now, go, bloody run. Hide if you see someone, then get out and run.'

'But you . . .'

'I'm all right, I'll have to tell Marsh I was here anyway. Go *now*.'

He pushed her out, shut the door behind her, and stood for a moment in a sweat of relief. She'd get away all right, and no one would stop a running woman. Jarvis wouldn't check the back anyway, he'd be so excited at catching him in the heinous crime of camp-breaking he'd never think about anything else. Poor Jarvis. He was in for a hell of a disappointment when the truth came out.

As he reached the hall the hussars were already walking through the broken door. Two had levelled carbines, one a drawn sword, but Jarvis had only a look of fierce satisfaction.

'Ryder,' he said, as if he loved the name. 'Ryder.'

It was a nice moment. 'Yes, Sar'nt-major. I've had a fight with a spy, I'm afraid, you'll find the body in here.'

There was no missing the dead Bulgar, his brains had puddled on the floor. One of the hussars ripped the dust sheet from a piano and quickly flung it over him.

Jarvis stared in confusion. 'What in hell . . . ?'

Ryder explained what he could. 'This man caught me listening to a conversation about a forthcoming attack on our ships. I'm sorry I can't say more now, Sar'nt-major, I need to report directly to an officer.'

'Indeed you do,' said Jarvis, recovering. 'You're going to one right now, and under full arrest. Camp-breaking and disobedience before we even start on what's happened here.'

Of course. 'Very good, Sar'nt-major, but it's only fair to tell you now I was following information about this spy.'

'You were following a woman,' said Jarvis. 'These men heard one screaming, and the neighbours say it came from here.'

His heart gave a little kick. 'They were mistaken. There are lots of houses here.'

'So there are,' said Jarvis. 'But only one with this outside the gate.' He snapped his fingers, and one of the hussars held up that bloody Crim-Tartar apron.

Nothing to do but bluff it out. 'That's nothing to do with me. There's been no woman here.'

Jarvis was looking over his shoulder. 'Really?' he said, and stepped past to pick up something from under the exposed piano. 'Then what's this?'

The embroidered headscarf Sally had worn. She must have taken it off. He knew she had, he remembered the feel of her hair under his hands. The thought stung with shame as he looked at her husband, and he felt it burning in his own cheeks.

'Exactly,' said Jarvis, rocking backwards and forwards on his heels. 'There's guilt in your face, Ryder. You came here to meet a woman, you and this man fought over her, and all this talk of spies is so much gammon.'

He could hear it himself, the bloody credibility of it, and so would Marsh. But they'd got to believe him, there was a Russian attack coming and too damn much at stake.

'All right,' he said desperately. 'All right. There was a woman, but not how you think. She was helping me track this spy. She followed him here to let me know the house.'

Someone laughed. One of the hussars was shaking his head

276

and chuckling, and even the others wore broad grins. Jarvis said, 'You're embarrassing me, Trooper. A 13th Light Dragoon ought to think of a better lie than that.'

He saw it in all their faces, the ridiculousness of it, a woman sneaking round after Russian spies. 'It's true. Whatever you think, it's true, and Captain Marsh will believe it.'

'With your record?' said Jarvis kindly. He held out his hand. 'Your gun, Ryder.'

His own revolver. His father's gun. He pulled it from his belt and passed it to Jarvis, hating the look of it in his hand.

Jarvis smiled. He didn't say anything, he didn't need to, the time for all that was over. He jerked his thumb at the hussars, said just 'Take him', and swaggered out into the sunlight.

14

23 to 24 October 1854

It cost Oliver three of Ronnie's cigars before the sentry would admit him to the guard tent. It was still a crime, he'd never done such a thing in his life, but Mrs Jarvis had begged him and Harry Ryder was his friend.

The emptiness struck him at once, a whole bell-tent with only one man in it. Ryder looked smaller than usual, stood at the far end with his arms folded defensively across his chest, but the look on his face made Oliver hesitate to go nearer. 'Ryder?'

'Hullo, Polly, come to say "I told you so"?'

It sounded like him, the same casual mockery that was like a slap in the face, but his whole body looked tense, as if he was straining against something Oliver couldn't see.

'To say I'm sorry. I've spoken to Mrs Jarvis.'

Ryder's arms dropped. 'Sally? Is she all right?'

She'd been worried sick about Ryder. He said 'I think so,' and tried not to look away.

'She's not told anybody else?'

'No, but she wants to. She thinks she can help.'

Ryder swore. 'Well, she mustn't, Polly, you've got to tell her. They already know I was meeting a woman, they'll only think it's her. She'll be sent home, Jarvis will disown her, she'll be going back to destitution. You've got to tell her, promise me.'

It was sounding more and more desperate. 'Yes, yes, of course. But don't they believe any of it? Surely Captain Marsh . . .'

Ryder gave a short laugh. 'Bog? Oh, he's following it up, but he won't find anything, will he?'

Oliver made up his mind. 'Then I'll back you up, I'll tell him what I know. I'm not in any trouble, they're more likely to believe me.'

Ryder's face softened a little. 'But what do you know, Poll? What have you actually seen? You didn't see the officer do anything at the Alma, you didn't see the man Mackenzie chased. You're the only one of us who's seen nothing at all.'

It was terribly true. 'But we've got to convince him somehow.'

Ryder shrugged. 'Oh, he'll believe me in the end, he's bound to when the attack happens. I've just got to make him listen before it's too late.'

'I know. The fellows are talking about a District Court-Martial.'

Ryder sliced the air with his hand. 'Damn the court-martial, what about the Russians? It's tomorrow, don't you see? Marsh needs to be alerting the officers in Balaklava, I've got to make him do it. You must warn the others too. This ship business is a distraction, there'll be a major attack somewhere and we've got to be looking out for the traitor.'

'All right,' he said miserably. 'But if we see him, what can we do?'

The tent flap rustled and the sentry poked his head through the gap. 'You – out. Ryder's for Captain Marsh, so hook it before the escort sees you.'

There wasn't time to do more than whisper 'Good luck!' and bolt for the entrance.

He was safely back at his tent when the guards marched past with Ryder, but the sight still made him squirm inside. He'd always hated it, the degradation of defaulters, but he'd never thought it could happen to someone he really knew. It was Ryder's own fault and he really had warned him, but it still felt dirty, infectious, and wrong.

He told himself it wouldn't matter. Captain Marsh was reasonable, he'd see Ryder had acted with good intentions. He'd stop this attack coming, and now he knew about the traitor he might be able to catch him too. Everything could still be all right. Oliver had only to do what he always did, place his faith in God and his trust in the officers, and hope to goodness they wouldn't let him down.

Captain Marsh had a whole tent to himself, with a camp stool, a field table, a bucket with a bottle cooling in it, and a stack of wicker baskets stamped FORTNUMS. He still looked uncomfortable.

He dismissed the guards, looked mistrustfully at the tent flap, then lowered his voice. 'Dash it all, Ryder, I hope you're satisfied. I've wasted half the day with a chap called Calvert in Intelligence, and there's not a thing to corroborate your story.'

Ryder remained at attention. 'Nothing, sir?'

Marsh made a huffing noise. 'Oh, I'll agree you ran into some doubtful characters. The owner of the house, for instance.' He selected a piece of paper with perhaps two sentences on it and gazed at it admiringly. 'Englishman, as it happens, a Mr Shepherd. Expatriate, of course, made himself a naturalized Russian. Might be all right, might not, but Calvert says he's moved to Odessa, so at least he's out of it now.'

'Yes, sir. Except that he was definitely conspiring in an attack on our army.'

'Only your word for that,' said Marsh, laying down the paper like a bad cheque. 'But this fellow Kostoff now. Thorough bad egg, our chaps have had an eye on him in Balaklava. No one's going to be too worried about the death of a type like this.'

A foreigner, in other words. 'It was self-defence, sir. TSM Jarvis saw the knife.'

'Oh, yes, yes, we know he went for the woman, the picquet heard her scream. No one's blaming you for his death, Private, there's really no need for all these lies.'

Ryder felt a pulse start to beat in his forehead. 'Lies?'

Marsh leaned forward over the table, fingers laced together, direct and man-to-man. 'Come on, Ryder. There's no threat of hanging. You'll have to be punished, of course, disorderly conduct, insubordination, camp-breaking, but hang it, why can't you just own up and take your medicine like a man?'

Ryder fixed his eyes on the canvas. 'Because I'm not lying, sir. One of our own officers is working with the enemy.'

Marsh sat up so abruptly half his papers fluttered to the floor. 'Dash it, you've got to stop saying things like that. It's sedition. You mustn't repeat it to anyone, you understand?'

'I haven't, sir, not even to TSM Jarvis. I won't say a word at the court-martial. We'll never catch this man if he knows we're looking.'

Marsh stared, and Ryder thought a hint of doubt flickered behind his eyes. 'Well then, dammit, you can jolly well stop saying it to *me*. Can't you see you're only making things worse for yourself?'

'Yes, sir. So why do you think I'm still saying it?'

Marsh looked back at his papers. After a moment he said, 'But you've got to give me something to confirm it, don't you see? This woman you say helped you. Give me her name.'

He swallowed. 'I'm afraid I can't do that, sir.'

'Why not, if she was doing nothing wrong?'

'I'm sorry, sir.'

'Your informer, then.'

Bloomer had trusted him. 'I don't know his name, sir. I heard it through someone else.'

'Gossip, you mean?'

'If you want to call it that.'

Marsh slammed his hand on the table. 'Hang it, that's what it is! Gossip and speculation! Opinions of troops on the orders of their officers! There's not a single fact in the lot.'

He kept his voice level. 'Except what I heard, sir. About the coming attack.'

Marsh snorted. 'Vague nonsense. Did you even hear them mention Balaklava?'

'I didn't think they meant Portsmouth, sir.'

Marsh's brows lowered at once. 'I'll overlook that, Trooper, you're in enough trouble already. We'll leave the rest for court-martial.'

It would be too late. 'I'd like to speak to Colonel Doherty.'

'The colonel's still very sick, I'm not bothering him with non-sense like this.'

He hesitated, but only for a second. 'He'll see me, sir. He knows me.'

'Oh, yes, yes,' said Marsh petulantly. 'He told me after the Bulganek. But he was very clear, Ryder, he said it was a slight acquaintance and merited no special treatment.'

Of course he did, Ryder had asked him to. His own pride, his own bloody fault, and men could die for it. He said desperately, 'Then Captain Oldham.'

Marsh's head shot up with outrage. 'I'm perfectly capable of running my own troop!'

Ryder breathed deeply. Last chance. 'Then you'll know, sir. How serious it would be if the attack happens and we've taken no action to prevent it. You'll know what it would mean.'

Marsh stared, then slowly slumped back down on his stool. He did know, he was bound to, he was a conscientious officer trying to deal with something beyond his comprehension. Ryder watched his fingers drumming on the table, then jumped when he saw them stop.

'Very well. God knows why, but I'll act on it. I'll speak to Captain Topham in Balaklava, put the marines on alert. But this had better not be another false alarm.'

Relief relaxed his shoulders, and he drew himself back into attention. 'It won't be, sir.'

'Good,' said Marsh, standing in dismissal. 'Before dawn, you say? Then we'll have the court-martial at nine. You're either a liar or a hero, Ryder, and by then we'll know either way.'

Evening in the hospital was its usual frightful din, and Woodall kept his head under the blanket to shut it out. The doctors said he'd be fit for duty in a day or two, but you could never tell with a head injury, he might be dying for all they knew.

A hand patted the hump of his shoulder. 'Are you Woodall?'

He peeped out cautiously, but it was young Mrs Jarvis and she was always kind. 'That's me.'

She crouched down by his pallet. 'I've a message from Harry Ryder. We're expecting an attack in the morning, and he wants us all to keep an eye out for our friend on the Staff.'

What had possessed Ryder to go blabbing to a woman? Then he remembered the Alma, a figure in a blue dress walking away from a fire and Mackenzie saying she was trouble. He looked at her doubtfully, but Mrs Jarvis was clean and respectable, not like some of the drunken harridans they called nurses in this dump. She wouldn't be party to anything wrong.

He muttered, 'What's he telling me for? Not much I can do in here, is there?'

'There might be if you come out tomorrow. There'll be an attempt on the harbour at dawn, but something more serious will happen later and we don't know where.'

Her casualness nettled him. 'But the harbour's here! We could be burned in our beds.'

She looked at him curiously, and he became horribly conscious of his unshaven face. 'You're quite safe, the marines are on guard. Ryder only wanted you to be warned, that's all.' There was a soft rustle of skirts as she rose and picked up the lamp.

'Wait a bit,' he said. 'Is he sure? Is it definitely tomorrow?'

The light cast dark circles under her eyes. 'I hope so,' she said quietly. 'He broke camp to get the information and if it isn't true they'll flog him.'

He stared at her retreating back in horror. Camp-breaking, flogging, what was he getting involved in? But an orderly passed her with a stack of mail and he quickly turned to face the other way, anxious not to look as if he was expecting something.

'Letter for you, Tow-Row,' said the orderly, chucking a grubby envelope down on his blanket. 'Looks like someone loves you.'

He snatched at the letter, holding it to his chest until the man had gone by. He was saying the same to everyone, 'Letter for you, someone loves you,' but Woodall knew that meant nothing. Bills, mostly, creditors found men even in the Army of the East, but his was personal and just for him.

But not Maisie's writing. Hers was beautiful with long curly bottoms to her 'g's and 'y's, but this was printed, capitals and small letters all mashed together as if the difference didn't matter. Only his sister Elsie, but still something precious and from home. He glanced furtively from right to left and opened it.

Words, a lot of them to the page, Elsie was mean with her money. The usual *hope this finds you well as it leaves me*, yes, yes, skip on and then this. *Well, Denny, I don't want to be the one says this but someone has to and you have to know. Your Maisie's skipped and gone with a theatrical man, and no one knows where except it might be Leamington. I don't know what she's took, but she's not been paying the rent these last two months, so the room's gone and the baillies have took the rest . . .*

It was the rooms he thought of first. The rent had always been a strain, but it had been worth it to marry Maisie, to know there was a little home for him outside the indignities of barracks. He thought of the way she'd come to see him when he was on duty outside the Palace, how she'd walk past with her head in the air then turn and flash him a big wink to make the other fellows jealous. He thought of getting leave to visit her, the way she'd leap up from the piano and wrap herself round him like a kitten. 'My Guard,' she used to say, 'my splendid, handsome Guard.' She'd always liked him best in uniform.

It was a mistake. Maybe she'd been frightened and alone and some smooth-tongued play-actor had talked her into it, but no theatrical man could compete with the glory of a Grenadier Guard. He thought again of the coming attack, and now it filled him with hope. He still had his rifle, he'd had it with him when they brought him in and he'd kept it safe under his blanket ever since. If there was an attack he could produce it and be a hero. He saw himself red-coated and gallant, firing shot after shot from the hospital windows, saving the women and invalids from hordes of marauding Russians. He saw his name in the papers, he saw Maisie reading it and weeping for her splendid, handsome, and heroic Guard.

Across the way the orderly was still handing out mail, 'somebody loves you', 'somebody loves you', 'somebody loves you too'. Woodall squeezed his eyes tight shut to hold the picture of a future that still might be his, but the tears trickled out anyway, spilling down the roughness of an unshaven cheek that no one would ever love now.

Mackenzie lay with his feet to the tent's centre and his head to its edge, a single spoke in a perfect military wheel. It was a sensible way for ten men to sleep, but tonight he'd like to have slipped out to look at Balaklava, and there was no moving without disturbing the others.

He gazed up at the darkness of the canvas and tried to picture it in his head. A fireship. That was a naval kind of thing, but he could see the idea well enough. Russian seamen would come stealing into the harbour, faces blackened likely as not, then swarm into a British ship at anchor, fill her hold with powder and sail her out innocently to rejoin her squadron. Mackenzie shuddered at the thought of an explosion right in the heart of that closely moored fleet. The steamers might not be so bad, but those old oak sailing ships? Havoc.

And a distraction, Oliver said, a diversion from the main attack. Where would that be now? The siege lines, was it, or maybe the British base itself? Mackenzie looked at the sleeping men about him, and wondered how their single regiment might protect a whole town. He listened to their soft breathing, the snoring of Lennox and wee grunts of Farquhar, the occasional furtive scratching of MacNab. He listened and waited patiently for the alarm.

And waited. The canvas flapped in the wind, but no other

noise broke the silence outside. Black gave way slowly to grey, and the dawn quiet was broken apologetically by the sound of the trumpet. Stand-to.

What had gone wrong? He was relieved the army was safe another day, but it would have been a fine coup for them to outwit the enemy and now it was themselves who looked the fools. And Ryder, what would come of him now? He pulled on his boots with a sense of great sadness, for he'd a terrible fear he already knew.

Heads turned all through the camp as Ryder was marched to court-martial. His chin was up and he walked ten inches taller than Jarvis, but Oliver thought he had a dazed look as if he still couldn't believe what was happening. He couldn't quite believe it himself.

'Told you so, didn't I, Polly?' said Fisk through a mouthful of biscuit. 'Should have listened to your Uncle Albie. You can't say he didn't have it coming.'

Bolton looked up from cutting his toenails. 'Not like that, though, Albie. It's no way to treat men.'

Fisk snorted biscuit crumbs. 'Come off it, Tommy, he was always ragging you, don't say you'll be sorry to see him get it.'

Bolton peeled off a slice of nail and inspected it with gloomy triumph. 'He saved my Bobbin in the water. I'll never forget him for that.'

They were talking as if he was dead.

The trumpet called them late morning, and the entire regiment shuffled to form a hollow square. A wagon had already been placed in the middle, and Oliver's last hope died. Everyone knew now, and even men from other regiments couldn't resist craning their heads to look as they passed. Someone from the 13th was for it.

Only their own troop knew who. As the little procession marched into the arena Oliver heard the name being murmured round the square, 'Ryder', 'Harry Ryder', 'it's Ryder'. He felt his own face redden with embarrassment and couldn't understand why. He tried not to look at Ryder himself, and keep him as a dark blue blur in the corner of his vision. Down the line he heard Prosser mutter, 'Sixpence gets you a shilling he's a nightingale, Telegraph. What about it?' Jordan said, 'You're on, chum. Ryder won't cry.'

Lord Cardigan called them to attention to listen to the proceedings of the court-martial. There seemed an awful lot of charges, and the familiar wording took on new meaning with every one. 'Leaving his post, causing his duty to devolve on a comrade' had made sense before, but not now he knew it meant latrine-digging when something needed doing that could change the course of a battle. Even the summary sounded wrong: 'insubordinate and outrageous and subversive of good order and military discipline'. What was outrageous about wanting to help the army and save men's lives? Doubts were clouding into Oliver's mind, he couldn't seem to think straight, and then the sentence came and smashed it into clarity. 'Fifty lashes'. Fifty. The maximum, for trying to serve his country.

They were doing it now, and he had to look. Ryder took off his coat and braces, stripped off the grey woollen shirt, and stepped forward to the wheel so his wrists could be tied to the spokes. The surgeon examined him, checked the barely healed wound in his side, said something to the farriers and stepped back. Fit for punishment. Oliver looked at that naked back, young, strong and muscled, and wanted to close his eyes. 'Damn shame,' murmured Lieutenant Grainger to their cornet. 'They're never the same afterwards, Hoare, you'll see.' Oliver knew what they looked like afterwards, those half-conscious men flat on the ground while the orderlies poured sea-water over them. What they felt like he couldn't imagine.

The farriers stepped forward and stood one each side of the wheel. It was their own farrier-sergeant first, he nodded at an order, wiped the back of his hand over his mouth, drew back his arm and brought down the whip with a crack. Oliver felt himself starting to shake. No mark yet, or not that could be seen from this distance, then *crack* again, and a thin red weal came up, a diagonal line from shoulder almost to the waist. It felt a betrayal to be watching, this was his friend, another great smacking blow and he closed his eyes.

Moody made a curious little grunt. 'I always said Ryder looked better with stripes.'

Grainger snapped 'Silence there', but it was too late for Oliver, he was already soaring with anger. It was for people like Moody that Ryder had done this, ordinary men in the army, and it was all brought to nothing because of the hatred of an NCO. He looked at Jarvis now, chest swollen with satisfaction, eyes fixed greedily on the circus that was the flogging of Harry Ryder. What kind of NCO was that? What kind of army was this?

The whip struck again but Oliver was looking round the regiment as if he'd never seen it before. Men in filthy, tattered uniforms because their packs still hadn't come back from the ships. Men who went without food and sleep at their officers' whims. Men who fell ill or died of wounds because there weren't enough stretchers or doctors or orderlies or supplies or enough of anything that might save their lives, but who could be tied up and beaten till their bones showed if the man who bullied them wore a grand enough uniform.

They were halfway through, and the second farrier stepped up. This one was left-handed, and his first stroke landed on still unbroken skin. Ryder's body jerked as it hit, and a new line broke out to cross the first, a giant X etched across his back, but he still didn't struggle, and still he made no sound.

Fierce pride blazed in Oliver. Ryder wouldn't break. He looked at the regiment again and saw something of the same strength in all of them, these men who lived like animals but fought like men. He remembered how steady they'd been under fire at the Bulganek, he thought of the infantry going in at the Alma, and suddenly he was filled with wonder. There might be bad officers and inefficient commanders, but these ragged men were the real army, and it was more glorious than he'd ever imagined.

Or it could be. There *were* good officers, people like Grainger and Doherty, there were things that could be done. From the wreck of his old dream he began to build another, a dream of an army where commissions went to men with ability, where the country they fought for gave them what they needed to do the job, where officers were people they could talk to, where men were treated with decency and respect.

He winced as the whip gave an especially loud crack. One day, perhaps, but not now. Until then Ryder was right, and from now on Oliver would listen to him. They would help this army despite itself, and they'd do it in any way they could.

Ryder bit down hard on the leather strap to stop himself crying out. Sam had been as gentle as he dared, but this one wasn't taking any chances. He braced himself for it, rode the blow, and puffed out breath and spit from the corners of his mouth. He could take it. They could hit as hard as they wanted, he could fucking take it.

He knew Jarvis was watching, but that only made his resistance more savage. Poor stupid bastard – did he really think this would prove anything? The next blow was vicious, a bolt of pain up his spine, and he felt his knees wobble with shock. He braced his feet firmer, clenched the spokes harder, bit down and waited for the next. The wind flicked a cold gust on the wetness of his back.

Another, and he rode it better. His body was nicely deadened now, he could go on for hours and it couldn't be more than another minute. The next smacked a dull ache through his kidneys, but he breathed out and held firm. Let them do their worst. They could break his body in pieces, but they couldn't get near him inside and that drove people like Jarvis mad. Another, and suddenly he was trembling, his back almost sobbing with the need for it to stop, but he mustn't break now, *not now*. Deep breath, but he'd mistimed it, the next stroke smashed air out of his lungs. Suck in quick, in and breathe out and wait for the next. Another. And another. *You can take it, you stupid bastard, hold on, you can take it*. Another, snatch breath and wait for the next.

There was none. Voices started talking outside his head and he shuddered back to reality as he realized it was over. Now then, now for it. He spread his legs further apart, dug his feet hard into the ground, and braced. He felt the lashings cut away from his wrists, but held tight to the spokes until the wobbliness faded and he was able to plant his full weight on the ground. Then he turned round.

It was worth it. His sight was blurred and the spectators little more than a wall of dark blue, but he heard the gasps like a single ragged breath running round the whole square. Over to his right came a ripple of laughter, and he turned to see the surgeon's assistant gaping with dismay at the prospect of throwing his bucket of brine over a man who was still on his feet. 'Oh, sorry,' said Ryder kindly, and turned again to bend for him. His eyes watered as the salt water smacked stinging onto his raw flesh, but his head was down and no one saw. He heard more laughter, blinked away the tears, and stood.

Cardigan sounded his usual unbothered self as he dismissed the parade, but it wasn't for his benefit Ryder was doing this, and he kept his eyes on the men of his own troop as they broke up with the rest. No one actually came near him, of course, but several grinned, Jordan stuck a thumb up, Fisk nodded, and Captain Marsh even murmured 'Good show' as he passed. Then there he was, there, Sergeant-Major Jarvis standing by himself, his face quite expressionless but his fists clenched in pleasingly impotent fury. Yes, it was worth it, and Ryder smiled till the bastard turned and walked away.

'You did so well, Ryder,' said another voice, and it was Oliver, Polly Oliver of all people, who'd walked up in front of everyone to stand beside him. 'I'll get Mackenzie, we'll find you at the hospital, then we can make a plan to put everything right.'

Jarvis's head would be nice, then perhaps some new skin for his back. 'Wonderful,' he said with an effort. 'Now get me to that cart before I fall on my face.'

Oliver was beginning to wonder if this meeting had been such a good idea. The hospital was a nightmare place, full of filth and misery, and they all had to squash round Woodall's pallet on a floor that was sticky and smelled of diarrhoea. It was in a corridor too, and they had to keep moving their legs to let people through, and speak in low voices because of other patients against the walls.

But it wasn't just the setting. They had a job to do, they should be planning together, but today the group seemed splintered and wrong. He could understand it with Ryder, who sat hunched forward with his braces down and was clearly in pain, but Woodall looked all right and his mood had been sour from the start. His only response to Ryder's story was to say, 'Flogged you then, did they? I bet that hurt.' Ryder looked blackly at him and turned away.

But Oliver was determined. He brought out the cards, let them play two hands, then said, 'We need to decide what to do next, don't we? Now we've come this close.'

'Who knows?' said Ryder. He twisted slightly at the waist, and Oliver saw sweat on his upper lip. 'What I don't understand is why this bloody attack didn't happen.'

Mackenzie gathered up the tricks. 'Could they have known we knew, do you think?'

Ryder went on twisting. 'I don't see how. Kostoff's dead, he couldn't tell anyone, and the instructions were going to this other chap, Borisoff.'

Mackenzie passed the deck to Oliver. 'But this officer now, he knew he was watched.'

'But not heard,' said Ryder. 'He left before they knew Mrs Jarvis was in the house.'

Oliver had his head down over the deal, but there seemed

a sudden heaviness in the silence. Then Woodall said, 'Mrs Jarvis? The woman who nurses here?'

'That's right,' said Ryder, with exaggerated carelessness. 'She's the one who helped us. Anything wrong with that?'

Woodall grunted and fixed his eyes on the growing piles of cards.

'Could it have been the wrong month that we had?' said Mackenzie. 'It's a strange thing for a man to be saying "24th", not "Tuesday" or "the day after tomorrow".'

He was right, that *was* odd, but Ryder dismissed it at once. 'No, it was the way the Bulgar asked it. Maybe he liked things spelled out very clearly.'

Oliver paused in the deal. 'Perhaps she just misheard? It must have been very frightening, she might have . . .'

'She didn't,' said Ryder immediately. 'You know her, Polly, if she were in doubt she'd say so. No, it's more likely Marsh has been careless, let something slip to the wrong person.'

'Your officer?' said Mackenzie, sounding faintly scandalized.

'Why not?' said Ryder aggressively. 'I'd believe that sooner than doubt Sally Jarvis.'

Woodall was watching him, and Oliver didn't like his look. He dealt faster.

Ryder picked up his hand. 'Either way, it's done, and we lost. That'll be the end of it.'

Mackenzie's hand paused on its way to the cards. 'But is it not with the authorities? This Mr Calvert in Intelligence, did you not say . . . ?'

Ryder was sorting his cards. 'He's an officer, not bloody God.'

Mackenzie's face darkened. 'There is no need to blaspheme.'

'Oh, isn't there?' said Ryder. 'Look, this Calvert's never even clapped eyes on our man, he doesn't know the first thing about it. And what makes you think he'll bother anyway? After this morning I doubt they'll believe anything I've told them.'

There was an awkward little silence. Oliver studied his hand, a mass of dull numbers with no pictures in sight. A 'Yarborough'.

'But we can still go on ourselves, can't we? We've done jolly well so far.'

Ryder laughed. 'You've got an interesting idea of "jolly well". But we can't get any further anyway. All we knew was that house, and they won't be using it again.'

He'd forgotten that. 'They'll still have to meet somewhere. We found this house, we'll find the next.'

'How?' said Ryder. 'Bloomer won't risk any more after today, and I'm damn sure I can't. Jarvis has both beady little eyes on me, and I'd like to keep what skin I've got left.'

'Jarvis?' said Woodall. A little tic moved in the side of his jaw. 'This sergeant-major who followed you – he was Mrs Jarvis's *husband*?'

Mackenzie stirred uneasily. Oliver looked at Ryder in alarm, but he only tilted his head back against the wall and looked up at Woodall with casual insolence. 'That's right. Don't you have wives in the Grenadiers?'

Woodall was breathing heavily. Oliver said quickly, 'It's my turn for trumps, isn't it? Sorry – pass.'

Ryder looked languidly at his hand. 'All right then – I call "bridge". How about it, anyone want to *contre*?'

Woodall was still staring at Ryder, and Oliver saw his throat move as he swallowed. 'You cad. You filthy, rotten cad.'

The silence was thick with hospital noises, footsteps and little moans, someone sobbing and an orderly clanking along with buckets. Ryder said, 'Don't push it, Woodall, I've told you how it was. Now are you *contre* or not?'

The cards were slipping out of Woodall's hands, fluttering and falling like dead leaves. 'He didn't know, did he? You and his wife, you planned this without telling him, you went behind the poor devil's back.'

Ryder smacked down his own cards, face-up and visible, the game ruined. 'We couldn't bloody tell him, he'd have stopped it out of hand. He doesn't give a toss about the war or saving lives, he can't see anything beyond his own spite.'

'And his own wife?' Woodall nodded knowingly. 'That wasn't spite made him follow you, oh no, he'll have been up to your little game.'

Ryder's voice was deadly quiet. 'There was no little game.'

Woodall threw away the rest of his cards. 'Not for him, no. How do you think it made him feel, poor beggar, knowing his wife was laughing behind his back with a private soldier, how the hell do you think he felt? No wonder he had you flogged, can you blame him?'

Ryder seemed to have forgotten his back, he swung round on Woodall like a man in a fight. 'Yes! If he suspected something he could have dealt with it man to man, instead of hiding behind his stripes and getting the army to do it for him. That's cowardly, and you know it.'

'I know this,' said Woodall. His voice was rising dangerously, and all down the corridor patients were turning to look. 'I know it wasn't his fault, or his wife's either. Poor little thing without her husband to guide her, how could she know it was wrong? You made her do it, Ryder, and that's a blackguard's trick. You deserved every lash of that flogging, and I hope they laid it on hard.'

Oliver felt a little tug in his fingers, Mackenzie pulling at his cards. 'Hand's over, Polly. We're finished here.'

Ryder stood. He didn't say a word as he shrugged back into his braces, but he was looking down at Woodall and his eyes burned. Then he slammed away down the corridor, hurling on his coat as he went, and the orderly backed against the wall to let him pass.

Oliver saw his whole plan shattering. 'How could you, Woodall? That was a beastly thing to say.'

Woodall actually laughed, a harsh noise like a crow call. 'And what would you know? You're just a green boy tagging after him, I'd take money you're a virgin.'

He felt himself flush to the roots of his hair. Through a hot mist he heard Mackenzie say, 'There are no boys in this army, not now. Oliver's a soldier, same as us.'

'Hasn't fought a battle,' said Woodall. 'Takes more than a uniform to make a soldier.'

Oliver looked at him in wonder. All the Guard's dignity had gone, he was a shabby man with dirty fingernails and patchy beard clutching at his blanket like a drunken beggar.

He said, 'I bloody am one, though,' and stood. 'All I need's a chance to prove it.'

Woodall jerked his chin. 'Touchy little beggar, aren't you?'

'He is that,' said Mackenzie, climbing leisurely to his feet and handing Oliver the cards. 'You'd maybe not know this, being unconscious at the time, but when you were shot it was this laddie risked his life for the ammunition to get you out of it.' He brushed down his kilt, shook out the tassels of his sporran, and looked Woodall directly in the eye. 'Ryder would have done it too, more's the fool of him, seeing how you've repaid him for the gesture.'

Woodall flinched. 'Well, I couldn't know that, could I?'

'It should no surprise you,' said Mackenzie serenely, 'seeing as that's what friends do. But then I'm thinking you maybe don't know that either.' He patted Oliver on the arm and walked away down the corridor, dwarfing the huddled invalids who lay to either side.

Oliver watched him go with a sense of despair. Their little group was breaking up, disintegrating, he had to do something to make things right. He looked back at Woodall, but the Guard was sitting hunched under his blanket and glaring at nothing. 'Woodall? Dennis?'

Woodall didn't move. Even his eyes were still and unblinking as he stared hopelessly at the empty wall.

Oliver turned and walked away.

The wind moaned down the emptiness of the Balaklava gorge. Ryder lowered his head against the rain, and strode on into the gathering dark.

He didn't move aside at the leisurely clip-clop of hooves behind him. They were redcoats, Heavy Brigade, they hadn't even been at the Alma, let them damn well wait. They swore at him as they squeezed by, and one said, 'Who's that bastard think he is?' but his companion said, 'That's the one took a licking today, don't kick a man who's down.'

Ryder stopped still on the track, and for a moment the biting wind was nothing more than a welcome coolness on the hot flush of his face. The pain in his back was suddenly excruciating, unbearable, and he braved the rain to strip off his coat. It was the bloody braces digging into his shoulders, he'd got to haul them down.

The wind found him at once, flapping in his woollen shirt and driving rain in his face. He stood with his coat in his hand and his braces dangling to his knees and wondered if it was actually possible to get any lower than he was right now. There was only one thing more wretched than a private soldier and that was a private soldier with the marks of the whip on his back.

Jarvis had done this to him. Oh, he'd been so proud of his little gesture of defiance this morning, but the truth was that Jarvis had broken him, had him stripped and beaten in front of his peers, and by God he was going to get him for it. The wind slapped his hair in his face, mocking him with his own futility. *What are you going to do, Ryder? Spit on his shadow?*

He laughed and hauled on his coat, easing the weight carefully over his shoulders. For a moment he thought of Sally's hands on them, then thrust away the memory like a disease. Woodall had called him a cad, but when he remembered that kiss he gave himself worse names than that. He had to leave her alone, stay out of her way, stop even thinking about her and hope she was able to do the same.

He turned again into the wind and walked on past Kadikoi. The rain was coming down harder now, driving in glistening horizontal streaks at his face, but he plodded steadily upward towards a camp and an army and a life that had lost all point.

'Ryder!' called a voice behind him. 'Hang on a minute, will you?'

He waited in resigned silence.

'Sorry,' said Oliver, arriving panting beside him. 'I never thought you'd go so fast.'

He started walking again. 'They didn't beat my bloody legs, did they?'

'No,' said Oliver, and was quiet for a few paces while he caught his breath. 'But I know it can take people badly. I was thinking of Joe Sullivan.'

Ryder stopped abruptly. 'I'm nothing like Joe Sullivan.'

'Of course not,' said Oliver at once. 'Sullivan really seemed to give up, didn't he?'

Ryder looked suspiciously at him, then walked on without a word.

Oliver came after him. 'You're not giving up, then? We'll still be going after the traitor.'

Ryder swore. He used every single oath he could think of, even the ones in Urdu. 'What's the point? We can't break the rules, we can't work within them, we can't do bloody anything except watch it happen and say "we told you so" afterwards. That's the army, that's the machine, what the hell can we do against that?'

They had to fight the wind as they turned out of the gorge, but Oliver never broke step. 'We can stand up for it anyway, can't we? Like you did today.'

He tried to laugh, but it sent a tearing pain up his back. 'Don't, Poll, please. That hurts.'

'You did,' said Oliver obstinately. 'You said one man can make a difference just by standing still. One man changed everything at the Alma. If he can do it, why can't we?'

Ryder stopped. The emptiness of the plain was all around them, a wilderness broken only by little fires from the cavalry camps and the Turkish redoubts. 'Maybe he's cleverer. Maybe he actually has the support of his superiors. It's just not the same.'

'You don't really believe that,' said Oliver. 'If you did, you'd never have gone in by yourself at the Alma.'

Ryder looked at him. 'You're a persistent little bastard, aren't you?'

'So are you,' said Oliver, and smiled.

The wind slackened as they approached the camp, and he listened to the trudging of their boots, crunching up the track together in perfect step. Rain had driven everyone else under canvas, and the place seemed deserted until Jordan came shooting out of a tent and nearly bumped right into them.

'Sorry,' he said vaguely, then quickly looked away. 'Oh. Sorry, Ryder.'

Pity. He had to stop that before it started. 'What's up, Telegraph? Any news?'

Jordan hesitated, then relaxed at his apparent normality. 'Not to notice. Look-On's talked to a Russian deserter who says there'll be an attack tomorrow, but no one's going to flap about that.'

Ryder felt a sinking sense of inevitability. 'The ships?'

'Not hardly,' said Jordan. 'Not going to swim for it, are they? No, the bloke says Kadikoi and Balaklava. Us.'

The camp looked empty, no sign of a stand-to. 'What are we doing about it?'

'What do *you* think?' said Jordan with a wink. 'Look-On believes it all right, but Raglan ain't buying. He says his poor cavalry ain't had enough sleep lately, he's not having them up all night on the word of a deserter.' He grinned amiably and hurried off into the dark.

'Ryder?' said Oliver.

Wind cracked in the canvas. Ryder turned his face up to the driving rain and saw thick black clouds racing through the darkening sky. He'd heard old soldiers say they knew when a battle was coming. When a big body of men is on the move the ground knows it, the birds know it, the air knows it, and the man who's bent all his mind on that same body of men knows it too. He listened to the wind rustling in the vineyards and felt suddenly very calm.

'It could be the same one,' said Oliver. 'Perhaps the reinforcements were late. Perhaps they just decided not to bother with the diversion. What do you think, Ryder?'

Ryder watched a flock of birds wheeling over the Causeway Heights towards the sea, crying harshly as they flew. 'I think we'd better sharpen our swords.'

15

25 October 1854, 4.30 a.m. to 10.55 a.m.

The trumpet called them out to the damp stillness of dawn. The canvas was sodden, the fires waterlogged, and the only things moving on the plain were themselves.

The ritual of gathering equipment was a joke. A supply tent had blown down in the storm, and the cartridges were heavy with moisture even as they counted them. 'Look,' said Jordan, holding one up. 'Look-On finally gets his chance with Fanny Duberly.' The cartridge wilted and bent under the punch of his fingernails.

Fisk guffawed, took it from him and tore away the sodden bottom. 'There,' he said. 'Now it's Prince Menschikoff.' Everyone knew the Russian commander had been emasculated by a Turkish cannonball at Silistra.

Ryder didn't join in the laughter. The morning quiet felt as menacing as last night's storm, and he wanted more than a useless carbine at his side. He passed his bridle to Oliver and walked boldly down the horse-line to face Sergeant-Major Jarvis.

Jarvis watched him approaching, piggy eyes alert for any sign of weakness or pain. Ryder had spent the whole night on his belly, his back was stiff as iron and his skin burned like hot tar, but he came to perfect, straight attention, fixed his eyes above Jarvis's head, and said, 'Reporting for my pistol, Sar'nt-major.'

He counted four seconds before Jarvis's face even moved. 'Not on parade, Private. A pistol's not regulation.'

God in *heaven*. 'It's a private possession, Sar'nt-major. I'm no longer under arrest, I'd like it back.'

Jarvis's mouth smiled. 'We're stand-to, Trooper, your private matters can wait. Report to me after parade.'

Ryder knew what he was after. He smiled, said, 'Thank you, Sar'nt-major,' and walked back to his horse without the smallest sign of discomfiture. If the bastard wanted to make a game of it Ryder could beat him with one hand tied to a wheel. Yesterday he'd done it with two.

Cardigan was obviously still snoring comfortably in his yacht, so Lord George Paget took the parade in a silence punctuated only by the snorting of horses, the murmur of NCOs and the squelching of footsteps as officers checked down the lines. Marsh paused in front of Ryder and said, 'Fit for duty, Private?' Ryder smiled for the benefit of Jarvis and said, 'Fit, sir.' Marsh nodded courteously and moved on.

A familiar rattling came from their Horse Artillery, the caissons setting off to fetch shells for the siege. 'All aboard for sunny Balaklava!' called Captain Shakespear as he did every morning. 'Anyone for the seaside?' The wagons set off with a bang, wheels crunching into the rain-filled ruts and spraying the parading cavalry as they passed. Just another day, supplying a siege that already looked like it would never end.

'Look-On's early, ain't he?' said Fisk, watching their bulldog-jawed commander prowling impatiently at the front of their lines. 'What's got him jumping?'

Ryder knew. Lucan could hardly wait for General Scarlett's report on the Heavies before he was off for the Causeway Heights with an entourage that seemed to consist of most of his staff. Paget watched the procession thoughtfully, then discarded his cheroot and trotted casually along to join it.

'Trouble, Bobbin,' said Bolton to his bloody horse. 'You smell it, don't you?'

Dawn was breaking behind the slopes of the Heights, and as light warmed the ridge Ryder made out the shapes of the first pair of horsemen on the skyline. His heart jumped as he saw they were moving, each trotting in a deliberate circle.

'The vedettes!' called someone in the Hussars. 'Look, they're signalling.'

So were the next pair, one circling clockwise, the other anti-clockwise. Infantry as well as cavalry were approaching.

'They're going faster,' said Oliver. His voice sounded dry and croaky. 'That's a gallop really, isn't it?'

'That's a gallop,' said Ryder. The faster the speed, the bigger the force, and what was coming looked like an army.

Lucan's mob were directly below the vedettes, and didn't seem to have seen them. They'd spotted something else though, and an aide was pointing towards Number 1 redoubt on Canrobert's Hill. Something looked different there, the flagpole was flying a second flag above the first, and then a crack of light drew Ryder's eyes to the source of a single, muffled bang. Cannon. The Turks were firing down into the North Valley.

'That'll be Russ,' said Jordan knowledgeably. 'They're coming at us over the Fedoukhine Hills.'

'You amaze me, Telegraph,' said the dry voice of Lieutenant Grainger from the serrefile. 'Really, you should be on the Staff.'

Amidst the laughter Ryder's eyes met Oliver's. This was what they'd dreaded ever since they learned the truth. Another battle where men might take orders from a staff officer working for the other side.

Hooves thundered towards them, Lucan's group galloping back from the Heights. Most were heading for camp, but Lucan peeled off for Kadikoi and the Highlanders, and Captain Charteris was charging clear across the plain for the Sapoune Plateau and Raglan's headquarters. No one seemed to be going for the infantry at Inkerman, but surely Raglan would see to that. He couldn't expect the cavalry division and a handful of Highlanders to defend the British base alone.

Paget skidded back to the lines in a spray of mud. Two staff officers were calling for Captain Maude, and almost at once Ryder heard banging and rattling behind as the Horse Artillery limbered up. Another rider wheeled off for Balaklava, shouting something about shells. 'And "W" Battery!' called someone else. 'Ask Sir Colin, all they can spare, we'll never hold them with this.'

Then another, more familiar sound rose shrill above them all, and Ryder faced front to see Trumpet-Major Joy with the trumpet to his lips. *Mount*.

No more doubts. They mounted drill-perfect, nearly seven hundred legs swinging over in unison. The thump as they hit the saddle had a certain squelch to it, and Fisk muttered 'We're going to have damp arses all day.' Colonel Douglas was giving a speech to the 11th Hussars, but when Ryder looked at their own front there was no Colonel Doherty to lead and inspire them, not even a major to take his place. After a moment Captain Oldham of 'A' Troop rode self-consciously to fill the gap. The 13th Light Dragoons were going into battle at last, and they were doing it with only a captain to lead them.

Another cannon shot boomed from the redoubts, followed by a crash of return fire. No isolated field guns this time, these were big bastards, 18- or 24-pounders, and over the crest of the ridge Ryder saw drifting smoke. He looked behind at their own 'I' Troop still furiously limbering up. Four 6-pounders and two short-range howitzers. They'd no caissons either, no shells but what they could carry on the limbers; the wagons had gone to Balaklava to feed that bloody useless siege.

'They won't send us in yet though, will they?' said Oliver. The light was brighter now, and Ryder could make out the unusual sharpness of his face. 'The Turks will hold them off.'

Another great blast of fire, this time from Kamara. The Russians were there too, big guns already in battery, and all aimed at Number 1 redoubt. He couldn't understand it, the 4th Light Dragoons were on picquet there, how could the Russians have Kamara? Then another boom, another battery to left of it, this time aimed at Number 2. The bastards were everywhere. They'd moved at night and struck at first light, the poor bloody Turks hadn't a chance.

He said flatly, 'We'll be lucky if they hold for an hour.'

Lucan was riding back. He took position beside Scarlett, and almost at once the Heavy Brigade began to move, advancing in column towards the beleaguered redoubts. Ryder glared at their receding backs in envy, but then the trumpet sounded and it was their own turn. 'The Brigade will advance – walk – *march*,' and in with the heels and off, following in echelon behind the Heavies, going at last towards the guns and smoke of war.

Sally stood by the empty fire and watched them go. Smoke was billowing over the Heights into the valley, and ahead of them something screamed into the earth and threw up clouds of debris as it exploded. The Russians were overshooting.

She knelt back down and went on crushing coffee beans. Jarvis would be panting for his breakfast when he got back, and there'd be others glad of a brew as well. An image of Ryder flickered into her mind, and she crunched it down hard with the pestle.

Boots and the hem of a pink skirt appeared in front of her, and she looked up to see Lucie Jordan standing irresolutely with a camp kettle. 'Out of sugar again, Luce?'

Lucie turned to look at her. 'They're awful close, those Russians. Hear them? I think they're at the Arabtabia as well.'

The firewood was damp, and Sally had to jerk her head to dodge a cloud of acrid smoke. 'Probably. No use just attacking one redoubt, they'll want all four.'

'There must be an awful lot of them then,' said Lucie. 'I mean – to do that.'

Sally looked up. She'd never much cared for Lucie Jordan, but there was an anxiety in the voice that touched her heart. 'Come on, Luce, your Billy's more than a match for a cannonball. Here, I've plenty of coffee, I'll make some while we wait.'

Lucie kicked her boot petulantly against the grass. 'What good's that? This isn't safe, we ought to be getting out to Kadikoi.'

Sally stared at her, then turned to look back at the Causeway Heights. The Light Brigade had stopped, thank God, but the Heavies were advancing into the smoke. The men were out there, *their men*, and she was suddenly so angry she couldn't speak. She bashed down again with the pestle and didn't reply.

'It's no good ignoring it,' said Lucie, her voice rising to a whine. 'Some are leaving already.'

'More fool them,' she said, without looking up. 'If our men can't hold here, what's the safety in Kadikoi?'

'The Highlanders are there, aren't they? Or we could go to the ships, we'd be safe there.'

Sally turned the beans with the spoon. 'You leave if you like. My husband's had to go out without his breakfast, and I'm going to be here to give it him when he comes back.'

There was a silence. Then 'Suit yourself,' said Lucie, with a toss of her head. 'But you'll look a bit silly making coffee when the Cossacks come.' She turned and flounced away.

Sally banged down the mortar with frustration. What else was there to do? She couldn't grab a gun and fight. The French *viviandières* brought the men supplies right on the battlefield, but an Englishwoman wasn't allowed even to do that.

The firewood spat stinging smoke into her eyes and she screwed them tight shut, but the blackness was filled with the booming of guns and screaming of horses and the voice in her head crying for something *she could do*.

Woodall sat miserably on his blanket, listening to the racket outside. There was a flap on somewhere, he supposed, but they might have a thought for the sick men in here. Some of them were dying.

Right now he wished he were one of them. His night had been filled with dreams of his friendless youth, ignored by the gentry, despised by the working men, hated at school for wanting to better himself and be decent. Nobody had wanted him till a recruiting sergeant told him there was a place for big strong men of good character. No one till the Guards, and then Maisie.

But he had had friends, and he knew it now. Ryder, Mackenzie, even young Oliver, they'd been real pals and he'd driven them away. Last night he'd rummaged in his blanket for things to give him comfort, but the photograph of Maisie was unbearable, the shaving mirror showed him a face he didn't recognize, and all he'd found of value was a pewter flask lent him by a friend. It was only rum, of course, but Ryder might have liked it and he'd given it to Woodall instead. He sat on his blanket clutching it like a lifeline, remembering the moment, and that Ryder had called him 'Woody'.

But he couldn't stay here weltering in his own filth. The noise was louder now, doors banging, Turks jabbering, something was up and maybe he could be useful. He laid down the flask, sat straighter and reached for his boots. Someone was talking in the main room, a loud voice with authority, and Woodall strained to listen. Someone was saying he was Lieutenant Colonel Daveney and demanding the attention of the wounded.

He limped to the door with the second boot still in his hand. The officer was saying Balaklava was under attack, and he needed more men to man the defence. 'I've a party of invalids here, and if you can stand and hold a rifle then I want you.'

I want you. The words were medicine, and Woodall never even felt the boot drop from his hand. He stepped full into the door-way and said, 'I can, sir. And I've got my own rifle.'

Across the room the officer's eyes found his, and Woodall's whole frame trembled with the recognition. The man was really seeing him, not that awful shameful thing he'd seen in the mirror last night, but him as he really was, *him*.

'Good man,' said Daveney. 'Anyone else?'

Woodall didn't stay to watch the rush of cripples looking for their chance of glory. He snatched up his boot, hopped back to his blanket, and fumbled out his rifle from underneath. He'd cleaned and kept it perfect, he'd a nearly full ammunition pouch, he was going to be the best find that officer could hope for. He yanked out his coatee and hurled his arms into it, thrust his foot into the second boot, and hurried out after the others into the freshness of the outside air.

Smoke and debris roiled back at the cavalry over the crest, and a black shape hurtled over with it. 'Over!' yelled the Heavies in front of them, and 'Over!' shouted their own ranks as they shifted their horses to dodge the oncoming ball. 'Look out, Lord George!' sang out a voice, but Paget skipped the wrong way and a cloud of dust enveloped him as the roundshot bounced through. A burst of laughter followed as an orderly cried, 'Ha, look at that, right between your horse's legs!'

To Ryder it was the Alma all over again. Russian artillery were hammering the Turkish redoubts right in front of them, while Lucan kept them sitting under fire as useless spectators. The Heavies were advancing and retreating, feinting menacingly and falling back, but that was no bloody good, they were only telling the Russians to come on and do as they liked, the British cavalry wouldn't lift a finger to stop them.

More roundshot roared over, and Ryder heard the terrible slosh as a cannonball ripped into the belly of a living man. Riderless horses were already weaving in and out of the ranks of the Heavies, and one poor staggering beast trying to reel back to its place had only three legs. Then a lightning crack split the sky over the ridge, a blast of orange staining the blue. Black rubble flew up, a block, half a wheel, the crazily jerking body of a man.

'Dear God,' said Oliver. 'That's our battery, isn't it? Oh dear God.'

Men hurried down from the Heights with a limp and mangled body, rushing him to the rear and the dubious safety of a road already wide open. 'Poor Maude,' said Lieutenant Grainger. 'Bloody good man. Poor Maude.'

The battery wasn't long after them. A black-faced and bleeding lieutenant ran to report to Lucan, then down came the limbers hauling the guns, every last shell expended for little result. 'W' Battery was still firing east of Kadikoi, but hopelessly outgunned by the Russians, and the Turkish redoubts had stopped even firing at all. The enemy infantry were going in, a grey swarm charging down the slopes and straight at Number 1, overwhelming the miserable sandbag defences like a wave. The Turks were running, breaking and running, abandoned by a British army who did nothing but sit and watch.

Number 2 was breaking too, the walls collapsing under the rush to retreat, while the white and gold standard of the Host of Azov broke defiantly from the flagpole on Canrobert's Hill. 'Oh, the bastards,' said poor Oliver, tears trickling down his furious face. 'They've taken our flag, oh, the bastards.' It was only a bit of cloth and Turkish at that, but Ryder's own throat tightened as if he were breathing smoke.

Musket balls pinged among them and cracked against the rocks, Russian fire from their own redoubts. Lucan yelled, a bugle called through the smoke, they were ordered to fall back. Threes *about*, and round we go, having done bloody nothing at all. They rode back almost as far as the camp, back to halt near the unmanned redoubts, British cavalry in retreat.

And not only British. Red-fezzed figures were pouring towards them over the plain, Turks running from the slaughter. Grey shapes trickled down the slopes after them, Cossacks on the hunt, lances sparkling in the growing light.

'Look at the Johnnies run,' said Fisk in disgust. 'We should have known they wouldn't hold.'

The Cossacks were in the back of them, bodies hurling in the air from the thrust of their lances. Ryder thought of India and pig-sticking, but these were men being tossed about like brightly dressed scarecrows, and over the galloping hooves he heard the anguish of hoarse screams. 'How could they hold when they saw us fall back?' he said savagely. 'Would you?'

Not that it mattered now. The Turks were gone, and there was no one but themselves between the enemy and Campbell's five hundred Highlanders at Kadikoi. Ryder braved the pain in his back to look round the plain, but there was no sign of infantry support yet, no one but Lord Cardigan trotting up to join them after a leisurely breakfast on the *Dryad*.

And a staff officer, a galloper from Raglan. Ryder looked closely, wondering if their man might have changed his horse and saddlecloth again, but the orders were genuine, they were actually being handed over on paper. Maybe this Calvert had said something, or maybe it was Angelo's doing. Maybe Angelo had been working behind the scenes all this time, and they weren't as alone as he'd feared.

But if the orders were genuine they still weren't palatable, and Lucan's response was probably audible at Kadikoi. 'Do *what*, sir? *Withdraw?*'

It wasn't a mistake, it wasn't treachery, it was the sheer imbecility of Lord Raglan. A grumbling Lucan led them back north, right back to the end of the Causeway Heights and the mouth of the North Valley. The camp was abandoned, its occupants undefended, and Campbell's Highlanders were on their own.

'The Regiment will fix bayonets!'

Mackenzie's hand went smack to the socket, pulling out the blade with a satisfying rasp.

'Fix – *bayonets!*'

Plunge in and the little twist to the click, then bang the piece straight to his body, atten*shun*! Trembling with tension he awaited the next order, but Colonel Ainslie was talking to Colonel Sterling and they'd maybe a minute or two yet.

But not much more. They'd a brave view from the brow of the hill that commanded the gorge to Balaklava, but there was little to see but Russians swarming into the redoubts and panicked Turks running towards their own line crying 'Ship, Johnny! Ship!' A naval officer stood with arms outspread, trying to stop and re-form them, but some were beyond it, poor devils, running blindly on towards the safety of the harbour. Heathens, of course, but the red fezzes called to him like men of his own coat and he didn't have it in him to join the calls of 'No buono, Johnny. No buono!' from others in their line. The Turks had fought a brave little fight down there, they'd held an hour and a half, and now it was their own turn.

'On our own, as usual,' said miserable Farquhar out of the corner of his mouth. 'It'll be the Alma all over again, my man, remember that Ranger? "Let the Scotch do all the work." That'll be the way of it now.'

Mackenzie smiled at the memory. 'We handled worse that day, Davey.'

'Oh aye,' agreed Farquhar, with hardly a movement of his lips. 'But we'd the whole army with us, if ye'll recall, and none of the women to worry about neither.'

Mackenzie turned to look behind their line. The camp was as it always was, the field kitchen brewing and an old wife hanging up her laundry in the hope of better weather than yesterday's, but the thought of Russian savages running amok in it with their bayonets was enough to cramp his bowels. And what was behind it was even worse to think of – their supplies, the hospital, the post office and escape route to the ships.

He turned back to face front. 'So we won't let them through.'

Farquhar looked sourly at him. 'Oh aye, you, me and five hundred other men will hold off the whole of the Russian army, will we?'

Boots were tramping behind them, a disciplined march and a voice calling 'Halt!' Even Sergeant Macpherson turned to stare as thirty Grenadier Guards formed unasked on their left flank, and two young lieutenants reported to Colonel Sterling. They'd maybe just come up from quarters in Balaklava, but the sight of the familiar bearskins gave Mackenzie a twinge of sadness at the thought of a man who would not be with them.

But others were. The Navy's Captain Tatham was re-forming the Turks on each end of their line, and behind them came a rag-tag bunch of invalids who'd maybe been on their way to the ships. There were near a hundred of them, mostly in the green of the Rifle Brigade, but a few bandaged figures from the line regiments, a couple of their own Highlanders – and one solitary Grenadier Guard in a squashed and dusty bearskin and beneath it the face of a friend.

Mackenzie's face split in a grin, and for a moment he saw Woodall smile back. 'You see, Davey,' he said in sudden elation of spirit. 'We're not alone now.'

Something pinged in his ear, his bonnet slid sideways, and he clapped his hand hard to his neck. Musket ball, but it had only skimmed him, probably at the limit of its range. But the cannon were not, and a blast from near the redoubts seemed to belch straight at them, a shell exploding in the right of their line. Men cried out, someone was down, and Lord in Heaven, there lay a leg on the grass, white hose and scarlet bindings perfect for parade. His hands tightened on the Minié. Fool that he was, he'd been looking at the battle like a picture, but the Russians were near enough to hit them and do it with iron.

'Fall back!' yelled Macpherson. Others were echoing it, and back they went, back and down to re-form. It seemed strange to be asking Highlanders to withdraw, but it must not be shameful or Sir Colin would not have ordered it.

'Lie down!' came the order now, 'lie down!' Memory of the last battle plucked at him, images of men pounded to blood and bone as they lay helpless in the grass, but he kept his trust in Sir Colin and laid his nose obediently into the mud. The ground trembled under him as a shell hit the other side of the hill, and at once understanding soared through him. This was not retreat. They were lying in wait as he'd done as a stalker, waiting out of range for the moment they would spring from the earth and confound the enemy with their appearance.

'Oh, this is grand, Davey,' he whispered. 'This is worth everything. This is grand.'

Farquhar seemed to convulse beside him, the man was shaking like an ague. Could he be took with the cholera? Mackenzie's hand reached tentatively to touch his shoulder. 'Davey?'

Farquhar turned his head towards him, and for the first time since he'd joined the regiment Mackenzie saw he was laughing. 'Oh, Niall,' he said, and was shook with another burst of merriment. 'When we go to hell to fight the devil, the man I want beside me is you.'

Sally emerged furtively from the makeshift shack they called the commissary store and saw the world had changed. The camp was almost deserted, and even those women she could see were scurrying away with bundles slung hastily on their backs. She looked across at the 8th Hussars' camp and saw only blasted Fanny Duberly with her quartermaster husband supervising servants as they struck the tent. 'Where's Whisker, Henry?' she heard the woman say. 'Where's my darling Whisker?' Sally could see the pony for herself, laden almost flat to the ground with bags of crockery and boxes of port.

She hoisted her own haversack. It was now heavy with contraband but she no longer felt any scruples. What was a drop of rum or a handful of biscuits compared with what the officers had, especially those like Captain Duberly who weren't even fighting and dying with the rest? She turned to join the Brigade – and stopped dead.

Cavalry were spilling down from the Causeway Heights. Hussars, she thought, but the colours weren't British, they were grey as clay. They were thundering down towards Kadikoi, and Lucie was right, there were an awful lot of them. Where were their own?

She saw them then, the Heavy Brigade rounding the ridge and starting to trot back towards the vineyards. Maybe Lord Raglan had seen the danger and sent them, but it was no good, no good, they could never reach Campbell in time. Her skirts spun like a dancer's as she swung back round to look at Kadikoi, but there was no one there, the brow of the hill was empty, there was no defence at all.

The Russian hussars were encouraged, they were speeding up to the gallop. They could go right through, take the gorge, open the road to the harbour, then they were finished, all of them, stranded in this stinking country with no way to the ships, stranded to be picked off at leisure. She dropped her suddenly useless haversack and waited to watch the end.

And the hill changed. A rim of black then bright crimson fringed the brow, and suddenly there were men there, a long line of red-coated Highlanders standing on the crest to face the oncoming enemy. The sun burned on their coats and glittered on their bayonets like a jagged crown. 'Square,' she thought, army wife as she was. 'They'll have to form square to face cavalry.' But the line still grew and settled, long and straight, a slender barrier two men deep, standing as they were to meet the onslaught of the charge.

Tears spilled hot down her face, blurring her vision till the Highlanders were no more than a thin red streak in the distance. She was on the strength of the 13th Light Dragoons, but at that moment she was of the whole army, and that frail line of resistance embodied everything she loved and was part of. Oh God, let them hold, let them somehow do the impossible and stand up to that charge, oh God and dear God, let them hold.

'Present arms!' and up with the rifle snug to his cheek, ready to fire at the word. But they were fast, these cavalry, and Mackenzie was not so very sure of the range. Infantry he'd faced, but this was new, horses galloping right at them with great big hooves and men with swords astride them.

There was shouting to left of him, Turks breaking and running in panic, belting down the hill to the camp and safety. Laughter in the ranks, and he turned to see one poor devil caught in the old wife's washing, and her belabouring him with a dolly stick, yelling him to go back to the lines. Maybe they ought to have the women beside them instead.

Campbell's voice turned him, calm as a loch in June. 'Now remember, men, there is no retreat from here. You must die where you stand.'

Die. Everything ending and the world going on without him. A voice growled, 'Aye, aye, Sir Colin, we'll do that,' and others echoed it, his own among them, 'Aye, we'll do that.' Campbell meant what he said, but they were Highlanders and so did they.

He planted his feet firmer into the earth. The stock was warm against his cheek, heated by his own blood. His finger was tight to the trigger, flesh and metal curled together for what they knew was to be done. Nearer and nearer rode the Russians, and '*Fire!*' came the order, his finger squeezed, the barrel tried to buck, but he held it steady and the shot flew clean. There didn't seem to be many down, he could see no empty saddles, but his hands were busy with other things. Butt to ground, cartridge out, bite, spit, over barrel and shake. Some fool was shouting 'Reload!' but that would be the Guards, poor creatures of ceremony that they were, he was already ball in and ramming, home and return. He was front rank, side nail to the right hip for the half-cock and hope the man behind remembered to place his higher. He did and they all did, not a tangle in the line as the caps went on.

He looked up for the range, but the Russians were wavering, the rush gone out of them, and a blast from the Highlanders' own battery shaking them further still. The fighting joy swept savage through their lines, and even Farquhar was crying '*Cruachan!*' in honour of their chieftain as they edged forward, forward to the bayonet and the real attack.

'Ninety-third, ninety-third!' roared Campbell. 'Damn all that eagerness!' His sword swept imperatively, and Mackenzie stepped back with the others, rifle again to the shoulder. He saw it then, what their chieftain had known, the cavalry weren't wavering but wheeling, turning to take the Highlanders' weak right flank. In front of him Campbell said to his aide, 'Shadwell, that man knows his business.'

So did Sir Colin. A single shout, and their grenadier company turned on the flank, bending the line so they could all fire to the east. Again '*Fire!*' the blast and cloud of smoke, and as it drifted and cleared Mackenzie looked up from the reload to see the Russians wheeling still further, riding away and back to the safety of their own lines. Behind him he heard the old wife still yelling 'Get out of it, you thieving cowardly bastards!' and the thwack of her stick on the shoulders of some hapless Turk.

Then the cheering started, a great roar that rose and spread along their line. Bonnets were sent flying, Macpherson shook his at the backs of the retreating Russians, and Farquhar, miserable croaker Farquhar, stuck his on his bayonet and waved it like a flag. Mackenzie lowered his rifle with hands that were still steady, and allowed himself a quiet smile of satisfaction.

'Will ye look at the look-ons,' said old Lennox, smacking his scrawny shank with enjoyment. 'D'ye think they were meaning to help us? Why, they're slower than snails!'

Mackenzie looked out to see the Heavy Brigade approaching from the fork in the valleys. But they were not headed for Kadikoi, or at least not now, they were turning for the Heights, and as he lifted his eyes he saw why. Horsemen were gathered on the ridge, a great body of them forming a thick, thick line. They looked the same kind of devils they'd seen off themselves, only many more of them, two thousand, maybe three.

The wee squadrons of maybe three hundred Heavy Brigade were turning to bring them to battle. Their progress was slow as they struggled through the vineyards, but there was another obstacle before them, and Mackenzie swallowed uneasily at the sight of little white triangles in regular straight lines. Two forces of cavalry were looking to collide, and full in their path lay the camp of the Light Brigade.

Sally saw them too. Russian cavalry, thousands of them, and on the ridge facing down to their own camp. She turned her head to the sounds of crashing and trampling in the vineyard, and here came the Heavies, their scarlet coats and brass helmets flashing bravely in the green vines. She looked back at the Russians beginning to move down the slope, and felt herself take a step backward, then another, until her heel hit a tent peg and stopped.

'Ah, Jesus,' said a tall big-boned woman by the 8th Hussars' tents. 'They're going to fight a battle right over us. Ah, Jesus.'

The first Heavies were thrusting into view, broken lines of cavalry struggling to re-form in a chaos of tents and washing and cooking fires, and Sally heard a rip as a tent went down. Her head cleared, she picked up her haversack, and moved back to the safety of the forge cart. No horseman on either side would try to ride over that.

Trumpets sounded shrilly as the Heavies came on. Their horses stumbled against picket ropes and dragged down tents, they crushed pans and kettles and bumped over a washing tub with a great whoosh of water, but still they came on, and when an officer trotted past Sally he actually touched his hat. Half-dazed, she curtseyed after him.

She watched them through the camp to the foot of the slopes, and saw with relief the Russians had stopped. They were waiting on the Heights, staring incredulously at the British thrashing about below them as General Scarlett tried to form his regiments into proper line. It was madness, and Sally's hand crept over her mouth at the sight of officers calmly turning their backs to the enemy in order to finish their dressing. Staff officers were joining them now, Lord Lucan himself screaming with impatience, but still Scarlett took his time. Above and beyond them Sally saw the Russians re-forming, sending out thick curving arms on either side like the claws of a giant crab. If the Heavies didn't move soon, the Russians would, and the fight would be right in front of their camp.

But at last the trumpet, and not the 'Walk-march', Scarlett was going straight for the 'Charge'. She watched in disbelief as he started up the slope with his aides, four men alone charging uphill and crashing right into the centre of the Russian mass. After him surged his first troops, hurtling at the enemy with a roar of sound that must have reached to Balaklava, a hubbub of trumpets shrilling, men shouting, steel clashing, and under it all the battle-cry that hadn't been heard since the Battle of Waterloo, the fierce low moan of the Scots Greys. Others followed them, the whole Heavy Brigade piling uphill, and to Sally's amazement the Russians were wavering under the onslaught. Three hundred men were holding off three thousand, and for now at least the camp was still behind British lines.

She allowed herself to relax a little, and moved away from the cart. A staff officer was trotting back from the slopes, and this time she didn't hesitate to curtsey. It was only a quick bob, her head came up as he passed, but she saw in front of her a black horse with a green saddlecloth, and above it a man in a cocked hat whose face she had seen before.

He was past without noticing her, and she stood for a second in the confusion of shock. He was here, right in the battle with God knows what plan, and no one and nothing to stop him. She looked frantically about her, but the Heavies were all on the slopes, the camp emptying again, and she saw no one but other women and a couple of looting Turks fleeing with armfuls of pots and pans. There was only herself.

She turned and ran. Not to Kadikoi and safety, she had to get to Ryder and warn the Brigade. The 93rd had held, the Heavies were engaged, but the Lights were still vulnerable to any order this traitor might give. She tore through the camp, dodging the tents and fires and picket ropes, running past the tumult of battle and plunging into the chaos of the trampled vines. The haversack banged against her back, the dress tangled in her legs, she stumbled and tripped and ran on.

She must be ahead of him, no horse could cross the camps and vineyards as quickly as she was doing it on foot, but the plain cleared as she neared the end of the Heights, and from here he could be at the Light Brigade in minutes. Her imagination conjured hooves behind her, a horseman following, then she turned her head and saw him, just yards away and staring, then his hand moved, something flashed, and the shot rang in her ears as the punch hit her shoulder, whirling her round and slamming her down. Pain crashed in her head and swirled in her thought like thick mist.

She fought it, and opened her eyes. He was turning, riding away, but not for the Light Brigade, he was crossing the plain to the Sapoune Ridge and Raglan's own base. She tried to roll over, to get up and keep running, but the movement chopped like an axe in her head, and for a little while everything dimmed into black.

Hooves roused her. Horsemen were coming, and the part of her mind that still worked knew she was lying right in their path. With thought came memory, and she turned in sudden terror to the head of the valley, but saw with shattering relief that the Light Brigade were still there. The horsemen approaching looked like Heavy Brigade, they must have won their action and were returning to join the Lights.

She crawled to the verge before the first horse reached her, and crouched at the base of the slopes to be sick. The pain wasn't so bad now, there was only a graze on her temple, and she supposed she must have hit a rock when she fell. Her arm throbbed a little, but that didn't look bad either, the ball couldn't have done more than skim her. She could move, she could still warn Ryder. She wiped her sleeve over her face, picked up her haversack, and forced herself to go on. The Heavies all passed her, her legs were shaky, she felt dizzy and sick, but she made herself keep going and those little figures of the distant Brigade grew larger and clearer all the time.

But something else was clearer too, and movement to her left took shape as a horseman plunged down the side of the Sapoune, heading like herself towards the Light Brigade. He was a wonderful horseman to tackle such a drop, but what else was he? She stared until her eyes hurt, but the horse was brown and the saddlecloth tiger-skin, and as he descended further she recognized Captain Nolan. Everyone knew him, and the paper he was brandishing must be a genuine order from Lord Raglan himself. Nothing that treacherous staff officer did could matter now, and the Light Brigade was safe.

She stopped and took a long, shuddering breath of relief. In front of her Captain Nolan reached the valley floor and galloped furiously on towards the cavalry, waving his piece of paper like a flag.

16

25 October 1854, 11.00 a.m. to noon

It was quiet at the head of the valley. The cannon in the redoubts were silenced, the patter of musketry had long ceased, and even the charge of the Heavy Brigade had been little more than a distant roar. Ryder stretched to ease his aching back and wondered if their own turn was ever going to come.

No one felt like talking. Oliver sat with his arms clasped round his knees, gazing into the South Valley to watch the return of the Heavies. Jordan was trying to light a pipe with damp matches, a constant scrape, scrape, then a rattle in the tin as he dug out another. Fisk was glugging back the last of his water, smacking his lips on the last drops and laying down the barrel with a deep sigh. Bolton was feeding his horse a handful of crushed biscuit, murmuring lovingly, 'All you need's a good gallop, isn't it, Bobbin? A nice long gallop.'

Most of their officers were still dutifully in the saddle. Marsh was fidgeting, checking his pistol, his scabbard, his horse's bit. Hoare had his sabretache out and was scribbling what looked like a letter. Grainger looked at his pocket watch, then shut it with a soft, firm click. Jarvis stood in parade position by his horse's head, everything regulation but for the eyes that looked only at Ryder, and the mouth that curved upward in a knowing smile. Ryder looked away, and cursed himself for doing it.

Hooves and clatter, the Heavy Brigade trotting back up to re-form. 'Hullo, look-ons,' called a red-coated Inniskilling, ostentatiously brandishing his bloodied sabre. 'Did you get a good view?'

'It's not fair,' muttered Oliver. His head was down, and his fair hair flopping over his face. 'When is it our turn – *when?*'

The same question Ryder had been asking, the one every man in the Brigade was thinking. Then he heard it, a rattle of hooves on the escarpment, a galloper coming from Raglan. Nolan was waving a paper in triumph, and that could only mean one thing.

'Now, Poll,' he said with sudden confidence. He stood up to watch the horseman galloping nearer and nearer, waving their fate in his hand. 'We're going in now.'

Oliver stood with fearful hope as Nolan crossed their ranks. He paused by Captain Morris of the Lancers, yelled 'You'll see, you'll see!' and galloped on. He was laughing with excitement, and Oliver felt it stirring inside himself. Three orders of nothing had flattened his enthusiasm, but now it was up and quivering, straining to be off like Nolan as he galloped the last yards, reined to a stop in front of Lucan and held out the paper with a flourish.

'It's not withdrawal,' said Fisk, lumbering to his feet. 'There'd be no bleeding hurry about that.'

The others were getting up too, brushing down their overalls, standing by their horses, all with their heads still turned towards Nolan and Lucan. Lucan was getting agitated and raising his voice.

'They'll want us to retake the redoubts,' said Jordan sagely. 'Look, our infantry's arriving down the Col; if you crane to the right you can just see them.'

Oliver gazed at the panorama in front of him. Roughly ploughed ground stretched to the rising slopes of the Causeway Heights, where it parted into two wide valleys. The first two redoubts were on little hills at the bottom of the South Valley, too far down to see from here. Numbers 3 and 4 were part of the ridge itself, but only the nearer Number 4 was visible and it seemed to be abandoned. Numbers 5 and 6 were unfinished anyway, but Jordan was right, little red figures of skirmishers were advancing towards them, and there would surely be more behind.

He turned his head left to look at the North Valley and the Woronzoff Road threading down it like a grey ribbon. There'd been Russian movement there all right, he'd sat and watched their cavalry cross it to climb the Heights and assault the Heavy Brigade on the other side. Like everyone else, he'd sat and watched them fall back, while Captain Morris pleaded fruitlessly with Cardigan to let them pursue. The road seemed empty now, though the Fedoukhine Hills were thick with grey and the sun flicked bright on the barrels of bronze cannon. Far in the distance down the bottom of the valley were more of them, a whole battery of perhaps twelve guns manned by a regiment of Don Cossacks. No. They wouldn't be going *that* way.

Lucan was shouting, and his words drifted back in the stagnant air. 'Attack, sir? Attack what? What guns, sir?'

Incredibly Nolan shouted back. An ADC yelling at a general! He seemed jolly wild about something, flinging his arm out back across the valley and crying, 'There, my lord, is your enemy. There are your guns!'

It made no sense to Oliver, but it obviously did to Lucan and everything went very quiet. A moment of mumbling, then Lucan trotted over to Cardigan, and Nolan turned for the 17th Lancers and Captain Morris.

'What?' said Oliver, confused. 'What are we doing?'

'The man said "attack", Polly,' said Ryder. He seemed so relaxed, his eyes full of laughter and his mouth twisted in that mocking smile. 'We'll doubtless find out where in a minute.'

Attack. This was it, then, the moment at last. He'd run under fire and felt rather brave about it, but this was the real thing, what he'd been trained for all this time. He wiped his sweaty palm on his overalls and took firm hold of Misty's reins. 'I'm ready.'

'Are you, Poll?' said Ryder. He'd been wrong about the laughter, there was something in his eyes that seemed inexpressibly sad. 'I think I am too.'

The trumpet was calling 'Mount!', Trumpet-Major Joy blowing like a picture in a history book about Waterloo. For a second

Oliver saw all of them like that, coloured drawings in a book studied by children. Then his foot was in the stirrup, up and over, down.

Captain Oldham took his place in the front rank, while the NCOs ordered the line. There was all the usual muttering and shuffling, the usual sense of miracle when they were dressed at last into long ranks two riders deep, and broken only by the gap between their two squadrons. The 17th Lancers were on their left, but beyond them the 11th Hussars were bunched more raggedly and Oliver heard the order 'The 11th to fall back and form a second line!' They were the first line, themselves and the Lancers, they were going to ride in front.

He grinned in delight. 'So much for Cardigan's favourites!'

'So much,' said Ryder. His voice had no expression.

Lord George Paget was falling back, presumably to command the support line of 8th Hussars and 4th Light Dragoons. Cardigan called after him in a voice as high and nervous as the neigh of a horse, 'I expect your best support, Lord George. Mind that, your best support.' Paget inclined his head and said, 'You shall have it, my lord.' He sounded very sombre, but Oliver saw with glee that in his casually drooping left hand he held a newly lit cheroot.

The Heavies were drawing up too, but they were right at the back and Oliver didn't grudge it them. He said, 'They can mop up anything we leave behind, can't they? They can watch while we show how it's done.'

Ryder looked at him, and something thumped in Oliver's stomach like a fist. 'Listen, Polly,' he said, and his voice was so normal that for a moment everything was all right. 'This is going to be bad, but it won't always be. When you're back here safe – and you will be – then don't think war has to be like this, don't be afraid to face it again. I want you to promise me you won't.'

He wanted to laugh, to think of a good rejoinder as Jordan always did. He looked down the line for Jordan, for Bolton and Fisk, but they were all facing front and wearing the same awful taut expression as Ryder. Bolton was praying, his lips moving in familiar words, 'Our Father, Who art in heaven, hallowed be Thy name . . .'

'Harry,' he said. 'What . . . ?'

Ryder's hand reached out and squeezed his arm. 'Promise me.'

'Of course,' he said, bewildered. 'Of course, if you want.'

Ryder smiled. His hand relaxed and let go, they were apart again, the regulation six inches from knee to knee.

'. . . as it is in heaven. Give us this day our daily bread . . .'

'Draw swords!'

At last, and it slid out beautifully, up and to slope against his shoulder. But Ryder was reaching over again, saying, 'Give me your handkerchief.'

'What?'

'Give it me!'

'. . . as we forgive those who trespass against us.'

He watched Ryder twist the handkerchief into a rope, run it through the hilt of his sabre and tie it to his wrist. 'I'm not going to drop it.'

'Not now you're not,' said Ryder. He dragged out his own handkerchief and gripped one end in his teeth as he did the same to himself.

'And deliver us from evil . . .'

'The Brigade will advance!' roared Cardigan. His voice was hoarse and his face red, but he seemed awfully calm and solid. 'First squadron of the 17th Lancers to direct!'

Oliver looked resentfully to his left, but couldn't help admiring the look of their neighbours. Their lances were at the 'carry', the little red and white pennants fluttering behind them like knights at Agincourt. They were commanded by a mere captain too, all their senior officers sick or dead of cholera, they were as young and orphaned as the 13th, and they were all in it together.

'. . . the Power and the Glory, for ever and ever, Amen.'

The bugles were sounding, Trumpeters Brittain and Joy both together, and Amen, he thought to himself. The Power and the

Glory, Amen. Forward they went, while the poor old 11th waited sullenly for the regulation two horse-lengths before they fell in behind. At the back would be Paget's support line, then behind him the Heavies, but Oliver was looking to his front and glory.

The ploughed land was bumpy beneath their horses' hooves as they stood in the stirrups for the trot. They weren't going to the South Valley. Cardigan kept them straight, and the rise of the Heights was facing them as they picked their way over the muddy ruts. It would be steep going to get to the redoubts uphill, but the Heavies had tackled worse, he'd seen them do it. They neared the slope, but still didn't seem to be wheeling, and he glanced at the Lancers to check direction.

But something was happening there, a flash of tiger-skin cloth as Captain Nolan leaped forward and away from his place by Captain Morris. 'No, no, Nolan, that won't do!' shouted Morris. 'We've a long way to go, we must be steady!'

Nolan was anything but steady as he swerved diagonally across their front, sword waving frantically, face white and staring like a man in a nightmare. He was charging right for Cardigan, actually overtaking the leader of the Brigade, and his voice carried back to them as an anguished cry of 'Threes riiiiight!' That was right, the right order, but the words were half lost in the roar of cannon from the Russian battery on their left. Boom and *crump* as a shell exploded to their front, black fragments hurtling back at them like demented birds. Nolan's voice rose to a shriek and the sword fell from his hand, but his horse wheeled round, carrying its rider back towards their own line. He was dead, he must be, the gold braid of his chest torn into a gaping red hole, but the arm was still up and the scream still sounding and echoing in the valley, horrible and unearthly. The horse vanished between their two squadrons, but the sound and terror stayed with Oliver and again a cannon went *boom*. Cries and neighing horses in among the Lancers, and bodies thudded hard to the ground.

It was madness, madness, why weren't they turning? They were in range of the Russian guns, if they went any further they'd be in range of the ones at the end too. Why didn't they turn for the Heights before they were blown to bits? He looked wildly at the Lancers for direction, at Cardigan in front, at their own Captain Oldham, then he turned to look at Ryder and understood.

They were meant to go this way. They were heading straight down the North Valley towards the battery at the end, charging artillery from the front with cannon to either side. No one was arguing, these were the orders and they were all going to die.

His knees spasmed and dug in, Misty lurched forward, but Ryder's arm was there again, pressing him back. 'Steady, Poll. We've still a good mile to go.'

Boom but no *crump*, a shell exploding in men and not earth. Men yelling, horses whinnying in terror, a lance falling across their line and cracking under Misty's hoof. Clouds of dark smoke billowed over from their left, and he was almost glad of it, he couldn't see the carnage in the Lancers or those terrifying black muzzles still silent in the distance. Dear God, another mile of *this*? He looked desperately down their line for Captain Marsh, saw him riding square and steady with perfectly straight back, then something sprayed between them, case shot tearing into their ranks, and Marsh was reeling, one white eyeball staring in ragged redness, he crashed over the saddle and was gone.

A splinter seared over his knuckles, a bloodied streak torn in his glove, a reminder of what was real. Their line was shifting and widening to let the dead men fall out of it, then closing back together without so much as an order, closing together and trotting on. They were still going on, and so, to his astonishment, was he. He was trotting as steadily as any of them, facing front and keeping his sword steady at the slope. What else was there to do?

Then realization sang through him, and in the choking grey smoke he saw with sudden clarity where he was and what he was doing. He was one man of a regiment, a trained light dragoon, and he was charging the enemy. It didn't matter what happened afterwards, all he had to do was charge.

And in front of them the great guns roared. Every muzzle belched orange fire, hurling roundshot and shell, every gun pounding into their thin blue line. Bolton was snatched away beside him, gone and blown backwards, his mare's saddle ripped away with the skin of her back. *Just charge*, he thought and rode on. The ploughed earth vanished, level turf stretched before them, and around him rose the wonderful thumping of hooves. Muskets banged to their right, men screamed and horses crashed, another great volley boomed out ahead, but through it all the hooves thundered on, faster and faster, his own lost in the rumble of hundreds as he rode on and charged with the Light Brigade.

Ryder was swearing as he rode. He cursed the guns and the Russians and riderless horses, he cursed the smoke and streaks of flame, the shells and the musket balls, he cursed that bastard Cardigan for refusing to let them ride above a canter or overtake his glorious self. Be damned to arriving on a blown horse, if they didn't go faster they'd never arrive at all. He stuck down his head and rode on.

The Heights exploded on his right, another bloody battery on the other side. Jordan's mount crushed against him to escape the blast, but as Ryder wheeled back Oliver smashed into his other flank, driven by the press of Bolton's horse as she struggled to find sanctuary in the familiarity of the ranks. 'Beat her back, Polly!' he yelled against the roar. 'Drive her off!' Jordan's leg crunched sickeningly against his own, and he jabbed out furiously with his elbow, screaming, 'Keep her back, Billy, you'll have us both down!' Dust flew in his face, Jordan's horse reared, then the pressure slackened and they were riding on in a moment's silence of the guns. They must have passed the range of the battery on their left.

The guns in front blazed again, those bastards were reloading every thirty seconds. He dug in his spurs to drive forward, dozens doing the same, they'd got to go faster or die. A shell whistled overhead, but he heard the crash behind as it exploded in the 11th

Hussars. A trumpet was sounding too, the 'Gallop' at last, but most were already doing it, and the Lancers pressing right up to the 'Charge'. 'Here!' shouted Fisk. 'Come on, don't let those buggers get ahead of us!' He was grinning wildly and brandishing his sword.

A ball smashed in from the right, bowling through their second rank and exploding in a mass of red and black, blood-spray and fragments, a horse trampling its own entrails as it tried to run. Horses in the first rank bolted in terror, Captain Oldham himself jolting suddenly in front of their line as if to lead a charge. The nearest men followed, whooping with enthusiasm, Jordan leaped after them, and then the front battery fired.

The first shell burst under Oldham's white mare. The black cloud engulfed all of them, every man who'd followed, every horse down, and Oldham's had lost both hind legs. The captain rolled over and leaped up, but a ball cracked in from the right and he crashed on his face, sword still clutched in his outstretched hand. Jordan was rolling too, arms over his face, screaming, 'Don't ride on me, don't ride on me!' Impossible to stop, Ryder swerved to avoid him and galloped on. A riderless horse pushed into the vacant space on his right, and beyond it he saw Jarvis, untouched and unhurt, riding on.

But they were riding into blackness now, smoke from the front battery swirling and blinding them. Even the muzzles of the facing guns were visible only in thick streaks of flame as one by one they bellowed into hellish life. No more volleys now, the shots were banging in succession as the gunners fired at will, but the black spray that flew out at them was deadlier than the balls had been. The bastards were firing canister, a thousand fragments of shot scything through their close-packed ranks. Screams lost meaning, mere high notes in the boom and roar, all that was real were the reins in his left hand, the hilt in his right, and the flanks of his horse between his thighs. The air was full of iron.

Oliver cried out, his head slamming round to Ryder as if from a giant slap, but it was the man beyond who was hit, a huge torso astride a bay mare and above it the remnants of half a head. Blood-spray drenched them all, blood and brains and a fragment of bone that stuck in his cheek like a dart, and it was only as the corpse rolled down and away that Ryder's mind seized the name. Fisk, he thought. That was Albie Fisk.

But a ball or shell, it had to be to take a man's head off, and even as Ryder wiped the filth from his face he saw with sudden clarity what that meant. Ball *and* canister, the enemy were firing double-shotted, the dangerous last resort of the desperate. The Russians were scared. They weren't seeing them as targets, they were seeing a terrifying charge of deadly steel rushing towards them, and by God they were right. This wasn't about dying, it was about bloody killing, and the realization spun his thought into hardness like steel.

The confusion vanished. He saw the right-hand battery had stopped, afraid of hitting their comrades in front, and knew they had only the one in front to beat. He could see the gun barrels and knew they were riding right in the interval of two great cannon. An officer yelled 'Close up! Incline left!' but when Oliver moved to do it Ryder snatched his sleeve and yelled, 'No, you don't, Poll, stay right on this line!' Oliver looked ahead, looked back, then smiled with understanding, and Ryder smiled back. They knew where they were going, they knew what they were going to do, they were head down and racing together, teeth clenched as they dug in their spurs and rode on through the iron hail.

And here it was at last, death and the end and the trumpet sounding 'Charge!' Air rushed under him as he stood to the crouch, arm thrusting forward, sword to 'Engage', green ground blurring beneath the pounding hooves. 'Come on, Deaths!' called the Lancers, but death was for the Russians and Ryder held it on the tip of his sword.

Through the smoke, right into it, then there were the guns, and there the men who served them, frantic dark green figures struggling like demons to reload in time. A portfire sparkled in a gunner's hand, a hoarse yell of '*Strelai!*' and then fire smashed into them, scorching his side with the blast of it, sweeping away the riderless horse next to him and hurling death into the line behind. But they were all but there, Ryder kept his eyes on the gap between the muzzles and charged right at it. The gun to his left was still loading, men screaming and working with pantomime haste, a gunner waiting with burning fuse, but too late, he was already up to it, boot grazing the burning muzzle, he was through and slashing down at the portfire, hand, wrist and all, chopping through the whole thing as he screamed in the terrified face 'Too *fucking late!*'

It was their turn now. Gunners broke and ran as the line crashed into them, dropping spongestaffs and prickers, roundshot and charges, dropping everything to run like rabbits or cower under the guns, anywhere away from the maddened cavalry leaping at them out of their own smoke. The Lancers were on them, skewering them in the backs, tossing them aside and charging on. Oliver was on them, through the gap and slashing out with the pent-up fury of that long and desperate charge. Jarvis was on them, roaring like a bull as he thrust down with his sword, Grainger was on them, drill-perfect with his cuts and thrusts, young Hoare was on them, hacking out wildly, his freckled face pale beneath the spatters of blood.

And Ryder was on them, wheeling round and round to reach more of them, sword whining through the air with the force of his blows. Hit them, hit them with everything, edge, point, even the hilt with the power of his fist behind it. A grey coat, stab it, a face above one, slash it, a Russian, kill it, kill it and move on. A gunner whacked at his arm with a rammer, but he reared his horse and smote left-right down to cleave the shapka to the skull. The smoke stung his eyes, the powder-smell burned his throat, the twisting and turning tore his back, but he'd ridden through hell to get here and all he felt was savage joy.

But the bastards wouldn't stand. They were turning and running in almost superstitious panic, and some of it justified. One gunner covered his face and screamed like a woman, and when

Ryder looked behind he saw a dragoon bearing down through the smoke with the top of his head gone, and his pale blue face streaked with drying blood. Moody was dead in the saddle, but his horse had brought him all the way.

But Ryder was alive and he wanted a fight, not a rout. He wheeled into pursuit, and saw others doing the same, Light Dragoons and Lancers all racing the retreating gunners to the back of the battery, Cornet Hoare even yelling 'Charge!' Ammunition wagons loomed up on the right, a tangle of hastily abandoned limber, he swerved left to avoid them, and reined to an abrupt halt. The smoke was thinner here, he could see open plain beyond, and trotting towards them was a thick mass of horsemen bristling with lances. Cossacks.

Here was their real enemy. Here were the oilskin-covered fur hats, the belted coats and savage faces they'd seen only from a distance, here were the bastards who'd mocked them with their refusal to fight. Well, they would fight now. He didn't wait for an order, no one did, they rose as one man in the saddle, levelled their swords, and charged.

A charge as it ought to be, no smoke, no cannon, only level turf sloping gently downhill to an already wavering enemy. The Cossacks were brave fighters, but they couldn't have ever seen a charge like the Light Brigade's, they were incredulous and in shock, and the rear ranks were already backing away when the dark blue line smashed into their front.

And this was it, this was how it should be, cavalry against cavalry not against iron and fire. He batted away the first lance like paper, back with his edge across the open throat, then drove forward for the next. Lances were no good in a mêlée, little more than sticks to be parried aside before striking home. He was cleaving through them, the bastards falling back and back, *Who's the cowards now?* They were scared of a few Lancers and Light Dragoons, but the second line was pouring in, Paget's support line already at the guns, and behind them would be the whole damned Heavy Brigade. He slashed at the next face, watched it leaping back out of reach, and knew they could drive the whole lot back to the Chernaya.

Forward they rode, all of them pushing together. That was Oliver next to him, but what his headmaster would think of that furious face and savagely slashing arm Ryder couldn't imagine. On his other side was Prosser, stupid Jake Prosser, but he'd got brain enough for this, he was stabbing at the Cossacks' faces and yelling 'Go to hell, go to hell, *go to hell*!' They were retreating, damn them, not enough to go round, and when Ryder lunged across to reach one already wheeling Jarvis roared 'Mine!' and swung his sword at the man like an axe.

He swerved past to clear ground, nothing ahead of him but the back end of horses, and nothing around him but Light Brigade blue. He reined Tally to a halt and forced himself steady, clearing the smoke and the anger with long, slow breaths from the depth of his lungs.

'I say, chaps,' said Hoare's voice, with an oddly high note in it. 'Where *is* everyone?'

He straightened. About the field were little knots of Lancers and 13th like themselves, but the men he was seeing would hardly make a troop, and he realized with dull shock they were all that was left of that beautiful first line. Some smoke-blackened 11th Hussars had made it this far, and he saw little bunches of 8th Hussars and 4th Light Dragoons pursuing Cossacks towards the aqueduct, but of the Heavies there was no sign.

'Look,' said Oliver, and he sounded more scared than in the charge. 'Ryder, look.'

He *was* looking, and didn't like it. Russian hussars were forming on their left flank, Uhlan lancers trotting down towards them from the Causeway Heights, and even the Cossacks had only withdrawn into little clumps to watch and wait from a safe distance. Those wonderful moments at the guns had felt like being an attacking army, but now they were just a small band of survivors and the Russians were closing in.

Jarvis turned stolidly to the cornet. 'Orders, sir?'

Seconds ticked away as the boy hesitated. 'We'd better find Lord Cardigan and the rest of the Brigade.'

One of the Lancers coughed. 'Lord Cardigan's gone, sir. He had a little cut-about at the guns, but we saw him ride back out.'

Bloody typical. Lead them in, dump them, and run for home. But the effect on Hoare was shocking, and he had to swallow twice before speaking again. 'Well, the Heavies, then. We'll find Lord Lucan and . . .' He stopped and looked uncertainly about him.

'The guns have stopped,' said Oliver. 'The cannon. I don't think . . .'

Ryder felt cold in his stomach. If the Heavies had been coming those two batteries on the flanks would have been hammering them all the way, but Oliver was right, the guns were silent. Cardigan had deserted them, Lucan had abandoned them, and the Light Brigade had been left to die alone. He said, 'We must cut our way out, sir. Back to the guns and out.'

Hoare nodded feverishly, especially at that word 'out'. 'Yes. Yes, come on. I mean threes about, gallop – march!'

They galloped, but not in a charge now, this was retreat. A band of Cossacks saw it and swooped after them, eagerly pursuing fleeing prey. Ryder remembered the fate of the Turks that morning, he knew what their own Lancers had done to the Russian gunners, he dug in his hooks and bloody galloped. They crested a knoll, he could see the battery below them, but Hoare was shouting 'No, no! This way!' and wheeling right, waving his arm furiously to make them follow.

He saw what Hoare was after, a solid little force of 8th Hussars and 4th Light Dragoons rallying round Colonel Douglas and the indestructible Lord George Paget, but the Russian hussars were already between them and moving in for the attack. He yelled, 'No, sir! The battery, there's no hope that way!'

But Hoare was the officer, Jarvis and the others already wheeling after him, and Ryder had no choice but to follow. The Cossacks were now to left of them, the Uhlans behind, the hussars in front, they were charging for the second time into the certainty of destruction.

'Break through!' cried Hoare, his young voice breaking under the strain of it. 'Break through to the others, break through!'

But the hussars were disciplined cavalry, not to be broken by a force of a dozen, however desperate. Hoare seemed blinded to it, he crashed right into them, pushing and pushing to reach the illusion of authority and safety on the other side, but the hussars closed round him, a sabre swiped him from the saddle and Ryder closed his eyes against the sight of a sixteen-year-old boy cut to pieces right in front of him.

'Back!' shouted a voice in his ear, Jarvis's mouth wide open as he yelled 'Left about wheel!' Ryder was already doing it, wrenching on the reins to bring Tally round, point her nose at the battery and home. There were only six of them now, the Lancers must have already gone, and somehow they had to fight through an army of hundreds.

Hussars were turning to face them, pistol and carbine balls followed them, and curving round like a flock of jackals came their own particular band of Cossacks. It was a race again, back to the guns from the other side, and then the Uhlans were in front of them, thick and impenetrable, nothing for it but to wheel and go round. Jarvis led, Ryder swerved after him, letting his sword dangle as he groped at his belt for his pistol, but Jarvis had taken it, never returned it, the bastard would be the death of them all. He snatched at his sword, got it and raised it, but a gunshot banged close and Oliver was down. Rolling and alive and maybe not badly wounded, he was struggling up and snatching his bridle to remount, but as Ryder reined to turn the Cossacks crashed into them.

Lances were in among them, spears thrusting at faces and bodies, and there went Prosser, shoved from his saddle like a doll on the end of a skewer. Attack was the only hope, and Ryder threw himself at the leader with a bloodcurdling yell. His sword plunged forward, but the Cossack swerved, a lance sprang in at his face, he dodged and felt another graze down his back. Pain fired in his head, leaving him dizzy and half blind. A blade jerked at his reins, the leather slid through his hands, then he was bumping against his mare's flank, crashing down smack on his mutilated back, and he heard himself scream aloud.

He was surrounded by horses' legs, and sat up to see five lances all pointed down at him. He felt his sword still anchored to his wrist and wrapped his fingers firmly round the hilt, but a lance cracked down across his forearm, and the point of another slid right under his chin. A coarse tuft of black hair decorated the shaft, and behind it he saw the metallic gleam of a sharp, cruel hook.

Somebody shouted above him. The lance point withdrew reluctantly from his throat, and slowly he let his gaze slide round. A hussar officer was trotting into the circle, waving imperiously at the Cossacks to back away. 'Surrender your sword,' he said in perfect English. 'You will not be harmed, you are a prisoner.'

He untied his sword, but the shame of it stung. All those dead men left in the North Valley, and he had no more than a few cuts. Jarvis was being disarmed too, but at least he was hurt, one leg of his overalls slashed open and bloody. He wondered who else had been taken, but the only double-white stripes around him were on the bodies of the dead. He made himself look at their faces, averting his eyes from what was left of Hoare's, skimming quickly over Prosser's, but feeling sudden hope at the absence of the one he knew best.

There was no sign of Oliver.

A haze of blue smoke still hung over the guns as Oliver finally reached the battery. It seemed almost a place of safety now, the starting point for the journey home. He had a pistol ball in his calf, but Misty was steady beneath him, he had other men about him again, and Lieutenant Grainger had appeared to lead them. The lieutenant's face was black with smoke, his uniform slashed with sabre strokes, his left arm hung limp and bloody, but he was a real live officer Oliver knew, and other dragoons had rallied to his voice. There were only eight of them altogether, but that was eight times better than being alone.

'Steady now,' said Grainger, as they threaded between the muzzles of the silenced guns. 'Save your speed for when we near the other batteries, then in with your hooks and race for home. Got it?'

They did, and every face was suddenly taut with the realization they had to run the gauntlet a second time.

'Spread out,' said Grainger. 'Weave all you like, never mind the line, just give them less of a target. Don't stop for anything, it's every man for himself and please God I'll see you all back there.'

He stepped his mount to one side, and Oliver was moved by the way he nodded as they passed, as if he was shaking hands with them, saying goodbye. With a curious twist of his mouth he said, 'The 13th will advance – trot – *march*!' and then they were off, racers out of a starting gate, bolting forward and back up the valley.

A brisk trot and no fire behind them, the Don Cossack battery had no one left to man it. Riderless horses darted in front of them, some tried to close up and run alongside, but none crushed into Oliver and his mare stayed calm. It was hard dodging the bodies, jumping over men and swerving round horses, it felt cruel and wrong, but they were all doing it, they were in it together and on their way home. Then the bang, the whizz and ping, the first musket-ball from the Causeway Heights, and Grainger yelled, 'Gallop, my lads, go it all you know!'

They galloped. Oliver put his head down until he could see nothing but ground shooting past under Misty's hooves, and prayed to just keep seeing it all the way back. No one was down yet, they'd taken the gunners by surprise. Probably they hadn't expected anyone to come back at all. But the muskets were still firing, bang, bang, bang along their path, and then a cannon opened up, thick smoke in his eyes, and suddenly he was shooting forward, the ground thudding up to his face as Misty screamed and dropped beneath him. He rolled clear, up on hands and knees in the dirt, scrabbling back to the horse that was his only way out, but she was dead, poor Misty, the shell had blown away half her hind legs. He sagged by her body, hearing the others gallop on for home, leaving him here by himself.

For a black moment he gave into it, curling into a ball behind the corpse of his mare, just wanting it all to be over and done, but even in the depths of self-pity he knew that wasn't the answer. Ryder was dead or prisoner, no one could save him but himself. The thought of Ryder flicked into memory, his friend saying 'Promise me' and looking as if he meant it.

He raised his head. The guns were quiet now, no one else to shoot at, and he himself was covered by the dead horse. He reached under the sheepskin for his cloak, and covered his blue and white with concealing grey. No one fired, and he reached up again to work free his blanket roll. The cards were in there, and he could imagine what Woodall would say if he came back without them. Besides, he'd need the blanket tonight when it got cold.

He tucked the roll under his arm and the Adams in his belt, and waited for the sound of hooves. Almost instantly they came, more survivors from the battery, and at once the guns began again from the Causeway Heights. But not this way, not at him, they were going for the riders as he'd known they would, and at once he lurched to his feet and staggered on up the valley. His leg hurt but not unbearably, he was moving forward, making progress with every step. A few musket shots clipped the ground around him, but there were better targets than one crippled soldier barely visible at the base of the Heights, and with luck he could make it all the way. It couldn't be much more than three-quarters of a mile.

After a while he started counting steps. Call each one a yard, there were seventeen hundred and sixty in a mile. Say it was a bit over half to go, say nine hundred steps. One, two, three, four, and a horse on its side frothing at the bit, straining to stand and falling heavily back on its shattered legs. He wished he'd a ball for it, but the Adams held only five and he couldn't risk running out with the Russians so close. Eight, nine, ten, a man with no face, eleven, twelve, thirteen, and something whirred overhead, a shadow passed over, and a large bird landed on the body of the faceless man. Fourteen, fifteen, keeping going and trying not to hear the squelch of ripping flesh. Keeping going all the way.

Artillery boomed again behind him, but now he was out of range. He'd got to a hundred and ninety when more horses galloped up from the battery, remnants of the good old 4th and 8th with Lord George Paget holding steady in the middle. They couldn't stop for him, naturally they couldn't, it was against the rules to risk lives for men already lost. He stood aside to let them pass, saying 'hundred and ninety, hundred and ninety' so as not to lose count.

Three hundred and twelve, and a lift of hope, a riderless horse standing on the track, but it shied away at his approach and cantered off towards the battery. Three hundred and eighty, and voices ahead, two Cossacks ambling down the valley sticking lances into the bodies of the dead and maybe only wounded. A third crouched to search a haversack, and yet another was wrestling a fine saddle from a fallen horse. Stop, hide, run, he just kept going with the revolver up and levelled in his hand. The two with lances saw him, saw the Adams, and crossed to the other side of the valley, but the looters hardly even lifted their heads as he passed. They weren't looking for a fight, any of them, only easy pickings from men who would never fight again.

Four hundred and forty, and he must be coming in range of that first battery in the Fedoukhine Hills. He wondered if he could run past, beat it by surprise and speed, but his legs were so heavy, and when he looked behind he saw a trail of his own blood dotted all along the valley floor. He ought to stop to bind his calf, but he had to get back, he'd bandage it later.

Slow hooves ahead, a single horse, and it was Bolton's mare, heading towards him with tragic eyes. She knew him, of course, but her back was half-flayed and he couldn't possibly ride her. He murmured 'Good girl, Bobbin', patted her nose and walked on, but she insisted on following, as if she found comfort in the familiar uniform. After a moment he reached up and took her bridle, leading her with him, leading her home.

The ground changed underfoot, naked ploughed earth. Every step was an effort, up and down through thick ruts of mud. There were hoofprints all over it, prints of men and horses who'd passed this way half an hour ago and would never come again. He was sure they'd been under fire here, but when he looked to the hills the grey ranks of Russians had disappeared, and there in the scrub he saw the sky-blue jackets and red trousers of the Chasseurs d'Afrique. The French had taken the battery, and he was safe all the way back.

He started to shake. He'd lost count somewhere, and couldn't remember how many yards there were in a mile. He couldn't even remember why he needed to know. He slipped in a rut, clutched at Bobbin's bridle, stumbled and fell on his face in the mud. Bobbin's nose came down to nuzzle him, but he just patted at it and let his arm flop back down. He must be nearly there, he'd just close his eyes and rest a minute, that's all.

The earth stirred slightly under his hand. Something was moving near him, and a faint swish snapped his eyes open in panic. Would a vulture attack a living man? He levered his face out of the mud and stared uncomprehendingly at blue cloth and the sudden unbelievable sight of a woman's lap. Above him came a slight clink, and then an arm wrapped round his shoulders to help him sit, and there was Sally Jarvis offering him a mug of rum.

'There, my love,' she said, and he'd never heard anything as beautiful as her voice. 'You drink this while I look at your leg.'

He drank the rum in a daze, and looked up almost fearfully, but she was still there, real and kind like a world he thought had disappeared for ever. He said feebly, 'What are you doing here?'

She smiled. 'There aren't enough bandsmen, and it's safe

enough.' He watched incredulously as she drew out a clean dressing from a bulging haversack and began to wrap it expertly round his calf. 'Poor Oliver,' she said. 'You've only about a cupful of blood left in you. What would Ryder say if he saw you like this?'

Reality woke again. 'I don't know. He might be . . .'

She bent lower over the dressing, and he saw with shock her own arm was bandaged. 'And Jarvis?'

'I don't know,' he said wretchedly. 'They could be prisoners. I'm sorry, I don't know.' He hadn't left it behind at all, that terrible valley, he'd brought it back with him like something that was never going to end.

She tied off the bandage and looked at him, still smiling and still kind. 'But you didn't see them killed?'

He shook his head numbly.

'Then there's hope, isn't there?' she said. 'And look at you, come back out of there like a miracle. Anything's possible, Polly Oliver.'

He smiled shyly, liking her knowing his nickname. 'I'd better get back.'

'Only if you're ready,' she said doubtfully. 'The bandsmen will be here soon.'

He didn't want to wait. He'd walked every step of the journey and wanted to finish it the same way, but his leg felt shaky when he stood and he was afraid he wouldn't get far.

'Lean on me,' said Sally. She slung the haversack round her back, wrapped his arm round her shoulder and clasped him firmly round the waist. 'Come on, we'll go together.'

She was completely steady under his weight, and he took Bobbin's bridle in the other hand. Together they set off over the ploughed field, a man, a woman and a horse walking out of the valley and back to the world of the living, just as Harry Ryder had promised him, an hour and a lifetime ago.

Ryder was torturing himself with the thought of tea. His mouth was so dry it made clicking sounds when he swallowed, and his body kept shivering as if he was cold inside. A lance prodded in the small of his lacerated back, he screwed up his face and stumbled on.

They'd taken his horse and haversack, of course, and all he owned now were the clothes he stood up in. Hardly even that, the way the Cossacks were going. One cut off the buttons from Ryder's coat as souvenirs, while Jarvis had to surrender his entirely for the sake of the braid. He looked curiously shrunken without it, just a short stout man in a grey shirt and braces with a little pot belly drooping over his belt. It made Ryder uncomfortable to look at him, but when he offered his own coat Jarvis just smiled contemptuously and turned away.

They stopped at the aqueduct to wait their turn to cross. There was only one narrow bridge, and Ryder took the chance to look round the milling crowd for other prisoners from the Brigade. He saw pitifully few and no senior officers.

Except one. One was very senior indeed, and as Ryder looked ahead he saw the grey cloak and weaver hat of a British staff officer being escorted to the bridge. No one was prodding *him* with a lance, he'd been allowed to stay mounted and was accompanied only by two Russian officers in fur cloaks. Understandable perhaps, respect for his rank – except that there hadn't been a staff officer near them when they charged. Not one.

The horse was black, the saddlecloth dark green, just as Sally had seen at Kamara, and Ryder was suddenly sure. He was sure of something else too, that the bastard wasn't here just as a spectator. He'd done something in the battle, that's why all those officers were swarming round to congratulate him; he'd done something that had been a huge success. Not the redoubts, there was no mystery about that. Not the Highlanders, and not the Heavies, they'd both been British victories. Only one disaster had happened here today, and Ryder was looking at the aftermath of it right now. Their order came in writing, it was brought by Captain Nolan, there wasn't a single thing that could be wrong about it, but Ryder stared at the back of the distant staff officer and knew without doubt he was looking at the man who'd destroyed the Light Brigade.

The hatred was choking him. Look at the bastard now, chatting and laughing quite openly with his captors, as if he didn't care who saw him. He swept off his cocked hat and Ryder willed him to turn round, *turn and show us your filthy cowardly face*, but he only gave a mock bow to his captors, tossed the hat disrespectfully in the air, then squashed it carelessly into his pocket. The little pantomime was rewarded with a burst of laughter, and with the sound of it still echoing in his ears Ryder finally understood.

The hat was a prop, a pretence as much as the horse and saddlecloth. Yes, this was him, the man they'd pursued all this time, but he wasn't a staff officer, he wasn't even a traitor. Their enemy was a Russian and a spy.

PART THREE

Inkerman

'[T]he bloodiest struggle ever witnessed since war cursed the earth.'

Alexander Kinglake, chronicler to the Crimean Expedition

17

25 October 1854, noon to 10.00 p.m.

The battle had stopped. Woodall wasn't sure it was actually over, but no one was shooting at anything and the Highlanders were sprawling on the grass lighting pipes. He'd fired two shots the whole time.

The Russians were making themselves quite at home in the conquered redoubts, but no one seemed to be trying to boot them out of it. The Fourth Division were busy manning an abandoned one the Russians hadn't bothered to occupy anyway, while his own First Division seemed to have been marched all this way just to stand and watch. Utter disgrace.

'Should have used the First to retake the redoubts,' he said to the Rifleman next to him. 'They wouldn't have given up for a few musket balls. They should have sent the Guards.'

He'd spoken louder than he meant, and an officer called out 'Quite right, that man!' to approving laughter from his little contingent of Grenadiers. Woodall reddened, but after a moment the lieutenant strolled over to join him. 'I know you, don't I? You're Woodall.'

It was their own Lieutenant Verschoyle and Woodall froze with alarm. 'I'm sorry, sir.'

'What on earth for?' said Verschoyle, amused. 'I've heard you're a very pretty shot. Are you still crocked up?'

Woodall touched the bandage beneath his bearskin, then let his fingers fall away. 'No, sir. I'll rejoin my unit when we're relieved here.'

'I think we're relieved now,' said Verschoyle, nodding towards the two regiments of Highlanders approaching from the Col.

'But they're looking for sharpshooters, old boy – have you thought about it?'

He had, he'd thought about creeping through brambles and lying out in scrapes all day, he remembered saying as much to Ryder, and how Ryder had looked when he said it. 'Yes, sir. I'd like to do it.'

'Good show,' said Verschoyle. 'They're looking for people to fill in for a couple of days, lost a few in a shoot-out with a Russian picquet. It's a Captain Goodlake running it at present, tell him I sent you. He's Coldstream, of course, but well – we're all Guards.' He smiled wickedly and sauntered away.

Woodall slung the Minié over his shoulder. Coldstream was bad, crawling in mud was worse, but it was a place to belong and a place to start. If it was heroic and dangerous he wanted it. He'd just go back to the hospital to collect his things before those thieving orderlies got their paws on them, then he'd –

'Are you off, then?' said Mackenzie, appearing in front of him with that sneaky silent approach all Scotsmen seemed to have. 'You're for the hospital?'

Woodall looked warily at him, but he seemed quite ordinary. 'No, I'm back to the lines. They've asked for me, as a matter of fact. Specialist work, sharpshooting.'

'Have they now?' said Mackenzie. 'Well, I'm glad to see you better.'

Woodall hesitated, thought of the word 'sorry', and couldn't quite manage it. 'Last night . . . it was bad last night, I was in a lot of pain.'

'Aye,' said Mackenzie, and actually put a hand on his shoulder. 'I was thinking you were maybe not yourself.'

A sensation of panic rose in his throat. He struggled not to look at his shoulder, looked at Mackenzie instead and said, 'My wife's left me. Maisie's gone.'

Mackenzie's eyes widened, but there was no contempt in them, only shock and understanding. 'Man, that's a bad blow. Why ever did you not say?'

Woodall blinked. Could he have? Might it even help put things right with Ryder and Oliver if he did? He considered asking Mackenzie to tell them for him, but the hillside was filling with kilts and feathers and big Scottish bodies as the other Highland regiments arrived, and his companion was already joining cheerfully in the banter being hurled at the newcomers.

'Ah, go back to your beds, you bunch of lassies,' he yelled at a private of the 42nd. 'You'll have maybe heard how the 93rd stood alone?'

The man didn't even grin. 'Aye, in the absence of better men. But is it true, what they say of the rest of it? About the Light Brigade?'

Mackenzie's smile faded abruptly. 'What?' he demanded. 'What, man? What about the Light Brigade?'

The Cossacks handed them over to the infantry at Traktir Bridge. The cavalry seemed to be returning to their camps at Chorgun, but they were taking mostly Turkish prisoners with them and Ryder wondered what was special about themselves.

Something certainly was. Light Brigade survivors were being herded together, and grey-coated Russian infantry clustered round them in a fascination that seemed mingled with awe. One stepped right up to Jarvis's face and sniffed his breath before stepping back to shake his head with incredulity. 'No drink!' explained a huge, jolly gunner, giving Ryder a slap on the back that nearly made him faint. 'No drink!' Another did a whole pantomime of actions, frantic galloping, cannon firing 'Boom, boom!' and finally a tapping of his head and an expressive shrug. It was starting to look as if the Light Brigade had acquired a status of celebrity for its own sheer lunacy.

But a reputation for heroism had its uses. A magnificent figure announced as General Liprandi came to say what splendid fellows they were and that a selection of the most fit would be taken to Sebastopol to meet Prince Menschikoff himself. Ryder's gunner beamed when he and Jarvis were chosen, and Ryder felt like smiling himself. It was ironic, perhaps, to be taken to the town they'd come to conquer, but it was a sight better than a camp prison for a man determined to escape.

Because he must. His information was vital, his commanders had to have it, and this time they'd be prepared to listen. There'd be no need for discretion or secrecy now it wasn't about a British officer but a Russian spy.

And he was sure. It explained so much that had puzzled them – why nobody ever recognized the man or his saddlecloth, why he was able to move about so freely without apparent duties of his own. His English must be perfect, but the Bulgar had even said as much – and why would he tell an officer his English was 'flawless' unless he knew him to be a foreigner? No, it was true, it had to be, and wouldn't even have been that difficult. The British Army was riddled with journalists and war-tourists, strangers no one ever questioned, and a man in uniform would simply be part of the landscape. All he'd needed was audacity, and it had been enough to carry him through.

Well, maybe it would be the same for himself. Sebastopol was a town at war, it would be crowded and chaotic, full of strangers and civilians, and there was a good chance he'd be able to disappear among them. Their infantry guards were friendly, even respectful, they weren't chained or closely watched, they weren't being treated like prisoners at all.

It was still a hard journey for wounded and exhausted men, and it was mid-afternoon when they finally rounded Careenage Bay. Their escorts led them to a heavily guarded stone archway cut under the bank of an aqueduct, and he realized this must be a side entrance to Sebastopol. He glanced casually up the bank, but there were more guards on the top and primitive houses built into the side, the bloody thing was impregnable. He looked down again and found Jarvis watching him with cool speculation in his eyes.

He turned away. Jarvis was yesterday's problem and supremely irrelevant now. He concentrated on what was ahead of him, staying alert as he followed the others through the little tunnel and into a woodland clearing criss-crossed with white paths. They were at the base of another of those ravines, uncultivated and overgrown, but leading gradually up into the town itself.

They emerged onto a metalled road, marched through a gateway in a low grey wall, and were suddenly in the Korabelnaya suburb of Sebastopol. It was part of the town, he even saw the dome of a church, but this was a military cantonment and still felt like war. The place was dominated by huge white barracks, marching soldiers, and lines of infantry drilling on a square.

They marched down a long straight street towards the grey docks, and as they neared the harbour he wondered if this might be his chance. Their escort was already thinning, some marching off to billets with the jaunty air of returning conquerors, and others piling into large troop vessels for their trip across to the main Town Side. By the time their own little group of ten was ordered down to the quay there were only half a dozen infantry and two officers left to guard them.

The quay looked chaotic enough too, sailors and grey-coated soldiers milling about yelling at each other or leaning against stone bollards to share a quiet pipe. A steamer was in, little puffs of white spiralling into the sky as if the ship too was enjoying a leisurely smoke while her slaves did the sweaty business of unloading. A regular *clang* and *clang* drew his eyes to a growing pyramid of iron bars being carried from a skiff to join the shells and gabions, flour-sacks and sides of red beef already piled on the crowded quayside. Food and armaments, the same old business of war.

But this wasn't Balaklava, and the patrolling soldiers weren't going to let a man in Light Brigade blue sneak unnoticed onto a boat. A boat it would have to be, a way across to the unguarded Severnaya, the North Side over the Roadstead where the siege didn't reach, but he'd need some kind of disguise to get on one, and his best chance of that lay ahead in the crowds of the main town just across the harbour.

349

They were crammed into two skiffs for the crossing, and to his disgust he found himself knee-to-knee with Jarvis. The sergeant-major seemed determined to keep control of him even here, he kept making odd stentorian noises and trying to catch his eye, but Ryder ignored him, hugged his knees and looked at their destination ahead.

The Grafskaya, their officer said to the boatman, the Town Side, the real Sebastopol, and there it was in front of them, drawing nearer with every pull of the oars. The domes and spires so far only glimpsed in the distance were becoming a real town with people in it, alive with the murmur of crowds and church bells ringing a peal of victory. In the pauses between the changes he heard a lighter, tinkling sound from a waterfront coffee-house and knew someone was playing the balalaika.

'What are you up to, Ryder?' whispered Jarvis hoarsely. 'You wouldn't be thinking of breaking out?'

In the middle of the harbour? He said 'No,' and kept his eyes on the approaching quay. There were a lot of civilians among the military, some hawking goods to the arriving soldiers, others maybe looking for a boat home after a day's work in the town.

'That's "No, *Sergeant-major*" to you, Trooper,' said Jarvis, his breath warm on Ryder's cheek. 'And you're lying, you little prick, I know you by now.'

That was interesting, Jarvis with the mask off. If the TSM hadn't been utterly insignificant in the scale of things Ryder might have prodded him further, but nothing mattered beyond the information he had to get back to Raglan. He said 'I doubt it,' and looked ahead.

Jarvis's hand closed on his leg, right on the site of his old wound. 'If you do anything irresponsible . . .'

Pain and fury finally broke his temper. He swung round and said, 'Then it's none of your business, is it?'

Jarvis's eyes bulged like little marbles. 'You speak to me like that again, and I'll . . .'

'You'll what?' said Ryder. 'You've had my stripes, you've had me flogged, what are you going to do now, *Sar'nt-major*?' The liberation suddenly struck him, and he gestured triumphantly at the Russians sitting around them. 'Who are you going to tell?'

Jarvis's face turned grey as the blood faded out of it. Then he gripped the side of the boat and said thickly, 'You're still in the army unless you're deserting. Is that what you're doing, Ryder? Deserting?'

The Russian officer was watching them curiously. Ryder smiled for his benefit and said, 'I'm not doing anything, now shut your mouth before you get us both shot.'

Jarvis subsided, but his breathing sounded loud enough to power the boat. Ryder went on smiling just in case, but the officer's attention had wandered and a moment later their skiff nudged gently against the landing stage and they were there.

'There' might have been London, only better. The landing stage was magnificent, white stone, white marble, level white steps leading up to tall great columns, and through them a square that made Piccadilly look like Meerut. Ladies in bright dresses walked on the arms of elegant white-gloved companions, a string quartet played Glinka, women with gaily coloured headscarves sold bread rolls, and a man with a samovar was yelling '*Sbitén!*' and being swamped by soldiers thrusting coins at him for a mug of the hot, sweet-smelling liquid.

But it was not so good for him. He needed assorted rabble, the kind he'd see in London, but he wouldn't pass for a moment in this clean and elegant crowd. If he'd been infantry he'd have had a grey greatcoat, he'd have been virtually indistinguishable from the Russian soldiers themselves, but his ragged blue coat and white-striped overalls made him as conspicuous as he'd been at Traktir Bridge.

It would have been so easy otherwise. Their guards didn't seem to have the slightest fear of their escaping, and two were taking advantage of their officers' inattention to share a yellow-papered cigarette behind one of the pillars. The officers were deep in conference with an elegant gentleman in a silky black fur coat, but Ryder's attention sharpened when he realized the man was following the custom of high-born Russians before inferiors and speaking in exquisite French.

'But not like this, my dear Borshevsky!' he said, waving a fastidious white-gloved hand at them. 'They're disgusting! Have them cleaned up, I'll send an escort in an hour or two.'

'Their wounds, your honour,' said one of the officers nervously. 'It may take a little longer . . .'

'Oh, just the bits that show,' said the gentleman. 'Tell Surgeon Piragoff they are priority – you understand?'

Ryder did. A hospital could be the perfect opportunity, full of civilians and, better still, civilian clothes. He had perhaps an hour to take advantage of it.

At least the place was close. The officers led them towards a grand building with Roman numerals carved on its handsome plinth, and as men came out with a bloodstained stretcher Ryder realized with astonishment this was the hospital itself. They passed through double doors into a vast open space with marble floor and a dizzyingly high ceiling, and he guessed in peace time it might have been an assembly hall for nobility. Now it was a field of beds and pallets and suffering men, just another army hospital like their own at Balaklava.

But different. There were no operating tables to shock the visitors, but a patient was being carried through another set of doors at the back, and a smell of ether drifted out to greet them. The floor was clean, the windows admitted daylight, and some of the men had wives sitting with them, comfortable looking women offering fruit and sausage from bulging carpet bags, while others had nuns kneeling beside them to pray.

But these were the only civilians. There were no discarded hats and overcoats, nothing he could steal in the way of disguise. The patients were all soldiers, probably men from the bastions wounded in the bombardment, and the only clothes visible were the grey coats spread over the beds as additional blankets.

His heart gave a little, soft thump. Why not? In a town at war, what better disguise than a Russian soldier? That spy had done it, passed right in among their own ranks without question; why shouldn't Ryder do the same? He didn't speak the language, but he knew *da* and *nyet*, and *spasebo*, and he would never forget the word *perzhalsta* he'd heard over and over again from Russian wounded at the Alma. Yes, no, thank you and please, he had four words of Russian and fluent French. It was enough.

If he could do it. Now was the time, their only guards were chatting happily with patients and their officers were arguing with a surgeon. The prisoners were unattended, a sulky line standing awkwardly against the wall, and he stared hurriedly up and down the beds, looking for a coat that was unused and unwatched. A man near him was asleep, he could just reach out and tweak the coat from over him, but the nights were cold and he was reluctant to rob a wounded man of another layer to keep him warm.

He looked again for anyone covered only by a blanket. There was one such soldier at his feet, but when his gaze travelled upward he recoiled at the sight of the staring eyes and slackly open jaw. No one had noticed him yet, and Ryder was filled with sudden pity at the loneliness of it, to die unnoticed in a room full of strangers. He knelt beside the body, murmured 'Go with God', and gently closed the staring eyes. Across the room a nun touched her crucifix in acknowledgement, Christian to Christian, then turned to give her attention to her living patient. Suddenly awkward, Ryder withdrew his hand – and stopped. The dead man's bed was only a straw-filled pallet, and behind his head was no pillow but a folded pile of grey cloth. A coat.

To rob the dead! But the boots on his own feet were testimony to his having already done just that, him and hundreds like him. In death they were all soldiers together, sharing what they had to keep going just that little bit longer. He cradled the dead man's head with one hand, slid the coat out from under it with the other and laid it gently back down. Then he stood.

No one had noticed. Others of their line were exchanging

fragments of French and English with the wounded Russians, both sides grinning with the pleasure of speaking with the comrade who was the enemy. The guards were still busy, the officers actually leaving, only Jarvis was watching him, and even Jarvis wouldn't turn in one of his own. Ryder draped the coat nonchalantly over his arm and waited his turn for treatment.

It was quick. This was a patch-up operation for the convenience of a Russian prince, and when Ryder revealed the blood-soaked dressing on his back the orderly only wrapped another bandage over it and waved him on. He returned to the line, replaced his shirt and buttonless coat, and simply put the greatcoat on top. One of the guards was looking, but he'd have seen British soldiers in greatcoats and this might easily have been Ryder's own. It wasn't quite the same, the Russian coat seemed to have a faintly yellow tinge compared to the British version, but it was near enough indoors. Outside it would look Russian, but then that was exactly what he wanted.

The last prisoner was just dressing when their escort arrived. New, smartly dressed officers and four bored looking infantrymen, it couldn't have been better. They didn't know the prisoners by sight, they never even bothered to count them, they just dismissed the old guards and led them outside.

Now. Now, it had to be now, he drifted to the back of the line and watched for a chance to slip away. His shoulders tingled with it, his ears echoed with new clarity of sound, everything about him was wide open and searching. A band played military tunes down a boulevard, and he noted it as a landmark. They were marching down streets now, but too civilized still, again it might have been London. Carriages rattled by, men bustled in and out of shops with ordinary goods displayed in the windows, tea and coffee, paper and ink, a tailor's shop, and in the window a frock-coat that might have been Raglan's own. Ryder winced and looked away.

But there was hope here, and he felt it in the rising boisterousness around him. More and more soldiers were turning into the street, some laughing, some drinking, and all heading in the same direction as themselves. From the open doors of a church came the voices of a choir raised in a soaring *Te Deum*. Sebastopol was celebrating a victory, and then they turned a corner and saw it for themselves.

Another big square, but this one was heaving with grey-coated soldiers, the crowd of Ryder's dreams, and all of them yelling in raucous song. In the centre stood a man on the base of a statue conducting with a bottle in one hand and his cap in the other. This was it, this was the place, but their escort kept them clear of the crowded middle and led them discreetly down the side. Even here there were chances, little unpaved alleys between the buildings, places he could duck into if the guards were distracted. One actually had two drunken soldiers sprawled asleep inside, complete with guns and forage caps, everything he needed, but the guard behind was too close and he had no choice but to walk by.

Then it came. The officer on the statue caught sight of them, stopped conducting, and gestured furiously to the crowd. At once the mob surged towards them, baying in approval, in vengeful anger, maybe even in friendliness, but what mattered was they were stampeding this way. Ryder backed against a wall as if in alarm, watched his guard swept past with the force of the throng, then swung round and plunged right into them, yelling without words as part of the crowd's own roar. He was bare-headed, but so were they, and when he snatched a bottle from a staggering gunner the man only beamed and clapped him painfully on the back. Ryder took a quick swig, felt the wine kick exultantly in his head, and began to work back through the crowd, away from the centre and back to the alley he'd spotted before. No one was shouting after him, and he wondered if the guards had even noticed he'd gone.

There it was, a dark little gap between a music shop and what looked like a classical theatre. The sleeping soldiers were still there. He pulled the cap from the nearest, seized a fallen musket, and was turning to go when a boot scraped against stone and a bulky figure blocked the light from the square. He swivelled at it, bottle in one hand, musket in the other, and stopped in shock at the sight of Sergeant-Major Jarvis.

For half a second they stared at each other, then Ryder hurled himself at him, dragged him inside the alley and slammed his back against the wall. 'What the hell, what the bloody, bloody hell do you think you're . . . ?'

'What do you think?' growled Jarvis, wrenching away Ryder's hands and shoving him back. 'I'm coming with you, that's what.'

Ryder stared in turmoil. He didn't even know if he could trust the bastard, and he certainly didn't want his company.

'Why not?' said Jarvis truculently. 'Easier with two, isn't it?'

He wouldn't have a hope by himself, not dressed in grey shirt and braces, and flaunting overalls with a British double-white stripe. Ryder swore under his breath and bent down again to the sleeping soldiers, fumbling to unbutton one of the coats. 'Grab a cap and musket and for God's sake hurry, someone could look in here any minute.'

The soldier was stirring, and Ryder tried to be gentler with the buttons. Jarvis hadn't moved, doubtless fuming over being given an order, but after a moment his hand came down, he lifted the cap off the second man, then hunkered down to help with the coat. The soldier opened his eyes, but Ryder quickly put the bottle to his lips, and he sucked as happily as a baby. They worked the coat and cross-belt off together, then lowered his head back on the belly of his companion. The soldier blinked, sighed contentedly and went back to sleep.

The coat was long for Jarvis, but at least it covered most of the overalls. The mutton-chop whiskers looked wrong, and his posture was far too English parade ground, but the white cross-belt looked convincing and Ryder took the other soldier's so at least they'd match.

He glanced out into the square and saw with alarm the mob was already thinning. 'Time to go. Back to the harbour and a boat to the North Side.'

'No, you don't, Trooper,' said Jarvis. He patted down his coat, then stooped for the other musket. 'We'll go back the way we came.'

Ryder's temper flared at once. 'Not if you're coming with me. Tag along if you want, but I'm damned if I'll take your orders.'

Jarvis's mouth set in a thin, hard line. 'Listen, you cocky little bastard, I've seen the North Side. We did a lot of patrolling while you were malingering after the Alma, and the only soldiers crossing the Roadstead are reinforcements coming in. We try and get a boat the other way, they'll have us as deserters.'

Ryder's fist tightened round his musket, but what the man said made sense. 'All right, we'll go back to the suburb. But follow my lead and for God's sake try and look less British or you'll be going on your own.'

Jarvis smiled, but Ryder meant it. The NCO could keep steady and follow orders, but he'd no more initiative than poor Hoare. He was wounded in the leg, he was slow and inflexible, he was a first-class bastard and the only reason Ryder was taking him at all was that stupid sense of loyalty to a man of his own side. He ran through their route in his mind and bent to search the nearest pack.

Jarvis glared. 'That's stealing, Trooper, there's no call . . .'

'If we're not in a troop ship we'll need money for the crossing.' He thrust a handful of coins into the pocket of his greatcoat, then snatched an empty bottle from the alley floor and passed it to Jarvis. 'Come on, it's quietening down out there.'

Jarvis looked at the bottle as if he didn't know what to do with it, but at least he followed. The crowds were definitely dispersing now, probably due to the presence of a couple of mounted officers, and Ryder set off at a spanking pace back towards the harbour. The military band guided him back to the boulevard, white puffs in the sky showed the location of the steamer, and he followed the cries of the gulls. He paused twice to give the hobbling Jarvis a chance to keep up, but the sergeant-major waved angrily, said 'Go on, go on,' and stumped after him in obstinate defiance.

Business at the quay was winding down towards dusk, and he only saw a few soldiers crossing in skiffs to the Korabelnaya. Darkness and crowds would be better, but there might be troops looking for them already, and if anyone found those soldiers in the alley they'd also know exactly what to look for.

'We can do it,' he said. 'Pretend we're drunk and we can do it.'

Jarvis didn't answer immediately, and Ryder felt a slight qualm at the sight of him. His face was flushed except for grey patches under his eyes, and he was leaning against a column to take the weight off his injured leg.

He said more hesitantly, 'Can you . . . ?'

'Course I can,' said Jarvis at once, straightening as if on parade. 'Course I bloody can. Let's –'

'Wait.' A group of infantrymen were weaving across to the colonnade, remnants of the victorious and drunken crowd staggering home. 'We'll go with this lot. If anyone's after us, they'll be looking for two on their own.' He watched them start down the steps, said 'Come on', and held out his arm.

Jarvis blazed with outrage. 'You keep your hands to yourself, I don't need help from a trooper.'

Ryder kept his arm where it was. 'Drunk and incapable, remember, Sar'nt-major?'

Jarvis took a deep, deep breath, skewered Ryder with his eyes, then took the arm. He clearly needed it, and his weight was enough to give Ryder a convincing totter of his own as they reeled together after the soldiers. They weren't two any more, they were eight, just another bunch of drunks heading for the barracks and home.

Three boatmen at once waved for their custom, and it was easy to see why. Drunk men didn't count money, they were shoving coins at the men and floundering into the skiffs without looking for change, and Ryder made sure to do exactly the same. Their boat was overloaded and travelled low in the water, but the closeness of the packed bodies was as reassuring as a tent, a living camouflage to carry them home. His young neighbour vomited noisily over the side and his companions jeered and slapped him with their caps, but Ryder only smiled with satisfaction. No one would want to come close to men like these.

He turned to look at the Korabelnaya looming ahead. Dusk was falling, but it was more than darkness that made the suburb look forbidding and hostile. There were no little braziers there, no traders, no music, only the giant metal-roofed dock buildings, the tall barracks behind, and beyond them the bastions and guns. For a little while they'd been in a world of lost civilization, and now they were going back to war.

Death followed Oliver out of the valley. Sally helped him down to Kadikoi, but all the way he was hearing the distant *pop, pop* of guns in the North Valley as the farriers shot the wounded horses. Kadikoi was different too, filled with silent and grim-faced Highlanders, while the church had been converted to a dressing station to deal with the overflow from Balaklava. It was filled with Light Brigade casualties but not one he knew by name. They were gone, all of them, Ryder and Jordan, Bolton and Fisk, Prosser and Moody, Cornet Hoare and Captain Marsh, even Jarvis was gone, and Oliver was quite alone.

He waited in the porch for his turn under the knife. It was strangely comforting there, almost English compared to everything else around him. The church smelled of incense and was decorated with luridly coloured icons, but the porch had a shabby corkboard with little notices on it, faded yellow paper with cryptic Cyrillic lettering, and a tear-off calendar that no one had changed since 13 October. He wished it really was the 13th. The bombardment hadn't started then, Ryder hadn't been flogged, the charge hadn't happened, he'd still been part of an army he believed in and his friends had been alive.

The surgeon cut the ball out of his leg with the ease of a farrier removing a stone from a hoof, told him he was a lucky lad and had lost nothing worse than blood. Sally talked while she put the bandage back on, she told him all about their staff officer and how he'd been at the battle himself, but even that didn't seem important beside everything he'd really lost.

What he needed most was the comfort of familiar things, but when he hobbled back to camp he found that too had been destroyed. Half the tents were down, some torn and trampled by the charge of the Heavies, some struck by people escaping the Cossacks, others looted by fleeing Turks. The horse-lines were pitiful, and their farrier-sergeant had tears streaming down his face as he sobbed to the quartermaster. 'Eighty, Joe, at least eighty from the regiment! God knows how many from us all!' Oliver tried not to think of poor Misty, the animal they'd given him to love and look after, but the feel of her nose was a memory of softness under his hand. He wondered if Bobbin would be thought worth saving or if she'd need to be destroyed with the rest.

He found his tent, but it was down and flattened and there was no one else there. He knelt to lift the canvas, but it was ridiculously heavy, and he let it drop with a defeated *flump*. He had his blanket, maybe he could sleep outside, but when he set a match to the scattered remnants of their firewood an NCO yelled 'No fires, Trooper, ain't you heard? We've the Russians just yards off in the redoubts, it's no fires till further orders.' He blew out the match and watched the glowing pinpoints of half-caught kindling fade slowly into black.

'Polly Oliver, by all that's holy!' cried a voice, and Billy Jordan came limping towards him out of the gloom. 'I was starting to think I was the only one.'

Oliver grinned with sudden happiness. 'I thought you . . . I saw you go down.'

'And stayed down,' agreed Jordan, dumping his haversack by the cold fire and throwing himself down after it. 'Not a horse to be had, chum, saving the five hundred trying to trample me to death. Biggest charge we'll ever get, and I spend it hiding behind a thorn bush.' He shook his head sadly and groped in his haversack. 'Here, have a peppermint.'

The sweets looked rather battered, but Oliver sucked one gratefully and found the taste clean and cool. 'Are you hurt, Billy?'

'Not so's you'd notice. Wonky ankle, cuts and bruises, I'm the fittest man in the regiment. D'you know how many of us were at parade tonight? Ten. Ten out of, what, a hundred and fifty?' His face seemed less fleshy than usual, as if it had tightened round his cheekbones.

Oliver tried to sound reassuring. 'There were some in hospital at Kadikoi, and there'll be more at Balaklava. And some might be prisoners, mightn't they?'

Jordan glanced at him curiously, then gave his arm a friendly little pat. 'All your tent, is it, Polly? That's rough.'

Oliver couldn't bring himself to speak.

'Come in with us, if you like,' said Jordan casually. 'There's only me and Trotter fit, and we could use a hand to put the thing up.'

Oliver felt a bound of hope. 'Will Mrs Jordan mind? She doesn't really know me.'

Jordan shrugged and got to his feet. 'Lucie's in Balaklava, the silly cow says it's not safe. Come on, let's get it up while there's still a bit of light.'

There wasn't much even now, but Trotter pitched in to help and they worked quickly in the growing dark. It felt good swapping stories after a battle, the way he'd heard the others do after the Alma. Trotter's was limited to, 'Well, we got to the battery, had a bit of a fight and came out again,' but Jordan had seen almost everything from his hiding place in the valley. He told them how Lucan had turned the Heavies round and abandoned the Lights to their fate. He told them how Cardigan had spent about a minute at the battery before riding for home. He told them everything he knew, and Oliver's grief began to warm into anger.

'We'd have been done if it weren't for the Frogs,' said Jordan, hammering in a picket peg. 'Lovely charge they made at Russ's battery on the Fedoukhine.'

Oliver tugged the canvas on the other side. 'Did they get cut up like we did?'

'Not they,' said Jordan. 'They did the sensible, didn't they, went round their bleeding flank. Wish we had their generals instead of ours.'

Oliver privately agreed. 'Why did we do it? Why did they make us do something so stupid?'

'Ah,' said Jordan. 'Ask me another, will you? Look-On's been ranting all afternoon, convinced he's going to be blamed for the whole thing. Seems it was one great big mistake.'

'Mistake,' said the taciturn Trotter. He banged at his picket peg with sudden ferocity, knocking it wildly skew. 'That's what they call it, is it?'

Jordan relieved him at the peg. 'It's what Look-On says. Seems we weren't meant to go that way at all, we were supposed to go for the redoubts, but Nolan pointed the wrong way.'

Oliver remembered that little vignette at the front of their lines, Nolan's outstretched arm and the frozen immobility of their officers. 'Lord Lucan should have made him explain. Oh God, Billy, you're saying it needn't have happened at all.'

Jordan banged down on the peg, cursed and sucked his thumb. 'Nah, the redoubts would have been just as bad. There was that battery in the Fedoukhine, we'd still have been in range of the Don Cossacks, those guns on the Heights were all ready and waiting, and they'd a great bunch of infantry there too.' He sucked his thumb again and looked at Oliver directly over the top. '*And* they were expecting us. The infantry on that side were standing in square, I saw them. They were expecting cavalry to come right for them, and a pretty hot reception they'd have given us if we had.'

He banged the peg again, and the sound hurt inside Oliver's head. 'Then why did Lord Raglan order it? Couldn't he see what was waiting for us?'

'Not him,' said Jordan. He tested the peg and sat back with satisfaction. 'He couldn't have seen much beyond the first two redoubts, not from up there. His ADC says he only ordered it because some officer said Russ was taking away our guns.'

'But they weren't,' said Oliver, desperate for something to make sense. 'Why would Lieutenant Calthorpe say that? We'd have seen them, they weren't.'

Jordan pointed his fingers at him like a gun. 'Quite right, chum, they weren't. Only a fool would have tried to drag cannon across the Woronzoff with us sitting on top of it like cats over a mouse-hole. Calthorpe didn't see it, no one did, only some helpful staff officer who obviously got the whole thing wrong.'

He stood to admire their handiwork, but Oliver stayed where he was, a sick weight of certainty sinking him into the ground. 'This staff officer. Who was he?'

'That's just it, ain't it?' said Jordan, straightening the canvas. 'Look-On asked Calthorpe, but Calthorpe didn't know. Nobody knows at all.'

Oliver did. This was what they'd feared all along and Ryder had been flogged for trying to stop it. Hundreds of men had died now, all thinking they were taking part in something glorious and important, hundreds of them dead and blown in bits, their guts trailed on the North Valley, their faces eaten by vultures, dead for glory and the whole thing had been one enormous lie. The memory of it was too much, suddenly all too much, and he felt himself shaking again, deep, painful shudders that racked his chest and throat and threatened to pour out of his mouth in a wail.

'Polly?' said Jordan's voice.

'Leave him,' said Trotter, and his hand came down on Oliver's shoulder. 'It's enough and more than enough, ain't it? I've seen older and bigger chaps blubbing today.'

He was, that's just what he was doing, he was blubbing like a silly kid. He clenched his arms round his knees and ground his teeth hard together, but tears came pouring out, his nose began to run, and suddenly none of it mattered, because his friends were dead, his dreams destroyed, and all of it had been for nothing.

*

The boat bumped gently into the quay of the Korabelnaya. Ryder scrambled awkwardly over the side, waved away the offered arm of a grinning boatman, and staggered to a stack of crates to wait for Jarvis.

This was where it would get difficult. Green-coated Ekipage patrolled the quay, two long-coated men with papers were arguing with a mounted officer, and an NCO was already bawling at two of their erstwhile companions. There was none of the main town's party spirit here, this was military business and the sooner they were out of it the better.

'What now?' said Jarvis, coming to lean beside him. 'Tag after the others?'

He was actually asking. Ryder hid his surprise and said, 'We haven't the language to bluff it. We've got to keep moving, get nearer the wall and hope for an easy way out.'

They had to find one soon. Darkness was falling, but it was also getting colder and the wind from the sea was biting. Jarvis was already hugging his greatcoat tighter round his body and Ryder suspected he was shivering. He gave the sergeant-major his arm, noted with interest the lack of objection, and lurched unsteadily away from the quay.

It was harder than it had been in the main town. Frivolity was laughed at there, but here he felt the eyes of disapproving NCOs on their backs and expected every moment to hear a shout. Maybe they would have, but a ship was disembarking, what looked like a whole regiment tumbling out, and the distraction helped them get safely round the corner of the first building. It wasn't the same road they'd come down, but Sebastopol was a new town and the roads were as regular and parallel as lines on a grid. If they kept on this one they'd be bound to hit the defences in the end.

It was still a nightmare. He prayed for the sanctuary of winding lanes and alleys, but the long straight road was as barren of cover as a parade ground, and the barracks beside them merged into a single unbroken line of stark white walls. Soldiers came out to light the lamps, and they scurried on faster, staying just ahead of the yellow pools that bloomed one by one behind them. Jarvis was clearly struggling to keep up, but Ryder pushed on relentlessly until they reached the broad street that ran parallel to the grey wall. A company of soldiers was marching along it, and Ryder pressed back into the shadow of the corner while he worked out what to do.

This stretch of wall wasn't guarded, but it didn't need to be, it was overlooked by the hulking shape of the Little Redan. But it was dark, there were shadowy stretches between lamps, and the bastion was watching for an invading army trying to storm in, not a couple of lone soldiers trying to slip out. There still might be a chance.

He looked at Jarvis, then at the wall. 'Could you climb it?'

Jarvis hesitated, and Ryder knew he was thinking about his leg. 'Is it worth it? The archway's guarded on the other side.'

'There's cover in the ravine. We've got to get off the road, we'll be spotted any minute.'

Jarvis said nothing. His breath was cloudy in the freezing air.

Distant footsteps were already echoing on the road behind them. Ryder looked round desperately, grabbed Jarvis's arm and pulled him towards a small row of houses standing back from the Little Redan. They must have taken the brunt of the British bombardment, and were every one abandoned, fronts piled with rubble and fallen slates, walls black with holes of blown-out windows. Not much in the way of shelter, but at least it was cover.

He hopped the low wall of the end house. The front room gaped in a frame of broken brickwork, so he simply stuck his leg over and climbed inside. Jarvis watched in mulish silence, but Ryder leaned over, took his hands, and lifted him bodily over the barrier. The wounded leg had obviously seized on him, and Ryder remembered exactly how it felt.

Plaster and debris crunched underfoot, and tiny bright flashes were shards of a broken mirror. This must have been a nice house once. A broken-backed chair still boasted a blackened antimacassar, the silky yellow tassels soft and innocent as afternoon tea. He shut his mind to the thought of it and groped forward to the stairs, desperate for height and a decent view. The boards creaked ominously but the structure was intact and at the top was the wreck of a bedroom with a shattered window open to the night. Jarvis sat down heavily against the wall, but Ryder moved gingerly to the sill and looked out to the Little Redan and the low wall. He could see clear over it, the metalled road the other side, the entrance to the ravine and surely, surely a way out.

'There were other paths, weren't there?' he said. 'Not just the one to the archway. If we can clear this wall we could try them, see if they lead into the Careenage Ravine on the plateau.'

Jarvis grunted. He was hunched over his knees and the unusual tightness round his jaw suggested he was clenching his teeth. 'Not yet, Trooper. No rush. Not yet.'

Ryder watched him with misgiving. Jarvis had been through the shock of the charge, his shin was cut open to the bone, he'd had to endure a long walk before his wound was dressed, Ryder had made him run, and he hadn't had a thing to eat since the night before. The man was freezing with cold and just about done. 'No, no rush. We can wait a bit.'

Darkness deepened, and with it the chill. He sat and leaned against the wall, huddled into his greatcoat, and wondered what the hell he was going to do. It would take more than a little sit-down to get Jarvis over that wall, let alone through the rough terrain of a ravine. He needed food and warmth, rest, sleep and something for the pain, and until he got them he wouldn't be capable of more than a short walk on the flat. He might manage the road they'd come by, but the gateway was guarded, so was the arch, there'd be passwords and checks, and neither of them could pass a close inspection. They didn't even have packs.

He pressed his hands to his head and tried to think. He could have given Jarvis a boost over the wall, he could have carried him down the ravine, but his back was raw flesh, and that was thanks to the sergeant-major himself. All of it was. If his back hadn't been useless he'd have beaten those Cossacks. If he'd had his revolver he could have saved them all. Jarvis had brought this all on himself, and there was no reason for Ryder to be dragged down with him. If he were alone he could be over that wall in just five minutes.

He knotted his hands and pictured it, the journey in the dark through the ravine. He could do it. There were landmarks he knew, and especially the windmill by the turning to the Light Division camp. Bloomer would be there, and Bloomer would get him home. Home was the cavalry camp, maybe Oliver would have made it safe back there. Then he thought of Sally, he pictured himself telling her he'd left her husband to die, and closed his eyes.

The cold was becoming unbearable. This was late October, and through the gaping hole of the window the stars had that bright clarity that augured frost. He had no tent, no cloak, no blanket, only his jacket and a stiff greatcoat that seemed thin as paper. Jarvis didn't even have the jacket. As he lifted his head he became aware of a new sound, the desperate, helpless shivering of a man too far gone even to pretend.

He made a face at the sky, and stood to take off his greatcoat. Jarvis was huddled almost into a ball now, and Ryder had to ease him forward before he could arrange half the coat around his shoulders, then hunch in beside him with the other half round his own. Jarvis's elbow dug uncomfortably in his ribs, but after a moment the man relaxed a little, leaned further in and allowed the touch to bond them all the way down. Slowly and gradually the shivering subsided into the softness of breath, and over them both spread the beginnings of warmth.

18

26 October 1854, 6.00 a.m. to 4.00 p.m.

Ryder woke to the sound of church bells. He blinked confusedly at the charred bare floorboards, then became aware of other noises drifting through the shattered window: wheels, chains, and the barking of distant orders. He looked distastefully at Jarvis's head on his shoulder, eased it back against the wall, and crawled to the window to look below.

Frost sparkled on the road, but familiar shapes moving over it jolted him into sudden wakefulness. Cannon. Limbered field guns were clattering past, and green-uniformed artillerymen bringing them to a stop by the gateway further down. Infantry were emerging from the three-storey barracks along the road, but they weren't for the Little Redan, they were marching to join others mustering on a distant square. It might just be a parade, but the church bells were still ringing, he remembered the incense on the soldier's coat at the Alma, and his unease began to grow.

The floorboards creaked as Jarvis crawled over to join him. Ryder made space at the window and looked out to see another regiment joining the muster, but these had black rather than white cross-belts, and he wondered who they were.

'Odd,' said Jarvis. 'Marines from the Black Sea Fleet. They expecting an attack or something?'

Not from the British. The church bells, the cannon, the mustering, the bringing in of men from the ships, everything pointed the same way, and Ryder gripped the ledge in sudden understanding. 'No, by God, they're coming out. The bastards are after another battle.'

'Bloody hell,' said Jarvis, and the flesh of his jowls seemed to sag. 'Haven't they ever had enough?'

Ryder was too elated to care. 'It's good sense. Who expects a battle the day after you've just had one?'

Jarvis looked sourly at him. 'And that makes you happy, does it?'

Ryder grinned at him. 'Look at those cannon. They're going through the gate, Sar'nt-major, they're going to march through that tunnel, and we're going right out there with them.'

When Sally finally left the hospital she found the cavalry had gone. Their tents were still standing, presumably to deceive the enemy in the redoubts, but the men themselves had moved nearer the Col and a picquet had to direct her how to join them.

It was a miserable sight that greeted her. The ground was bright with frost, but men were lying huddled together like animals in the open air, their blankets lost with their dead horses, and not so much as a fire to keep them warm. Reveille was calling as she arrived, and she doubted more than half had had any sleep at all.

She skirted tactfully round a group of officers, but stopped abruptly as a familiar voice rose angrily among them. Colonel Doherty! He must have heard the news and dragged himself from his sickbed to look after his men. His face was grey and strained but his voice sounded as strong as if he'd suffered no more than a chill.

'It's broad bloody daylight, man,' he was shouting at an elegant ADC. 'The Russians don't need fires to tell them where we are. You tell his lordship from me that I'm ordering fires, and if he doesn't like it he can damn well relieve me of my command.'

The aide saluted and fled, and Doherty turned calmly to Lieutenant Grainger. 'Much obliged, Lieutenant, get the wood parties out as soon as you can. Leave the butcher's bill with me.'

He did look very poorly still. He might be the colonel of her regiment, but he was also a man she'd nursed and she couldn't just walk by. She waited for Grainger to leave, then bobbed a curtsey and said, 'Forgive me, sir, but should you be out in this cold?'

He said, 'I should have been here yesterday,' and she was shocked by the haunted expression in his eyes.

She said quickly, 'Very good, sir,' but he blinked as if only just realizing who she was, then lifted a hand to stop her going.

'I'm . . . very sorry to see about your husband. Do you know what you'll do?'

She lifted her head. 'I'll wait for him to come back, sir. There'll be time to think about other things if he doesn't.'

'Quite right,' he said approvingly. 'Take all the time you need. You'll always be welcome on the strength of the 13th.'

But she'd have to take another man, and something in her squirmed away from the idea. It was what people did, it was the sensible thing, but somewhere in her mind was the memory of a young man who held her as if he loved her and kissed her as if he needed it, and after that it was hard to think of anything less.

She said 'Thank you, sir', but his attention was fixed again on the casualty lists, his eyes unmoving as if they stayed on one name, and she understood quite suddenly they were both thinking of the same man. She whispered again 'Thank you' and crept away quietly, wondering just how well Doherty really knew Harry Ryder, and why he'd been so distressed when Syme told him of the flogging.

But Ryder was gone too, like so many of them. Poor Cornet Hoare, who'd cried in her arms when the officers' mess had bullied him. Poor Jake Prosser, who worried about his smallpox scars and was convinced no woman could ever love him. Poor Tommy Bolton, who'd only come to the cavalry because he'd loved the pit-ponies in his Durham mine and wanted a live beast of his own to look after. They were all gone, and it was pure selfishness in her to think only of her own loss and what she would do if her man didn't return.

But if Ryder does, said a voice in her head. *If Ryder comes back and Jarvis doesn't, what then?*

Then nothing. She slammed down her haversack and took out her bottle of rum. Ryder was not for her and never would be. There was gentleman in him somewhere, she'd thought so long before she saw him with Doherty. When he'd finally worked off that terrible anger of his he'd be looking to make something of himself, and the last thing he needed was to get there and find a Sally Jarvis wrapped round his neck. If she loved him she'd let him go, and she did love him, she'd known that for some time.

She took the rum and went round the men, pouring a drop in every mug that offered. They were all her family now. And maybe somewhere only a few miles away someone would be caring for the two she loved best, nursing them, perhaps burying them, perhaps helping them both to come home.

It was time. The first guns were already through the gateway, a column of infantry approaching down the street that crossed their window, and another waiting to turn in from the side road. Their discipline was visibly shaky too, and Ryder had watched disbelievingly as the men were first shriven by the priests, then poured full mugs of liquor from a seemingly endless supply of casks. Maybe the Russians were hoping to turn their soldiers into Light Brigade heroes.

But drunk or not, they'd still be bound to notice a couple of soldiers nipping out of a ruined house to wriggle into the middle of them. Their only chance lay in the house's corner position. They'd have to tag onto the end of one regimental column and hope the one following would assume the stragglers had simply joined from the other road. He'd have much preferred the anonymity of the column's centre to the exposure of its rear, but if there was an alternative he couldn't see it.

He said, 'Good luck, Sar'nt-major,' and stuck out his hand. Jarvis hesitated, then clasped it firmly and let go.

They walked gingerly down the creaking stairs, waited for the column passing the front to clear, then climbed quickly out of the hole in the wall. Jarvis managed it unaided and Ryder began to hope he could make it yet. He leaned against the wall and watched the side column begin to file past for the turn, not one of them thinking to look left at the yard of an abandoned house. They could do it, just hop over the wall and do it, and he wondered why he felt sweat in his armpits and cold on the back of his neck.

'Is my back clean?' muttered Jarvis. 'The coat, is it clean?'

It was speckled with white ash from the bedroom wall, and Ryder felt heart-pumping panic as he brushed his hands frantically over the TSM's back. 'And mine, I never checked it, is mine?'

He turned his back and told himself one day this would be funny, one day he'd laugh at Jarvis wiping his arse, but not now, nothing was funny now. Jarvis said, 'That's done it, you're clear,' and his voice was steadying and normal. Ryder turned and saw there was space after the men passing them, the end of the column right there.

'Now,' he said. '*Now.*' Two strides, a hop, and he was over the wall into the openness of the road. He hurried up behind the last rank and steadied his pace to theirs, staring straight ahead, trying not to see the emptiness about him, then Jarvis appeared beside him and he was safe in the invisibility of a column. The man in front glanced round and grinned, seeing nothing more suspicious than a couple of latecomers trying to catch up. Ryder gave an embarrassed shrug and grinned back.

They passed safely through the gateway, but behind came the tramping steps of the next column and Ryder was painfully aware of the gap between them. Hidden in the middle it wouldn't matter, no one saw more than the head and shoulders of the man in front, but the column behind could see their backs and legs, and he felt their visibility skewer him between the shoulder-blades. They'd get away with it for now, men heading to battle had other things on their minds, but let the monotony of a march set in and someone would see they wore no packs and their trousers were grey, someone would notice and shout. He concentrated on marching in step, left-right, left-right, invisible in the uniform ranks, but as they turned down into the ravine he saw Jarvis already starting to limp.

Sweat began to prickle on his upper lip. He saw cover all round him, long grass and straggly bushes, but if they broke for it they'd be taken for deserters. He kept marching with his head up, as if staring ahead might make him less noticeable from behind; then his boot knocked into the heel of the man in front, and he saw the column was slowing to a halt.

Something was happening. Ahead lay the hub of paths he'd noticed on the way up, and another column was crossing their own, marines with black cross-belts heading down one of the side paths he'd guessed would follow the Careenage Ravine. But there was a third column approaching down another path, men dressed like themselves and heading in the same direction, and they too were creating delay as the lines overlapped on the route to the arch.

Delay – and confusion. He whispered, 'Change columns, get in the middle,' and Jarvis nodded in fervent agreement. Their own column started moving again, a stop-and-start shuffle as the ranks bulged and overlapped, and Ryder broke across in two steps to plant himself on the outside of another marching line. His neighbours looked startled, but he groped at his greatcoat as if buttoning himself after a furtive piss in the bushes, and was rewarded with a conspiratorial smile of understanding. A second later and Jarvis tucked in beside him, and as they funnelled into the bottleneck for the arch another pair stepped smartly up on their right to make a four. No one commented, no one even stared, and then the sky darkened over him as they passed through the tunnel. No challenge, no password, not for an army. They were through the arch and out, turning smart right for the Chersonese Uplands and home.

And the marching was easy. The road was level, to his left was the low wall that bordered the Careenage Bay, and when the bay met the Roadstead they continued hugging its shore. It made sense for a stealthy attack, they were keeping Mount Sapoune between themselves and the Allies, and it wasn't until they reached the Volivia Gorge that they turned south, off the road and onto the bumpy terrain of the Uplands. Somewhere ahead of them lay British-held Shell Hill, and their chance to break for freedom.

Beside him Jarvis stumbled, and at once Ryder's unease returned. The sergeant-major had managed all right on the road, but now his gait was stiff and uneven, and after five minutes he was virtually staggering. Ryder slipped a hand under his elbow to support him and prayed he could hold out long enough to get them in reach of the British lines. At least his neighbours didn't seem to have noticed. Their faces showed only grim indifference as they marched on, left-right, left-right, men going into battle and probably feeling the way the British had before the Alma.

Jarvis stumbled again. Ryder steadied him, but the NCO's face was contorted with pain and he was obviously only minutes from collapse. Maybe they should risk it and just run, maybe the Russians wouldn't fire for fear of giving away their approach, but Jarvis couldn't run, he could hardly bloody walk, and the Russians didn't need noise to capture a cripple. No. They had to get clear and out of sight before anyone could think to come after them.

He scanned the ground. Grass, stunted oak, thorn bushes, boulders, gullies, lots of places to hide if your companions didn't actually see you doing it. Over, further, and dark blobs ahead in a fold of the slopes, horses standing alone and cropping the arid grass. Two, no, three of them without riders, saddled but empty, standing by themselves as calmly as ponies on Exmoor. He saw the black lambskins of the Light Brigade, knew what they were and what they'd run from, but they were here, they were transport and speed and a chance. He pressed Jarvis's arm and indicated them with his eyes.

'Not a hope,' muttered Jarvis. 'We run at them, they'll bolt.'

'Just one,' he whispered back. 'They're big, one can take two men. Don't tell me we can't get at least one.'

The horses were only twenty yards from the track and clearly unbothered by the movement of troops. Their own rank would draw level with them in maybe one minute.

'All right,' said Jarvis suddenly. 'But I've only got one leg that works, remember that.'

Ryder grinned. 'You can bloody limp it, we'll still be away before the Russians react.'

His neighbour glanced round. Ryder wondered if the English had been too loud, and hastily gave a vague mumble, brushed his forehead and tried to look hungover. The lad smiled broadly, said something incomprehensible, and actually patted his shoulder.

Nearly there, and the horses hadn't moved. It was a hard thing to do in cold blood, he needed an emergency to respond to, but there was nothing but themselves marching safe and about to throw themselves into danger. Left-right, left-right, *now*, and he shoved Jarvis out of the column to stagger blindly onto the grass.

Good, he looked ill and dazed, no one suspected, and Ryder darted after him, a Good Samaritan helping a man who'd fallen out. A mounted officer started towards them but Ryder grabbed Jarvis's shoulders and staggered back with him, right for the horses, noses up and watching with interest, go for them, grab one, *go*. A whinny of alarm, the first was off, the second backing away with the look of an elderly virgin finding a man in her bedroom, but his hand was up and grasping, leather, a bridle, he clenched it and shoved Jarvis at the stirrup.

'Get up, get up!' He was yelling now, the pretence over and done. 'Go on, *go*!' He boosted the sergeant-major from behind, leg over and up, and the approaching officer actually slowed in surprise. Ryder laughed as he turned, hand up to Jarvis for the pull, but nothing caught him, the horse was wheeling, her flank bumping hard into him as she turned. He staggered, snatched again at the bridle, but it was whisked out of reach, he was groping after a horse already galloping away. He called 'Jarvis!', desperate to believe it an accident, but the Russian officer was yelling too, and soldiers breaking after him from the ranks.

He was alone and unarmed against four thousand Russians and Jarvis had left him to die.

He ran. Nothing else for it, he wrenched away from the reaching hands of the nearest soldier and bolted like a rabbit over the slopes. The musket banged on his back, his feet stumbled over ruts and bumps, terror stabbed him as his ankle twisted and nearly bent over. The man behind was quicker and nimbler, a hand brushed then seized his arm, jolting him back and round. He rode with it, swinging round faster than the pull, fist hammering out to connect with the face of the boy who'd marched beside him. Crack on the cheekbone, see him down, swivel again and run.

It was hopeless. Hooves pounded behind him, the officer coming up, he couldn't outrun a bloody horse. He scrabbled to unsling the musket, sprang a foot on a boulder to gain height, and there was the rider, smash out with the butt, hit him and drive him back. Useless. He'd caught the arm, but a horseman wouldn't retreat from an infantryman with a musket butt, he was wheeling to come again and in his hand was a drawn sword. Whatever the man thought he was, enemy or deserter, he was going to bloody kill him and find out afterwards.

Ryder swung back to face him, desperate and at bay. The sword flashed down, he smashed it away with the musket, then leaped from the boulder and ran. A lance would have caught him, but a sword might be dodged, he twisted and ducked and ran. Pain scorched down his back as the tip of the sabre caught him, but he dived away, sobbing and cursing, still running and with a chance. Use the ground, get trees between them, rocks, and then the miracle, a stone-slide of a gully, he threw himself down and rolled. Stones flew down with him, face and hands tearing over them, hip smashing agonizingly into a rock, but he was going at speed and no horseman could risk following. He jarred to a halt against a tree, forced up his head and saw the rider safe on the skyline looking down.

He waited a moment on hands and knees, panting to catch his

breath, then looked up at the sound of distant shots. Small-arms fire from the direction of Shell Hill, the British picquets must have spotted the approaching enemy. He looked back in triumph to see the horseman still watching, and somewhere his brain finished the thought: the alarm was given, the Russians had no more need for silence, which meant they could –

He was already flying for the boulders as the shot split the air. A stinging blow burned down his scalp, a spray of sharp dust flew in his face, he squeezed his eyes shut and felt the judder through his skull as his head struck rock. He was lying on pebbles, he felt the bumps all down his side, but daren't open his eyes to see. His eyelashes were gritty and stinging, tiny splinters of stone, if they went in his eyes he was blind. He lay still as dead, feeling blood trickle down his face and hearing his heart like a drum.

Moments passed and his mind came back to him. The horseman had paid his grudge, he'd have gone back to his men and the battle, and Ryder could move if he wanted. *If he could.* All the little pains were talking at once, as if he were being turned on a spit with everything hurting in turn. He made his hand trace the line in his scalp, a clean furrow in the skin oozing out blood as if he had plenty to spare. His leg was throbbing, a familiar ache he thought he'd long conquered, but the skin was cold with wetness and he knew the wound had reopened. His back was the worst, and his other hand crept down to explore the rent in his greatcoat, the slash in the coat beneath, the parted rags of the shirt, the dressing sliced through and the raw bleeding flesh beyond. The sword had gone through all of it, and if it hadn't been for the thickness of two dressings the blade would have cut to his spine.

But it hadn't. A ridiculous pleasure coursed through him with this single small triumph, and he slid the hand from his head to stroke the grit from his eyelashes, wetting his fingers to make the particles stick and lift away. He wouldn't be blind. He wouldn't give up. He couldn't just die here without getting his information to Raglan. His eyes opened slowly, cautiously, testing for pain, but there was no more than the sting of sand, a faint prickling that blinked away with tears. He saw blue-grey rocks, a boulder spattered with blood he knew was his own, and a gully that tapered into a dead end. Above him was a battlefield.

But not everywhere. The Inkerman area was getting it, but the only force attacking the west side would be that much smaller column of marines. If they'd kept to the cover of the Careenage Ravine they'd be breaking out by now and he could use it himself to get back. He could follow it to the Victoria Ravine, to the windmill and Light Division camp, everything as he'd planned it last night, before he made himself stay to help Jarvis.

Jarvis. Every other thought receded until he could see only those layered jowls and malicious eyes. He could smell the sweat of him, feel the weight of that wheezing body as he'd supported it with his own. Never mind his life, never mind his information, he was going to get back somehow just to get even with Troop Sergeant-Major Jarvis.

Inch by inch, hand over hand, he crawled up the side of the gully. Handholds were there when he reached for them, a spindly tree trunk, a handful of bramble, the curve of a boulder, he reached out and found them and hauled himself up. He was out of the gully and facing the steep slope of the Careenage Ridge. Behind him came the pounding of artillery, cannon on Shell Hill, heavy firing down towards the Inkerman defences, and underneath the guns the roar of fighting men. He paused a moment, wondering if their spy was already among them, but there was little scope for misdirection when the enemy leaped out and started firing cannon.

But if he wasn't here today he would be tomorrow and Ryder had to go on. His leg kept buckling, his head throbbed, and blood crept in his eyes, but step by step he made it up the ridge and started gratefully down the other side. The crashing of cannon receded, but now he heard other, lighter sounds, small-arms fire ahead. He couldn't see anything, the ground was clear, but the firing grew more and more intense and then a ball whined straight past his head. He threw himself down, cursing his own stupidity. Of course he couldn't see anything, the firefight was in the bloody ravine.

It sounded savage too. As he edged closer he heard more shots flying and ricocheting off the stony slopes, whistling out to spend themselves in the ridge behind. The marines must be down there, they hadn't broken out after all, and someone was making a very determined effort to stop them. Those were the people he needed. All he had to do was walk on until he got behind the fight, then climb on down to join them.

But he was hardly even walking now, his legs were soft and clumsy and his back wrenched with pain at every step. The fight was driving forward as if the defence were falling back, and his progress felt dreamlike, walking but getting no nearer. Still he went on, yard after yard, and gradually the shots grew louder and more distinct, howling back and forth down the walls of the ravine. The resisting force weren't falling back any more but had found somewhere to make a stand. He forced up his head and saw orange flashes cracking from behind a grey line of earthworks, a trench across the junction of the Mikriakoff Glen and the Wellway. The men firing from it would be British.

He thought he could make it. The ravine was growing shallower to its end, but the Russians were still firing from inside. A few were on the slopes and banks, but if he kept low to the ground they mightn't notice him as he edged the last yards to that trench. He crouched down for one last effort, and the ball spat right past his ear.

Idiot, idiot, fool and idiot, he was wearing Russian cross-belts over the coat, of course his own side would fire on him. He stayed low, waved frantically, and yelled, 'British! I'm British! Prisoner coming back in!'

Another ball flew past, this time from the ravine. Now he'd got the Russians on him, imagining there were men coming to take them in the flank. Frustration and rage threw him forward, two good strides then down again, crouching behind a miserable bunch of thistles. Someone shouted from the trench, but the words were lost in gunfire, he heard only their Englishness and the single word 'yourself'. They'd take orders from a Russian, but give them a bloody Englishman and they suddenly remembered the rulebook. He shouted back 'I'm Ryder, 13th Light Dragoons, now let me in, you bastards!'

He heard gruff laughter. Someone yelled 'Come on, then' and he saw with astonished gratitude two men turn to give covering fire at the Russians in the ravine.

One last gasp. He gulped a breath and jerked forward, up from the ground and into the open. Crouching and stumbling, falling and lurching, another ball zipping overhead. A fit man could have run it in ten seconds, but his body couldn't even stagger, the bloody thing was giving up, and his next thrust forward only pitched him on his face.

And someone was coming at him, feet thudding fast over the ground. He rolled to face the danger, saw a grey coat stooping over him, struck out and hit only cloth. A reproachful voice said 'Cut that out, will you?' and strong arms wrapped round his chest, lifting and supporting him onto tottery feet. A hand grasped his wrist, his arm was tugged round a set of broad shoulders, and the face by his own was a friend's.

'Come on,' said Woodall, tightening the grip round his waist. 'I've got you, come *on*!'

A musket banged, and he was propelled violently forward, half-dragged, half-carried, his feet skimming the grass as they ran. Shots still pinged about them, but they were already leaping over a soft mound, then a sharp jolt down, loose earth sliding under his feet and he landed with a thump in a crowded trench. 'There,' said Woodall triumphantly, propping him against the wall. 'You're in the lines, you're safe.'

He wasn't. As he took in his surroundings he realized the trench was no more than a shallow dug-out, and the grey-coated men packed into it couldn't number more than sixty. How many Russian marines had there been – seven, eight hundred? His companions were firing with nonchalant steadiness, independently loading and firing, loading and firing, guided only by shouts of 'Breaking out left!', 'Watch your right!', and the calm voice of an officer calling 'Come on, chaps, you can hold them', but they couldn't, not possibly, and he was no safer down here than he'd been in the open. He struggled up to look for a weapon.

'Stay *down!*' ordered Woodall, slamming him back against the wall. 'I'm not saving you again, stay down!'

Ryder winced with the pain. 'Careful, you great ox, mind the back.'

Woodall blinked in surprise, then actually grinned. 'And you mind your manners,' he said. 'You're with Her Majesty's Guards now, you'll do what you're ruddy well told.' He wadded his handkerchief, placed it on Ryder's head, said 'Hold it there', then turned calmly back to the parapet. A second later he fired.

Ryder watched him with confused wonder. It was Woodall all right, the voice was as pompous as ever, the bearing just as stiff, and the little red scratches on his jaw only bore witness to the ferocity with which he'd obviously tried to shave a week's growth of beard. But he was loading and firing as naturally as a man making tea, thinking of nothing but what he was doing, and spitting his cartridge tops with total unconcern for where they landed. When he missed a shot he yelled 'Damn it!' and didn't care who heard him. He was a soldier among soldiers, and that wretched haunted figure who'd clutched at the blanket in Balaklava had vanished as if he'd never been.

And Ryder envied him. That was what he wanted, to fight with his own side, not sit back helplessly when every man was needed. A soldier without a weapon was unmanned and useless, and Ryder was stained with the memory of his own surrender. He sat up and said, 'Come on, Woodall, I've got to have a gun.'

Woodall hesitated, then seemed to understand. He called down the line, 'Anybody down? We need another rifle.'

Impossible to believe not one had been hit, but it was still several minutes before a rifle was passed down. The stock was bloodstained and sticky, but it was a weapon and with it came a cartridge pouch and percussion caps. Ryder seized it gratefully and squeezed himself round to face the parapet.

'Can you load?' said Woodall, squinting down his barrel and firing another shot. 'The Minié's complicated, you know, you don't just point it and fire.'

Ryder grinned at the familiar superiority and began to load as Ginger had painstakingly shown him. 'Will it go bang, do you think?'

Woodall's head shot round, but then he saw what Ryder was doing and relaxed. 'Look, stop putting me off, will you? I'm trying to fight a battle.'

'So am I,' said Ryder, and rammed the ball. 'You and me, Woody, let's drive those bastards back.'

Woodall's face lightened. He said, 'Come on then, donkey-walloper,' and in a few seconds Ryder planted his barrel beside him. The Russians were mostly pressed into the sides of the ravine or hiding in the brush, but then a couple broke cover to fire at their flank and Ryder pulled the trigger with an almost physical sense of release.

'Reload,' said Woodall. They started together, but the Guard was finished and shooting before Ryder had even pressed on his cap. This was his weapon and his war, he was completely at home and gave the impression of actually enjoying it.

Ryder would have enjoyed it more with another six hundred men beside them. 'Where's the rest of you? The First Division, where is it?'

'Aren't any "rest",' said Woodall. 'We're just a bunch of sharp-shooters caught on the hop, that's all.' His barrel tracked back and forth as he scoured the ground for movement. 'But there's a bigger column of the bastards peppering away on Shell Hill, and if we don't hold this lot here the Second Division will be getting it from both sides.'

Ryder remembered the vast force he and Jarvis had marched out with, and knew the Second would be hard put to resist them even without the marines in their rear. 'We can't hold them much longer, can we? Not with so few?'

'Oh, can't we?' said Woodall. 'We've held them two hours already, and I don't see them breaking out, do you?' He fired at a grey shape creeping from the brushwood and turned again to reload.

But they were definitely getting bolder. The shooting grew more sporadic, just enough to keep them pinned down in their trench, and every few minutes a bunch would surge out to rush their position. The Guards' officer was calling as calmly as ever 'Breaking right! Pot that fellow, Ashton!' and using his own pistol with devastating accuracy, but if the Russians tried a concerted dash they'd be overrun in seconds. The barrel of the Minié was growing warm to Ryder's touch, and when he reached for another cap his fingers fumbled and dropped it.

'Fiddly things, aren't they?' said Woodall kindly, snapping on his own with a sharp click. 'Don't worry, I've got dozens.'

So had Ryder, the tin was full of the tiny metal cylinders, but when he next turned to reload he found his cartridge pouch empty. Others seemed in the same position, he saw men patting their pockets and turning to mutter to their neighbours, a chilling reminder that they couldn't hold much longer. He whispered, 'Woody, have you got . . . ?'

Woodall's mouth tightened as he saw the empty pouch, but he reached at once inside his greatcoat and dug out a packet of his own. 'Here,' he whispered. 'Here.' Their fingers brushed as he passed it over, the ordinary intimacy of men who fought in the line.

Ryder reloaded with renewed urgency. The enemy were breaking out everywhere, spreading into the brushwood right where he'd been lying, where he'd be lying still if Woodall hadn't come for him. A shot chipped the lip of the trench, spraying earth into his face and stinging his eyes; he couldn't even see to bloody load. More gunfire behind, a whole volley, and he swung round blindly to confront the new threat, but the shots were blasting clean over their heads, over them and into the Russians. He blinked his eyes clear and glimpsed dark green in the rocks at the mouth of the Wellway, men fanning out in skirmish order, dropping behind rocks and bushes, standing against trees, dropping on their arses and firing between their feet in Plunkett's Position right in the open. The Rifle Brigade, the bloody beautiful Rifle Brigade was here and they were reinforced at last.

'Keep firing, chaps!' called their own captain. 'Now we'll jolly well show them!'

They hardly needed to. The Russians seemed demoralized by this unexpected relief, and after a few desultory exchanges they disappeared into the cover of the ravine and began to retreat. Ryder lowered his rifle warily, expecting them to cross the open ground to join their own main force, but in the silence of their own skirmish he became aware for the first time of a different sound to the gunfire from Shell Hill. The noise seemed both louder and more distant, dominated by guns facing out towards the Russians from the front of the British Heights. Somehow the Second Division had held long enough to move their own artillery into place, and the enemy advance was stopped in its tracks.

'Bloody Light Division,' said Woodall sourly, retrieving his fallen handkerchief and whacking it back on Ryder's head like a bad-tempered nursemaid. 'Turning up at the last minute to take all the credit, you'd think they'd have more shame.'

Ryder looked at him, and the horror and tension of the last twenty-four hours balled into a single tightness in his chest that could only be relieved one way. He laughed until his guts hurt and the tears were wet on his cheek, and beside him Dennis Woodall was laughing too.

19

26 October 1854, 4.00 p.m. to 11.00 p.m.

The gunfire from Inkerman grew quieter and more sporadic, and Mackenzie was not sorry when the Highlanders were stood down without being called to engage. He'd have liked another crack at those Russians, but it had been the turn of other men to be heroes today, and he was growing impatient to learn what had come of his friends.

The Light Brigade were easy to find, poor souls, wandering the plain like lost children as they retrieved their bits and pieces from the abandoned camp by the redoubts. He rejoiced at the sight of Polly Oliver alive and dragging a ten-man tent all by himself, but the laddie had a bandaged leg and red eyes, and seized Mackenzie's hands with fingers that trembled and clenched white. 'Ryder's gone, Niall,' he said. 'Did you know that? Ryder's gone.' He was shivering in the afternoon sun.

Mackenzie buried his own sorrow, and helped carry the heavy canvas to the new cavalry camp by the Col, but it was more than shelter that Oliver needed. He was twitching all the while the tent was going up, and it was all Mackenzie could do to make him sit still inside it. At last he dug out his coffee ration and said sternly 'Relax now, will you, and let's make us a brew. The guns have stopped, it's over for the day.'

Oliver groped dutifully for a mess-tin. 'But Woodall might have been in it. And Bloomer, I haven't seen his cart go past all day.'

The laddie had lost half his friends the day before, it was understandable he'd no wish to lose more. 'Ah, they'll be grand,' he said comfortably. 'Woodall's never fit enough to have been in action today, and Bloomer was born to be hanged.'

Oliver creased his forehead. 'I thought you said Woodall was joining the . . .'

He stopped abruptly at the sound of hooves. Someone was galloping, and a voice yelled, 'My God, look who's back!' Oliver hurtled at the door flap, bashing the canvas out of his way like gauze, and Mackenzie followed with a sudden hope in his heart.

Men stood in amazement as a horse reined to a stop in front of them, its rider clad in a grey coat and the overalls of the 13th Light Dragoons. He dismounted heavily, and turned to show a face of mutton-chop whiskers and many chins.

Oliver's shoulders sagged. Mackenzie said casually, 'A friend of yours, is it?'

'Jarvis. He's the man who had Ryder flogged.'

Oh, *was* he now? An excited little group was following the man, and Mackenzie strolled among them for a closer inspection. A woman at a fire stood to meet them, and the blue dress and fair hair identified her at once as the lady he'd met after the Alma.

'That's Sally,' whispered Oliver. 'That's Mrs Jarvis.'

He'd not have guessed it from the brusqueness of her husband's greeting. The man said only 'Tea, woman', then turned to a shabby lieutenant with a bandaged arm and a tired face. 'Sergeant-Major Jarvis reporting for duty, sir,' he said, and snapped off a salute that made his whole stout little body quiver.

Mackenzie studied him, this man who'd thought it a fine thing to flog his friend. He was swelling his chest like a pigeon as he told how he'd escaped from a whole army of Russians by stealing a horse under their noses, but he was not so very formidable at close quarters and Mackenzie decided he could take him if he'd a mind.

'Any other prisoners, Sar'nt-major?' asked the officer, producing a notebook. 'Anyone of our regiment?'

Oliver tensed beside him, and Mackenzie hushed his own breathing to listen.

'Oh yes, sir,' said the sergeant-major importantly. 'TSM Linkon, oh and Smith, sir, I saw them both. Private Harris I saw, Duke and McCann, but no one else. Of course we weren't all together, it was mostly only glimpses.'

'It's a start,' said the lieutenant, writing furiously. 'It gives us something to write to the families.' He closed the notebook and shoved it in his pocket. 'Ryder's gone, presumably? You were last seen with him.'

Jarvis held up his head like a man at court-martial. 'Afraid so, sir. He *was* a prisoner, but he got himself shot trying to escape.'

Oliver made a stifled exclamation. The sergeant-major glanced round only briefly, but the flash of malice in his eyes made Mackenzie catch his breath. That man was a liar.

'Well, can't be helped,' said the lieutenant, sticking his pencil behind his ear. 'You're wounded, Sar'nt-major? You need an orderly?'

'Not me, sir,' said Jarvis heroically. 'Scratch in the leg, that's all. I've had it patched at Kadikoi or I'd have been back here before now.'

That at least might be true, for the hospital had been heaving when Mackenzie set out, filled with the casualties of two battles. They were still coming through now, wagons rattling down to Balaklava, but Mackenzie's eyes brightened as the last cart turned towards the cavalry camp instead. It bore a green stripe round its body, and the redcoat driving might perhaps be Bloomer.

Mrs Jarvis was giving her husband tea, and the lieutenant stepped tactfully back. 'All right, Sar'nt-major, I'll inform the colonel, and leave you with your very capable wife.' He smiled at Mrs Jarvis and walked away.

The sergeant-major sipped complacently, then let his eye fall on Oliver. 'Don't look so down in the mouth, Trooper, it's the best thing that could have happened to you.'

Oliver started. 'Sar'nt-major?'

Jarvis smiled. 'You were shaping up a nice little soldier. Ryder was a thorough bad influence.'

Oliver was silent. So was Mrs Jarvis. Mackenzie looked at their faces and stepped boldly forward. 'You'll excuse me, Sergeant-major, but if Ryder was shot might he not be still alive?'

Jarvis looked him up and down and gave a little snort. 'Not a chance. First shot winged him and he sobbed for mercy, but the second put him out of it, I saw it myself.'

Another bloody lie. 'You didn't see him die.'

'Sawnie,' said Jarvis almost lovingly. 'I saw his bloody brains.'

'Polly!' cried a voice behind, and there was the dead man himself, leaping off the cart as if he'd just nipped to Balaklava for more shells. 'Told you so, didn't I say you'd make it?'

Ryder it was, a man who'd never cried for mercy in his life. He'd his old limp back, his head was bandaged, and his dragoon's coat seemed to have lost every one of its buttons, but he walked through the camp as if he owned it. A trooper cried 'Bloody hell, trouble's back' and he said just 'Shut it, Telegraph', cuffed the man affectionately, and came on.

Everyone watched him. Behind him strolled Bloomer and the impressively bearskinned figure of Woodall, but it was Ryder people stared at, Ryder and the sergeant-major who stood rooted by his wife's fire as if he'd never move again. The man was pale as suet, eyes shrinking to hide in the folds of his face, and the bristles on his jaw showing dark, dark blue.

The camp hushed as Ryder approached the fire. Jarvis braced himself, but Ryder merely sidestepped him to get to his friends. 'Niall, you old hero,' he said, thrusting his hand into Mackenzie's own. 'I heard about the 93rd.' To Oliver he said just 'Hullo, Polly', but he grasped both his hands and the grin split his face. Mrs Jarvis he greeted with a smile that said a wee bit more than it should, but he said only 'Is that for me?' and nodded hopefully towards her teapot. The sergeant-major made a little choking sound, and it was only then that Ryder paused, let his smile fade, then turned around to face him.

Mackenzie caught his breath. This was a lowly private confronting an NCO, but Jarvis held himself stiff and upright while

Ryder seemed relaxed to the point of insolence. He looked the sergeant-major up and down, gave a casually lopsided smile, and said, 'Hullo, Jarvis, hope the horse was a good one. I picked the best I could.'

Now that was a silence. The sergeant-major should be bellowing outrage at being addressed in such a way, but Mackenzie heard only a faint wheezing from that puffed-out barrel of a chest. Ryder waited courteously with his head on one side, and somewhere in the crowd a man laughed.

The sergeant-major's tongue flicked furtively over his lips. 'Trooper. I could have sworn you'd had it.'

'It's not your fault I hadn't,' said Ryder. 'Sar'nt-major.'

Jarvis's eyes darted from side to side. He said, 'You watch your tone, Trooper, you watch your mouth,' but his voice lacked authority and his shoulders were hunching like a Shetland bull's.

Ryder laughed. 'Scared of what I might say?'

Jarvis twitched. It was a tiny movement, quick suppressed, but Mackenzie heard the response all round him, clothing rustling and boots creaking, while beside him Bloomer muttered 'Now then' and stepped back. Mrs Jarvis's face had turned stark white.

Not Ryder. He looked at the sergeant-major's frustrated fury, and a kind of light leaped into his eyes. 'Is that it, Sar'nt-major? Do I frighten you?'

Jarvis almost spat his answer. 'You? A man who surrendered without so much as a scratch on him? The kind of man whose only wounds are on his back?'

A muscle ticked in Ryder's cheek. He moved forward, and Mackenzie took one stride to block him. 'Come on, man, we've a fire, you'll want a brew before you –'

An arm struck across his chest and Ryder turned him a face he hardly knew. 'Get away, Mackenzie, I'm warning you.'

He couldn't, the fool would get himself flogged or hanged. He stumbled back at him, but Ryder was stopped still and staring, and in the silence Mackenzie heard the voice of a woman.

Mrs Jarvis had moved between them and was taking her husband's arm.

'You shouldn't be standing, Jarvis,' she said calmly. 'You're wounded, your leg's hurt, please sit down.' She indicated an upturned box by the fire.

Now there was a clever woman. Ryder would never hit a seated man, no, nor a wounded one, and Mackenzie saw his shoulders subside. Jarvis grumbled 'We're talking, woman', but he sat as his wife bade him and the watching men seemed to shift and relax.

All but Ryder. The fight might be out of him but there was no mistaking the balked look on his face. He wiped the back of his hand across his mouth and said, 'All right, I can wait. I'll have to report to the officers anyway, won't I?'

There it was again, that flash of fear in the NCO's eyes. 'I'll go with you.'

Ryder smiled. 'Why? You already know what I'm going to say.'

Mackenzie was beginning to think he did too. Others maybe felt the same, for there was an awful lot of murmuring going on around him. He heard the words 'Ryder' and 'Jarvis' and 'horse'.

Jarvis sprang up and said, 'Dismiss, damn you! By God, there'll be some drilling tomorrow morning. Back to your business before I put the lot of you on a charge!'

The crowd began to disperse, but they were still muttering and Mackenzie guessed the story would be all round camp in an hour. Jarvis seemed to know it too, for he sat back down with the slump of a man defeated. His very chest seemed to have shrunk inside his shirt.

Ryder glanced down at him, then picked up Mrs Jarvis's teapot. 'Oh come on, Sar'nt-major, you must know I won't tell the officers.'

Jarvis stared, but Ryder seemed concerned only with the tea. He said, 'May I, Sal?' and poured without waiting for a response.

Jarvis said hoarsely, 'What do you mean?'

Ryder drank back the tea in one long draught. Mackenzie watched his throat moving convulsively at every swallow and began to understand a little of what the man must have been through. He finished at last, said, 'Bless you, Sally, I needed that,' and turned to go.

'Wait,' said Jarvis, and his voice was little more than a croak. 'What do you mean, you won't tell them?'

Ryder paused. 'It's between you and me, isn't it? Do you think I'm the kind of coward who brings in the army to do his dirty work for him?'

The sergeant-major flinched violently, but Ryder was already walking away. 'Come on, Polly, tell me what's going on here, then I'd better go and report.'

Mackenzie followed them, but with an uncomfortable feeling he found hard to dismiss. No doubt the sergeant-major deserved what was done, but it seemed to the Highlander a sad blow at the natural order of things. He glanced back half regretfully, but Jarvis was staring at Ryder's back and the sight of his expression stopped Mackenzie mid-stride. This was an NCO, an important link in the hierarchy, but he'd a look in his face that in a private soldier would surely be called murderous.

There was no need to grovel for admission this time. Syme was emerging from Doherty's tent as Ryder reached it, and his whoop of recognition brought the colonel himself to the entrance. He said, 'What the devil are you yelping at, Syme?' then saw Ryder and stopped dead.

For one, two seconds they stared at each other. The Old Man's face was still grey, but his shoulders were straight and his eyes held their former alertness. There was something else in them too, and Ryder had to swallow hard before he remembered to salute.

'Ah, ah, yes,' said Doherty, hastily clearing his throat. 'Well come on in, Trooper, I imagine you're here to report.' He turned and stalked back into the tent.

Ryder followed through the flap and found the colonel waiting for him with outstretched hand.

'Escaped, did you, boy?' he said, shaking his hand vigorously. 'Well done. Well done.' He seemed reluctant to let go.

'I'm sorry, sir. Did they tell you I was dead?'

'They did,' said Doherty, eyebrows bristling. 'I think TSM Jarvis has some explaining to do.' He released Ryder's hand and stalked round to his chair.

Ryder took a deep breath. 'There's no need, sir. It was a misunderstanding. I'll tell Lieutenant Grainger.'

Doherty looked sharply at him, then lowered himself carefully into his chair. 'Going to deal with it yourself, hey? That the idea?'

'There's nothing to deal with, sir.'

'Humph,' said Doherty, with a hint of his old fierceness. 'Well, keep it out of the troop, Harry. I can't have personal feuds interfering with the regiment.' He settled back in his chair and added soberly, 'This one's done quite enough damage already.'

Ryder wondered how much he knew. 'Sir?'

Doherty glowered at the desk, then lifted his chin to look him square in the face. 'I hope I needn't tell you how damnably sorry I am, Harry. About – what happened.' His hand moved in a vague circle, a strange gesture for something as brutal as flogging.

He didn't want to talk about that. 'Not your fault, sir. You ordered me to leave it alone.'

Doherty rubbed his hand over his face. 'I'd still have stopped it if I'd known. Poor Marsh, not blaming him, damned awful position to be in, but I'd have stopped it if I could. I could at least have told them you meant well, that you were in earnest about this traitor.'

The Old Man's mood was sympathetic, there'd never be a better time. 'I was wrong about the traitor.'

Doherty looked up. 'What's that? What makes you . . . ?'

'He's not a staff officer, he's not even British. He's a Russian spy.'

The colonel's face was almost comical. He stood like a man in a dream, then shut his mouth with a snap. 'Good God, boy, if you could convince me of that you'd give me the best night's sleep I've had in a week.'

'There's one easy way to prove it, sir. Do you have the casualty returns for yesterday?'

Doherty's face clouded again as he picked up a sheaf of papers from his desk. 'Dreadful, just dreadful. Incomplete, of course, but we'll know more when the Russians name their prisoners.'

'Then here's the question, sir. Are any staff officers listed as missing?'

Doherty lowered the papers, a startled look in his eyes. 'That's just the thing, Harry. Lord George has one listed as prisoner, someone must have seen one taken, but the fact is there's none missing. Damned odd thing, Grainger commented on it too. Are you telling me . . . ?'

The relief of certainty was almost shocking. 'Yes, sir. Yes, I –'

'Sit down,' said Doherty, shooting out from behind the desk. 'You're done in, boy, I should have realized . . .'

'No, sir, thank you, I'm all right.' He blinked away the dizziness and tried to think straight. 'I'm sure I can tell you more when I've talked to my friends, but we'll need facts confirmed, and we'll need your help.'

'You'll have it,' said Doherty. 'Anything you want, name it. Give me the facts and I swear we'll act on them.'

He hesitated. 'My friends, sir, they're from other regiments . . .'

'Give me their names,' said Doherty, returning briskly to the desk. 'I'll send to their COs, get permission for them to stay overnight. We need to move fast now, Harry; I want a complete report by the morning.'

Ryder gave him the names, marvelling at the difference between reporting a Russian spy and a British traitor. 'That's all I need, sir.'

Doherty laid down the pen. 'All you'll ask for, you mean. You deserve a lot more.' He hesitated, then bent to a large box in a corner of the tent. 'Here, take this for tonight. We'll sort out something more permanent in the morning.' He passed over a green bottle bearing the familiar label of Moët et Chandon.

Ryder blinked at it, aware of a sudden lump in his throat. 'There's no need, sir.'

'Isn't there?' said Doherty and his voice sounded unusually gruff. 'Wish I could undo it all, Harry. Now off you go, you've a job to do.'

He walked out in a daze. A few hours ago he'd been hunted and desperate, as low as a man could be, and now he was strolling to meet his friends with the thanks of his colonel and a bottle of champagne. He felt himself grinning like an idiot, and didn't give a damn who saw him.

Dusk was falling, but a fire burned outside their tent and Woodall was making coffee. Mackenzie lounged on his back smoking his pipe, and Bloomer was making a great to-do with clinking mugs. They'd got candles too, and behind them the tent glowed with yellow light like a saint's niche in church. The flap moved and the firelight shone on Oliver's blond head as he came out with a little coloured box Ryder had never thought to see again. Only Polly Oliver would have ridden down the North Valley and back still carrying a pack of cards.

'Oi, Tow-Row,' said Bloomer. 'You got another mug for Ryder? He'll be sans kit, remember.' Woodall threw him a mug without speaking, but a moment later he muttered 'And it's Woody, actually. My friends call me Woody.' Mackenzie took the pipe out of his mouth as if to say something, then stuck it back in and just smiled.

Ryder smiled too, enjoying the sight of them together. Bloomer was new to the group but he fitted like a piece in a puzzle and made them complete. Looking at them made it easier to forget the sour smell of a man he'd nursed last night with his own body and who today had tried to kill him. And Doherty was right, he did have to forget it. Jarvis had let personal hatred get in the way of fighting the real enemy, and Ryder mustn't make the same mistake.

He strolled out of the shadows and held out the bottle. 'Little present from Colonel Doherty.'

Four faces gaped at him, then Bloomer sprang to his feet. 'Fizz,' he said with respect, grasping the bottle firmly in a hairy fist. 'Fizz, no less. This colonel, would he be the one . . . ?'

'He would,' said Ryder gravely. 'He's also arranging for you to stay tonight because he wants us to talk about our traitor.'

Bloomer's jaw slackened. 'Wants? He actually *wants* . . . ?' He gave it up and blew out his cheeks in disbelief.

'I'm glad,' said Oliver, with a new chill in his voice. 'I'm afraid I want to talk about him too.'

His tone sobered them. Bloomer put the champagne reluctantly aside, Woodall poured coffee, and they settled by the fire in all the solemnity of jurors sitting down to a trial.

But Ryder's calm shattered as he listened to Oliver's story. The bastard had shot at Sally. He'd sprung the trap that caused the Light Brigade's charge and the deaths of two hundred men. Raglan, Lucan, Nolan, they'd all played their part, but it was this man who'd forced the action and led Raglan to give an order which would any way destroy them. Ryder had suspected it, now he knew it, and wanted only to kill this man with his own hands.

Oliver came to an end. 'It's maddening that nobody knew him,' he said. 'It seems so silly, but I think everyone just assumed someone else did.'

It was Ryder's turn. 'Sillier than you know, Poll, since he isn't even British at all.'

Movement rustled round the fire as if everyone had stretched their legs at once. 'It's no possible,' said Mackenzie. 'How could a foreigner get himself so close to our leaders?'

Ryder explained. The perfect English, the lack of security, the politeness that never asked questions, he went through it all and reminded them of the telling conversation with the Bulgar. 'It wouldn't be so hard, Niall. Every day, yes, sooner or later he'd be spotted, but he only seems to turn up when there's a battle and everything's in chaos.'

Bloomer pursed his lips. 'He'd need uniform. He'd need the full rig-out.'

Ryder spread his hands. 'The frock-coat's easy, any European gentleman would have one. But a weaver hat's uniform, it would need to be exactly right.'

Oliver nodded. 'Could he have got one from a prisoner?'

'Not before the Alma,' said Woodall. 'They didn't have any prisoners before then.'

Mackenzie's pipe made a little clink as it dropped against the kettle. 'But they tried, didn't they, Woody? You'll mind of it, that day on the beach? Sir George Brown himself?'

Woodall sat bolt upright. 'Bloody hell, yes. Those Cossacks on the cliff. They went right after a staff officer and nearly got him.'

'They did that,' said Mackenzie. 'And maybe they got something after all. He fled in such haste the hat flew off him, do you not recall?' He made a slow see-sawing motion of his hand through the air. 'I mind the shape of it falling to ground.'

'Yes,' said Woodall, gesturing wildly. 'And something else, do you remember *this*? I sent them packing, and I said there were two of them and you said no, you thought there were three.'

'So I did,' said Mackenzie, nodding violently. 'That's the right of it. They had a force right in the heart of us, and when they went they left one behind.'

They grinned at each other, then Woodall sat back with sudden self-consciousness, and Mackenzie relit his pipe. The quiet seemed even heavier than before.

'Right back then,' said Oliver wonderingly. 'You think he joined us right at the start?'

'Perfect time, Polly,' said Ryder. 'All that confusion, remember? Rain and dark, people separated from their units, we could have had the Tsar there and not known.'

Oliver looked at the tents around them as if he expected to see a shadowy figure listening in the gloom. 'But not a staff officer. We were all desperate for orders and direction, you couldn't be a staff officer on that beach and not be besieged by people asking questions.'

'He wouldn't have to be a staff officer from the first, would he? Any kind of officer would do; we all looked alike in that rain.' He ran his hands down his own coat and realized again how easy it was. 'No one looks, Polly, don't you see? Two of us marched right in with the Russians today and nobody noticed.'

'Four,' said Woodall importantly. 'Our Captain Goodlake, him and Sergeant Ashton got cut off at the start of the fight today. They came back same as you did, right in the column of Russians, and they weren't even in disguise.'

Mackenzie puffed on his pipe. 'Ah, but the coats look the same. These men on the cliffs now, they were Cossacks. Maybe a wee grey cloak on them, but the jackets were any old colour. One was green.'

'He could have stolen clothes,' said Oliver. 'It was that night de Lacy Evans's servant was stabbed, wasn't it? Our officer said some things had been taken.'

Bloomer fingered his chin. 'A tile maybe, bits and pieces, but not a full rig-out, I'd have heard about that. He wouldn't need it neither. We had dead 'uns everywhere, a cove could pick up a tog and kicks to fit him in no time. I had one or two off them myself.'

Oliver looked at him in horror. 'You robbed the dead?'

Bloomer rolled his eyes. 'Oh, come out the pulpit, Polly, take a gander at what Ryder's wearing. It wasn't for myself neither, I even give a Benjamin to one of you horseboys, didn't I? Cove called Joe Sullivan, though I heard he rolled over not long after.'

Ryder pictured the dead face in the rain, and something turned over inside his chest. He said, 'What's a Benjamin?' and was surprised to hear his voice shake.

Maybe Bloomer heard it too. He said simply, 'It's a coat. Joe was on the shallow that night, so I give him a cover-me-decent. A greatcoat.'

He knew it. 'He wasn't wearing one when we found him, was he, Niall? Nothing to keep out the rain.'

'I mind of it,' said Mackenzie gently. 'There was no coat on him then.'

There was a little silence. Woodall cleared his throat and said, 'Doesn't have to have been our man, though, does it? Sullivan fell, anyone could have found him.'

Ryder's fingers were hurting, and he realized how tightly he was clutching his mug. 'Joe didn't fall. He was too strong and steady for that.'

Oliver said hesitantly, 'He'd been flogged though, he was –'

'And so have I,' said Ryder. 'It was over a week since Joe was whipped and I can tell you, it's not that bad. He didn't fall, he went up those cliffs, someone killed him and threw him down, and that's not a soldier looking to pick up a stray coat, that's an enemy, the spy, the same bloody bastard it's been all along.'

He had to put the mug down, he was crushing the bloody thing. Useless, cheap tin.

A hairy paw reached down to pick it up and Bloomer's voice said, 'Chuck us the kettle, Woody. I'll make some more coffee against the cold.'

'Aye, there's a chill right enough,' said Mackenzie, and his hand patted lightly on Ryder's shoulder. 'Shall we move in the tent now, do you think? Seeing as we've this grand palace all to ourselves.'

He pulled himself together. 'Yes – yes, it's getting damp out here. Come on, Poll, let's get the gear in.'

He himself had none, but it was a ten-man tent for just five of them and compared to last night it was luxury. Oliver had arranged candles on an upturned box, but there was still a central space for them to sit round, an emptiness that became immediately suggestive. They exchanged furtive looks as grim sounds of coffee grinding began from outside.

'It wouldn't be right to go on talking without Bloomer,' said Oliver.

'Not at all,' agreed Mackenzie, sitting up expectantly. 'We need his opinion.'

'He could be a while, though,' said Ryder.

Woodall clapped his hands together and rubbed them with anticipation. 'Come on then, Polly, where are the cards?'

It felt right for them to be playing again, everything as it was on the night they'd just talked about. The tent kept them secret as the wagon had done, and Ryder remembered the sound of the rain on the groundsheet, the sporadic shouts from the Second Division, the distant crash of the sea. They played a hand in clubs, but were only halfway through the second when Bloomer appeared at the tent flap and began to pass in their mugs.

'Oh, that's friendly, that is,' he said, squeezing in with his own. 'Wait till my back's turned to get the broads out. What is it – biritch?'

'It's called "bridge", actually,' said Woodall with a sniff. 'It's a new kind of whist.'

'I know what it is, you cake,' said Bloomer, nodding at the exposed dummy hand. 'I learned it off prisoners after the Alma. That's biritch, that is, what some call Russian whist.'

The cards blurred in Ryder's hand, a slew of meaningless red and black, the letters and numbers cryptic as code. Bloomer was saying 'no, bir*itch*, listen, say it quick and it sounds the same', but nothing was the same because he knew now, so did Polly, so did Mackenzie, sitting still as photographs, both of them, and then Woodall shut up and knew too.

'What?' said Bloomer suspiciously. 'What?'

He let Oliver tell it, a story of four innocents who'd sat on a beach and let an enemy officer teach them cards. His own mind was only just facing it, what it meant and what he'd done. They were debating it now and he tried at least to listen, hoping some-one had an argument to make it not true, but they were going down one after the other like skittles. No, he wasn't a staff offi-cer, but then he wasn't bloody English either, he could dress as anything he pleased. He'd been wearing an officer's cap when they first met him, but that could have been de Lacy Evans's. He'd told them about the robbery himself, but then he'd had to, there were people hunting for him and a sergeant had even looked under their own wagon.

Everything fitted. The greatcoat, the timing, even the friendliness they'd liked so much. Of course he was bloody friendly, he needed their help to camouflage him from anyone looking for the rogue intruder. He'd been using them, he'd used all of them, and most of all he'd used the unspeakable fool that was himself. Even the cards at his feet seemed to mock him, the truth that had always been there and he'd never seen.

'And that patrol,' said Oliver, shock making his voice wobble. 'The one where we were lured into an ambush. He was with us, wasn't he, Harry? Do you think he did it on purpose?'

Ryder remembered him talking to Doherty, giving directions, making him go on. And the village they'd watered at, that was how the Russians knew they'd found it, that was why they'd burned it the day of the march. Everything, all of it, was down to this one man.

Mackenzie gave him a gentle kick. 'Ah, don't fret on it. And it's himself who's the fool now, thinking himself safe all this while and never an idea we're even looking for him.'

He had to tell them. 'He does know, Niall. He knows because I told him.'

Four faces turned to him as if pulled by a single string. He couldn't look at any of them and studied his coffee as he told the whole humiliating story. He explained it, the frustration of working without officers, the need for an ally somewhere, but he couldn't excuse it and didn't try. He said, 'I didn't give names, I only said what we knew, but it was all of it and more than enough. I told him about the saddlecloth and that's why he changed it. I even told him the bombardment was starting the next day, and the next thing we knew he was riding for Sebastopol. We thought there was a traitor in this army; well there is, and it's me.'

He put down the mug and waited.

'The bombardment,' said Oliver hesitantly. 'I've heard people

400

say the Russians could have seen our men cutting the embrasures the night before.'

He couldn't look up. 'We believed it was the traitor when it fitted our theory and made us feel important. Are we going to change that now it's no longer convenient?'

'No, cully, we're not,' said Bloomer, and his voice was suddenly very grim. 'I was there, I saw what happened, I know what it cost and I know we were blowed upon.'

Ryder knotted his hands until the knuckles shone white. He remembered Bloomer describing the direct hit on Mont Rodolphe, fifty men burned to black in a single instant.

Something gripped on his shoulder, a single hard squeeze from a meaty hand. 'I knows something else too,' said Bloomer's voice. 'The nob was with us the day before – remember? He was in our dog-leg fixing it for his pals to come chucking grenades. He spoke to us lobsters, he spoke to our officers, if there'd been a bleeding dog he'd have spoke to that too. You may have told him about the bombardment, but there's a score of us did the same.'

He couldn't even feel relief at first. His hands were hurting, he prised them apart, then turned to look in Bloomer's face.

'That's right, pal,' said the Fusilier. 'So stop hugging your guilt and drink your bleeding coffee.' He thumped Ryder on the shoulder and sat himself back down.

His raw skin throbbed from the thump. 'Doesn't make me any less stupid though, does it?'

'That depends,' said Mackenzie serenely. 'Did you tell him anything else now? This attack there was meant to be on Tuesday, did you say anything about that?'

'I would have done,' he said, and couldn't hide the bitterness. 'I couldn't get hold of him, that's all.' It made him sick to think how close it had been, how easily he could have told the bastard about Kamara, how Sally could have walked alone into a trap.

'Then there's no harm,' said Mackenzie. 'He was just what we'd all been seeking, a regular officer friendly enough to listen. No harm in it at all.'

Woodall cleared his throat. 'May even be good. You've seen him, haven't you? In broad day? You'd know him again.'

'Aye, and I would too,' said Mackenzie. 'Ryder held a candle while I poured the devil his coffee. I mind the face of him very well.' His fingers closed tightly round his mug, and behind those tranquil eyes something burned.

Bloomer pulled at his nose. 'I'd know him too, cully, but what good is it? Not likely to come strolling my way again, is he? Not now he knows we're fly.'

'But in a battle,' said Mackenzie. 'If he tries his tricks again, he'll no succeed with the 93rd.'

Bloomer snorted. 'That's prime, that is. Say I stops him with the 7th. Say Ryder gives him the bum's rush with the horseboys. What's that leave? Sixteen thousand?'

'It doesn't matter,' said Oliver quickly. 'Colonel Doherty will warn the commanders, we won't need to do a thing.'

'The commanders,' said Bloomer, and rolled his eyes. 'All right, maybe there won't be no more lying billy-doos from Raglan, but what about the swaddies? Is he going to tell them not to take orders from anyone they don't know? Nah, be your age, Polly, this wants more than warning. We've got to catch this Joe and do it quick.'

He was right. Ryder looked at the candles stuttering on their tin lids and pictured a storehouse at Balaklava, the voice of an officer who'd said he could call him 'Angelo'. Irony? He remembered the man's humour and felt a sudden certainty that his real name was Michael. What other clues had he given? What was there in that conversation he could use?

His mind stopped at the sound of gunshots outside. Muskets – and the boom of a distant cannon. Impossible, not again, and for a second he saw the shock on all their faces, then the trumpet called and it was real. He extinguished the candles and crawled after the others into the night.

Darkness, and men running blindly for horses that had died the day before. A few were getting saddles up, the poor remnant of the Light Brigade, but many stood as helpless and horseless as himself. Woodall had a rifle, and Oliver took out his Adams, but Ryder had neither sword nor gun, and could only stand in frustration as he listened to the hundreds of hooves galloping towards them out of the dark.

But only hooves. He heard no shouts, no more gunfire, just hooves and snorting and the whinnying of frightened beasts. An officer yelled 'Hold your fire, hold your fire!' and then shapes began to form, looming nearer, cavalry horses galloping into camp, but all with empty saddles. The back of his neck felt suddenly cold. It was as if their own horses were come back out of the valley, carrying only the ghosts of the riders they'd left behind.

Jordan's voice cried, 'Russian horses, by damn! They've had a stampede!' A horse charged right by him, white vapour puffing from its panicked nostrils, and he saw it was true. Russian horses, scared by an alarm in the redoubts, looking for the safety of horse-lines and familiarity, and the Light Brigade camp had seemed to provide both. Laughing men trampled the scrub as they grabbed at bridles, soothing the animals, leading them to capture, a voice crying 'I'm calling mine Menschikoff!' and then another, nearer and softer, saying 'There, it's all right, I'll look after you, you're safe.' Polly Oliver holding the reins of a massive grey, stroking its nose and murmuring. It wasn't his lost mare, but perhaps at that moment it might as well have been.

For some it really was, and one horse cantering by wore a saddlecloth of the 4th Light Dragoons. Then another, and he stared in disbelief at a familiar chestnut form with his own saddle on its back. 'Tally!' he called, and then louder, '*Tally!*' She saw him, and trotted over, calmed at once by a familiar voice. He patted her in a daze, noting his own black lambskin still in place, just as he'd fastened it himself. She was a Russian horse, but they'd ridden together through the fire of the charge, there was a bond between them, and when he'd called her, she'd come.

His hand froze on her bridle. *When he'd called her, she'd come.*

'Ryder?' Oliver was beside him, holding the grey's bridle with shy pride. 'Are you all right?'

He grinned in sudden exaltation. 'Come on, Poll, let's get the beasts seen to, then it's time to open the champagne.'

Oliver's smile echoed his, but without understanding. 'Because . . . ?'

'Because Bloomer's right,' he said. 'Because we've got to catch this bastard, and I know just how we're going to do it.'

20

28 October to 5 November 1854

Ryder's boots crunched in the morning frost as he tramped down the track for Kadikoi. The last time he'd walked this road the wind had been howling, his back had been bleeding, and a cavalryman who'd never fought a battle had toiled at his side. Now the air was still and cold, the stripes on his back were healed by the three on his sleeve, and he walked with only the invisible company of an agent of Mr Calvert who was watching him all the way.

It was all Doherty's doing. He'd checked everything, he'd even had a quiet word with Sally, but it was he himself who'd provided the final proof. The ADC who accompanied them on patrol that day had given his name as Major Soames, and Doherty had only to ask General Airey to find no such man existed. He was red-faced with fury when he told Ryder about it, and tugged his beard hard enough to pull it out, but all he could say was, 'It's got to stop, my boy. Whatever you like, just make it *stop*.'

Nothing had been too much trouble for him. He'd briefed Calvert himself, he'd let Grainger into his confidence so Ryder was released from duty when he needed it, and he'd even told Jarvis enough to stop him interfering. He couldn't clear Ryder publicly, the affair still had to be secret for the sake of morale, but everyone knew he was admitted to Doherty whenever he chose, and no one was surprised when he appeared with his brand-new sergeant's stripes. It was the highest honour in the Old Man's gift, and if it couldn't take away Ryder's scars it was still more than he could ever have dreamed of before.

But not quite. What he really wanted was the man who'd

caused all this in the first place, and at last they stood a chance of getting him. The mysterious Mr Calvert had issued a few words of command, the entire Turkish sick camp had been moved, and the well at Kadikoi was once more open for business. Doherty wasn't sure Angelo would bother to check it, but Ryder had no such doubts. The thing had been blocked for near three weeks, they could have found out anything in that time, and of course the bastard would want to know. Not to check would be like playing biritch without looking to see what was in dummy's hand, and this man was a far better player than that.

Better than himself, probably. He'd spent hours crafting the letter, enough to draw him, not enough to scare him, it had to be a queen to finesse the king. At last he'd written only *Must see you. I learned something at Sebastopol and am very confused. I must go to my officers but will wait a week in the hope of hearing from you first.* Angelo wouldn't dare let it go, the queen might be a trick-winner if Ryder had evidence sufficiently dangerous, he'd have to cover it with the king – and then Calvert would take it with his ace.

Here was the field, and there was the well. He wondered if Angelo had noticed it was clear yet. He wondered if he was watching now. Ryder was taking no chances, which was why he was delivering the message himself and alone. He folded the paper small, groped to find the gap behind the rafters under the little tiled canopy, and slid the letter inside. There was his bid. No trumps, he was calling 'biritch', just two men and their cards and their skill. 'Come on then, you bastard,' he whispered. 'Just you and me. *Let's play.*'

Sally watched him every day. Every morning she walked the Kadikoi gorge on her way to Balaklava, and every morning he was walking back from the well with slumped shoulders and a look of sulky determination that told her at once there was no answer.

Jarvis watched him too, and in a way that frightened her. He hardly ever drank, he kept himself clean and steady for the army, but the day he learned of Ryder's promotion he threw back the rum till it sweated from the pores of his skin. 'You know how long it took me to make sergeant, Sal?' he said as she cleaned the vomit from his new coat. 'Eleven years. Eleven years of never putting a single foot wrong. Ryder doesn't give a whore's tit for the army, he's only in it for himself, and the cocky little shit gets it in less than two.'

'It's war, Jarvis,' she said, wiping his face and thanking God his wound still kept him off duty. 'Promotion comes quick when men die, you've always said so.'

'Dead men's boots,' he said, and laughed as if it were funny. 'But there's better men could have had it, corporals high on the list. This is for some stupid story about a spy.'

'But it's important, isn't it? That they catch him?' She reached for his cheek again, but he'd pulled right back and was looking at her as if she were dangerous.

'What do you know about it? What's it got to do with you?'

She hesitated, but there could be no harm in it now. Colonel Doherty had told him the most important things, and he should be allowed to know as much as his own wife. So she told him what had happened at Kamara, then put away her basin and started to make tea.

He looked at her with unfocussed eyes. 'You expect me to believe it was you who listened to those spies? That whole ridiculous story?'

'Of course,' she said, wishing the water would boil and she could get some tea down him. 'You believe Colonel Doherty, don't you? You know it happened, why shouldn't you believe I was there?'

He made a spitting noise and glared at the fire. 'I bloody *know* you were there. I checked at the hospital, didn't I? I know you sneaked out to meet a private soldier of my own troop. Doesn't mean you were out hunting spies, does it? Doesn't have to mean that at all.'

She stared at him in consternation. 'Oh, Ned. You've been

thinking . . . All this time you've been . . . Oh, my love, why didn't you tell me?'

He turned his head sideways to look at her. Sometimes he was angry if she said 'my love' in public, but his eyes were only sad. 'Why didn't you tell *me*, Sally? Sneaking round behind my back.'

She felt his unhappiness like a blow. 'You wouldn't have let me go. And if I'd told you afterwards, what would you have thought then?'

'I don't know,' he said. 'But you're kind that way, Sal, you're a fool, always have been. You'd tell a lie to help a presentable lad out of a hole.'

'Kind's not stupid,' she said. The water was ready, and she breathed in the tea smell as she poured into the pot. It was the third time for these leaves, they wouldn't take a fourth, but if she mashed them well it would still be a decent brew. 'I did it because it was important, and it *is* important, Colonel Doherty says so.'

'Doherty,' he said, and the sneer was back in his voice. 'Doherty's got himself a nice new pet now, hasn't he? Sergeant Ryder can do what he likes, go where he likes, Sergeant Ryder can do no fucking wrong.'

She wondered how to comfort him. 'It's only until Ryder catches the spy. That's what he's doing, he says the spy knows him and they're going to lure him into a trap.'

His voice sounded thick, and she hoped he wouldn't be sick again. 'He knows him. What – by name?'

'That's right,' she said, stirring the pot vigorously. 'He knows Ryder's after him, and we're hoping he'll want to stop him.'

He was silent. She looked up sharply, but he was still conscious, just sitting staring at nothing. 'Ned?'

After a moment he laughed, a terrible unhappy sound that confused her with tenderness. 'Tell me, Sal. Is there anyone in the whole fucking Crimea who hasn't made a fool out of me?'

She reached out, but he grunted angrily and struck her hands away. Touching was for night under the blanket when he couldn't sleep, not here in the open where someone might see. She said 'Who? Who's been . . . ?'

'Oh . . . no one,' he said, hunching himself up aggressively. 'Everyone. My own wife to know more than a sergeant-major in the 13th Light Dragoons.'

She was sure he'd meant something else, but he was too drunk to make sense. She poured the tea and hoped he'd stay awake long enough to drink it.

'Not my fault, was it?' he said to his boots. 'I did my best. All I've ever done is do my best.'

She held out the tea, but he didn't take it. He didn't even seem to see it.

'Makes no difference anyway,' he said. 'Deserved it, didn't he, the cocky little shit? Look at him now, always needling me, making people laugh. Oh, you just wait till this is over, Sal. You just wait.'

She offered the tea again, but he was collapsing slowly on his side and after a moment he began to snore.

She fetched his blanket, tucked it round him, and sat to drink the tea herself. 'When this is over,' he said, but it hadn't really started, and she was beginning to be afraid. The spy simply had to be caught before another battle came, and when she looked across at the Russian fires in the redoubts she knew it couldn't be long.

They were so close now! They would only need minutes to bring their cannon in range of Kadikoi. The British base was so small and vulnerable, and all but cut off from their siege lines now the Russians controlled the Woronzoff. The Col was open, but it was a longer route, and reinforcements could never move between their two forces in time. Cavalry could do it, of course, but there weren't many left of them, not now. There weren't many left of any of them. Cholera, the Alma, the disaster in the North Valley, people said the whole British force was down to about sixteen thousand men. They could hardly resist a determined attack as it was, and the spy in their midst would be the end of them.

She wasn't alone in her fears. A few days later the dawn patrol reported a large force heading south for Sebastopol, and there wasn't a man in the camp who didn't know what that meant. 'That's it, then, isn't it?' said Jordan, looking out towards the Russian-held redoubts. 'They're reinforced, they've got enough to attack. Domino, chum. We're finished.'

Finished. The morning was grey with rain, but Sally hardly noticed it as she set off for Balaklava. Jordan was right. She was only a woman, she knew nothing about the campaign and less about the war, but she knew a British army was about to be slaughtered thousands of miles from support and home.

She was nearing the turn to the field when she saw Ryder coming back from the well. They couldn't talk, of course, this Angelo might be watching, but she wiped the rain from her face and managed to give him a smile of encouragement.

And Ryder smiled back, a real, proper smile that made him look ten years old. They passed with three feet between them but she heard his whisper and it lifted her heart. 'Got him, Sal,' he said, and his eyes blazed with a hope she hadn't seen since they landed in this terrible country. 'He's answered, he wants a meeting, and *we've bloody got him*.'

He was a good player, this Angelo. He'd set the rendezvous for midnight by the windmill and ordered Ryder to come alone. It was true the Chersonese Uplands had plenty of cover and darkness would make Calvert's men even easier to hide, but success at biritch was down to counting losing cards rather than winning ones, and Ryder couldn't afford to hold any at all. A major Russian attack was inevitable now, and there would be no second chance.

Oliver obviously felt the same. He was grave all evening, and Ryder had an uneasy feeling he was doing a lot of praying. When it was time to leave he lent Ryder his cloak and said, 'You're going to be a hero, do you know that? It's what we all dream of.'

Ryder could guess at least one man who did. 'What's a hero, Polly? How do you know when you are one?'

Oliver considered. 'Well . . . You might get a medal.'

He was a good kid, and Ryder only wished he had a better army. 'Medals are for officers. All you or I will get is a campaign medal that says we were there. We'll probably get one for the bloody Alma.'

'There are other things,' said Oliver. 'Your name being read out at school. A plaque in the chapel. Something in the newspapers. I've a sister at home, she'd like that.'

'Well, I haven't,' said Ryder. 'And you don't get mentions for playing cards.'

They shook hands solemnly, then Oliver muttered, 'God bless you, Harry,' and stumbled back into the tent.

Ryder walked quickly away. He didn't want sentimentality tonight, he had a game to play with lives at stake. He needed only one companion, and it was stuck firmly in his belt under the cover of his jacket. Strange to think it was only Jarvis's bloody-mindedness that had stopped the Cossacks getting his revolver when he was captured, but he supposed even that bastard had his uses. What mattered was he had it now and all six chambers loaded.

The rain was only a fine drizzle as he crossed the valley, but the night was chilly and he was glad of Oliver's cloak. He'd like to have taken Tally, but that would have suggested collusion by his officers and Angelo wouldn't neglect the precaution of getting there early to watch him arrive. It was an hour's walk in the cold and wet, his back hurt and his leg ached, but he wasn't going to do a thing to rouse his opponent's suspicions.

The ground changed under his boots as he hit the track by the Col, the crisp, decisive steps of a man with a purpose. There would be a picquet watching from the Sapoune Ridge, but two of Calvert's men were with them tonight and he rounded the slope without challenge. The silence gave him a strange sense of invisibility, as if he were a ghost passing by.

He smiled at the thought, and started the steep haul up the pass. There'd be no more picquets now till the Guards' camp and no one else was likely to be strolling the wilds on a wet night in November. There were only two people in this isolated world of his: himself and the man he was going to destroy.

Oliver couldn't sleep. The tent felt cold and empty and he was worried about Ryder. It was ridiculous really, it couldn't be much more than eleven o'clock, but he had a nagging feeling he ought to be doing something and doing it now.

Quick, light footsteps came from outside, someone walking past the tent. He sat up and listened, but there was no alarm, no voices, nothing to suggest the picquets were on the move. A moment later the footsteps came again, erratic and hasty, passing the other way.

He pulled on his boots and crawled out into the damp night. The grass was soggy, the air felt heavy, and the rows of tents stood still and silent as giant mushrooms in a field. A flicker of a dress caught his eye, and he turned to see a woman walk hurriedly past the sick wagon, then stop, agitate her hands, and turn back. She clutched a thin plaid tightly about her shoulders, but her hair was dishevelled and her face pale and distracted.

'Mrs J,' he said, in concern. 'Sally, what is it?'

She spun round, then relaxed. 'Polly, oh thank God. Have you seen Jarvis?'

He moved closer. 'No – why?'

The wariness on her face crumpled into naked anxiety. 'He went out a while ago. I thought he was just going for a piss, but he's not come back, I can't find him anywhere. I'm afraid he might . . . He's not been himself lately, I thought he might . . .'

Her fear caught at his own. 'He's gone after Ryder, hasn't he?'

She flinched. 'Just to have it out with him. You know how it's been.'

Mrs Jarvis minding what he thought, Sally needing his help. 'It's all right. I'll go after him. No one need know.'

She caught at his coat as he turned. 'But what can you do?'

'I won't have to do anything. I'll just wait for Ryder and walk back with him.' He looked at her in sudden doubt. 'Nothing's going to happen until after the appointment, is it? The sergeant-major knows how important . . .'

'Yes,' she said quickly. 'Oh yes, he knows.' She released his coat and stepped back like an obedient child. 'Thank you, Polly.'

Her gratitude warmed him as he hurried through the camp. He was doing something useful, and anything was better than lying in a tent worrying like a silly kid. Anything.

The landscape grew lonelier as Ryder walked on. Even the sky looked empty, the moon shrouded in mist and the stars lost in cloud. It was a welcome change from the bustle of camp, the tents so close together, the ever-present smell of rancid salt-pork and the sweat of men who'd long since given up any idea of bathing.

The pain hit like an axe between his shoulder blades. His neck snapped forward, head scrambling back into sense with the shock of his hands smacking on gravel. Another blow to his side, he was hurled off the track, crashing down with his face in prickly gorse. He rolled and struck out, fist swiping through air but then a body at the end of it, a man who slipped aside chuckling, then fingers were clawing into his hair, a boot thrusting into his ribs, he was flipped over like a sack of rubbish, and the hand on his head pressed his face into thick grass. A voice above said, 'Do stop fighting, will you, old man? You asked for the chat, the least you can do is let us have it.'

Angelo. Strange how obvious truth was when you had a mouthful of mud and a hand in your hair. He wasn't interested in the rendezvous where Calvert's agents were waiting to catch him; he'd sent them miles from anywhere and caught Ryder half an hour out from home. He'd done it in style too, and Ryder's sideways glance showed him what had hit him: the trailing lash of a long, thick whip. A second strip of hide was attached to it by a large brass ring, and he knew he was looking at the dreaded Russian knout.

All right, then. The whip was a long-range weapon, little danger if he stayed close. Get the bastard off balance, get a hand to the revolver and a shot would alert the picquet on the Sapoune. If it was the right shot he wouldn't need the picquet at all. He thought a moment, then allowed himself a tiny groan as he made his body go limp. Angelo stayed motionless above him, then Ryder heard a little thump as the whip was discarded on the grass. Now then.

Something cold and sharp under his ear, then Christ, a knife going in, he'd forgotten that bloody stiletto. He struck out backwards with his arm, and there was that chuckle again, the laugh he'd admired for its carelessness until he learned what not caring really meant.

'Please don't,' said Angelo, leaning forward to pin down his forearms. 'You're perfectly conscious, so am I, and I want you to tell me what gave me away.'

He was after more than that, or a ball from the side of the road would have settled it. Ryder spat out grass and said, 'You first. Same question. What gave me away?'

A soft weight moved over the backs of his legs, the bastard was straddling him. 'Oh, my dear man. When a suddenly promoted trooper visits his colonel twice in a day? You do know we hold positions a few hundred yards away, don't you? You have heard of a telescope?'

Damn him. 'There could be other reasons for that.'

'So there could,' said Angelo, 'if I hadn't watched you this morning. A lady in a blue dress passed you, a lady we both know you know well, but not a word was said between you. Very ungallant, unless you were acting a little play.'

Was there nothing he didn't know? Ryder was floundering, duelling a man far above his class. Only one thought made sense, and that was the gun in his belt. The Russian couldn't know it was there, and if only he'd loosen the grip on his arms . . .

'Your turn,' said Angelo politely. 'I'm intrigued. What mistake did I make?'

It was hard to believe he'd made any. 'Biritch, that's all. Russian whist.'

A tiny pause, then the weight shifted above him as Angelo laughed. 'Now truly, that's too funny. There's a lesson there, Ryder. The biggest mistake is always kindness.'

A bigger one was laughing when holding another man down. Ryder wrenched back his arm and heaved upwards to throw him off balance. Angelo's grunt of surprise hit him like wine, the man was human, he could be beaten, and Ryder's hand was already in his belt, on the stock, the barrel pulling out smooth. Then fingers clenched round his wrist, Angelo's weight bore back down on him, their legs were locked, he couldn't twist free, but he had the gun, one shot would do it, and his thumb strained at the curl of the cock.

The knife chopped down, a flash of white metal slashing at his fingers, and he couldn't stop himself jerking back. Angelo was straight in, gripping the barrel and thrusting it under Ryder's own chin. The knife in his other hand snaked up to Ryder's eyes, and froze in the air in front of them. Ryder's blink brought his lashes to brush against the blade.

'Your choice,' said Angelo. 'Shoot and bring the picquet, but your brains will be out too. Fight and be blinded, it's all one to me. Or, of course, you could always drop the gun.'

Ryder dropped the gun. The picquet might come, but without his help they'd never find Angelo in all these miles of dark.

'Thank you,' said Angelo, scooping it up with his other hand. 'Now if you don't mind, I preferred you how you were.'

Ryder hesitated, but the pistol smashed into the side of his head and his shoulders were forced to roll round with it. For now, all right, for now, but there'd be a chance and he wanted to stay in one piece to take it. He lay passive as the Russian straddled him again, and tried to listen for what he was doing with the Colt. Would he keep hold of it, or lay it down somewhere within reach?

A soft splash, a clunk of metal, then the point of the knife back at his neck. 'Now we can be reasonable again,' said Angelo. 'I need you to tell me what you know about my plans.'

The bastard had dropped the gun in a puddle somewhere, but the Colt was better protected than Russian pistols. The chambers were greased, the firing faces of the caps hard down on the nipples, there was a chance they mightn't all be too wet to fire. If Ryder could distract him again, push him right off and kick that damn knife away, maybe he'd have a moment to find the gun and bloody fire it.

Angelo ran the haft of his knife down the line of Ryder's spine. 'This must be painful, isn't it? What if I did it with the point?'

Distract him, keep him talking. 'How do you know about . . . ?'

'Oh, I watched,' said Angelo with engaging frankness. 'You really shouldn't have allowed it, Ryder, a gentleman can't let himself be flogged like a peasant. But then he can't let himself be taken prisoner either, and you did that too. That's why I know you'll tell me what I ask.'

A cold draught ran down his back as the Russian's hands pushed up his coat. 'But you know what I know, you bastard, I told you myself.'

The hands were still working, shoving up his shirt to expose the dressing underneath. 'I mean afterwards,' said the soft voice. 'I mean Kamara.'

They learned nothing at Kamara except an attack that didn't happen. 'How would I know?'

Pain tore down his back as the knife sliced clean through the dressing, scoring the half-healed skin beneath. He sucked in his breath and pressed his forehead against the turf.

'Because your lady friend was there, and not by coincidence. Because my friend Kostoff has disappeared. Did you kill him?'

'No.'

'You were there. Why else would they flog you?' The knife ground down another line, the bands parting thread by thread beneath the blade. 'Did your lady friend kill him?'

Ryder clenched his teeth. 'We fought, it was an accident.'

The knife tapped thoughtfully against the throbbing flesh of his back. 'Better. Now tell me what you heard.'

Why was it so important? 'Nothing.'

A tiny touch of steel, the knife tip picking between bands of the dressing, and then grazing backwards and forwards over the raw wounds. 'We've lots of time. Why do you think I picked a rendezvous so far away? No one will miss you for at least half an hour.'

Ryder screwed his hands into fists in determination not to scream.

'Tell me what you heard, and what you have told your suddenly obliging colonel,' said Angelo. 'Unless, of course, you'd like me to carve my name on your back.'

Something important must have been said there, something Angelo needed to be sure wasn't compromised. 'Nothing, I swear it. I didn't even get there till you'd gone.'

The knife began to cut, slowly and deliberately, slicing down the long line of a vertical letter. Ryder squeezed his eyes shut and forced his mind away, reducing the pain to a burning tingle that would pass. But his ears sharpened as other senses dulled, and he heard the sound he'd made himself as he'd walked here, the distant slap of boots against wet gravel. Someone was coming up the track. He made himself cry out to give the warning.

'Foolish,' said Angelo. 'The picquet can't possibly hear you.' He finished the stroke and took the knife back to the top.

Ryder's hope soared. The bastard hadn't bloody heard. Keep him talking one more minute and they'd have him. 'Don't,' he said, and was disconcerted at how easily he made his voice shake. 'I'd tell you anything if I knew.'

'If you were that kind of man you'd have screamed earlier,' said Angelo. He began the second cut even deeper than the first.

Ryder cried out, and wasn't even sure he'd meant to. 'Listen, you bloody bastard, if I knew anything useful, do you really think they'd have flogged me?' The knife stopped, Angelo wavering, but he had to keep talking to cover the sound of steps that were closer now and running. 'I'd have been a hero, wouldn't I? You'd know, you've been watching, you'd –'

Angelo whirled round. His chance, and he slammed the pain aside to heave hard upwards, twisting round, hurling himself to one side and for the gun. His hand fanned furiously over the wet scrub, soggy heather, for God's sake, it was here somewhere. Angelo was flinging back round, Ryder kicked him full in the chest, and groped again in the black undergrowth. A rock, a dip, water on his fingers then a touch of metal and his hand was on it, his own gun, his father's, and God help the man who tried to stop him now.

Angelo sprang, and Ryder hit him with the gun in his fist, smashing that filthy lying face with the cleanness of metal. Bone cracked, nose, teeth, jaw, who cared, he was going to make pulp of all of it. Angelo fell back, Ryder leaped after him, but air whistled round his head, the weighted lash cracking where his neck had been, he'd forgotten the bloody whip. It would have to be the gun, his thumb already fumbling back the cock, but the powder was spoiled, nothing, and Angelo laughed and flexed the whip.

A dark shape hurtled at them out of the dark, feet thumping furiously, legs flashing a white stripe, Jarvis, bloody Jarvis, and Angelo slashed out with the whip in a crack that tore the air. Ryder screamed 'Watch him!' and jerked the trigger, another misfire, but Jarvis was reeling back from a blow that had opened his neck with a single flick.

Close distance, close distance, and Ryder hurled himself forward like a cannonball, smashing out left and right with the useless revolver. He struck nothing, Angelo was dancing backwards, snatching in the whip for another strike. Shoot him then, the gun had been on its side, there must be *one* chamber still dry, but it wasn't the third, and here came the lash, moonlight turning it to white lightning as it flew. Ryder leaped aside, but the lash looped and cracked, streaked sideways and at Jarvis, the NCO yelled and was down. Angelo drew back the knout for another blow, and Ryder ran at him, pulling the trigger as he came. Fourth chamber damp, nothing, Jarvis rolling on the ground with only his hands to ward off the whip, cock and fire the fifth and *bang*, the gun came suddenly alive in his hand, and Angelo staggered backwards with his arm across his face.

Got him, but he was still on his feet near Jarvis and hadn't dropped the whip. Fire the sixth, nothing, but Angelo couldn't know that, he couldn't have heard all the clicks. Ryder pointed it anyway and yelled, 'Get back from him, leave him alone!'

Angelo swung round, eyes white in a face blackened with blood, then he lowered the whip and laughed. 'This for a man who betrayed you?'

'Drop it,' said Ryder, suddenly calm. 'Drop the whip.' Lanterns were moving on the Sapoune, help would be here any minute.

Angelo saw them too. He took a step backwards and said, 'I don't think so.'

Ryder kept the gun steady. 'Don't you think I'll shoot?'

Angelo smiled. 'I'm sure you would have – which is why I know you haven't a shot left to fire.' He inclined his head in the tiniest of bows, swept round and ran into the darkness.

Ryder chased after him. It was hopeless and he knew it even before he rounded the knoll and saw the waiting horse. Angelo slashed out with the whip to keep him back, then he was up in the saddle, turning the beast and away. Ryder lowered the gun in fury.

He walked back to find Jarvis sitting up and groaning, bleeding down his neck and obviously in considerable pain in his side. 'My fucking ribs, that's what, that fucking son of a poxed-up whore, his whip got my fucking ribs.'

Ryder's feelings settled into blank unreality. 'What the hell are you doing here, anyway?'

Jarvis stopped massaging his ribs. 'Lucky for you I am, isn't it?'

Evasion. 'You thought you'd wait for me to come back? Ambush me in the dark?'

Jarvis's eyes burned. 'No, I bloody didn't. You may not understand this, Sergeant, but I wanted us to do this man to man. Like you said.' He heaved himself slowly to his feet, wincing at every movement. 'Instead of your way. Starting whispers behind my back. Making people laugh. Nothing so bloody manly about that.'

Ryder shrugged uneasily. 'Nothing so bloody manly about abandoning a man who helped you either.'

'Just saved you, didn't I?' said Jarvis. The man was indestructible, brushing down his coat as if it mattered more than the damage to his body. 'Doesn't that cover it?'

Horsemen were galloping down from the Sapoune, but Ryder suddenly felt very tired. 'No. Because I want to know why.'

Jarvis's hands stilled on the coat. 'Maybe because you're a jumped-up cocky little bastard who's been spitting on my regiment ever since he joined it. Will that do?'

Maybe it would. Ryder saw himself as he had been, looking on a British NCO as the enemy and befriending a Russian monster instead. 'He said you betrayed me.'

Jarvis stared at him, trapped. 'You'd believe him?'

Calvert's men were almost down to the road. 'Not if you say it's a lie.'

Jarvis watched the horsemen riding nearer and nearer. He said abruptly, 'No, damn you, it's not. I kept you in camp on his say-so. I thought you were messing with my wife.'

Ryder was aware of a sick, sinking feeling in his guts. Woodall had said that, he'd said Jarvis would suspect. 'But you must know she'd never . . .'

Jarvis slewed round. 'I didn't imagine it, if that's what you think. He as good as told me. How the hell was I to know he wasn't a real officer, that he was a poxy bastard Russian spy?' He jerked his head in the direction Angelo had gone. 'He put me through hell just to bring you down, and it was all a bloody lie.'

For a moment he remembered Sally in his arms. For a moment he thought of the kiss that would be the last they'd ever have.

Then he remembered her stepping back, and knew it had to be her choice and not his.

'Yes,' he said. 'It was a bloody lie.'

Oliver caught up with them at the base of the Sapoune. There was a mounted picquet with them and he thought at first they'd been arrested, but the horsemen turned off towards the Uplands and the two battered cavalrymen toiled on alone. Their condition seemed to confirm his worst fears, but to his astonishment Ryder was supporting Jarvis and the sergeant-major didn't seem to mind.

'Hullo, Polly,' said Ryder, without apparent surprise. 'You're in perfect time to help a couple of crocks down to Kadikoi.'

There was a bitterness in his tone Oliver immediately understood. 'He got away?'

'He got away,' said Ryder. 'I've marked him, though; there'll be some kind of wound on his face. He'll need to lie low for a bit, and if Calvert gets the word out over the next couple of days we might stop him doing any more harm.'

He'd obviously done some tonight. Oliver rather gingerly offered his shoulder to the sergeant-major, but Jarvis leaned on it with obvious relief and even muttered 'Thanks'. Something had changed here, and when Ryder told his story Jarvis never even interrupted.

'It's Kamara that worries me,' said Ryder. 'He was dead set on that, Poll, he had to know what we knew. All right, we didn't hear everything, but what the hell did they say that's so damned urgent he'd risk coming out in the open like this?'

'That attack you went on about,' said Jarvis. 'Come on, it's got to be that.'

'But it didn't happen,' said Ryder. 'It was meant to be on the 24th but it didn't bloody happen and I've got the back to prove it.'

Jarvis snorted. 'You got your back for being an insolent bastard who broke camp. Don't try to lay it on me.'

Ryder looked at him with something almost like affection. 'How's the ribs, Sar'nt-major? Would you like to walk to the hospital alone?'

Jarvis bared his teeth at him, and they staggered on in a silence that seemed oddly amiable.

It was long after midnight when they finally reached the hospital at Kadikoi. The candles were still lit and the orderlies seemed happy to patch up a couple of NCOs who looked as if they'd been on the wrong end of a bull fight, so Oliver handed them over and went to wait in the porch, just as he'd done on the day his world changed.

Nothing else had. Church life went on as if there were no war, and a little old woman like a gnarled chess piece was muttering under her breath as she trimmed the lamps and wiped away blood splashes from the white plaster walls. It was Sunday tomorrow, and there would be a service here despite the human debris lining the walls.

The porch hadn't changed either. The same curling notices were here, in the same fascinating Cyrillic script it was hard to believe made sense to anyone. The calendar was here too, just as out of date as before – in fact exactly as out of date as before. Someone had moved it on since Oliver was last here, but now it read the 23rd when the day just started was 5 November. Why would anyone update a calendar by ten days but not the whole way?

The old woman bustled into the porch, eyed Oliver as if he were something that needed dusting, and poured water into a vase of pale yellow flowers. They gave off a faint smell of jasmine, and his memory opened to England and schooldays, to history and something called the Julian calendar from a hundred years ago. He thought he remembered hearing that not everyone had changed yet, that Orthodox Greece still used the old system. Wasn't Russia Orthodox too?

The old woman flicked her duster over the notice board,

reached out to the calendar and tore off the top leaf. The number underneath blazed out fresh and clean, today for the first time, the thick black numerals spelling out the number 24.

In Russia this was 24 October. The attack on the harbour and assault on the Allies were scheduled for today before dawn. Not last week, not twelve days ago, but now.

21

5 November 1854, 2.00 a.m. to 6.00 a.m.

Mackenzie lay awake in the sleeping wheel of men. Footsteps were approaching, then the canvas rustled, and a cold draught rushed inside.

'Mackenzie,' said a voice he knew. 'I'm looking for Niall Mackenzie, is this the right tent?'

He sat bolt upright. 'Ryder!'

'Get out of it, will you?' grumbled Lennox, snatching back his disarranged blanket. 'Let decent bodies sleep.'

They were all waking now, muttering and protesting as he crawled apologetically towards the entrance. Farquhar hefted a boot at him and said, 'Close the flap after you, you selfish bastards, it's freezing out there.'

Indeed it was, and Mackenzie's feet chilled on the wet ground as he emerged to find Ryder with a man he was startled to recognize as Jarvis. 'What is it? Did you no get him?'

Ryder told him while he put on his boots. 'Polly's gone to Doherty, but God knows what he'll do, the main assault could be anywhere. We're off to warn the marines, will you come?'

Camp-breaking, and in the middle of the night! 'I will that,' he said. 'Give me a minute whiles I see the sergeant.'

Ryder stared. 'There isn't time for . . .'

Mackenzie stared back. 'I'll not go behind his back. Start without me, I'll catch you long before Balaklava.'

He'd be catching them before they cleared camp. Ryder had a pale and groggy look to him, and the sergeant-major had a bandaged neck and thick strapping under his coat. That was quite a fight they'd been in, and from the sound of it worse to come. He turned and ran for Mr Macpherson.

The tent was but two down. He opened the flap, patted the sleeping sergeant's shoulder, and said, 'You'll forgive me, Mr Macpherson, but I need to go out for a wee while.'

The sergeant looked blearily at him. 'What in the name of . . . ?'

'I'm camp-breaking, Sergeant. I'm wanted at Balaklava to fight off some Russians, but thought I'd best tell you before I went.'

Macpherson looked at him without expression. 'Did you.'

'Aye,' he said patiently. 'You'll mind of that intelligence business the cavalry colonel wanted me for, it's to do with that. There's an attack coming on the ships and we need to warn the marines.'

Macpherson sat up. 'Ah, havers, man, who says?'

There was not the time for explanations. He said 'Someone I believe,' and backed respectfully out of the tent.

Ryder and Jarvis had moved faster than he'd credited, and had already disappeared into the gorge. He retrieved his rifle and set off briskly after them, but Ryder's urgency was beginning to hammer in his head, and after a moment he began to run.

Ryder fought with panic as they ran down the gorge. Dawn wouldn't break until six, but what did 'before dawn' mean? Three o'clock? Four? Now?

Jarvis kept up. His ribs must be jolting agonizingly despite the strapping, but he'd far too much pride to allow Ryder to outstrip him. Mackenzie could doubtless have outrun them both, but he loped comfortably along beside them and only the set expression of his face betrayed his own desperation. No one spoke. Their pounding feet and gasping breath began to sound oddly close and distinct, as if the world outside them had been muffled to silence.

'Fog,' panted Jarvis. 'See it settling? Fog.'

The mist was certainly thickening and a wisp floated past

Ryder's face like a miniature cloud. If it was like this at sea, what chance would the fleet have of spotting the danger in one of their own vessels drifting towards them? Missed signals wouldn't matter, nothing would until the explosion erupted right among the packed ships that were their only way home. Ryder pictured the fire spreading from rigging to rigging, put down his head and ran.

Balaklava at last, the first white houses looming out of the dark, the slopes about them broken by grey lines of dry-stone walls. The fog grew more opaque as they descended to the sea, and Ryder was unable to make out even the lamps of the distant fleet. At least the silence began to be reassuring. If anything were wrong he'd be hearing shouts, maybe gunfire, but there was only their own running footsteps and the distant monotone barking of a bored dog.

On past the clusters of military buildings, crude military fingerposts, and the sign for 'Commisariat' spelled with one 's'. He could see the harbour below now, grey fog and haloed lamps, the gloom pierced only by the skeletal nakedness of masts without sails. They rounded the first line of storehouses, wound through stacks of boxes and piles of iron girders, passed six white tents pitched in the dirt, and there was the quay ahead of them, clear and smooth and peaceful. A lamp shone outside the tiled shack of the harbourmaster's office, and the figure leaning against the wall wore the reassuring red coat of a marine. There was another huddled under an open shelter with a canvas canopy, and a third sitting against the wheel of a gun carriage. The cluster of ships lay still at anchor, and the only movement was the gentle bobbing of a dinghy moored to the jetty. Jarvis bent double and gasped for breath, but over his head Ryder and Mackenzie exchanged a grin of exhausted relief. They were in time.

'Far enough,' said a man emerging from behind a storehouse with levelled rifle. 'This is a prohibited area, what's the password?'

At least the marines were alert. 'I've no idea, I'm bloody cavalry, aren't I? Look, we need to speak to an officer, there's an attack coming, we've got to –'

The marine jerked the rifle at him. 'I said, what's the pass-word?' His face was expressionless, and his sleeve bore the same number of stripes as Ryder's own. 'You could be bloody anyone.'

Ryder's temper exploded. 'For God's sake! The Russians are coming, and I've got to see your officer.'

The sergeant glanced contemptuously at Mackenzie's kilt, at Ryder's torn coat, at the bandaged and stooping figure of Jarvis. 'You don't give me orders, Sergeant. This is a prohibited area, we don't allow rabble on the quay after dark –'

'Rabble!' Jarvis jerked upright, and thrust himself in front of the marine. 'That's "*Sergeant-major*" to you, Sergeant, I do give you orders, and by God I'm giving one now.' His breathlessness was gone, his ribs forgotten, he stood straight-backed and impos-ing, his chest swelling with wrath and his voice a parade-ground roar. 'I want every man in your command out here *now*, then you'll fetch me your officer.'

If there was one way to beat a bastard it was to confront him with a bigger one. The sergeant threw a helpless glance at the marines already emerging sleepily from their tents, looked back at Jarvis, and capitulated. 'Aye, aye, Sergeant-major, I mean yes, Sergeant-major, it's Captain Broomfield, I'll send a man . . .'

'You'll go yourself,' said Jarvis, hissing the words with venom. 'And *at the double!*'

The sergeant turned and fled.

Jarvis swivelled his gaze to the open-mouthed marines. 'Now then, speak up. Have you let any civilians onto this quay tonight?'

They shuffled nervously under his gaze, and Ryder saw a cor-poral exchange a glance with his neighbour. He said quickly, 'No one's in trouble. There's going to be an attack on the ships, and there's local help involved. If you've seen anyone, for God's sake say.'

The corporal glanced round again, took a deep breath and stepped forward. 'Only some Bulgars, Sergeant. Just selling wine.'

Jarvis's brows lowered ominously, but Ryder intercepted him. 'It's a cold night, no harm in a drink. Where did they go?'

No one seemed to know. 'They did go on the quay,' said one. 'I saw them selling to . . . someone on guard, but I turned in after that. It was gone one o'clock.'

Two hours ago. 'Were they carrying anything? Just bottles?'

The corporal sounded very sobered now. 'Great sacks. There were five or six of them, all with leather sacks. I assumed they were bottles, but . . .'

Ryder was already turning for the quay. Powder, it had to be, they were packing the fireship ready for the Russian sailors, but which one was it? The sentries must have seen something, he'd have to –

'Hey!' called an irate voice, and an immaculately dressed captain came marching towards them with a crumpled aide and the marine sergeant in his wake. 'What the devil do you mean by it, disturbing an officer at this time of night? How dare you shout at my sergeant in front of his men?'

The old game of hierarchy, when the Russians could be on them any moment. Jarvis dutifully reported, but the first mention of Ryder's name sent Broomfield into fresh fury.

'Ryder!' he said, swinging vengefully round on him. 'You're the fellow who had us stood to all night on some damn-fool wild-goose chase. You're at it again, aren't you? Answer me – aren't you?'

Ryder had had enough. 'Sir, there've been saboteurs on the quay, I need to talk –'

'Oh no, you don't,' said the captain. 'You need to learn . . .'

Ryder turned and strode onto the quay. The captain shouted 'Guards, stop that man!' but it was the guards he wanted anyway. He ran straight for the redcoat leaning against the harbourmaster's office and called, 'Listen, those wine sellers, did any of . . . ?'

He stopped. Broomfield was shouting 'Abbott, arrest him!' but the redcoat didn't move. He leaned against the lintel as nonchalantly as ever, but his head was lolling forward and his body kept upright only by the bayonet that skewered him to the wall.

Ryder fought a wave of nausea. Men were pounding towards

him along the quay, but they were irrelevant now and he turned to look for the other sentries. They too were unmoving, and the one under the shelter had fallen on his side. Dead, all of them, and the Bulgars already in a ship somewhere, one of the two dozen moored round the harbour.

Footsteps stopped behind him, and he heard a gasp. 'Abbott,' said the marine corporal. 'My God. Jimmy Abbott.' Beyond him Captain Broomfield stood in shocked silence, his face suddenly wiped of expression. Mackenzie took one look, unslung his rifle, and turned to study the headland.

The corporal recovered first. 'It's true then, Sergeant? The Russians are coming?'

'Ryder,' said Mackenzie. 'Below the fortress – see it?'

The headland was only a black mass in the dark, the ruined Genoese fortress a jet pillar rising out of it, and between them the night sky was thickened with fog. But Mackenzie was right. The air was still, no clouds were moving, but the fortress wall seemed to be darkening, then paling, darkening, then paling, as if by the passing of shadows.

Ryder drew his revolver. 'Not coming, Corporal. They're already here.'

Woodall liked the fog. It had the home feel of a London Particular, suggesting the rattle of hansom cabs and hazy glow of gaslight, the smells of wet cabbage and horse dung and in winter the roasting of chestnuts. He could picture himself walking the pavements with jingling coins in his pockets, refusing to toss with the pieman for the pleasure of taking his whole pay home to Maisie.

He turned abruptly and began to pace the other way. There was nothing like that *here*. Picquet duty was standing in wet clothes in a cold you could catch your death in, and the only smell was an unpleasant sourness he had a suspicion came from his own clothes. No spares, and he wasn't sitting round naked in a November fog while he waited for his own to dry. He wriggled his toes in the slimy softness of his socks and wondered if he mightn't risk washing at least those.

'Hang about,' said Truman, coming to a sudden stop beside him. 'Is that bells?'

Church bells from the sound of them, muffled and distant, somewhere in Sebastopol. 'It's Sunday, isn't it?'

'It's four in the morning. You don't think they're shriving the troops for another battle, do you?'

Ryder had said they'd given them a church service last time. Woodall peered round at the swirling fog, the dark shapes of rocks and trees that seemed to loom up then float away even as he watched. 'I hope not. We can't fight in this beastly fog, it's like a bonfire.'

Truman grinned. 'Very appropriate.'

Woodall looked blankly at him. 'Why?'

Truman rolled his eyes. 'Come on, chum, it's November the 5th. Guy Fawkes Night.'

Chum. Woodall glanced furtively round at the rest of the picquet, but unfortunately no one seemed to have heard. He said brilliantly, 'Well, let's hope we don't get the fireworks to go with it.'

Truman didn't laugh. He rubbed his palm against his scrubby beard, and said, 'Let's hope.'

'And run like hell!' said Broomfield. His face was as pale as the fog. 'Tell Captain Tatham we've only got minutes.'

And not many of those. The marine set off at a breakneck pace, feet slamming the quay as he turned off for the path, but the shapes on the headland were already forming a cluster and starting to move downhill. It was too dark to count, but Ryder could be sure there'd be enough to tackle the two dozen marines now spread round the approaches. Angelo would have known exactly how many he had to beat, he'd been strolling round this area quite openly and unchallenged. One of the men who hadn't challenged him was Ryder.

'No sign of the Bulgars, sir,' said the marine sergeant, panting back up along the quay. 'All the guards are dead, every one of them, but there's no ships moved.'

Of course there weren't, they were waiting for the sailors. 'They'll be on board one of them, sir, the hold already packed with powder.'

'Yes,' said Broomfield meaninglessly. 'Yes. Now which?' He looked down the rows of masts and licked his tongue along dry lips.

The corporal had his wits about him. 'She'll be a small craft, sir, they'd have to take her out under sweeps or we'd see them setting sail. What about the cutters? *Persimmon* and *Starling*, they're both in.'

'Yes,' said the captain, and seemed steadied by the names of craft he knew. 'Yes. Show him, Corporal. Take three men and show him.'

'Aye, aye, sir,' said the corporal, and turned swiftly to the marines. 'You, you, and you – fix bayonets. If there's powder about I don't want no shooting, right?'

Five should be enough to tackle six Bulgars, but not if those Russian sailors managed to join up with them. He muttered to Mackenzie, 'You've got our backs, Niall. They mustn't get to a ship, all right? They mustn't get past.'

The Highlander was already tucking himself into the wall and bringing up his rifle. 'Aye, I ken.' He looked up for a second, steady blue eyes in a taut, pale face. 'They'll not get past Niall Mackenzie.'

God help them, they wouldn't. Ryder turned and ran after the redcoats already sprinting down the quay. A dark blue shape came pounding up on his right, and he marvelled at Jarvis's tenacity. Far too conscientious to break camp under arms, he hadn't a single weapon to defend himself but was coming on anyway.

A rifle cracked behind him, then another, the Russians already in range and the marines shooting to keep them back.

'*Persimmon*,' gasped the corporal, pointing ahead at a single-sailed ship no more than thirty feet in length. 'Gawd, she's weighing!'

Ryder heard the steady grinding of the capstan as the anchor was hauled up. The Bulgars weren't waiting for the sailors, they'd heard the shots and were taking her out right now. He tried for one more spurt, but his bloody ripped-up back was refusing to give him the thrust. The marines were all ahead of him, and there was the cutter, anchor already slithering over the hull in a loud cascade of water. Only a single taut mooring held her to the quay.

'Over you go, lads!' sang out the corporal, throwing himself at the ship. The tide was down, the wooden side no more than shoulder height from the quay, and the marines swarmed over it with the ease of long practice. Ryder caught up with them, but the corporal yelled back 'Not with that pistol, Sergeant!' and disappeared over the top.

He was right, damn it, and Ryder could only stand uselessly at the quay with a pistol he'd carefully reloaded and now couldn't afford to fire. One spark wouldn't just destroy the cutter and all aboard her, it would take out the frigate beyond. He could hear the fight going on above him, thumps and yells, and a crash against the side that rocked the whole vessel. How many Bulgars were there? 'Five or six' to start with maybe, but how many had joined them after the guards were killed?

And how many sailors coming? The shooting behind was fast and furious now, and he swivelled round to see grey figures already ducking and weaving among the stores as their guns blazed fire at the marines.

'Look out!' roared Jarvis, and he whirled back to see a man leaning over the cutter's side. Something white flashed in the murk, a knife in his hand, he was reaching over to cut the mooring and take the cutter out to sea.

He had to risk it, had to. He crouched to give the highest trajectory, nothing behind the man but harmless sky, pointed the Colt and fired. Too high, damn it to hell, and the knife already swooping at the rope, but a pole flashed past Ryder's shoulder, a boat-hook crunched down to pin the cutter to the quay, and the man skipped back with a yelp. Ryder's thumb scraped back the cock, again *bang*, and the Bulgar slumped forward, draping over the prow like an obscene figurehead. The knife landed tinkling on the quay.

Ryder turned and stared at the sight of Jarvis holding grimly to the boat-hook. 'Where the hell did you find that?'

'Where do you think?' said Jarvis, jerking his chin at the pile of stores behind them. 'And it's "Where did you find that, *Sergeant-major?*"'

For the shortest of seconds their eyes met. Then a ball struck the stone between them, a tiny white flash and a flying chip of stone, and Ryder swung the pistol round to see Russians on the quay itself. Grey coats, black belts, sailors from the Black Sea Fleet, the men he'd fought with the sharpshooters, and some of the best fighters in the world. He fired at the nearest and yelled, 'Damn it, Mackenzie, where are you?'

Mackenzie's fingers were slippery with sweat as he reloaded. They were good, these Russians, but they were also grey men in darkness and fog, picking off redcoats standing in lamplight as if they were so many ducks at a fair. They'd all the cover in the world too, threading between the stores and houses like mongrel dogs, not fighting in a line like men. He adjusted the sights, picked a big man thundering towards the cutter, and fired.

'Hold them, marines!' bawled the sergeant beside him, the complacency gone from him like a cast-off coat. 'For God's sake, hold them!'

They couldn't. The marines were grand shots, men said they could pick off an officer on a ship five hundred yards away, but there were o'er few of them now, struggling to find cover in the bright light of the quay. And here came more of the grey devils hurtling down to the ships, and himself not loaded, his fingers too slow, and he'd given Ryder his word.

And he would keep it. He snatched the gun from the dead marine, pointed it blank at the nearest Russian and fired. Only a smooth-bore, no precision to it at all, but at this range it blew a hole in a man's body, and down went the front man, down. Two others just behind, but that marine sergeant fired and took another, there was only the one man still ahead of the pack and Mackenzie would stop him himself. He stepped from the office into the frightening nakedness of the open, but in his hands was the musket and at its end was a blade.

The sailor skidded to a stop, levelling his own bayonet, and Mackenzie lunged straight at him. The coat was thick, the belt tangled his blade, he'd done no more than scratch, and had to use the barrel to knock away the man's own thrust. He stabbed at the neck, the man down and decently dead, but two, three others were springing at him now, teeth bared in that chattering snarl he remembered from the Alma. But he'd an oath to keep, he scythed round with the bayonet to keep them back, and he'd a snarl of his own to make too. '*Tulach Ard!*' he roared at them, battle-cry of the Mackenzies for centuries before he was born. '*Tulach Ard*, and take that, you bloody heathens!' He sliced one cheek to shoulder, punched his left into the jaw of the next, and gashed at the arm of the one looking to sneak up on him. He was tingling from head to foot with the joy of it, ready to take on them all.

A volley, beautiful, clean and loud from above and all three of them falling right there on the quay. It could never be the reinforcements, there hadn't been time, and then came a great roar that brought round his head like a man hearing a miracle.

'Stand, 93rd! You'll charge when I say so, and not before!'

Mr Macpherson. He'd maybe a dozen men with him up on the bank, Farquhar, Lennox, men from his own tent and the sergeant's, he'd trusted Mackenzie and brought them himself. For a moment his eyes blurred, and he turned in haste back to the shack and his own Minié.

'Bloody hell,' said the marine sergeant, grinning as he brought his musket back to the present. 'You Sawnies are all mad.'

Mackenzie grinned back and found his hands were steady again on the rifle. There was shouting behind, more trouble at the ships, but Ryder was there, he'd deal with it. There were more of the Russian devils running towards them, but the 93rd would deal with *that*. They had the enemy on the run now, and the business was as good as done.

It was Jarvis who was yelling, his voice calling 'There, *there*!' Ryder squeezed off another shot at the advancing Russians, then turned and saw it, a second cutter further along, its anchor already whooshing clear of the water.

Two! Of course there'd be two, one would never be enough for all these sailors. He cursed and pelted after Jarvis. Behind him the corporal was yelling, 'Back over, boys, there's a second!' and he guessed the first cutter was secured, but the one ahead was bigger and could do massive damage if the Bulgars managed to take her out.

And one was already leaning over to cut the rope. Ryder kept running, but Jarvis was ahead and whirling his boat-hook like a dervish, slamming it over the cutter's side even as the rope parted to the knife. There were three Bulgars on the deck above him, and bloody Jarvis was trying to hold the ship firm with just the strength of his own body.

Ryder yelled 'No!' and swung up the Colt, wavering, wobbling, impossible as he ran. He stopped to fire but the bang wasn't his, the shot wasn't, one of the Bulgars had fired a pistol, and Jarvis sunk to his knees as the hook clattered down on the stone. The cutter was moving out under oars, shoving away into clear water, but Jarvis was down and Ryder's own steps trailed to a halt as the marines shot past in pursuit of a ship already out of reach.

Voices babbled about him, 'Follow in the dinghy', 'There's no point', 'Blow her here', 'We can't, we'll hole the *Ajax*!' He knelt on the quay as Jarvis's body slumped towards him, with a hole in the chest he could have stuck a fist through. The gold braid was blackened and blown apart, and the man was dead. Ryder lowered him to the ground, careful not to jar the broken ribs Jarvis himself had ignored, and for a second he closed his eyes.

'Sergeant,' said the corporal. 'Sergeant. She's gone, what shall we do?'

Go to hell. 'Can we get a ball in her once she's clear of the ships?'

'Not here,' said the corporal. 'If we sink her she'll block the harbour entrance. I'll tell the captain to ask the battery.'

Of course. Captain Barker's 'W' on the slopes above. They could get her as she went round the headland, still a good safe distance from the fleet. The visibility would be very poor in this fog, but it was still a chance.

He climbed slowly to his feet, and became aware the gunfire behind him had ceased. The quay was teeming with the red coats of Captain Tatham's reinforcements, and he even saw a few kilted Highlanders in the crowd. A cluster of sullen Bulgars stood under heavy guard, but the only Russian sailors he could see were sprawling on the ground or scrambling away back up the hillside towards the Genoese fortress. He looked in sudden concern at the harbourmaster's office, but Mackenzie was already strolling towards him, bloodied from head to foot but apparently his usual calm self. Everything looked like victory, except for the dead man at his own feet.

'That's a sore pity,' said Mackenzie, looking down at Jarvis. 'He was a bonny fighter at the end. Did you see him with yon boat-hook?'

He had. 'Will you help me take him back, Niall? Sally will want to see him.'

'I'll do that,' said the Highlander. 'My sergeant's given me a free hand whiles this business is over.'

Brisk footsteps sounded behind them, Captain Broomfield arriving with his aide. 'Well, you were right, Ryder. *Persimmon*'s crammed with powder, absolutely crammed with it. She'd have taken out a steamer or two if she'd got close enough.'

Starling might do it yet. 'Will Captain Barker help us, sir?'

'Well, I've sent to him.' The cutter was already nearing the first bend, oars pulling strongly through the still water. 'We're flying a signal to warn the fleet just in case, but I'm afraid they won't see it in this damnable murk.'

The aide coughed. 'We could ring the church bells, sir. It's the Balaklava signal, but it would warn the admiral something's up.'

Ryder turned in horror, but the captain brightened. 'Worth a try. At least it'll call senior officers on the watch instead of some damn snotty who won't see a thing till it blows up in his face. Off with you, my lad, report to Captain Tatham and ask to ring the bells.'

'Wait,' said Ryder. 'Sir, please wait. The bells will bring reinforcements, Lord Lucan, Sir Colin Campbell, everything the Russians wanted to draw us from the main attack. The fireship was meant as a distraction, we can't let it succeed.'

Broomfield's irritation returned at once. 'Now look here, Sergeant, enough's enough. Captain Barker'll do his best, but it's damn foggy out there, he'll be shooting almost blind, and I can't risk it. We're going to warn the fleet.'

'There's time,' said Ryder desperately. 'Can't we at least let Captain Barker try?'

The captain wavered. 'This other attack. Where is it, is it far?'

Ryder heard the flatness in his own voice. 'We don't know, sir. We don't know anything at all.'

Broomfield's spine stiffened. 'Well, I know my duty, and that's to do everything in my power to save our ships. Off you go now, Bennett, and look sharp about it.'

The aide set off at a sprint, and Ryder turned hopelessly away. They'd tried all they could and Jarvis had died for it, but Angelo's plan was going to succeed after all.

Mackenzie pulled a rag from his coat and began to clean his bayonet. 'It's maybe no so bad. If it's Kadikoi again then it's only minutes we'll be losing before we can get the men back.'

'And what if it's not?' he said. 'What if it's the Uplands, Niall, what then?'

The relieving picquet turned up at five, by which time Woodall was chilled to the bone. His rifle was heavy with moisture, and he'd have to draw the charge before it was fit to fire, but he cheered himself with the imminent prospect of fire, breakfast, and washing his socks.

He marched briskly with the rest, pausing only as they passed the windmill to wonder what had happened last night with Ryder and the spy. Surely he'd have heard something if they'd caught him, gunshots or shouting or something, but the night had been quiet except for the bells and those ruddy wheels on the Woronzoff Road. The Russians always used the night to move their supplies around, safe from the attentions of the British marksmen.

The odd thing was he was still hearing them. He glanced at Truman, wondering if he should say something, but no one else seemed bothered. It was the fog, that's all. The Russians knew they were still invisible no matter what the time was. That was all.

He shouldered his rifle more comfortably and marched on towards the Guards' camp and home.

Ryder lifted his head at the muffled bang from the headland. All about the harbour men fell hushed as they listened for the explosion they hoped would follow. Seconds ticked, but there came only a sound like a faint, distant splash, and Ryder's heart sunk with the dispirited murmur that spread round the quay.

'Hopeless, you see,' said Broomfield, with a kind of dismal satisfaction. 'What else could you expect in this fog?' He looked back at the town and said petulantly 'Where the *hell* are those bells?'

Maybe Captain Tatham was hesitating. Maybe he'd do it a little longer, and give 'W' Battery another chance. That might have just been a ranging shot, and the next . . .

Another bang. Again the hush, and again only the faint splash followed by the low rumour of a sigh.

'Sir!' said an agitated voice, and the aide was back at Broomfield's elbow. 'Sir, Captain Tatham says no bells. This man brought a message from Lord Lucan.'

Ryder turned in astonishment and saw a horseman clopping casually down onto the quay to join them. He had fair hair and rode a grey horse, and wore the overalls of the 13th Light Dragoons.

Ryder felt himself grinning stupidly. 'Hullo, Polly. The Old Man came good, did he?'

Oliver nodded solemnly. 'He took me to Lord Lucan *himself.*'

Broomfield's eyes darted between them in frustrated suspicion. 'Oh, so we'll have *you* to thank, will we, when Her Majesty's ships are sunk and we haven't given –'

Another bang, and then the sky split in a giant flash of lightning. Even the fog shimmered with sparkling yellow dust, while the harbour shook and reverberated to the roar of a thunderous explosion. Ryder spun round with his hands clamped to his ears, and saw a thick column of black smoke rolling and spreading beyond the headland like a deeper, cleaner darkness in the murk. As the rumble subsided, he heard little distant splashes as if flying debris were falling back down to the sea.

A marine shouted and threw his shako in the air. Someone laughed, another whistled, and above the quay men cheered and clapped, waving their caps in salute to the invisible 'W' Battery on the headland. Oliver clapped too, eyes wide with awe, and whispered, 'Oh, well played, the battery. Well played!' Ryder shoved away a sudden sharp memory of Hoare, and sat heavily on the harbour wall. His bloody legs were shaking.

A red figure thumped down beside him, Niall Mackenzie sitting to reload his precious Minié. His sleeves were rolled up to expose forearms smudged with blood, but when his eyes met Ryder's he gave a gentle smile.

Oliver dismounted, and took off his shako to wipe the hair from his eyes. 'You've done it, Harry. You were right all along. No one's ever going to doubt you now.'

Maybe. He looked up and saw Broomfield still standing there, fidgeting uncomfortably and jingling what sounded like coins in his pockets. 'Sir?'

'Oh, it's well enough,' said Broomfield quickly. 'Fleet's safe, and that's what matters. Pity about the cutter though. Nice little craft, the *Starling*.' He gave an awkward little nod and wandered rather hastily away.

'Ah, forget him,' said Mackenzie comfortably, sliding out the rod to ram the ball. 'You've saved two, three of Her Majesty's ships there, to say nothing of the men aboard them. Your Angelo would no be so happy about that.'

No, he wouldn't, the bastard, and Ryder allowed himself a first savage surge of triumph. They'd saved the fleet, and thanks to Doherty no one had left their posts to come to their help. The distraction had failed too.

The reminder sobered him. What had happened here was nothing, and the main attack was still to come. He watched Mackenzie calmly slotting his rod back into place, then looked out at the sky over the harbour. The glow of the burning cutter had faded, but the fog still seemed paler than before, and behind it gleamed the first pink tinge of dawn.

22

5 November 1854, 6.00 a.m. to 8.10 a.m.

Bleeding fog. Bloomer peered through the floating mist of the White House Ravine and decided it was coming on a regular thick 'un. The fresh rag tied round his Minié lock was damp already, and he could have squeezed a quart pot out of the one over the muzzle. How was a man meant to keep his powder dry in this?

Lieutenant Butts hadn't even bothered with a rag. The poor flat was prowling round the picquet in proper charley style, barking-iron in his hand and open to the wet. Bloomer wondered how long before he gave up and just stood and shivered his heart out with the rest.

A dull report popped to the north, high up the Careenage, then more of them, a regular banging match starting up at West Jut. The sharpshooters, must be, and Bloomer's fist was already shoving the rags off his gun. They'd seen something, the flash-barkers, and it might be coming this way.

'I can't see . . .' said Butts uncertainly, standing on his toes like a bleeding dancer. 'I can't . . .'

Bloomer ignored him. This was his world, the Limehouse murk in the lonely hours, ears strained for the padding feet of Lascars or a peeler's whistle. Then he heard it, the rattle of stones in the gully, men running down the Careenage Ravine towards them.

'Take your cover!' he bellowed, and dived for the nearest boulder. 'Russkies in the gorge!'

In it and on them, and a ball splintered into the rock as he ducked behind it. A damp body thumped against his side as Morry slid in next to him, and young Peachy was diving for the shelter of a ruined wall, but there were plenty in the open still

441

and the balls whining in like death out of the clouds. Donnelly down, Stevens, and Christ, little Pilchard shot in the back and screaming like a woman. Bloomer looked for a target, but these were grey men in thick fog, nothing to see but muzzle flashes, and nothing to do but stay down.

Not Butts. He was rallying a dozen to the white house above, but they'd hardly took three steps when a crowd of ghostly figures oozed round the ruins to take them from behind. Bloomer fired and got one, *that* was no ghost, that was a Russian in grey coat and white cross-belts, but when Butts spun round with his pistol it just went click with no bang. The thing was damp as a whore's muff, and their officer good as unarmed.

Bloomer wasn't, but he'd got to reload and the beggars were coming from all sides. Morry got his piece in, but same story, click and no ruddy bang. Then they were all at it, everywhere clicking and cursing, and Peachy crying 'Corporal, my rifle *won't work!*' with a shock in his voice like a child's. The Minié, the gun that had saved them at the Alma, the one big edge they'd had over the Muscovites from the start, the Minié was letting them down.

Bastard fog, it would be the death of them all yet. He was loading fast as he could do it, Morry firing cap after cap to clear his own charge, but the Russians were picking them off like rats in a barrel. The sergeant was down, so was Dawson and old Bandy, and others legging it as riflemen swarmed down on them from behind. Butts's lot was surrounded and surrendering, so was another down the Careenage end, only a few managing to bowl off into the wilderness of the Uplands. Time for a wise man to consider his options and hook it.

He heaved round to face Morry and Peachy. 'Back up the slope at the double, find cover and wait for me.' He dug in his pack for his NCO's spanner and handed it to Morry. 'And draw your bleeding charges while you wait.'

Peachy had eyes round as pennies. 'Aren't we meant to delay the enemy before we fall back? Fight and give our side time to bring up the guns?'

Gawd help us. 'We have bleeding fought,' he said patiently. 'We're more than half dead or took, and the rest already cutting. Now look fly, and leg it when I tell you.'

He turned to face front. The Russians were done skulking now and running into the open to mop up with the bayonet. Bayonet meant they'd fired, these would be first rank and already empty, now was the time and 'Now!' he whispered. 'Bloody now!'

Morry took off like a scared cat, and that scrabbling of stones would be Peachy following. Flat-capped heads turned at once, and one upping his piece, blast him, he'd one up the spout after all. Bloomer settled his own and fired. Down and hallelujah, but he himself was up and out of it, panting up the rocky slope for the cover of the brush above.

A couple came scudding across to block him, bayonets set to lunge. He bashed one away with his barrel and thrust hard in the other, the man screaming at him open-mouthed. The blade caught in the pull-out, it was up with the old Marylebone kick, boot in the belly to shove the man off, then turn panting for the other. Young and nervous, this one, weapon ready but hands trembling, Bloomer swiped at his mug and yelled 'Yah!' The kid stepped back wobbly, and Bloomer hadn't the heart, he really hadn't, he turned again for the crest and raced for the top. When he looked back down the boy hadn't moved.

Bloomer laughed. His blood was up, the warmth driving the fog from his bones, and there were Morry and Peachy waiting for him in the brush like a little gang of his own. 'Charges drawn?'

Morry passed him the spanner. 'Back to the battery, friend?'

Bloomer looked north towards their base. He couldn't see a blasted thing, but there was gunfire on the east side of the Careenage, and a moment later the boom of one of their own Lancasters. 'Nix on that,' he said, and turned to reloading. 'We'd be between the Russians and our guns. We'd best go straight to the battle, wherever that . . .' He stopped at a low, deep-throated roar rumbling off to the north-east.

'Shell Hill,' said Morry. He'd a compass in his noddle, that one, find his way home with a bag over his head. 'It looks like the twenty-sixth of October all over again.'

Bloomer snorted as he snapped on his cap. 'Let's hope this time there's enough to go round.' He slung his rifle and turned to grin at them as he strode forward into the brush. 'Here we go, boys. This way for Inkerman and all the fun of the fair.'

Woodall stirred his socks in the pan and listened uneasily to the sound of the guns. The next boom sent a circle of ripples over the surface of the water.

'Whew,' said Parsons, crouching and straightening as if it would help him see better in the fog. 'This is big, comrades, the buggers have got guns on Shell Hill.'

'Not just any guns,' said Truman, sitting up sharp. 'Hear it? Crown to a guinea that's Whistling Dick.'

The long whining whistle of the 32-pounder howitzer was unmistakable even before the *crump* that shook the ground. This time the Russians meant business.

Truman reached for his boots. 'We're for it, old sons. The Second will never handle that lot on their own.'

Woodall looked in horror at his soaking socks. Impossible to wear them like that, his feet would swell. The wood and water fatigues had already gone out, everything normal, it could still be a normal day . . .

'Stand to your arms!' bellowed an NCO, and he had time only to thrust his naked feet inside his boots, grab his rifle and run to fall in. No breakfast, no sleep, they were being marched out without even time to check their equipment.

A moment later it came, 'Left four deep, quick *march*!' and off they went to the Post Road, heading towards the roar of the guns. A scruffy lot they looked, and he could have wept to remember those splendid red and black lines marching in perfect order at the Alma. Now they were huddled into grey coats, bearded, ragged and filthy, and even their bearskins were gritty and matted. He was as bad himself, and it was only when he saw the blaze of artillery on the heights ahead that he realized something else was different too.

It hadn't even occurred to him to be afraid.

As they walked into camp Ryder saw only craftsmen and anxious women, all standing in silence as they looked towards the roar of the guns. What was left of the Light Brigade had already moved out, and was drawn up in long blue lines nearer the Col.

The reason was standing at the head of the valley. The fog lay thickly there, but the shifting clouds revealed a dark grey mass of men and horses behind, a Russian army right at the base of the Causeway Heights. They weren't doing anything, just watching and waiting, but their presence was a weapon all its own.

'Pinning us down,' he said. 'If we go to help the infantry they'll swoop on Balaklava.'

Mackenzie shrugged. 'It could be worse. Had we all sped to the harbour they'd be through the Col this minute and falling on our infantry from the rear.'

The harbour seemed irrelevant now; everything did in the voices of the great guns. Even the deserted camp seemed to scream with urgency and the sense of being left behind. Oliver dashed to the tent to fetch their swords, but Mackenzie stayed with Ryder as he led the horse with Jarvis's body and wondered what the hell he could say to Sally.

He didn't need to say anything. Oliver had warned her they'd been going into action, and as soon as she saw their burden she stopped and covered her mouth. He hardly dared look at her as he explained, but she was an army wife, she only thanked them quietly and said, 'Leave him with me now. You'll need to stand-to with the others.'

He did, and was ashamed that she knew it. 'He saved me, Sal. He wasn't even armed. He was a hero.'

Her skirt rustled as she knelt beside her husband. 'He would have liked that. It's all he had, you know, really. The army.'

Ryder looked down at her bent head. 'He had you.'

'Yes,' she said, and looked up at him with sadness in her eyes. 'He had me.'

The guns roared again from the Uplands, a ragged salvo of *boom-boom-boom*. He said inadequately, 'I'm sorry. I'd better . . .'

'Go,' she said, and smiled softly. 'He would have. Go.'

He turned and fled for the horse-lines, but was startled to find Mackenzie still keeping pace with him. 'I'm going for my horse, Niall, I've got to join the regiment.'

'I ken that,' said Mackenzie calmly. 'I'm coming with you.'

He wouldn't break step for something so ridiculous. 'Don't be a fool, you can't ride with the Light Brigade.'

'Then I'll run after you,' said Mackenzie. 'Do you no see it, Ryder, what kind of battle this will be?' He gestured at the grey-ness of the plateau, the thicker fog clumping at the base of the Sapoune. 'How will a man know even his own commanders in this?'

Ryder stopped. Mackenzie was right, it was the perfect setting for Angelo, for any man whose business was confusion and mis-direction. 'But I wounded him. He's hurt.'

'So are you,' said the Highlander. 'You should be under the surgeons right this minute, but you're going into battle and so will he. And I'll be biding right along with you, since in all this grand army there's just the four of us know his face.'

Woodall's ears hurt from the nearness of the guns. He couldn't see the ruddy things, only distant flashes in the murk, but the ground trembled under his boots and the mist carried black specks that stuck on his lips and eyelashes.

And this was Home Ridge, their main base on the Uplands! He'd have thought the so-called British Heights would be safe, but Russian artillery was pounding at them from Shell Hill, great big beasts of cannon that made their own 9- and 12-pounders sound like pop-guns. He wasn't too impressed by their defences either, the dry-stone and mud crestwork that in places was no more than two feet high.

But they weren't to stay here. The Line had obviously got themselves in trouble somewhere, scouts were talking to the Duke, and a moment later came the call 'The Brigade will advance!' Brigade indeed. The Coldstream hadn't come in from picquet yet, there was only themselves and the Scots Fusiliers and both woefully under strength. Seven hundred exhausted men the lot. But they were needed, the Guards never let the army down, so off they tramped, round to the east and Fore Ridge, the other prong of the V-shaped prominence that comprised the British Heights.

It wasn't much quieter. Dark shapes solidified in the fog as they passed the Hill Bend, another British battery and firing for dear life. The gun-captains were in charge here, each alone in the little world of his gun and his team, and quite oblivious to the Guards marching with such dignity a few yards to their rear. Their hoarse voices competed in savage desperation, 'Ready!' 'Ball!' 'Sponge out, damn your eyes, you want to blow us all to hell?' In Woodall's opinion they were already in it. Fog and smoke hung over them, guns black against the grey as they belched out orange fire. Every recoil rolled the monsters back like living things, and men rushed to haul them forward again, sweating slaves to their own machines. The images stayed with him as they tramped on past, and the voices followed him all the way. 'Load!' 'Stop your vent!' 'Fire!' 'Fire, damn it!' 'Fire!' 'Fire!' *'Fire!'*

As they toiled up Fore Ridge the ground opened in front of them like a widening pit to offer a first real glimpse of the battle. Fog clouded tantalizingly over the valley floor, but shapes were moving in it, yelling and spitting fire like a miniature version of the battle of the giants overhead. No red coats, Woodall noted sadly, it was British grey against Russian grey, but the ground was heaving with them, and where it thronged closest the orange bloom of rifle fire was replaced by the white flash of steel.

A ball flew overhead and crashed into the earth beyond. In range. A minute later a shell, iron fragments whizzing at them out of the fog and slashing a jagged tear down his sleeve. He'd have to ruddy sew that up when they got in. He marched on in the ragged grey column, horribly aware of his bare feet chafing in the discomfort of his boots.

They were heading for Mount Inkerman. He wondered if they were for the Barrier, that bit of wall the picquets used to shelter under in bad weather, but they went on west towards the slopes of the Kitspur, and he saw what it was they had to do. There was only the Sandbag Battery up there, a useless redoubt they'd long ago taken the guns out of, but it was a British outpost and those were Russians swarming over it, some even standing crowing on the parapet. Right then. Right. The enemy had taken it, and the Guards were here to take it back.

Another shell whizzed into them, and one of their officers' horses was down. 'Coo!' said Parsons, holding his bearskin hard on his head and grinning round at them like a street urchin. 'Coo!' Woodall ignored him. Orders were being given, the Scots Fusiliers halting behind, the Grenadiers were to go in first and they were going in *now*.

They turned downhill. Smoke and flying earth mingled with the deepening fog, but crimson and gold flashed in the greyness ahead of him, the colours being carried aloft. Lieutenant Turner held the Queen's, rich and red as their own hidden uniforms, but Lieutenant Verschoyle carried the Regimental, red, white, and blue of the Union with that golden III to mark the Third Battalion of Her Majesty's Grenadier Guards. Woodall's chin came up. Every movement of his swinging arms, every stride of his boots in step with the others, these things were suddenly precious in a way he'd never understood until now. They *were* a Brigade, the Guards Brigade, and by God, they were going in.

Ryder couldn't wait any longer. Inkerman was blowing to hell from the sound of it, but still the Light Brigade stood uselessly at their horses' heads while Lord George Paget lit cheroot after cheroot from the stub of the last. Ryder thrust his bridle at Oliver, said, 'Hold her, Polly,' and strode up to Lieutenant Grainger.

Grainger smiled wearily at him. 'Hullo, Sergeant, come to tell us how to run the war?'

'I have to be there, sir. You know why.'

Grainger turned to the Russians still waiting on the cusp of the South and North Valleys. 'They're pinning us down, can't you see? The picquets say it's Gorchakoff himself.'

Ryder cleared his throat. 'I understand, sir. I'm asking permission to go alone. Just me and Oliver.'

'Outrageous,' said Grainger, and looked directly at him. 'But the Uplands are no good for horse, we may never be ordered out at all. Take Oliver and go, I'll tell the colonel.'

Ryder saluted and started to turn, but Grainger's voice arrested him. 'Oh, and do take that Highlander, won't you? If his lordship condescends to leave his yacht he won't take kindly to an apparition of that kind.'

Ryder understood. A man in a kilt didn't look his best on horseback, and Cardigan would probably faint at the sight of Mackenzie. There were only sick horses left for him to choose from, and the beast he'd got was poor Bolton's mare, her back protected by a soft blanket but her height dwindled by the size of the man astride her.

He said, 'I'll take him, sir. And thanks.'

The tiredness fell away as he waved at Oliver and Mackenzie to join him. This was more like it, this was the thing, no officers, no orders, no one but the three of them riding together up the Col to a battle that called like the beat of a drum. Their hooves hit the track together, and the fog parted and closed behind them like the smoke of war.

Woodall kept his eyes on the colours and tramped steadily down. Musketry now, balls spitting and whining in among them, and in front a man sagging to his knees, but their line was broken by brushwood, the fog could hide a Grenadier as well as a Russian, and Woodall felt no more than a twitch at his sleeve as a ball whipped by.

Faster and faster they went, and now the fire was hotting up, shot, shell and musket balls pelting at them like driving rain. Men were falling, and nothing to do but elbow past them and go on, get through it and at them. Then Sergeant Norman yelled, 'Give it them, my lads!' and up went the Minié, tight to Woodall's cheek as he picked a Russian on the parapet and fired.

Click. Nothing. Horror smacked him as others exclaimed with the same discovery. What had possessed him not to draw his charge as soon as he got in? The crisp volley that ought to have swept the Russians clean off the hill was no more than a few ragged shots and a lot of ruddy cursing. His cheeks burned with his own stupidity – and the Scots Fusiliers watching from above! He was already lowering the barrel before Captain Tipping called it, his voice high and agonized, 'Give them the bayonet, my boys! In with the steel!'

He'd give them steel all right, shaming them like that, he was charging with the others and roaring as he went. The balls were nothing now, one clipped Truman in the shoulder but he was coming on anyway, they all were, on the slope to the Battery, up, up, up, and there was one in front of him, in and twist and out. The coats were a puzzler, thick and foiling the blade, but 'Faces!' shouted someone. 'Blow the coats, go at their beastly faces!' That was the stuff, and as he leaped up onto the ledge his rifle was already high over his shoulder to slash down the skull of the cowering Russian in front of him. Down and thrust him aside for the next, but there was no one there and his rush sent him thudding into a wall of sandbags. The Battery! They were there, and he hurtled through the embrasure into the space behind.

It was empty. Beyond the centre mound he saw flat-caps racing for the opposite embrasure, fleeing down the hill to the safety of St Clement's Ravine below. 'After them!' yelled Parsons, and the cry was taken up all round, 'Gone away, gone away!' 'Tally-ho!' Then Captain Tipping was in front of them with a revolver in his hand, shouting 'Stand, Grenadiers! Stand and hold your ground!'

Woodall lowered his rifle. The officer was right, of course, they'd won the high ground and it would be mad to abandon it for a few fleeing Russkies. He sat down on an overturned gabion and pulled out a new cap for the Minié.

'Here,' said Truman, passing him a thin metal tool. 'It's Sergeant Powley's, pass it on when you're done.'

Woodall took it gratefully and began to unscrew the nipple. 'We'll be all right here, won't we? We can hold this against anyone.'

Truman wriggled his wounded shoulder. 'Russians didn't, did they?'

He tore open a cartridge to sprinkle dry powder over the wet charge. 'They're not the Guards. They haven't our guts, nor our guns.'

Musket fire crashed on the far side of the Battery. 'They've got something,' said Truman, and ran for the wall.

Woodall made his fingers work faster. Nipple back on, new cap, fire into the ground, and the relief of the bang, his gun back in order. He chucked the tool to Parsons and started to load, but he was hearing other noises over the yelling and gunfire, men near him shouting and cursing in frustration. He snapped on his cap, made for the wall, and then he understood.

The sandbag walls were eight to ten feet high, but there was no banquette, nowhere for a man to stand to fire over the top. It was lower at the shoulder-joins, but there was only firing room for half a dozen at each and men were already clustering back round the embrasures to find space for their guns. A couple of idiots were clambering up the mound of the derelict magazine, but Captain Higginson had hardly yelled the warning before a musket cracked and the first man crashed heavily to the ground.

Woodall stared frantically round him. A working gun was no use if he couldn't fire the ruddy thing; he needed height to reach over that wall. He seized the nearest gabion, wrestled it to the sandbags, and furiously scraped up more earth to fill it solid. It took his weight, it would do, and he was up on it in an instant, lifting his head over the top layer of sandbags.

Fog and Russians. A thick mass was charging up the hill

towards them, only the red cap-bands and white steel of bayonets picking out men from mist. He fired at the nearest, and propped his elbow on the sandbags while he struggled to reload from his precarious perch.

'Watch it!' yelled an NCO from the embrasure. 'There's the Scots Fusiliers down there, don't be firing on our own chaps.'

About ruddy time those Scots turned up. He could see them himself when he next got his rifle up, the black bearskins picking them out clearly from the enemy, but they weren't coming up to support the Battery, they were turning off and charging at something else. 'Hoi!' called someone. 'Over here, you stupid Sawnies!' Woodall heard men guffawing round him, but his own mouth was suddenly dry. From his height he could see what they were up against, two dense columns of Russians emerging from the Quarry Ravine, a whole army against a couple of hundred of their own Guards.

And the Grenadiers couldn't help them. Stuck behind these stupid, blinding, good-for-nothing walls, they could only pour a fraction of their real firepower into an enemy that seemed to be growing as they looked, more and more of them materializing out of the fog and the earth. The Fusiliers were turning them all by themselves, the Grenadiers useless spectators, and it wasn't to be borne a moment longer. Others were already breaking for the embrasures, and he was with them, with them, empty rifle but a bayonet on the end of it which was all a Grenadier Guard would ever need.

Jostling, shoving, elbows jabbing, he was through the bottleneck and out on the freedom of the slope with baying Russians right there in front of him. Stab the first, stamp and out and slash the second right across the mouth, another looming, give him the butt smash on the jaw. Another man near, but it was Truman beside him, the two of them together against the whole grey hordes.

But not alone. They were all out now, all of them, and swooping on the Russians with vengeful fury. Back the beggars went, driven down the slopes like whipped dogs, but the ledge was a kind of overhang giving cover for them to lurk and regroup, they'd got to be booted out of it and quick. He was charging after them, so was Truman, so was Parsons, so were all of them, the Russians screaming defiance as they backed off step by step.

And then another yell, another howl, this time of triumph and from behind. Woodall stopped, scrubbed his sleeve across his mouth, and turned to look back.

The Battery. The Sandbag Battery they'd taken so gloriously was swarming with Russians again, at the embrasures, at the joins, one of them crowing from the mound itself. They'd lured out the Guards and taken it from the other side.

Oliver was shivering. Ryder had insisted on returning his cloak, but the clamminess of the fog turned to moisture on his hands and cheeks, and chilled his lungs as he breathed. The cold seemed almost visible in the whiteness of the air, giving even the rocks and trees an alien quality as if they were riding into another country far away. The guns grew louder with every step.

'Home Ridge,' said Ryder, turning left off the road. 'There's reserves up there, let's find out what's going on.'

Oliver thought of the enormous reserves at the Alma, and was shocked at how few men remained on Home Ridge. A Rifle battalion was drawn up in readiness on the lower slopes, and sections of the 20th and 95th Foot stood with the frustrated expression of dogs kept on a leash, but otherwise there seemed only to be little parties of stragglers wandering round aimlessly in the fog, looking for orders, for an officer, for a unit to which to belong. Picquets driven in perhaps, wounded looking for a dressing station, but an Irishman was bellowing 'The 88th! Has no one seen the Rangers?' and a group of bewildered privates from the 77th sat huddled on the grass like abandoned baggage. The only other unit of any size was the 30th, and they were bundled up against the lower crestwork, half of them asleep. Their clothes were blackened and bloody, and it was clear they were survivors rather than reserves.

There was no need to ask where the rest were. A group of senior officers were examining the field through telescopes, but musket and artillery fire seemed to boom from everywhere, the whole Uplands engulfed in the smoke of battle. Oliver looked down over the field, and slowly felt his blood warm. They were part of this, or soon would be. They might not be fighting in the line, but if they won out today they could save a regiment, a battle, perhaps even a war.

'Well, cock your leg and cry "Sugar," ' said a familiar voice. 'If it ain't the bleeding cavalry come to save us.' Bloomer, of course, sprawled on the grass with a mixed group of refugees, sucking a piece of grass and grinning up at them with knowing eyes.

Ryder dismounted at once. 'Bloomer, you old warrior. Seen any fight yet?'

Bloomer took the grass from his mouth and spat. 'Regular wallflowers, that's what *we* are. We've been told to play with the 95th, but they've packed half of them off already with His Nibs the Duke of Cambridge.'

'Cambridge?' Oliver couldn't keep the surprise from his voice. 'But surely he's . . .'

'The Guards, right,' said Bloomer. 'Give that man a coconut. But there's a row on at the Sandbag Battery, and he's sent for the peasants to help.'

He mustn't think about Woodall now, they were here for something bigger. 'What else is going on? Have you heard anything?'

Bloomer tilted his head. 'Anything in particular, young Polly? Or should I say any*one*?'

'Someone,' said Ryder. 'He got away from me, Bloomer, we're here to finish the job.'

'Ah,' said Bloomer in a long exhalation of breath. 'Well, I told you, didn't I? Going to come to this in the end.' He stroked a fat finger lovingly up and down the barrel of his rifle.

Mackenzie looked startled. Oliver remembered how he'd felt himself when Bloomer first suggested it, but that was before the

North Valley. Now if he saw in front of him the man who'd murdered the Light Brigade he knew he wouldn't hesitate.

Ryder clearly wouldn't either. 'Of course. If we can find him.'

Bloomer pulled a face. 'I'd leave the nags if I was you, it's legwork down there.' He heaved round his bulk to face the other linesmen and said, 'Right, cullies, lend us your lugholes. These coves need to find a staff nob, black nag, green spread, cocked felt. Anyone copped a sight?'

Oliver blinked, but nobody seemed to see anything odd in the question. A ragged private from the 49th said, 'Not many on horseback today, they're too much of a target. They got General Adams that way.'

'Oh, I've seen a few,' said a corporal of the 41st. 'Duke of Cambridge is up. Don't know about the others, though, they all look alike.'

'Not this one,' said Ryder. 'He's been wounded, face and head. There might be a dressing.'

The corporal's face cleared. 'Oh, *him*. Nose like a Sunday morning and bandage round his neck? He was nipping between us and the Barrier all the while.'

Ryder's voice sounded deceptively casual. 'And where were you, Corp? In the thick of it, obviously.'

'Oh, nowhere important,' said the corporal. 'Just that hill above the Inkerman Tusk. You know – the one you were just talking about. The Sandbag Battery.'

Woodall stuck down his head and charged. They'd got reinforcements arriving, Coldstream and all sorts, he wasn't having them retake the Battery under their noses when the Grenadiers had already done it twice.

The last yards were always the worst. It was so ruddy steep they were all puffed out by the time they reached the Battery, a bunch of gasping wrecks the Russians could pick off at leisure. Well, not this time, oh no, Woodall was going all the way.

He threw himself forward, yelling as he ran, and by his side Truman was yelling too. For a second their eyes met, both open-mouthed and roaring, then they grinned, looked away and ran on.

And here was the Ledgeway, he would *not* stop, he was pumping his legs over it right to the embrasure, Russians backing off and away, then he was in, ruddy well shoved in by the force of the men thrusting behind. Some of the Russians were making a fight of it, backing away with bayonets levelled, and the crowd of Guards were driven right in after them. Parsons was going it like a terrier at the front, and the whole crush between them, but when the Russians turned to bolt there was Parsons down with more cuts than a man could count. Woodall pulled him away to the wall and turned back to the fray, but the fight was over, both their own colours coming in, and the Battery was theirs. They'd been in and out so many times it was hard to tell, but the flags were the one thing that never changed.

He went back to the wall. Truman was bending over Parsons, but he stood as Woodall reached him and simply shook his head. Shame. Poor old 'Nasty', he'd never had much going for him, but he deserved a better end than that.

He leaned back against the sandbags to reload, and felt an odd sinking sensation as his fingers encountered one lone cartridge in his pouch. He vaguely remembered it now, opening the last packet, but that had been nine shots ago and this was all that was left.

'Me too,' said Truman grimly. He groped for Parsons's pouch, but that too was flat and empty.

Woodall felt in his coat, and breathed in relief at the familiar touch of paper, the packet he always made sure to keep hidden. 'There's another ten here. Five each.'

Truman's face split in a long, slow grin. 'Thanks, chum.' The hand he held out was calloused and dirty, the nails broken and blackened, but Woodall shook the cartridges into it without a qualm. Six shots each in all, say the Russians came again three times . . .

Gunfire again, blast them, and he wasn't loaded. Someone

was, a Scots Fusilier firing blindly into the grey, but there were scores of Russians thrusting forward and at the parapet before his cap was even on. He threw himself at the gap, slamming and smashing out with the gun that was now no more than a club, yelling 'Get out of it, get back!' A bayonet stabbed at his face, but he was already ducking and felt it only slice the top of his shoulder as it passed. His left fist closed on the heaviness of the top sandbag, and up it came, swiping right, left, knocking them down like ninepins, and his voice hoarse in his own ears screaming 'Get back, you bloody bastards, *get back!*'

The fog thickened as they descended into the valley, but Ryder never doubted the scale of what lay beneath. The thumping of artillery was familiar, so was the brittle hammering of musketry, but not even at the Alma had he known such yelling, such clashing of wood and steel. Little skirmishes roared up at them out of the gloom, bands of stragglers locked in hand-to-hand combat, while distant voices rallied invisible armies, 'To me, 21st!' 'Come on, 63rd!' and somewhere far behind them the war-cry of the 20th, the distinct deep ululation of the Minden Yell.

The slopes of Fore Ridge grew thick with brush, some of it four and five feet high, and they kept in cover as long as they could. The big guns couldn't tell friend from foe down here and were fighting it out overhead, but musket balls cracked from trees and rocks, they flew blind in the fog and ricocheted from all sides. Mackenzie's red coatee was the big danger, the only splash of colour in the whole monochrome world, and Ryder insisted on wrapping Oliver's cloak over it before they emerged onto the valley floor.

It was safer than it looked. They were only three fleeting shadows in the fog, of no interest to men watching out for whole battalions that leaped up out of nowhere and fell on them with fixed bayonets. When foreign voices and the tramp of boots warned of a Russian column passing ahead, they had only to crouch against a jutting crag to melt into the black-fissured grey of the stone.

But the Russians weren't just passing, they were prowling with muskets low, bayonets fixed to make spears pointing at the earth. Then one jerked, stopped and stabbed down, not at earth, not at ground, but at a grey shape that lifted horrifyingly with the blade only to be scraped down off it again with a high black boot. These were men they were spiking, British wounded and dead lying on the valley floor, the bastards were butchering the dead.

Mackenzie made a choking noise and turned his face to the stone. 'Heathens,' he said. '*Heathens.*' His knuckles were white on the barrel of his gun.

Another stabbed, and a man squealed, a wounded soldier being hacked to death in front of them. Ryder dug his nails deep into the palms of his hands, but there were just three of them, they could only hide and watch as helplessly as children. Above them was the world of Alma and Balaklava, of open lines and heroic charges, but here beneath the shrouding fog was the terrible underbelly of war.

There was another reality too, and the stone felt cold against his back as more and more of the marching figures loomed and passed in the mist. Even this one little column was numbered in the hundreds, and he'd seen scores of them from the heights of Fore Ridge, maybe thirty or forty thousand coming against their own seven or eight. The guns too, a never-ending line of them blasting out all along Shell Hill and beyond, eighty, ninety, maybe even a hundred when the British must have less than forty.

'The French,' muttered Oliver, and Ryder knew he too was starting to count. 'They must know we're in trouble, they'll come.'

There was no sign of them yet. The only colour Ryder could see was a distant glimpse of red coats vanishing round the flank of the Kitspur. That must be the Fourth Division, he'd seen some discarding their greatcoats to fight in red, but why were they going round there? The frail defence of the Barrier was all that stood against the enemy pouring out of the Quarry Ravine, so why were the Fourth ignoring the wide open gap to march east?

But everyone was, even the Russian column finally coming to an end in front of them. The fighting was hottest on the Kitspur, a fierce shouting and frenzy of movement, with even the stragglers catching the infection and following the hordes turning for the Sandbag Battery.

'Why?' said Oliver wonderingly as they stood and rubbed their limbs after the crouching of concealment. 'There's nothing there.'

'Is there not?' said Mackenzie, and pointed through the fog at the distant slopes. 'See it? That'll draw every British soldier on the Chersonese, aye, and every Russian too.'

Ryder followed his finger to the rounded hill of the Sandbag Battery and felt something move in his throat. Two little patches of colour flew above its crown, one as red as Mackenzie's coatee, and both standing out like beacons against the greyness of the sky.

There was no ruddy end to them. Woodall could hear the Coldstream firing busily on their right flank, the Scots Fusiliers on their left, he knew there were wings of linesmen in support either side, but still the Russians kept coming, wave after wave, as if the Quarry Ravine was bottomless and they were boiling up from the centre of the earth.

They weren't even Russians now, just moustached faces thrusting forward one after the other, open-mouthed and screaming. They were musket balls thudding into men's bodies or spraying up earth from the ground, bayonets jabbing over the parapet, hands clutching at the sandbags, legs trying to climb over, flat-capped heads to be clubbed and bellies to be stabbed. Woodall's feet were sliding in his boots, but he dug in his heels and fought forward, bashing and hacking and yelling with the best.

His cartridges had long gone. Truman had ducked back into the enclosure to raid the pouches of the dead, but he doubted there'd be time to load anyway. Captain Burnaby was darting into the gaps with a pistol, shouting 'Hold them, my boys, keep the beggars back!' but Woodall's own body was the front line, his and the men next to him behind a wall now hardly three feet high. Some hurled stones to defend themselves, some scraped up handfuls of earth and chucked it in the Russians' faces, but the Russians were using the mounting corpses as a ramp, trampling their own dead to hurtle over the wall. Too many at once, and sandbags were scattering, he was thrown back and down as a whole pack charged into the enclosure.

Truman was in their path. Woodall lost sight of him, there were only grey backs and the rise and thrust of bayonets, then the Russians swept on leaving Truman in a bloodied heap on the ground. Guards on the walls leaped to run after them, driven to a frenzy by the longed-for sight of enemy within reach. Someone was yelling, 'Come on, come on, plenty for everyone!'

But there weren't. The few Russians inside weren't anything like enough for the frustration of men who'd been forced all this time to stand impotent behind high walls. Some were rushing out of the embrasures to get at more of them, and even Captain Burnaby was climbing over the parapet to join the fight below. The battle seemed to be outside for a while, so Woodall clambered to his feet and went to find Truman.

He was still alive, but spluttering bright red blood down his chin. Woodall propped him against the magazine, but the ripped and broken belly told him there was nothing to be done. Truman knew it too. He made a face like an irritated child, said 'All up, chum,' and gave Woodall the faintest of smiles.

Woodall tried to think of something uplifting to say, but his wretched mind was blank, he was hearing only that word 'chum' and wanting to cry.

'Fun though, wasn't it?' said Truman, and spat out blood. 'Like playing King of the Castle as a kid.'

Woodall struggled. 'I've never played it.'

'No,' said Truman, and there was something sad in his eyes. 'I don't suppose you have.' His face screwed into spasm, then his mouth fell open and the blood poured out unchecked.

The sound of gunfire seemed to come from a long way away.

Woodall turned wearily back to the walls, but saw with a growing unease they were now half empty, abandoned by their defenders in the dash outside. He walked back to his old place to look over the parapet.

The valley was in turmoil. Everywhere he looked men were hurtling down the slopes to join the battle on the valley floor, red-coated linesmen thronging in among the fighting mass of grey. Only the 46th and 68th were fighting in red today, it had to be the Fourth Division, but why were they here, why had they abandoned the heights? Others were catching the contagion, the Coldstream starting to swoop downhill and even the Scots Fusiliers edging from their post on the ridge to advance on the Russians below. What possessed them? It was against orders, against sense, what the hell did they think they were playing at?

'Charge,' said a voice, vaguely familiar and somewhere above him. 'Charge!'

Then the whole enclosure was at it, loyal, level-headed Guards yelling 'Charge, charge!' and rushing to the embrasures, leaping and vaulting over the low shoulders of the work, taking a way out anywhere they could find. 'No!' yelled the Duke, 'No!' yelled General Bentinck, 'No!' yelled Lieutenant Verschoyle, holding firm to the colours, but they were all ignored, everything forgotten in the need to be let loose on the Russians outside. One man had done this, one order, and Woodall looked frantically round to see who had given it.

And there he was. On horseback outside the enclosure, little to see but the cocked hat and beneath it a bandaged neck and battered face Woodall knew he ought to recognize. No staff officer would come out looking like that, and this man wasn't one. He oughtn't to be here, he should be dead or captured in the ambush Ryder had set, but somehow the spy was right among their own ranks and leading them all to destruction.

23

5 November 1854, 8.10 a.m. to 2.00 p.m.

Ryder knew. The Guards hurtling pell-mell down the slopes, their officers' vain shouts of 'Halt, halt!' – it was the bloody Alma all over again and the same evil mind behind it. He yelled 'Come on!' and began to pound harder up the gully.

'It's all right,' panted Oliver, struggling to keep pace. 'The Russians are running, I can't see an ambush.'

'Look up,' said Ryder savagely. 'Can't you see, we're losing the high ground.'

They'd already lost it. The flags still flew in the Sandbag Battery, but there was only a small wing of linesmen left to protect it, while everyone else was plunging into the valley or pursuing the fleeing Russians into St Clement's Ravine behind. The Fourth Division should be round there somewhere, but devastating gunfire round the Kitspur's flanks suggested they too were in trouble. The whoops of distant victory were already changing to cries of alarm, and again came the gunfire, again and again, pierced only by the frantic call of an invisible trumpet begging for help. There bloody well was an ambush somewhere, and creeping round here too. Russians were emerging from cover and firing from the hillside, the valley was only an invitation to death.

Some Guards had already seen it, and were pelting back for Fore Ridge and the safety of their own Heights. There were troops up there, thank God, swarming round the highest point at Mount Head, but as the Guards neared them a little bloom of whiteness flowered in the fog, then another, and the bang of musketry echoed round the hills. The troops were Russians, Russians on the British Heights, firing down on the helpless soldiers below.

No time to ask how, no time for anything but to climb. The Battery was alone and unprotected above them, Russians already starting to move towards it from Mount Head, and nothing in their way but those linesmen on the ridge. That would be the 95th, one of the most solid regiments in the Line, they only needed to hold long enough for reinforcements to sweep the Russians off the Heights. He climbed higher and higher, until the linesmen became individuals above him, hopping from one leg to the other with cold while they looked enviously at the fight below. There'd be an officer here somewhere, someone he could –

'Charge!' yelled a voice. 'At them, 95th! Charge!'

'No!' Ryder shouted. 'No, hold your ground!' but he was one lowly cavalryman with hardly the breath to speak, and the Derbyshire men were already breaking ranks to pour headlong down the hill. An officer shouted 'Who gave that order?' another cried 'No, men, stay where you are!' but still they were pelting downhill, thicker and thicker, down and down. He ran with arms outstretched to stop them, but they came charging on, a heavy body cannoned into him, his legs swept from under him, and his head thumped hard on the stony ground. Black-trousered legs stampeded all sides of him, the 95th running down and out of reach.

Mackenzie pulled him out of their path, and he didn't bother to resist. The linesmen were gone, and the Heights left empty for the Russians advancing on the Battery. Only one man was up there now, a horseman turning away into the fog, and Ryder didn't need to make out the shape of the cocked hat to know who it must be. Angelo had won again.

Oliver swept off his shako in defeat. 'They'll get the colours. We can't stop them.'

They were moving now, those two defiant banners, hurrying out of the Sandbag Battery as if their bearers had only just realized the danger, but the cluster of Guards around them couldn't number more than a hundred. Flags, that was all, nothing for a man to die for, but the thought of Angelo laying hands on them was suddenly unbearable.

He struggled to his feet and said, 'We can try.'

Woodall pressed close to the colour party. The Russians were after his flag.

And looked like ruddy getting it. Urgency screamed in the officers' voices as they urged them all faster, faster, on along the ridge to where the Scots Fusiliers should have been, where the 95th should have been, and where suddenly there was no one at all. A few stragglers were clambering back up to reach them, but their only hope was to beat through the Russians on Mount Head to the safety of the British lines.

It wasn't much of one. Officers were pleading with the Duke, 'You must go, sir, you simply can't be taken,' and a moment later their commander galloped away from them, riding hard for Mount Head with only his aide by his side. Woodall watched breathlessly as he scraped by the left flank of the approaching Russian infantry, but the horses won the day, the Duke was through and past with only a few stray musket balls flying harmlessly round his departing shadow.

But now it was their turn, and they had to do it on foot. Woodall glanced behind and saw how few they were now, sixty at best, with thousands closing in on them from all sides. He said, 'This looks sticky,' but the man next to him wasn't Truman, he was a linesman and a stranger. Woodall was in the worst mess he'd faced in his whole life, and he was quite alone.

'Carry high the colours!' called an officer, and up went the Regimental at their front. The Queen's was even nearer, Lieutenant Turner was only a rank in front of Woodall, and the great red flag was spreading and shining right before his eyes. There was no wind to swell it, but Turner was waving it, flying it broad and high to draw the eyes of any stragglers, to bring any British soldier with a soul running to their aid. Woodall's eyes filled with water, but still the colours waved and nobody came.

Except the Russians. A roar of voices was growing behind them, enemy flocking from round the Battery to chase this greater prize. The lot from Mount Head were spreading to take them front and right flank, there was nothing to do but run and keep left. Order crumbled, other men's boots banging into his heels, some turning aside to fire at Russians climbing up from the valley. Verschoyle would make it, surely he would, charging in the same path as the Duke, but the advancing Russians were curving round at his rear, cutting off Turner's band of defenders from following.

Then here it was again, the bang of musketry and clash of bayonets ahead. 'Close in!' called English voices, 'Close round the colours!' and he was, he couldn't get any closer, they could have covered the lot of them with a ruddy sheet. But there was behind to watch too, and he swung round to face off the Russians coming the other way.

They were coming all right, a great rampaging pack of them, but a group of maybe fifteen Guards were spreading across the ridge to block them. Captain Burnaby had come back to save them, he was making a rear-guard to help them get away. It bought time, it bought him the seconds to swing back and thrust at the Russian running in from his right. Another behind him, two, they must have cut past Burnaby. Woodall stamped and lunged into one, lowered his head and rammed it smash into the other's face. The colours were already yards away, he turned to follow – and stopped.

Burnaby was right. Fighting by the colours only slowed them, giving the Russians time to move in. To defend them he had to let them go, to stand here and let nobody past. He turned again, planted his feet square on the turf, brought up his rifle and realized with dull astonishment he was waiting to die.

And here it came. Another Russian through, Woodall braced to meet him, but something jerked him back, the man he'd already downed was grabbing round his knees. He was wobbling, tottering, kicking out at the clinging man's face, screaming and weaving with his bayonet at the other. Yet another coming, a man thundering up the slope from his right, he yelled 'Get back, back!' and spun the bayonet to face him, but the colour was blue, not grey, and the face was Harry Ryder's.

For a terrible second Woodall wondered if his mind had snapped, but a pistol cracked and the Russian in front fell, that was really Ryder springing to his side, and behind him ran Mackenzie and Polly Oliver. He was surrounded by friends, they'd seen him in danger and come for him, and his head whirled in a sudden intoxication of happiness.

More Russians were running at him, maybe a dozen, but he kicked away the one at his knees and wondered why he'd found it so hard before. He heard the ring of steel as Ryder and Oliver drew their swords, he heard Mackenzie fire, and stood ready with his own bayonet to face whatever came. They stood side by side, the four of them, and when the enemy were near enough they charged. The joy of attacking, fighting forward, the rifle thrust out, not tucked into his own body, he roared in the faces of the Russians as he cut them down. There were more coming behind, Burnaby's men must be down, but still he was stamping and thrusting, aware of the whistling of Ryder's sword clearing space to his left, of Oliver's to his right, of the occasional crack of their pistols, and beyond them a terrifying war-cry he knew must be Mackenzie.

Then something else was dashing in from their flank, a great rush of men cheering and yelling, he glimpsed scarlet trousers and knew it was the French. The Frogs were in, *now* the Russians would catch it, but there were still these beggars in front to deal with, and even as he bashed the butt down on a man's skull he was turning with eagerness for the next. Another, but he stumbled over a corpse as he lunged, and an icy pain ripped into his chest, the shock tightening like a hand round his throat. He stabbed out blindly, but his knees were buckling, Ryder's voice cried 'Woody!' then he tasted blood in his mouth and knew.

He was on the ground, men's feet stamping round him, but his breathing was bubbly and painful, and he wanted to see his friends. He strained up his neck to peer through the fog, and saw high in the distance a square of red that caught his heart and stopped his breath. The Queen's colour was past the Russians, it was safe and starting round to the British lines at Home Ridge. Its red and gold were blackened with smoke and tattered by gunfire, but he gazed until his eyes darkened and knew it was the most beautiful thing he had ever seen.

Ryder slashed after the last retreating Russian and dropped to his knees by Woodall's side. The French had it now, they were charging after the fleeing enemy, the bloody army could give him a moment to look to his friend.

Dennis Woodall was dead. The ugly red wound splattered through his greatcoat was seeping, not bleeding, and the eyes gazed openly at nothing. Ryder brushed them gently closed, and wondered what had brought that little smile to the dead face, what made it look so peaceful. Above him he heard Oliver mumbling softly and knew he was praying.

'A brave end,' said Mackenzie sadly. 'He was a fine soldier.' He began to reload.

That was all really, and Ryder knew it. There was no room for sentiment here, this was just another dead soldier in a battle, another victim of the bloody madness caused by a man Ryder had allowed to escape.

He looked up in despair into the grey world. The fog was thinner on the ridge, floating and wispy, opening little glimpses of clarity in the murk. The Grenadier colours were already out of sight, but he heard the distant cheering that greeted them from the British lines beyond. The sound drifted back over the slopes to the shadowy figure of a horseman standing in a fold of the hills, as if he too had stopped to listen. The fog eddied and drifted, wreathing him in smoke, then parted to reveal a cloaked figure in a cocked hat, whose head was just turning to Ryder as if he knew himself watched. There was a bandage round his neck.

Then he was scrabbling to his feet, snatching uselessly at his empty revolver, remembering Mackenzie's rifle, shouting 'Niall – there! Shoot him – there!'

Mackenzie turned on the first word, and had the Minié up on the third, but the horseman had already turned to ride away, an ordinary respectable British staff officer. A fraction of a second, Mackenzie hesitating, Ryder screamed '*Now!*' but the horseman heard him, he was turning again, and then the bang, two of them, like an expanded echo. Angelo was toppling, but it was the horse that was hit, he himself rolling free, and Ryder turned to see Mackenzie dropping to his knees, his bonnet blown off, his curly hair growing redder and redder, then his whole body slumping gently to the ground. God, no, not another, not Mackenzie too.

Then he was screaming again, this time without words, and running as if there were no such things as pain and tiredness, pounding after the unhorsed Russian, the man who'd done all of it and had to be made to pay. Oliver was with him, he heard the frantic panting and thudding of feet, and the gasps that told him the boy was crying as he ran. He should save it, the time for that was later, now they were going to kill.

Angelo knew it, he was going all out for the safety of the Quarry Ravine. He had distance on them, he could reach it in two minutes, but he'd been hurt in the fall, his running was awkward, lop-sided and clumsy, and slowly they were gaining. A smooth crop of rocks, Ryder ran up and over them, dug in his boot and sprang. Angelo swung wildly round with the revolver, but Ryder's sabre was already slashing down, crunch across the forearm, drop it, you bastard, drop it and fight like a man.

The pistol fell, but Angelo jumped back to snatch out his own sword. It was good British steel, better than Ryder's own, but what mattered was the arm that wielded it, and Angelo's was wounded and Ryder's young and strong and driven to rage at the death of his friends. He never even thought of the cavalry drill, it was a man not a target he was hitting, and he did it with hate.

Once to beat the sword away, back across the cheek, down across the front of the chest, up to slice the jaw, then step back to stab the knee and bring the bastard down where he belonged. Down he came, thump on the grass, bleeding and coughing, human and beatable and finally beaten. Ryder drew back his sword to impale him to the ground.

'No!' cried Oliver behind him. 'Not while he's down!'

Ryder gripped his hilt harder and damned British decency to hell, but it was no good, the words had been said, the notion was in, and he was back in the old, clean world they'd left behind above the fog. He lowered the sword, and looked down at the man who'd done so much to destroy it. A quick death was too good for him anyway.

'You're right, Poll. He's a prisoner, we'll tie him up and take him to Raglan.'

The Russian's eyes burned in the wreck of his face. He lifted his head in a grotesque parody of dignity, and said, 'Better to finish it now, damn you. The game is over, and I dislike post-mortems.'

It had never been a game. 'No post-mortem. Just a good, honest British trial.'

Angelo's jaw was broken, but still the lips smiled. 'Do you really think Lord Raglan will allow the world to know what fools the British have been? There will be no trial, only a quiet exchange as is usual between gentlemen.'

'Not for spies,' said Ryder. 'We hang those.' He turned to Oliver and said, 'Help me with him, Polly, we've got to get him –'

Oliver's mouth was opening, eyes wide in panic, and Ryder swung back round. Angelo had flung sideways and in his hand was the revolver retrieved from the grass. Ryder leaped forward, but the barrel was already flashing orange and the bang came with Oliver's cry. Oliver, standing shocked and white, hands pressed above his belly and thick red blood oozing out between his fingers. Ryder whirled round at the Russian, hacking down at the hand, the arm, then slicing across the exposed throat. Dead, but he slashed back again just to be sure, and only then did he see the little smile of victory on the Russian's face. The bastard had played for this and won.

He flung away the sword and turned back to Oliver, but the boy was on his knees, hugging his body as if trying to hold it together. Ryder seized the dead Russian, rolled him over and ripped off the clean back of his shirt. Fine, white linen, unsullied by Angelo's blood, he wrapped it round Oliver's torn side and took the Russian's cloak to tie the dressing in place. His fault, *his fault*, Angelo hadn't given a damn about Polly, he'd only shot him to make Ryder give him a clean death.

'We did it though, didn't we?' murmured Oliver. 'We got him. He won't be betraying anyone else.'

It didn't seem much of a victory, not now. He was becoming aware again of the world outside their own little pocket in the fog, the rumble of artillery and rattle of musketry, the business of war that the death of a single spy couldn't stop. But there were nearer, sharper sounds in among them, shouting and the pounding of feet running this way. He looked across at the Quarry Ravine and glimpsed white cross-belts in the fog, more Russians pouring out to assail the Barrier and the British Heights behind.

'Time to go, Poll,' he said casually. He slung Oliver's arm round his shoulder, gripped tightly round the waist and hauled him carefully to his feet. 'All right?'

Oliver looked at him dazedly. 'You can't, you've got to leave me. That's the rules.'

Ryder thought of those wounded men being scraped off Russian bayonets. 'Not me, I want one of those medals you were talking about.'

Oliver looked steadily at him. 'You said they were only for officers.'

'Maybe they'll make an exception. Now get moving, or there'll be nothing left to pin the medals on.' He took the weight and eased him gently forward, manoeuvring them step by step back from the Quarry Ravine. It would be safest to head for the Barrier, but the Russians were going there, they'd have to slide round them and look for British help near Fore Ridge.

'Mackenzie,' muttered Oliver, as Ryder paused to lift him bodily over a rocky outcrop. 'We must go back for Mackenzie.'

'He'll be all right,' said Ryder, praying desperately it was true. 'There were all those French there, they'll look after him. It's probably only a scalp wound.'

'Yes,' said Oliver. 'Yes.' His eyes were wide and dark, and a tiny line of pink saliva was dribbling down his chin.

Ryder cursed under his breath and hurried them on. The Russians weren't close enough to be worrying, they were too intent on the fierce fighting round the Barrier, but Oliver was going to die if he didn't get a surgeon fast. It shouldn't matter, he'd be just another dead soldier like Woodall, like Jarvis, like Bolton, Fisk, Marsh and Hoare, like Ginger long ago, but still he pushed himself harder across the bumpy ground, lifting Oliver, half-carrying him, all but dragging him over the scree, anything to save this stupid, ignorant boy who'd been fool enough to believe Harry Ryder could be a hero.

They were back at the slopes leading to the Sandbag Battery, but there were no lines of defence here, no doctors or reserves, no British soldiers to protect the British Heights. Even the French had disappeared, and when he looked up he saw glimmers of turquoise round the Battery and more stringing out along Inkerman Tusk. A few British troops were wandering in the fog, but they were refugees like themselves, turning in hope to the sound of footsteps then seeing only wounded cavalry and looking away. Ryder laid Oliver down on the soft grass and looked about him in despair.

'Isn't there anyone on Fore Ridge?' said Oliver, craning to see. 'Surely there's . . .'

There were Russians on Fore Ridge, still massed round Mount Head, and now Ryder knew how they'd got there. The ground was empty of British forces from the Barrier to the Sandbag Battery, a gap in their defences a quarter-mile wide.

He said, 'It's no good, I'll have to get you to the Barrier. The Russians will be pouring through here any minute.'

Oliver's hands were moving restlessly over the grass. 'They'll get to Fore Ridge. Behind it. Our guns, the camps. Balaklava.'

There was no point pretending. 'Yes. Come on, I'll carry you.'

Sweat was breaking out on Oliver's forehead and he screwed his eyes shut. 'We've got to stop them. If this is the gap, we've got to hold it.'

If it hadn't been Polly he'd have laughed. 'What – you and me?'

Oliver retched, a racking, bubbling sound that brought Ryder's head up fast. 'You can. At least a bit of it. You always said . . .'

Ryder crouched in front of him and seized the flailing hands. 'Don't you bloody die on me, Polly, I won't have it. Where's my medal then?'

Oliver's mouth stretched in a little smile, then drooped and relaxed while his eyes closed in a parody of sleep. His breathing was very faint.

Ryder clutched the limp fingers, then gently let them drop. Unconsciousness took the boy out of pain, but he'd die without help, and Ryder couldn't reach it. It wasn't going to come to them either, not while that gap remained, inviting the Russians to pour in and take it, win the battle and the war, drive the British and their incompetent commanders all the way back into the sea.

Hold it, said that voice in his head. *Hold it. You can.*

Trust Oliver to believe in him only when he was talking utter rot. Yes, one man could make a difference, but it would take a regiment of them to hold this gap. A regiment . . .

He looked again into the swirling fog. Footsteps, movement, occasional voices, groups of one or two, maybe three, but if he added them all together? But that was stupid too, he couldn't make them, he was no one, just a . . .

He glanced down at the bright yellow chevrons on his own dark sleeve. They were meaningless bits of cloth given to him for nothing more heroic than being flogged, but to people like Oliver they meant something, and to men like Mackenzie too. Jarvis had used them to make things happen at the harbour.

He turned into the fog, saw shadowy red figures in front of him and shouted, 'You men! Here to me, at the double!'

They came. Four linesmen, running with eagerness, glad of the presence of authority. 'Yes, Sergeant?'

Fourth Division, the 68th. 'Are there any more of you?'

They could only shrug and look vaguely about them. A lance-corporal said, 'Our officers were killed, up by St Clement's Ravine. The general's dead, Cathcart's gone. We'll be rallying some-where, but I don't . . .'

'We'll rally *here*,' said Ryder, gesturing an arc to spread round the slope. 'Spread out, find yourselves cover, and hold back any-thing breaking through to Fore Ridge, got it?'

He didn't wait to see if they had, there was more movement ahead of him, a wounded man being supported by two compan-ions, three more bodies to fill his gap. He leaped after them, calling, 'You, back here! I need you in this line.'

There was no line, he was making it as he went along, but it helped them believe in it as a proper plan. The next group came unasked, a bunch of Connaught Rangers drawn to the sound of activity, then some Coldstream Guards who burst enthusiasti-cally from cover at the sight of organization. In two minutes he had a score of them, then two dozen, throwing out the line to cover more and more ground. It was still pitiful, more of an out-post than a line, but it would block a whole column trying to break through, and could harry the flanks of anything smaller slipping by.

It might even do more, and as he brought in a trio from the 49th he realized how little their weakness showed. The fog curled thickly about the base of the slope, showing only the shapes of men moving among the rocks and the occasional glint of a bay-onet. The Fourth Division were most visible of all, and as he watched his new recruits take their places he realized suddenly the value of what they had.

'Coats off!' he yelled down the line. 'Never mind the cold, get your coats off and show Ivan who he's bloody fighting.'

A heavily bearded private of the 20th looked at him squint-eyed. 'But they'll see us, Sergeant, we'll stand out like blazes in red.'

'Of course!' he said, and laughed at the simplicity of it. 'We can't beat them, so we're going to bloody scare them. Come on, spread out, make them think we're twice as many, they'll run all the way back to Odessa!'

The difference was magical, a thin red line appearing out of the mist. Nothing as a fighting force, but it needn't be if it only stopped the Russians realizing how weak they were. The idea was catching now, and men began to improvise their own improvements, heaving rocks into the line, wedging discarded muskets into forks of trees, sticking shakos on the top of boulders, making a ghost army that would be all the oncoming Russians needed to see.

'They can still come round us,' said the corporal of the 68th, as he scavenged for cartridges in the pouches of the dead. 'We haven't the firepower to stop them.'

Ryder began to load his revolver. 'It won't be for long. Lord Raglan must know about this, he's bound to send reinforcements.'

'Already did,' said the corporal. 'He sent us, didn't he, only then he changed his mind. We had a staff officer come after us, I saw him talking with old Cathcart.'

Ryder's fingers froze on the ball, and the memory of that last smile on Angelo's face filled him with icy understanding. The bastard thought he'd defeated them even in death. Well, not yet. Thanks to Oliver there'd be one last round, the very last, and this time Ryder was going to win.

He rammed the ball cleanly into its chamber and gave the corporal a confident grin. 'Doesn't matter. We'll just hold here till he sends someone else.'

The corporal seemed content as he took his hoard of cartridges back to the line, but Ryder walked back to where Oliver lay on the grass. The boy was still alive and his eyes were open, but his face was grey as the Russian coats and the end couldn't be long.

'Listen, Polly,' said Ryder, and saw the blue eyes fix on him as if he mattered. 'I'll hold here if you *hold on*. Is that fair?'

Oliver was actually trying to answer. He kept his eyes on Ryder's and whispered 'Is that a challenge?'

Poor kid. The poor, dying boy who still believed in rules. He touched his fingers to the cold face and said, 'Put in a word for us, will you, while you're just lying there? We never needed it more than now.'

Now. Someone yelled, and here came the Russians already, hundreds of them pouring up the side of the Quarry Ravine. He was still loading frantically as he ducked back to the shelter of a twisted oak, caps on, and no time for grease. Men were waiting on him, he called 'By sections from the left, fire in turn!' then pointed the revolver and yelled '*Fire!*'

Bloomer crammed his shako lower on his head, and cautiously raised his eyes above the brushwood. They were still in the middle of a battle, he could hear it from all sides, but at least the ground in front seemed clear. It had been Russian till they'd hooked them out of it with Captain Bellairs's lot, then the Russkies again, swooping round from behind the Barrier to drive them back, then the Frogs came charging in, then the Russians again, and Gawd knew who had it now. What he needed was a bit of land that did what it ought and stood still.

He stooped to help Peachy out of the brush. The kid had a nasty pale look to him and the bandage over his eye was slipping, but he still seemed game for whatever scrap was going. Morry looked the same as he always did, solemn as a rabbi, adjusting the bloodied rag round his neck and saying, 'Back to the Barrier, my friend? That at least will not move.'

'Sez you,' said Bloomer. 'Where is it, then?' Everything looked the same in this fog, grass and rock and dead men.

Morry hesitated. 'My nose says west, my ears say east. There is firing that way too.'

Bloomer regarded him without favour. 'Well, my head says we go for the nearer. East it is.' He pulled Peachy's arm over his shoulder and set off with determination to find the source of the firing. Someone was making a stand somewhere, and given the pair of crocks he was stranded with, that was worth twenty of the dashing-about game.

The gunfire grew louder as they made towards it, and there was a sight of yelling too. It was coming from the base of the rise to the Sandbag Battery, but Bloomer could have sworn there'd been no one there an hour ago. There was now though, a great curved line of men taking shape in the mist, a whole outpost of them, and most in the proper red of the Line.

He nipped higher up the slope to see what they were firing at, and creased his brow at the mass of Russians advancing from the Quarry Ravine. Hundreds of them, easy, but when he looked down to the rear of the British line he felt his own jaw drop. From above and behind there was no hiding its weakness, and he saw now it was only the patches of red that were men, no more than fifty the lot. The rest were rocks and bundled top-togs, and some just piles of stones, a galloping piece of fakery to humbug the Russians to their front.

He let out a sigh of pure enjoyment. 'This is the place for us, boys. *They're* not going anywhere, not a bunch of lunatics like that.'

Morry looked more doubtful. 'They can't hold long, my friend. The Russians will see their firepower is too small for so big a line.'

'So we'll boost it, won't we, you cake,' said Bloomer without heat. 'Two more guns we're bringing them, and even Peachy will be another lobster coat.'

'I can shoot,' said the lad, sliding his arm from Bloomer's shoulder. 'The left eye's all right, you can't keep me out of a scrap like this.'

Bloomer eyed him with pride. 'All right then, tiger-cub, let's get stuck in.' He bustled forward to the next knoll, then paused for a closer squint. He saw bearskins among the line, a couple of coves in the green of the Rifles, and standing at their left flank a dark blue figure he recognized, but shouting in a voice he did not. 'Hold them, boys,' he was calling. 'That's it, you've scared them, watch the bastards run!'

Ryder. Harry Ryder, but not as Bloomer had ever seen him. There was nothing relaxed about him, none of the usual 'be damned to you' cockiness, he was running from man to man in the line, cheering them on and crying 'Shout! Shout, you beggars, let them bloody hear you!' He'd a barking-iron with him and was pausing to fire from every gap between his soldiers, spreading the fire to make a whole line of shots that came from just one man.

'Dear oh dear,' he said admiringly. 'Mark that, will you, Peachy, that's no way to die old in your cot.'

But it was working. The Russkies weren't up to it, not they, they were on lower ground and in fog, they were seeing a row of bangs and flashes, a line of shapes and red coats with men moving fast behind it, they were hearing enough shouting for a regiment. They dithered, dallied in confusion, then began to back away.

'That's the game,' he said, unslinging his rifle. 'Come on, let's puzzle them some more.'

If four dozen men could pass as a regiment then three flashes of fire from the hillside could look like reinforcements. He flipped the sights to a careless three hundred yards, pointed the barrel at the oncoming Russians, and fired. So did Morry. So did Peachy. Bloomer started reloading, but there were only backs to peg away at now, the Russians were out of it and off.

They'd be back, they always were, but there'd be three men of the Royal Fusiliers in the line to meet them. As they set off down the slope Bloomer was filled with a comforting sense of coming home.

*

Ryder fought on. His pistol was empty and no more balls for it, but it was iron in his fist and he'd a sword in the other, he could punch and slash all he needed till there was time to pick up a rifle.

He never doubted there would be. He'd lost count of how long it had been, how often the Russians had charged, but always they held them back and the line had never broken. The sky was lightening overhead, the sun nearly at its height, but still they were fighting and he knew in his heart they were going to win. The fog was clearing, their weakness laid bare to the enemy, but there were more of them than there had been, linesmen, Guards, Riflemen, even stray French infantry, men swelling their ranks from all over, and every one determined to die before they broke.

This was what Oliver had wanted, and Ryder put the thought of it into the next blow of his sword. Polly was part of this too, so was Woodall, so was Mackenzie and even Sally, all the little band of them who'd seen what Angelo was and made it their mission to stand up and fight him. Well, they were doing it now, and as he smashed his pistol into another man's face it was Angelo he was seeing, Angelo he was killing, die, you bastard, *die*.

But they were backing off instead, veering round their flank to easier pickings on the British Heights beyond. He'd known he couldn't hold the whole gap, hundreds got past every time, but still the frustration made him curse aloud.

'They won't get far,' said the lance-corporal, lashing a giant handkerchief round his wounded ankle. 'Look behind us, we're not alone.'

Ryder knew it, he'd been hearing gunfire and the yelling of infantry for a long time, but now he found he could see it too. The fog was dissolving into floating ribbons, and all around him were little pockets of resistance, distant skirmishes, glimpses of individual heroism. Four linesmen were fighting through dozens of Russians to bring an ammunition mule to the Barrier, two NCOs bringing in a wounded officer in the face of a hail of fire from the Kitspur, and a bunch of Zouaves were charging up Home Ridge to beat off an attack on the British guns. Distant

Shell Hill was a cloud of smoke and tumult of firing, the Sandbag Battery swarmed with bearskins as the Coldstream stormed it in triumph, Inkerman Tusk was bright with red-trousered French-men, the Heights thundered with the ceaseless pounding of artillery, and away to their left was the constant crash of volley fire from the Barrier, that steady little wall that had stood hour after hour against numbers sometimes ten times greater than its own. This was the biggest battle Ryder had ever seen or heard of, and set beside it their own ragged action seemed suddenly very small.

But it wasn't. Waves of Russians were still attacking them, and as he ran the line with the last of the cartridges he saw the same astonishing heroism right in front of him. Some had died for it, like Bloomer's friend Morry who'd gone on crawling down the line with ammunition long after his foot was shot away. Others had no intention of dying, and when the Rangers' guns were empty they simply hurled rocks and Irish curses instead, jeering at the Russians as they lured them onto their bayonets. A Scots Fusilier was using his rifle like a club, standing on a pile of dead Russians to smash down on the heads of their comrades below. A dark-haired young Frenchman was still firing, but he was stand-ing forward to do it, covering the retreat of a blinded linesman who was being dragged to safety behind him. Bloomer was in his element, brawling joyously with fists and rifle butt, roaring like the terrifying and glorious bruiser he really was.

They were all heroes, every one of them, and as Ryder stooped to pick up a rifle his eyes blurred with a sheen of tears. The scale of the battle didn't diminish what they were doing, it made them part of something huge and unbreakable. This was what an army really was, and why not even an incompetent commander could destroy it. This was why all the Angelos in the world would always fail in the end.

It was already happening, and the Russians to their front were beginning to waver and break away. Cheering drifted down from the Sandbag Battery, and all along the line men stepped back to take breath and look around them. Ryder called, 'Reload while you can! Bloomer, get me a volunteer for an ammunition party!' but the ground in front stayed empty and he became aware of a new quietness around him. There was less firing from the Barrier, it was lighter and more sporadic than it had been. The fighting round Shell Hill still sounded tremendous, but the weight of the battle was shifting away from them, moving north and back to the Russians.

His legs were trembling as he walked back to the left flank. Some of the men tried to cheer him, and the lance-corporal reached out to bang him agonizingly on the back, but it all seemed very far away, and he was seeing only that little huddled patch of dark blue lying still at the end of the line. This was Oliver's triumph, and Ryder could only pray he'd lived long enough to know it.

He knelt down beside Oliver's body. The eyes were closed, no awareness in him, but a tiny rise and fall of the chest told Ryder his friend had kept his end of the bargain. He should be dead, should have died hours ago, but somehow and impossibly Oliver had held on.

'Good show,' said a voice, and he looked up to see a mounted major of the 21st Fusiliers beaming down at him out of a smoke-blackened face. 'Damned good show, and there'll be something in it for you, I shouldn't wonder. Give me your name, I'll write to your officer.'

The irony twisted in his gut like a ball. A 'mention', no doubt, the glory Polly always wanted, but all the boy got for it was agony and at best a trip to the horror of Scutari. He took a deep breath and looked the officer square in the face.

'Thank you, sir,' he said politely. 'The name's Oliver. Charles Oliver, of the 13th Light Dragoons.'

Ryder slung his boots in a corner of the tent and sat down heavily on the ground. The battle had dragged on into evening, there'd been a day and two nights of burying the dead, he was exhausted, filthy and unshaven, and every bit of him ached. Outside came the clatter of field kitchens, the voices and laughter of men cooking supper, but he wanted nothing more than to close his eyes and sleep.

At least there was room to stretch out. It wouldn't last, someone would spot he'd a tent to himself and shove another load of smelly bodies into it, but for now he lay full length on his blanket and reached for the cloak to cover him. It was Polly's, of course, his own gone long ago, but they'd put it round Mackenzie and it was all he'd found when he climbed back up the Kitspur. The Highlander was gone, and there was only Oliver's cloak on the ground like a reminder of something that was over. The boy had been taken straight to the ships, he'd be on his way to the hellhole of Scutari, and all Ryder was left with was what had been in the tent: a bottle of brandy with maybe four nips in it, a box of cigars, and a battered pack of playing cards.

And that was maybe just as well. He'd always managed best alone, and as he lay in the dark he cursed himself for drifting into such a pitiful state of dependency. He'd been fine till he came to this miserable godforsaken country, spent three nights on a rain-sodden beach, and allowed himself the luxury of friends. That was a mistake in war. It was a mistake any time to get involved with someone you were bound to lose.

Sally was another, and the thought nearly made him reach for the brandy bottle. He'd known it was no good really, the ghost of Jarvis would always be between them, but he'd needed her so much, and more than ever now. He hadn't pressured her, he'd been prepared to wait, but she hadn't, she'd gone off this morning and shipped with the wounded to Scutari. He'd tried to tell her what he felt, but she'd only taken his face in her hands and said, 'You've lost your companions and you need a friend. You're a soldier who's fought a hard battle and you need a woman. But one day you're going to find you need more than that, and then you'll go down on your knees to thank Sally Jarvis for saying no.' That was one thing he wouldn't miss about her, her ability to make him feel twelve years old.

The canvas rustled, and Jordan's voice said, 'Blimey, what are you doing in bed at this time? You're not dead, are you?'

He gritted his teeth. 'You will be if you don't bugger off.'

'Not me, Sergeant,' said Jordan, sounding reproachful. 'The Old Man wants you, I told his aide I'd dig you out.'

Ryder threw off the cloak, and saw Jordan gazing round the tent with envious eyes.

'I say, this is a bit lonely, isn't it? Would you like me and Trotter to –'

'No,' said Ryder, shoving on his boots. 'I can think of nothing I'd like less.'

'Charming,' said Jordan, sticking his hands in his pockets. 'Just thought you might like some company. I mean we all thought you and Mrs Jarvis . . .'

Ryder turned to stare at him. 'What?' he said softly. 'What did you think, Jordan?'

Jordan's hands crept out of his pockets and the smile slid off his face. 'Nothing. Nothing, Sergeant, swear to God.'

'Good.' He groped for his shako and stooped for the tent flap, backing Jordan out as he went. 'We wouldn't want the wrong kind of news going on the telegraph, would we?'

'Course not,' said Jordan obediently, but as Ryder walked away he heard him mutter 'Humourless bastard'. He grinned to himself, and felt better.

Doherty was in his tent, swathed in a greatcoat and muffler, but still looking stronger and more cheerful than when Ryder had last seen him. 'Ah, Ryder, at ease, just a quiet chat.' He nodded to dismiss the aide, and Ryder realized they were to speak again in complete privacy.

'Sir?'

'All right, Harry,' said Doherty, sitting back on his camp stool with an alarming creak. 'Come to the point, what? Private Oliver. Sad business, all the rest of it, but I've had this letter, d'you see, and he's to be recommended for a medal.'

Ryder couldn't conceal his surprise. 'Medal?'

'Yes,' said Doherty, searching vaguely among his papers. 'May not happen, of course, it's only planning at this stage, but Her Majesty's considering a new medal to be awarded regardless of rank.'

About time. 'I can't think of anyone who deserves it more than Oliver, sir.'

'I can,' said Doherty, and looked up. 'The letter describes him as a sergeant.'

Ryder thought fast – the fog, confusion of the moment, maybe a swap of jackets because Oliver was wounded – but when he looked into the patient shrewdness of the Old Man's eyes he swallowed and said just 'Sir'.

'Quite,' said Doherty. 'Why'd you do it, hey? Don't want the recognition – is that it?'

No, he just wanted it for Polly. He tried to explain how Oliver had always loved and believed in the army, how he'd trusted Ryder and pushed him into attempting things he'd never have tried for himself. He said, 'Because he was the real hero, sir. If anything I've done has been of use then it was Polly Oliver who made me do it.'

Doherty listened with his head bowed, then sat back with

a sigh. 'All right, I'll wink at it. The boy can have his medal – if he lives and there is one.' He reached for a bottle of wine, and poured two generous glasses. 'I don't agree with you about him, mind. A fine soldier, a good man, but he'll never make an officer. You, on the other hand, will.'

Ryder stared. 'Sir?'

'Do stop saying that,' said Doherty irritably. 'You sound like the village idiot. Sit on that box, have some wine, and try to have an intelligent conversation.'

Ryder sat abruptly. It was the same biscuit box he'd sat on before, that terrible night before the Alma.

'Don't think I'm doing you any favours,' warned Doherty. 'We lost damn near forty officers at Inkerman alone, and Lord Raglan's asked every regiment to make up one of its sergeants. You're the obvious choice, that's all, and we both know why.'

He sipped the wine and let his mind clear. 'I can't afford it, sir. The uniform, the equipments . . .'

'Taken care of,' said Doherty. 'I can authorize the money, I've done it before. It's the rest that's the hard part, Harry, trying to fit in out of the ranks. I'm thinking you might do better with a fresh start. Another regiment. Where there's been no unpleasantness.'

The flogging, of course. No man could be asked to respect an officer they'd seen flogged. Ryder stared at his glass and felt his cheeks burn.

'It would mean infantry, I'm afraid,' said Doherty. 'But their need's greater than ours, and of course you have the right experience. Besides, this chap Calvert wants you.'

He suppressed the urge to say 'Sir?'

'Yes,' said Doherty, as if he'd said it anyway. 'He thinks there's more to Intelligence than just catching the odd spy. This Shepherd of yours, for instance, chap who owns the house in Kamara. Him and his Bulgarians. The Russians are thinking bigger and Calvert says we need to do the same.'

Ryder stirred uncomfortably. 'I'm not a policeman, sir.'

'Not what Calvert wants,' said Doherty. 'He thinks this is a different kind of war, one where we need to stop following the Russkies and come up with a few new things ourselves. Says we need more men like Goodlake and his sharpshooters, like you and your friends, men prepared to work on their own initiative and hit the enemy in unconventional ways. He wants a unit of such men and he wants you to lead it. What d'you say?'

His own unit, unhampered by line officers, able to carry out his own plans without interference. For the first time since the battle he felt a tingle of returning excitement, a sense of a future and a place for himself in this war. 'I say yes, sir. Yes, and thank you very much.'

Doherty sat back with a pleased grunt. 'Good. I'll miss you, my boy, won't say I won't, but it's a first step to getting you back where you belong. Going to use your own name, hey?'

He didn't hesitate. 'Not till I've earned it by clearing my father's. I'll do it one day, sir, but till then I'm Harry Ryder.'

Doherty considered, then bowed his head. 'Well, maybe some sense in it. Don't want your father's name associated with that . . . other business, do we, hey?' He finished his drink and stood in dismissal. 'We need to assign you a regiment and Calvert will want your advice in choosing the men, but otherwise it's official from now. It's your last night of freedom, Ensign Ryder, and if I were you I'd enjoy it.'

He didn't think there was much chance of that. The men were relaxing as he walked back through the dusk, eating, drinking, playing cards and dominoes, but he'd done with all that anyway. He wouldn't miss the regiment, he had no friends left in it, and tomorrow he'd stand no chance of making any. Doherty was right, an officer had to be free of personal entanglements.

He'd like to be free of personal history too, but some of it was engraved on his back. 'That other business,' Doherty had said; 'any unpleasantness'. That was something else he'd need to hide if he was to have a bearable life in an officers' mess. More secrets, more lies, and back to not trusting anyone at all.

The grass was already frosting in the night air. The cold suited

485

his mood, and when he saw some bastard had lit a fire right out-side his tent he was almost glad of the excuse for a row. But it wasn't Jordan, the man bending over a simmering camp kettle was a red-trousered Frenchman, and next to him was the bulging shape of Bloomer, curled up before the flames like a fat-bodied spider. 'Evening, cock,' he said, grinning from a mouth that seemed to have lost three front teeth. 'We was wondering when you'd turn up.'

'Bloomer,' said Ryder feebly, but a third man was turning from the shadows, and he didn't need to see the kilt and bonnet to rec-ognize Mackenzie. He had a bandage round his leg, another round his middle, a third round his wrist, and the trail of a fourth protruding from under his bonnet, but the sight of him dissolved the last of Ryder's anger in a smile that made his cheeks ache.

'Bloody hell,' he said. 'You look like a badly wrapped parcel.'

Mackenzie looked at the bandages as if he'd forgotten they were there. 'Aye, well, I'd a few wee holes in me, but they're heal-ing fine. Yourself?'

There was no simple answer to that. 'You must all have a drink. Polly's gone to Scutari, but he left the bottle, he'd want us to have it. I've some coffee somewhere too.'

'We found it,' said Bloomer with cheerful amorality. 'And your mug, we're nearly ready. Bert's doing the brew, he says he's a proper dab at it.'

Ryder looked doubtfully at their companion, and recognized the dark-haired Frenchman who'd helped the blinded soldier at Inkerman. 'Bert?'

The Frenchman shrugged amiably. 'Albert. But the Bloomer says no English person can say it, so I am happy to be Bert.'

'So you should be,' said Bloomer severely. 'Good British name. Now hurry up with that coffee, I heard some cove mention brandy.'

Ryder ducked back into his tent to fetch the bottle. He'd have to tell them, it wouldn't be fair otherwise, but there couldn't be any harm in one last night of company. After tomorrow he wouldn't be seeing any of them again.

He stood a moment, listening to the banter outside and feeling the familiar roundness of the bottle in his hand. Maybe it didn't have to be that way. Doherty said he could choose his unit, and he was going to need NCOs. Who better for an unconventional scrap than Bloomer? Who better to have by his side than the steady, reliable Highlander with the fighting spirit of a berserker Viking? Maybe one day there'd even be another, a young idealistic cavalryman who'd survived through one of the longest, bloodiest battles there'd ever been, and might even survive the horror of Scutari.

On sudden impulse he stooped to pick up the cards. Why not? They were four, weren't they? It was dark in the tent, but he could picture the box as clearly as if it were bright day. A Light Dragoon called Stokes had brought them out brand new from England, shiny, colourful, and full of hope, and passed them on to a charity boy called Oliver who'd been his friend. Oliver had chosen to share them with the bitter, sharp-tongued corporal who'd never done a thing to deserve it, and as he slipped the box into his pocket he knew finally that he was grateful. For this, and for all of it.

He stepped out into the firelight. Four steaming mugs were immediately thrust at him, and he crouched to divide the brandy equitably between them. They clinked together, drank and sighed pleasurably, then he put down his mug and produced the cards.

'Ah,' said Mackenzie, straightening with enthusiasm.

'Ah,' said Bloomer, whipping out a pad and pencil stub.

'Ah,' said the Frenchman. 'I have heard. We do not have this game in France, but perhaps you can teach me.'

He'd learn, just as they had, and Ryder let Bloomer explain as he began to deal. He watched himself doing it, one, two, three, four, the movement as natural as it had ever been, his hands building shape into the world with the dealing of a pack of cards.

Epilogue

The world was a floor that moved, walls that creaked, and the moans of the soldier next to him who'd waited nearly two days for a doctor to look at his shattered jaw. The world smelled of blood and sounded like men crying, but Oliver knew it was hell and put it aside. He lived in his own head, and it was quiet there, it felt like school after lights-out and the only thing to fear was whether he could construe well enough in the morning.

But it was night when he woke, or at least it was dark. The pain was still there, but dull like a headache and he didn't need to cry. Water he needed, but he was used to that, and somewhere in the nightmare Sally Jarvis had been there, giving him little sips from a canteen and saying the ship's surgeon had removed his spleen. Sally. Mrs J. She'd been with him all through it, and in the peak of horror he'd felt her hand on his head and been comforted.

There was no Sally here, and the stillness filled him with dread. Had they arrived? Was this the infamous hospital at Scutari where men came to scream and die in their own filth? But the room was quiet, the sheet on his chest was as stiff and clean as at school, and even the smell recalled carbolic soap, the cleanliness of the San, and a matron who dealt with his broken finger after a cricket match and said, 'Well done, Oliver, jolly good catch.' This *was* the School, he could see it now, the high ceiling and rows of beds and a single lamp moving in the dark; it was the School and he must be dead or how could he be back here? He struggled to sit upright, and gasped at the twinge in his side.

At once the wavering light swung towards him, and a woman's voice spoke in the gloom. 'What is it, soldier? Are you in pain?'

It wasn't Sally. The hair under the frilled cap was dark, the face was hard and faintly disapproving, and the voice far too educated for a nurse. He shrank back into his pillows and whispered 'No, miss. I don't know where I am.'

She moved closer, lifted a glass that had been beside him all the time, and put it to his lips. Water, real water, and it tasted clean. She said, 'You're safe in hospital in Scutari, and you're going to get well.'

He looked doubtfully at her. 'Scutari?'

She laid the glass down with a clear, precise clink. 'I am running things now, soldier. There is a lot to do still, but I think we can say we have made a start.' She smiled as she said it, and then her face wasn't severe at all, it was warm and kind, a lady whose word he wouldn't dare to doubt.

He settled back in the comfort of certainty, and watched her resume her walk down the long hall. He could hear other sounds in the darkness now, the murmurs and rustling of men stirring in pain, but the lady's dress swished against the floor as elegantly as in a drawing room, and as she passed along the rows of beds he thought the light of her lamp shone like hope.

Historical Note

Into the Valley of Death is fiction, but much of what happens in it is true. Some may be truer than we know.

The main characters are fictional. There was no 'G' Troop in the 13th Light Dragoons, and neither Ryder, Oliver nor any other of its members has any basis in fact. Woodall, Mackenzie, and Bloomer are all inventions, as are their intimates. Outside these closed circles, however, almost everyone is real. Some, like Raglan, Cardigan and Nolan, are well known to history, but others are just as factual. The mysterious 'Mr Calvert', for instance, was actually the former Vice-Consul Charles Cattley, who used this alias when he ran the Secret Intelligence Department in the Crimea. Even the 'bit-part' characters existed, from Lieutenant Verschoyle of the Grenadier Guards down to the Sergeant Priestley who lost a foot at the Bulganek and the legless man who did indeed cry 'Go it, beauty Guards! Go in and win!' at the Alma. The heroism of individuals like Captain Goodlake of the sharpshooters and Captain Burnaby of the Grenadier Guards was certainly real, and far surpasses that of my own invention. The boy who planted the flag of the Royal Welch on the Greater Redoubt was Ensign Anstruther – and the Maltese terrier at the Alma was 'Toby'. The nurse in the Epilogue is (of course) Florence Nightingale, who arrived at Scutari on the day of the Battle of Inkerman.

Apart from Cardigan's brief appearance in the first chapter, the only 'real' character I have allowed to interact significantly with my fictional ones is Lieutenant Colonel Charles Edmund Doherty of the 13th Light Dragoons. Little is known of him, but he did lead the ill-fated patrol of 18 September, and was sufficiently ill on 25 October to miss the Battle of Balaklava. He did serve in India in 1840, and had indeed previously authorized payment to help an NCO acquire the equipments needed for officer rank. Everything else said or done by Doherty in this book is fiction, and I hope it does no disrespect to his memory.

As with characters, so with action. Events witnessed by demonstrably real characters can mostly be assumed to have really happened, while those outside their view are almost invariably fiction. The patrol of 18 September, for instance, happened much as described here, except for the sequence when Ryder and his friends fight the Cossacks out of sight of the regiment. There are, however, two exceptions to this rule. Although 'commando-style' attacks were indeed made on the British trenches, I know of none on 15 October 1854 and Bloomer's account is pure fiction. Neither was there an attack on Balaklava Harbour on 5 November 1854, and nobody who takes part in this skirmish really existed, except the 'off-stage' characters of Captain Tatham and Captain Barker. I have deliberately given a false name to the irritating marine captain so as not to cast aspersions on the very gallant force that in reality defended the British base.

For the rest I have tried to stay within the boundaries of what is true, although there are inevitably omissions and simplifications during the long battle sequences. I have, however, consciously manipulated time only twice. The incident of the stampeding Russian horses that provided remounts to the Light Brigade is true, but it happened on 27 October rather than the 26th. The first cavalry disembarkation from the *Jason* happened 'towards evening' of 14 September, but the attempt on General Airey and Sir George Brown as described by *Times* correspondent William Howard Russell, was made in the morning. One other detail of that incident is fictional: there is no evidence to say either Airey or Brown lost a hat.

Which brings us to the shadowy figure of Mikhail Andreievich Kalmykoff. The character is a creation, but he is based very firmly on someone who is not: the 'unknown officer' who recurs throughout the first seven weeks in the Crimea. He may have been one man, he may have been several, his actions may have derived from stupidity rather than treachery, but he existed and was certainly responsible for considerable damage. Alexander Kinglake, the official chronicler accompanying the Expedition, drew from interviews with eyewitnesses when he wrote of the unknown voice that called 'The column is French – don't fire, men!' at the Greater Redoubt, and of the unknown mounted officer who told the bugler of the 19th to sound first the 'cease firing', and then the 'retreat'. His account of Colonel Chester's intervention is even more specific, describing him gesturing as if to say 'Nonsense . . . the column is not French . . . Fire into it!' before being 'struck first by one shot and then almost instantly by another', a circumstance quite as peculiar as Ryder points out.

Nor did it end there. What Kinglake describes as the next 'apparition' occurs with the Grenadier Guards, to whom the unknown mounted officer gave the order to retire before galloping away 'without having been surely identified'. The situation was saved by Colonel Percy, but meanwhile the officer had ridden to the Coldstream and given the same order, which happily they resisted. The only question mark is over the order for the Scots Fusiliers' withdrawal, which Kinglake 'believes' was given under Bentinck's authority – but that does not mean the general concurred with it. Captain Gipps describes the moment with obvious emotion: 'At this moment someone (alas, who was it?) rode or came to our commanding officer and told him to give the word for us to retire.'

Even excluding this incident, Kinglake believed the matter merited explanation – and there were others of which he knew nothing. It is from regimental sources that we know of the mysterious order given to the Black Watch not to fire on the Russians because they were French – which was indeed foiled by a sergeant insisting 'there's no mistaking them divils'. Captain Nolan's diary refers to a battery that was given the same misleading order, although he makes no mention of an unknown officer. The *Recollections* of Albert Mitchell of the 13th Light Dragoons give us the patrol of 18 September, which certainly looks like an ambush, and was (unusually) accompanied by an anonymous staff officer.

Kinglake leaves the question at the Alma, but the mystery continues at Balaklava. Controversy usually focusses on the failure of communication between Raglan, Nolan, and Lucan, but in offering only the traditional Kinglake version I have ducked this issue entirely in order to concentrate on the question of why Raglan gave the order in the first place.

The issue of the infamous 'Fourth Order' is far too complex to deal with properly here, but as Major Colin Robins, Mark Adkin and Terry Brighton have all pointed out in recent studies, the outcome would have been disastrous even had the Brigade advanced along the Causeway Heights as intended instead of straight down the North Valley. Raglan's explanation for the order is that it was to 'prevent the enemy carrying away the guns', but there is no evidence the enemy were even contemplating doing so. It would have been an astonishing thing to attempt in the circumstances, and even Kinglake admits his Russian sources did not confirm it. Brighton goes further and says Russian historians 'assert that no such operation was taking place at that time'. So why did Raglan think it was?

Because, as Brighton puts it, 'a staff officer whose identity has never been established' shouted out that the Russians were dragging away the guns. No single conference has been subjected to so close a scrutiny as this one, and it seems inconceivable the name would not be mentioned – unless, of course, nobody knew it. As Mark Adkin expresses it: 'An unnamed officer's warning had lit a fuse at precisely the right moment.'

As also at Inkerman. There is no talk of an unknown staff officer here, and no evidence to suggest General Cathcart's disastrous departure from orders was the result of anything other than his own pig-headedness. I have, however, used real incidents on which to build the fictional denouement, and the unauthorized headlong dash by the Grenadiers, the Coldstream and the 95th Foot remains a mystery today. Kinglake casts about for psychological reasons to explain why so many Grenadiers in the Battery burst out 'almost at once' with the word 'Charge!' while Captain Wilson is at a similar loss in the Coldstream, recalling only his vain attempts to pursue his errant charges with a cry of 'Halt, halt!' Only with the 95th do we have a more specific explanation, and it is alarmingly familiar: as Kinglake describes it, 'All at once, by *some voice still unknown*, the word "Charge!" was uttered in a tone of command.'

But any attempt to impute sinister motives to all this is pure conjecture. That the Russians made determined attempts to mislead and delay the British attack is certainly true, and the incident where they pretended to be British in order to spike the French guns is recorded in Fanny Duberly's diary entry of 23 October, but 'Kalmykoff' himself remains firmly fiction. His interaction with my own heroes is, of course, entirely so. It is true that news of the bombardment leaked and the Russians opened fire first, but that could indeed have been because they observed the British cutting embrasures for their guns. There was no attack on de Lacy Evans's servants or theft of his property, and all the details of Kalmykoff's clothes and trappings are invented. None of the facts produced by my heroes as corroborative evidence have any basis in reality – except one. Lord George Paget's casualty lists do include one staff officer taken prisoner at Balaklava, and yet none was found to be missing. Paget's source clearly saw somebody going with the Russians who looked like a British staff officer, but was actually no such thing.

Whatever the truth of it, Kalmykoff's evil personality is in no way intended as a reflection on the courageous and honourable Russian officers who fought in the Crimea. I have not, however, invented the atrocities. Instances of wounded Russians shooting those attempting to help them are supported by eyewitnesses, as is the widespread bayoneting of the wounded at Inkerman. In defence of the Russians, there had certainly been atrocities committed by the French in the villages, and more than one church was looted in full view of the defenders of Sebastopol.

I have tried not to exaggerate the attitudes of the British either.

The piety of Oliver and Mackenzie is strongly rooted in the reality of the time: officers of the 93rd Highlanders read from the prayer book on the march to the Alma, and Russell gives a moving account of encountering individual soldiers praying on their knees the night before. Oliver's insistence on 'fair play' was also common, and many soldiers recorded instances of officers demanding they 'spare' the enemy even in the midst of battle. Private Bancroft of the Grenadiers recalled trying to fight off a Russian who was gripping his legs, only to be told by his sergeant not to 'kick a man who was down'. This attitude did not, however, survive the campaign. Chivalry in war was perhaps the greatest single casualty of the Crimea.

Not all its legacy was evil. The monumental inefficiency of the Crimean campaign was an important catalyst for change, and even its battles have left their traces today. The victory at the Alma is still remembered in a previously obscure Christian name, and on the signs of countless pubs and roads around Britain. Balaklava gave us Tennyson's 'Charge of the Light Brigade' and the phrase into which Russell's original 'thin red streak' was mutated: the Thin Red Line. Inkerman became known as 'The Soldiers' Battle', and did more than any other to eliminate the system of privilege where rank could be attained only by money. The tragic heroism of the Guards at the Sandbag Battery will in particular never be forgotten, and the unit now comprising the 3rd Battalion of Her Majesty's Grenadier Guards is known as 'The Inkerman Company' to this day.

For even more than a 'Soldiers' Battle', the Crimean was a 'Soldiers' War'. If all we remember now is the incompetence of the high command we do a great disservice to the men who suf-fered, fought, died – and achieved victory under it. Queen Victoria did not forget, and the medal mentioned by Doherty which was to be available to all ranks was, of course, what we now know as the Victoria Cross. The medals were struck from the bronze of Russian cannon captured at Sebastopol, a tradition supposedly continued to this day.

It's certainly appropriate. British naval supremacy had long been acknowledged before the 1850s, but the Russians were of the firm opinion that the British 'could only fight at sea'. Alma, Balaklava, and Inkerman changed their minds. It is fitting therefore that the highest medal for valour in the British Army should have its origin in the conflict where the legend of its indomitable courage was born.

Acknowledgements

To write about the long-forgotten heroes of the Crimean War has been a privilege, and I am very grateful to Alex Clarke at Penguin for allowing me to undertake it.

To even attempt it would have been impossible without the first-hand accounts left by those heroes themselves. I have tried to preserve the authenticity of these by using their contemporary spelling (including the erroneous 'Sebastopol' for modern 'Sevastopol' and the 'off' rather than 'ov' suffix for Russian names), and also wherever possible by reproducing peculiarities of style and voice. Among the many I've consulted I owe special thanks to: Albert Mitchell of the 13th Light Dragoons, Timothy Gowing of the 7th Royal Fusiliers, Captain Tipping of the Grenadier Guards, Captain Wilson of the Coldstream Guards, Colonel Sterling and Surgeon Munro of the 93rd Sutherland Highlanders, and Lord George Paget of the Light Brigade. I must also gratefully acknowledge the massive debt owed to the contemporary chroniclers of the Expedition: the writer Alexander Kinglake, and *Times* Correspondent William Howard Russell. These men were *there*.

But there are others who might almost as well have been, and I would have been lost without the invaluable guidance of the Crimean War Research Society. Of the many members who have given me help and encouragement I would particularly like to thank Tom Muir, Major Colin Robins OBE, FRHistS, and The Hon. Secretary David Cliff, who has bravely given my manuscript a 'historical proof-read' for accuracy. I have also been honoured with assistance from scholars in the Crimea, and am especially grateful to Daniel Berjitsky, senior research historian at the Sherimetievs Museum, for bringing the reality of the Siege so vividly to life. Most of all, I would like to thank Manita Mishina of

Sevastopol, who not only shared unstintingly her own extensive knowledge of the campaign, but even persuaded eminent local specialists to walk me round the various battlefields. Manita has been the unsung heroine behind many other works on the Crimean War, and I am delighted to have the opportunity to acknowledge her quite unique contribution in this field. I have been extremely fortunate in the help of all these experts, and if I've still managed to go wrong then I'm afraid I have only myself to blame.

In the modern world, thanks are due also to Kevin Lees of the 'Jersey Militia' for educating me in the various firearms of the period; to my copy-editor Trevor Horwood for his meticulous and sensitive work on the manuscript; to my agent Victoria Hobbs for her unwavering faith and support; and (as always) to my friends and family for their severely tried patience. To write this book has been a dream of mine for many years, and it is only the generous support of so many people that has enabled it at last to come true.

He just wanted a decent book to read ...

Not too much to ask, is it? It was in 1935 when Allen Lane, Managing Director of Bodley Head Publishers, stood on a platform at Exeter railway station looking for something good to read on his journey back to London. His choice was limited to popular magazines and poor-quality paperbacks – the same choice faced every day by the vast majority of readers, few of whom could afford hardbacks. Lane's disappointment and subsequent anger at the range of books generally available led him to found a company – and change the world.

'We believed in the existence in this country of a vast reading public for intelligent books at a low price, and staked everything on it'
Sir Allen Lane, 1902–1970, founder of Penguin Books

The quality paperback had arrived – and not just in bookshops. Lane was adamant that his Penguins should appear in chain stores and tobacconists, and should cost no more than a packet of cigarettes.

Reading habits (and cigarette prices) have changed since 1935, but Penguin still believes in publishing the best books for everybody to enjoy. We still believe that good design costs no more than bad design, and we still believe that quality books published passionately and responsibly make the world a better place.

So wherever you see the little bird – whether it's on a piece of prize-winning literary fiction or a celebrity autobiography, political tour de force or historical masterpiece, a serial-killer thriller, reference book, world classic or a piece of pure escapism – you can bet that it represents the very best that the genre has to offer.

Whatever you like to read – trust Penguin.